Oh Aton, Perfect, Unchanging, Giver of Life

. . . upwelling fountains of gas form flattened, mushroom caps that are the size of the Earthly State of Texas. Existing in constant motion, these columns thrust up the spicules of hot gas which feed the chromosphere; they also push around the magnetically active regions which control the shape of the superheated solar corona.

In short, these granulated columns of rising gas direct the divergent flow of electromagnetic energies that most affects the lives of humans on that little green world. If not for the movement of these convection cells beneath the surface, the star would shed its energy in a single, impartial, uniform glow.

In fact, that was how, for thousands of years, the humans of that green world thought about their "day star," their sun, their god Aton: as a single, unchanging beacon, uniform in its benevolence, unswerving in its outpourings, impartial in its gift of energy, consistent in its love.

Of course, they were wrong.

Other Baen Books by These Authors

The Mask of Loki

Roger Zelazny

Wizard World
This Immortal
Isle of the Dead
The Dream Master
Four for Tomorrow
The Black Throne
   (with Fred Saberhagen)

Thomas T. Thomas

ME
First Citizen
The Doomsday Effect
   (as by "Thomas Wren")
An Honorable Defense
   (with David Drake)

FLARE

ROGER ZELAZNY
THOMAS T. THOMAS

BAEN
BOOKS

FLARE

This is a work of fiction. All the characters and events portrayed in this book are fictional, and any resemblance to real people or incidents is purely coincidental.

A Baen Books Original

Baen Publishing Enterprises
P.O. Box 1403
Riverdale, NY 10471

ISBN: 0-671-72133-X

Cover art by Dean Morrissey

First Printing, September 1992

Printed in the United States of America

Distributed by Simon & Schuster
1230 Avenue of the Americas
New York, NY 10020

Part 1

Minus Ten Million Years . . . and Counting

The day comes lovely to the sky's edge,
living Aton, opener of life's gate.
Rising at the eastern rim of the world,
you fill the lands with your glory. . . .

Great, glowing, high above the Earth,
you send rays to brighten the land,
filling with light all that you have made.
You are Re, making all things captive,
binding them with your love.
Distant, you shed your light upon us.
Striding on high, your footprints are the day.

—From "Hymn to the Sun"
by Pharaoh Amenhotep IV (later Ikhnaton)

● Chapter 1

Concatenating Bangs

Ping!
　　Ping!
　　　　Ping!
　　　　　　Ping!

Or whatever the sound might be when two hydrogen nuclei — in effect, a pair of stripped protons — collide repeatedly at pressures of two hundred billion atmospheres and temperatures of fifteen million degrees Kelvin.

Conditions of such pressure and temperature exist within the cores of G-type yellow stars. However, the scales for measuring them, expressed in "atmospheres" and "degrees," only have relevance to the temporary environmental stability of a small green planet which orbits at one hundred and fifty million kilometers from the surface of such a star.

Ping!
　　Ping!
　　　　Ping!
　　　　　　Ping!

Protons are tough little nuts, even under such extremes of temperature and pressure. Each one is welded together as a simple combination of quarks, which are various and not simple at all. Quarks are, depending on your point of view, either the building blocks of matter, or the slippery interface between matter and energy. Take your pick.

Because protons have a positive charge — a descriptive quality of matter that, again, only has relevance in an Earthside laboratory or an electronic circuit — and because particles having similar charges repel each other with a ferocity beyond all human understanding, the colliding protons immediately spring apart, unscathed.

In fact, any single proton must collide, on average, forty trillion *trillion* times with one of its associates before anything will happen. At the rate of one hundred million collisions per second, under the jostlings of extreme pressure and with the agitations of extreme temperature, one proton in the star's core will suffer a physical change once in fourteen billion years. On average. And fourteen billion years is three times longer than the star itself is likely to remain active. So the average proton, loose in a star's core, can expect to lead a hectic but otherwise uneventful life. Such as it is.

    Ping!
        Ping!
            Ping!
                Pong!

But once in forty trillion trillion times, a collision will fuse the two protons together. One of them sheds its charge with the release of a positron (or positively charged electron) and a neutrino (which is like a little fragment of subatomic glue), becoming a bare neutron. Because positively and neutrally charged particles *can* stick together, they do, forming a nucleus of deuterium. This is called "heavy" hydrogen because the nucleus is freighted with an unaccustomed neutron.

Anyone might suppose that, because the instance of fusion is so rare among protons, the next step might be dissolution. With the next jostling *ping!*, in the next hundred-millionth of a second, the deuterium nucleus will fall apart. Then, from the dense crowd of particles surrounding it, the neutron will collect its positron and neutrino, which cannot have gone far in such a short time; it will patch itself together and resume its life as a proton.

But that is not what happens. The proton-neutron marriage endures for an average of six seconds, or only six hundred million more collisions, before another proton joins up.

    BANG!

This collision leaves each of the partners individually unchanged, but releases a unit of energy — the chargeless, massless photon, vibrating at the extreme frequencies of gamma radiation. This photon goes on its way, leaving a ménage à trois, the helium nucleus. This is called "light" helium because it's missing a second neutron to complete its normal structure.

After another million years or so of further bumping on the crowded proton dancefloor, two of these light helium nuclei will themselves chance to collide. Their collective four protons and two neutrons will swing around each other, *dos-si-dos*, and form a new configuration. This will be a stable nucleus of regular helium — with two protons, two neutrons — and a pair of free protons, which go back into the dance and begin looking for other partners.

Meanwhile, the photon that had emerged from the second fusion collision radiating like a gamma ray will take part in no more combinations. The positron that was ejected from the first collision will soon meet a free electron, its antiparticle, in the plasma soup and annihilate it. The product of this mutual destruction is a pair of energetic photons, which are also radiating up in the gamma region of the electromagnetic spectrum.

So, in all, while six protons slowly turn themselves into a helium nucleus and a pair of stragglers down in the core of an average yellow star, three high-energy photons are created and released.

Three tiny sparks of light are produced in three separate collisions that are relatively widely spaced over time and distance, among trillions of other collisions that produce not so much visible energy as our archetypal *ping!* These tiny sparks spring forth into a crush of matter so dense and opaque that atoms themselves must shed their electron clouds and flow as a kinetic plasma. Is it any wonder that the core of a G-type yellow is blacker than the darkest edge of space?

Blacker, but not colder. These three energetic protons will contribute their energy to the heat of the star's core as they pass, bouncing off protons and light helium nuclei alike, on their way through the shuffling crowd.

In this pitch and toss of photons moving back and forth across the core, none has a preference for direction. Each photon strikes a larger particle and rebounds — or, in technical terms, is absorbed and immediately reradiated — like wild dancers slamming their way across the floor. Their direction is random. That is, none can *choose* to move toward the sidelines and spin away from the dance. And anyway, each photon will move only a fraction of a centimeter — one more measure valid only in Earthly terms — before striking another particle and reradiating in another direction.

While none of these photons has the thought of escaping the core and moving out into the star's higher layers, still some — a small fraction — happen to do just that. These represent the "excess" energy in the core; that is, the amount of heat greater than is needed to keep up the pressure and hold the core from collapsing under the inward push of gravity from the overlying material. These few excess photons do reach the dancefloor's sidelines and are shed upward, toward the star's surface.

In the dense, opaque layers above the core, each photon continues the game of absorption and reradiation, bouncing one step forward and two steps back. And as the photon encounters the cooler layers above, it may also lose some of its energy; the frequency of its vibration becomes slower, its wavelength longer. On average. A few photons may maintain their potency over the long haul, but not all of them, certainly. In general, gamma rays at the core become x-rays in the intervening layers, then ultraviolet rays just below the surface, and then mostly visible light — again an Earthly, human term — at the surface.

In the outer region, about two-thirds of the way to the surface, the stellar gases cool from fifteen million degrees to about two million. These cool gases become nearly opaque, so the distance that any photon can travel by bouncing around becomes insignificant. At the same time, however, in this region the temperature difference between the bottom, innermost layers and the top, outermost layers becomes much greater. Also, the cooler gases throughout this region are less dense, and so less stable. Thus, hotter material from the star's innermost depths flies upward like steam bubbles in a saucepan, in a process called "convection." This action then drives the cooler, relatively denser material near the star's surface downward in an endless, rolling boil.

So, in the opaque region of the star's interior, the photons stop traveling by their bounces over centimeters and fractions; instead they ride with the roiling atoms of the convection layer. It is as if they were taking express elevators up to the surface regions of the sun.

Any single photon — or, to be precise, the track of multiply absorbed and reradiated photons — spends about ten million years in passing from an initial fusion collision in the core to its visible-light escape at the surface. For most of this immense time, the photon is bouncing forward and back in the packed interior, and for a shorter time the photon rises effortlessly in dark columns of boiling gas.

At the surface these columns — like thunderhead cells along a stormfront, or bubbles rising in a pot of porridge — shape the outward face of the sun. These upwelling fountains of gas form flattened, mushroom caps that are the size of the Earthly state of Texas. Existing in constant motion, these columns thrust up the spicules of hot gas which feed the chromosphere; they also push around the magnetically active regions which control the shape of the superheated solar corona.

In short, these granulated columns of rising gas direct the divergent flow of electromagnetic energies that most affects the lives of humans on that little green world. If not for the movement of these convection cells beneath the surface, the star would shed its energy in a single, impartial, uniform glow.

In fact, that was how, for thousands of years, the humans of that green world thought about their "daystar," their sun, their god Aton: as a single, unchanging beacon, uniform in its benevolence, unswerving in its outpourings, impartial in its gift of energy, consistent in its love.

Of course, they were wrong.

Ping!

   Pong!

      Pong!

         Pong!

The initiatory collision of one proton with another — that once-in-a-forty-trillion-trillion event which sheds a positronic charge and ultimately gives birth to a triplet of wandering photons — is only the usual sequence in the sun's core. It represents, over time, only the average of all possible interactions.

This dance of separate particles and photons is controlled by the workings of probability, a science which will be much studied on the small green planet. Probability and the laws of chance say that, over all time, in the universe taken as a whole, the high points and the low match up and cancel each other out. They level all possible experiences to a nice, stable median point in a smooth curve.

But this is only one picture of reality. It's a working conceptual definition — not reality itself.

Now and then, here and there, the framework of probability breaks down. Sometimes the real world swings wide and deep in establishing that balanced median. And so, in that particular time and place, the long run and the universe as a whole are temporarily forgotten.

More and more of those initial *ping* collisions may happen to produce many more nuclei of deuterium and loose photons than the forty-trillion-trillionth of a chance would indicate. At that point, the consequences can be immediate and astounding.

BANG!

   BANG!

      BANG!

         BANG!

Then highly unusual things can start happening.

Chapter 2

The Dolphin League

> *Have news!*
> > *Good fortune!*
> > > *Glad tidings!*
> > > > *Good news!*

Among the convection cells in the upper layers of the solar atmosphere, the creature slides, buoyant as a soap bubble. He passes the rising columns of superheated gases and the falling sheets of freshly cooled gases, all the while maintaining his equilibrium.

Of course, the atmosphere is not really a gas made up of free-roaming atoms and molecules. At its ambient temperature of about 5,800 degrees, the sun's photosphere is far too hot for that. The heat strips the simple molecules of their atomic structure, reducing them to a plasma, a bath of charged particles: ions, positively charged protons and hydrogen nuclei, negatively charged electrons. All of them shudder and dance under the bombardment of high-energy photons. The photosphere is a fluxing soup of activity and potential.

> *Warmth!*
> > *Flow!*
> > > *Energy!*
> > > > *Lift!*

Against the blast-furnace, jet-engine, fire-bell scream of hot plasma rising from the convective zone, the creature's voice booms out in organized subsonics. The mechanism for these pulsing cries is a simple bladder, twanged rhythmically against the relatively lighter mass of the surrounding plasma.

The wonder is that any structure can exist in that high-energy hell. But between the dense, hot, gamma-ray core and the thin, still hotter, visible-light corona lies this region of comparative stability. Here the attraction between positive ion and negative ion can occasionally override the disruptions of pressure and heat.

Electrons and protons align themselves, negative to positive, under a static charge — not quite an atomic bonding but not a fluid plasma, either. Call it a confederation of potentials and influences. And call the creature a "plasmote." The seed of his structure is a magnetic field, of which many and varied configurations race and swirl through the solar atmosphere.

Once joined, these ion webs build to form membranes and envelopes, pockets of quiet against the storms of gamma energy, magnetic flux, and convective flow. So the plasmotes harbor regions of greater and lesser density, achieving sustainable dimensions in the writhing soup. They accomplish their motility with the pump and thrust of bellows or the thrash of a loose and raveling ion whip, depending on their individual natures.

And deeper within the relative quiet of the plasmotes' envelopes, more subtle structures are allowed to form and grow. The deep silence of these pockets enables coded sequences, yes-and-no, on-and-off, which carry and maintain a complex matrix of information. Scores of captured neutrons interrupt and punctuate these numerical values and strings, giving them phrasing and meaning. The free energy flux of gamma radiation, rising from below, excites these coded sequences, passing electron pointers through them and directly driving the processes of consciousness.

The plasmote is a creature of pure, scintillating awareness, with his only available expression in voice and movement. His only activity is to propel himself ahead of his world's delights and dangers, crying news of them, so that others of his kind may hear and respond.

Cold!
 Flow!
  Plunge!
  Danger!

If the plasmote finds delight in the upwelling lamination of warm, energy-laden juices surrounding a rising column of gas, then his greatest danger is found in the narrower regions on either side.

To venture too far within the column, seeking out its radiant core, is to risk disruption of the plasmote's delicate membranes and sacs. There the turbulent fountain of unequal pressures yields rending velocities and certain death.

But to venture too far outside the column is to risk capture by the downdraft of cooled material that moves within the interstices between the rising, granular cells. These convection drafts can carry the plasmote down toward the core, where rising temperature and pressure will as surely interrupt his tender, magnetically oriented structure.

So, like booming dolphins of the temperate zone, the plasmotes navigate the hexagonal borders of the convection fountains. There they pass, exulting in stability and warning each other of the perils at hand on either side.

Come!
   Feel!
      Expand!
         Rejoice!

Like dolphins and whales, the plasmotes gambol in the photosphere and know no equal to themselves. They exist in many forms: as pulsing sacks, writhing whips, or funneling jets, as contemplative, near-stationary billows full of densely matching logics, or as hyperactive kites with almost no logic at all. But all plasmotes are concurrent. All are viable. And all are mutually exclusive, mutually supportive.

The plasmotes form no families or tribes, no states or principalities. They share no secrets, create no religions, forge no bonds, work no magic. They build no lasting relationships among themselves other than a joyous passing acquaintance.

No plasmote has ever been seen to be born of another, either by partition or conjunction. None, in fact, has ever been created anew. Neither has one ever died of old age, or disease, or the stresses of movement and life. None has died at all — except by a carelessness that leads to sudden rupture on one side or to the long plunge into pressure and heat and darkness on the other.

The sun boasts no lesser forms from which these beings might have evolved. No plas*mites*, as it were. So there exist no backwater swamps of obsolete, failed plasmotes. And they can find no fresh spawning ground for hopeful, future plasmotes. These simple beings have only the rupture and the plunge, and the safe path they dance between those alternatives.

The plasmotes can trace no evolution in themselves, nor have any idea of how or where they come from. Like dolphins and whales, they are simply unique in their environment. A thoughtful observer then might wonder if their antecedents were introduced from another place, another time. But if this is so, the plasmotes do not remember or record it. They only swim forward, singing.

Chapter 3

On the Green World

Ramapithecus
  Australopithecus
    Pithecanthropus erectus
      Homo neanderthalensis

East Africa, circa One Million B.C.

Ga-ah chased the little lizard on the ground, because that was where it went. She knew she could move faster up in the trees, where she could use both her gripping fingers and her curling toes for aid in the scramble, where she could literally fly from limb to vine to limb. But the lizard was on the ground, down among the leaf clutter, and she did not want it to escape. Lizards were good to eat. But lizards could also burrow down in the leaves and disappear, so Ga-ah had to chase it where it went, to keep it from getting away.

Dart left, dart right, the lizard was quick. It knew Ga-ah was after it, and so it ran fast. So Ga-ah had to run fast. The lizard darted under a wall of bushes, and Ga-ah used her strong hands to bend back their branches, clearing space for her legs and hips.

Her large, wide-set eyes, adapted to the shading of the high forest layers, could pick out subtle flashes of color. Lizard gray-and-green against the broader pattern of leaf gray-and-green. Ga-ah's deeply cupped ears, which stood away from her head, adapted to the conflicting breezes of the forest canopy, could detect the scuffling of lizard claws from the plainer rattle of leaves on the wind. But her snub nose, which was not adapted for anything special, could tell her little about the lizard's line of flight. Lizards did not have much smell, anyway, or they did not smell much different from the leaf-molds of the forest floor. So Ga-ah looked and listened, ignored her nose, and followed.

Through the low-lying brush she went, her arms batting away the clutches of leaves, her feet stomping the hard soil. Was she following the lizard? Or was she driving it forward? Ga-ah could only tell that it was moving deeper into the bushes and moving more slowly, more warily now.

The air around her became brighter, hotter . . . whiter. Sweat trickled down her face and stung her lips, tasting like blood but slightly sour. Tasting like fresh lizard. Ga-ah eagerly shoved another branch aside and pushed herself forward.

Then she stopped.

The world was still green, but it was a burning, whitely glaring green. The bushes faded out into the spiky stalks that Ga-ah sometimes found beside the forest streams. But these stalks, bending to a wind which did not flutter but blew straight, went on forever, as far as the eye could see, then even farther.

Ga-ah covered her face with long, curling fingers. Too bright. This was like climbing to the very top of the forest, where the tree limbs became loose and springy and would not hold her weight. Where the great white showered down on the cool green, offending her eyes. Where the wind sang a loud, steady, thrashing song, offending her ears.

She widened the space between one finger and another, peeking out through the thin shade. Still too bright, but at least Ga-ah could see for a little ways. She could see the lizard, a dark gray blot against the bright green of the bending stalks. It was running over their suppleness without any sound she could hear above the deep sighs of the dry wind.

As if knowing it had won, the lizard stopped. Supporting its body upright on back legs and tail for a moment, it turned one eye over a sloping shoulder and flicked its tongue at her. Then the lizard raced on, incredibly staying on its rear legs, as if it drew energy and courage from the white-gold light falling all around it.

Ga-ah looked up, past the lizard, to the half-dome of sky above. So big here. So hard and blue. One side was bounded by the trees at her back, the other side by nothing. This was a great piece of sky here. In the forest, she could only see little bits of this sky, revealed only when the wind tossed aside the branches, way high in the treetops.

Something else was in that sky, too. Up higher, where she could not look. It was too bright for Ga-ah's wide-set, delicate eyes. Too bright. Pure white. Hurtful. It was something the lizard did not fear, but she did.

Ga-ah put her hand back over her eyes, turned around, and pushed her way back through the screen of bushes. She disappeared into the more friendly forest gloom that was her heritage.

But not her future.

> *Bringing dogs and goats inside the fence*
> *Planting wheat and barley in the fields*
> *Harnessing horses and oxen to the plow*
> *Pulling cotton fibers and weaving fabrics*

Parsumash, circa 6500 B.C.

Haddad watched his apprentices pound the green rocks to powder. Under his breath, he counted the ritual strokes of their pestles against the stone basin. He studied the flexing and tightening of the smooth, brown skin over their arms, the whip-snapping of tendons, the writhing of veins as those arms chopped at the fragments of malachite. Only when the green powder was as fine as the river silt could the next stage of the process begin.

Then slaves brought out jars of charcoal — wood burned under a blanket of soil, so that it turned to hard, black nuggets instead of fragile, white ashes. These nuggets, too, had been ground to a fine powder. The slaves added handfuls of the charcoal to the malachite, still in its basin, and the apprentices mixed it evenly with their pestles. When the joining was done to his satisfaction, Haddad directed them to take up their reed pipes while the slaves ran to get torches of pitch pine.

Breathe in through gapped mouths, blow out through hollow reeds. The apprentices exhaled their life-force gently, steadily into the pipes, whose ends were buried under the green-black mixture at the sides of the bowl. Meanwhile the torchbearers passed their burning wands over the powder's surface. Tiny sparks of charcoal flew up and ignited. The bearers dipped their flame lower, and the embedded grains began to glow.

Soon the blowers were puffing out their cheeks, and their brows were furrowing, glinting sweat with their exertions. One of them weakened. Haddad looked up sharply, saw the man's eyes cross in his face, his mouth slacken, his hands flutter on the reed tube.

Haddad gestured impatiently to one who stood in reserve. That one pulled the sagging man out of line, caught up the pipe, and resumed the steady blowing.

In a few moments, the mixture in the basin caught fire.

It always went like this. But only Haddad understood and directed the sequence, because he alone knew the numbers of handfuls of malachite and charcoal to mix, of strokes to make, of breaths to take, of torches to light. That knowledge was his contribution to the magic.

The river watered the land's grasses, making them green, one of the colors of life. From the sky the sun's red fire — another life color — slew those grasses in the field, making them pale and brown, one of the colors of death.

Sparks struck from the river rocks ignited those dried grasses, making them burn yellow-hot — more life color — like the sun. The rains watered the forest's trees, making them green, while the yellow-hot fire under the earth blackened their flesh, turning it the color of corruption.

The malachite stone under the earth was green, color of life. When malachite mixed with the dead trees, in the presence of the body's breath and the yellow fire, then a new thing would be born. And behold, it would have the red color of life and of the sun.

That was the principle: life and death, body and breath, in constant revolution, driven by the sun's everlasting power.

Haddad concentrated hard on this burning mixture, furrowing his own brows. By expecting, hoping, and waiting, he tried to make the change come. And he was always vastly thrilled when it did.

There!

Death and corruption burned away in a thick smoke. It left, scattered across the bottom of the basin, a cluster of shimmering beads. These beads glowed first yellow like the newborn sun of morning, then red like the tired sun of evening. As the apprentices continued to blow and the last of the corrupt powders burned away, the beads scurried around on the smooth stone like live things. When one met another, they joined, forming a larger bead, red and yellow.

Breathe in, breathe out, the apprentices continued to feed a fire that was no more. In its wake, the sunlike beads flowed together into a single, reddening lump. As their breath failed and the pipes sagged out of their mouths one and all, the lump flattened and grew darker yet.

But that darkness was illusory, as Haddad knew. In a few more moments, when it was cool, he could take up the lump and pound it against the face of the stone. And then, unlike any other substance of Haddad's experience, this "firerock" could be worked into smooth shapes. It would take these shapes more readily than a chip of flint or piece of river stone; it would hold them more certainly than a sliver of bone or cattle horn.

Haddad could draw it into fine threads that were just as smooth but stronger than yarns of sheep's hair. He could make the metal into funny faces, or bowls, or bits of ornament. And, also unlike any other substance, the more he worked it, the brighter and redder and more like the evening sun it became. It would glitter and shine like nothing else, except perhaps the setting sun on the face of the river.

That was the magic, and Haddad was extraordinarily proud of it.

It would be another thousand years before Haddad's distant descendants would begin experimenting with the magic that he passed down to them. They would mix various sands and rocks with the base green malachite, altering the cycle of life and death. In the course of these additions, one artisan would sprinkle in a measure of tin — a soft, white metal with even less practical use than the copper that Haddad's magic created. Added in the right proportion, however — anywhere from five to twenty percent of the mix — the white metal would stiffen and strengthen the red copper, making a tough, durable slab that Haddad's descendants would call "bronze."

This new metal was harder to work than the other, and it did not turn the same satisfying, sunlike red in return for their effort. But in just a few years more, another of Haddad's descendants would discover how easily this bronze took and held a cutting edge.

Then the fun would begin.

> *Invasion of Egypt by Hyksos horsemen*
> *Invasion of India by Aryan nomads*
> *Invasion of Britain by Celtic tribesmen*
> *Invasion of Greece by Achaean noblemen*

Thebes, 1374 B.C.

If he was wrong about this, the Lord Osiris would surely eat him. Or feed him alive to jackal-headed Anubis.

Amenhotep stared moodily outward from his seat in the shade, his eyes sweeping across the palace's inner courtyard.

There, in the sun, upon the surface of packed sand, his women were playing. Each woman had three balls of leather stuffed with bran and tied up with string, all about as wide as Amenhotep's fist. The women threw them in the air in intricate patterns, sometimes crossing their arms between one throw and the next, sometimes jumping and kicking out with their legs before a throw. The object of the game, as Amenhotep understood it, was to catch the balls in succession. Anyone who failed at this then had to bend down and let another ride on her back as on an ass. The more skillful rode and threw their balls, until one of them also failed in the catching. Then she, too, bent and was ridden in humiliation.

Women's games, played in idleness.

Under the stern, ever-watchful eye of the sun.

Amenhotep had been taught that the gods of his land were many and divided, like those flying skin balls. Their affairs were many and complex, like the game of tossing and catching, with arms crossed or legs kicking. And the forfeits in those affairs were complicated, like being ridden as an ass. All of this was because Khem, the land divided by the river and the flood, was a complex place and needed subtle and complicated guardians.

Like Osiris, ruler of the underworld. Whose brother Set had killed him and scattered the pieces of his body into fourteen sacred places across the land. Whose sister-wife Isis gathered up the pieces and made him whole again. Whose son Horus in turn killed Set and became ruler of the divided land, becoming father-many-times to Amenhotep himself.

But if the godhead were truly divided — like Osiris' body, like the community of Isis and Horus, Anubis and Maat, Nut and Set — then the land would also be divided. As the desert is separate from the fields of grain. As one bank of the river is separate from another. As the water is separate from the land. Yet Amenhotep knew this was not so.

Could a man not walk from the wet fields into the dry desert and his feet never leave the land itself? Did the river not rise each year, in the great flood, covering the land with its body? Could a man not walk down the bank of the river into water rising above his knees, above his waist, and still his feet be upon the solid land? Was not the distant sea still more water that covered the land of the sea bottom, and did not the sailors feel the anchor stones *thunk* against it when they tethered their ships for the night?

The land was all one thing, in flood or in drought.

The cup of the land and its river of water was for the people, whether they were at work or at play or at rest.

The dome of the sky with its river of stars was for the sun, whether he rose and lighted the land, or slept and darkened the day.

The land and its people were mortal and divided.

The sky and its sun were immortal and singular.

And, as the land went on under the river and beneath the sea, so the sky went under the land. The sun followed it down below when he disappeared for the night. Thus night and day were all one thing; they might appear to be divided only because the sun was in hiding for part of the time.

Only the sun went on forever, unchanging.

Only the sun was supremely powerful.

Shining as Aton, he was merciful in his fruitfulness, drawing the green shoots from the mud. He was terrible in his heat, drawing the blowflies out of an improperly tended corpse. He was the rising of the river and the baking of the land. And, when he hid beneath the world, then men slept and for a time joined the dead in their blind confusions.

Amenhotep had long understood this in his belly. Yet now the knowledge was also clear in his head, for he had worked it out by himself. The new idea stood in opposition to everything his father and his priests had told him about the gods. But still, he could see it so clearly.

Only, if Amenhotep were wrong about it, Osiris would eat him with a great and toothful smile. And perhaps Osiris would not even wait for him to die and surrender himself for judgment. So a prudent man, however much he believed in his newfound wisdom, would do well to take steps that would guard himself against calamity.

Any peasant of the fields might smear mud on his doorpost, untell his name in the rolls of the priests, travel to another town, and be done with it. With another name, that man would then escape the wrath of the gods, unmade as they were.

But Pharaoh's name was everywhere. The cartouche of Amenhotep-his-father, and now Amenhotep-the-son, was carved into every wall of the temples and cut on the steles at every crossroads and in every marketplace.

What was Pharaoh to do?

Change the name. For good luck and succor, he would

take a new name under his new belief. He would call him-self "Aton Is Pleased," and thereby seek protection and guidance from the all-ruler. And to make this conversion complete, he would strike the old name and add the new on every papyrus roll, incise it on every stone and into every wall. And thus the old gods, unmade as they were, would look and look for Amenhotep — and never find him.

The change, such an amount of writing and carving, would require a great deal of work. But then, did not Pharaoh have slaves to command? And would not the scale of effort impress all the people of Khem with his sincerity?

Still, the change would deface the stone of the temple walls, marring the royal likeness with the blot of scratching out and etching anew. But then, did not Pharaoh com-mand the hands of the masons? They would simply have to cut a little deeper into the rock. Then the new name, "Ikhnaton," would cast a longer shadow among the bless-ings that Aton showered down upon his Pharaoh.

And that was as it should be.

Empire of the Persians
Empire of the Athenians
Empire of the Carthaginians
Empire of the Romans

Rome, 477 A.D.

Beowin was busy smashing noses when Roderic found him.

"Come on! There's gold still to get here," Roderic called. "And Alaric has a temple he wants to pull down. We need your strong back for that."

Beowin squinted up at him. "In a minute. Have to finish this."

He had set the marble bust at a slight angle, tipped back on its base, with the nape of its neck resting firmly against a piece of stone. Beowin eyed the angle critically. "Needs to be just right," he explained. Then he hefted his war axe, taking a measured two-hand grip, with the blunt edge facing forward.

If it was Roderic who was going to smash the statue, he'd have hit it from the side. And he'd have left it on the pedestal in the first place. Then one hard blow against the temple, reinforced by a couple of running steps, would shatter the whole thing. Or one sideways blow against the nostril if, like Beowin, he just wanted to take off the nose.

But Beowin was doing it differently. And that made a kind of sense, for Beowin had a lot of practice at this.

"Why do you spend so much time with the faces?" Roderic had once asked his friend. "And why the noses, particularly? Why not the eyes? Or the ears or lips?"

Beowin paused to consider the matter seriously. "Someone will find them, one day," he said at last. "Maybe a friend or relative. Maybe someone who never knew them at all. And there they are, these Caesars, with their fancy noses all broken off." Beowin clamped his own nostrils between two fingers. "Abd den dey talk like dis!" He unclamped his nose and laughed out loud.

Evidently, Beowin imagined these stone forms were somehow spiritually linked to the bones of the dead. Maybe the Romans had thought so, to have made so many of them. Then one day the spirits would rise up and become abashed by their new deformities. So Beowin had made an art of breaking off just the noses.

So he always took the bust down carefully, set it on the ground and braced it with a stone, then checked all the angles. Like an old Greek philosopher with a straight-edge and a compass. Now he was standing beside the statue's ear, bending over the face with great attention. His two-handed grip extended just the right length along the haft on his axe. He tapped the flat end against the tip of the cold, white nose. Then Beowin drew the axehead up in a high, half-circle swing, twisting his whole body with the effort. He brought it around and down.

The nose exploded off the face in a cloud of white dust. The blow left a deep gouge between the cheekbones and under the eyes.

Beowin spat into the hole. He left the bust lying against the stone. If Roderic had been doing this himself, he would have set the head back on its column, for show.

"A temple, you say?" Beowin looked up with a grin. "Any pretty priestesses?"

"All gone, I'm afraid. . . . But Alaric thinks they might have hidden gold under the roof, in the eaves."

"Well then, priests? Their men are kind of delicate and not at all strong."

"Gone, too."

"Damn!"

But Beowin came along with him anyway — that is, until he saw another statue with a whole nose. Then his friend's attention wandered immediately. So Roderic left him in the Forum, trying to lower the full-body statue without breaking off the head or hands. Clearly he wanted just the nose to be missing when someone found it. Roderic went on to the temple site alone.

The whole world was moving. Alaric and his band of Goths, as well as the Vandals, the Lombards, the Saxons, and a dozen other tribes that Roderic knew only by reputation, all were loose in the vineyards and fields which the old Romans had kept for themselves so long.

Beowin was a fool to bother with the statues and their noses — Roderic understood that clearly enough. A man had no time to waste on artworks and such windy considerations as what a dead Roman's friends would think when they saw him "widoubt hid dose."

The thing to do was get the gold, the jewels if any, now and then a cup or plate of polished metal, any weapons that would fit a horseman's hand, and ride on. Leave the furniture. Leave the statues. Use any women they found for a night at most, and then leave them, too. And ride.

For there were worse things in the world than rape and pillage, Roderic knew. Pushing in behind the Goths and Vandals, raiding hard against the Celts and the Saxons to the north, came another people. Dark-clothed riders from the steppes. People of the dawnlands. Small people, bowlegged from sitting their horses for weeks at a time. Smelly people who lived in skin tents. Who knew nothing of gold or women. Who'd kill you soon as look at you, and they'd do it for the pure pleasure of killing. Who drank the blood of their enemies — which was to say everyone who came in their path — and left the bones for wild animals to pick over. Who spoke no tongue that anyone could understand. Who stopped at nothing.

The only wise course for men like Alaric and his band was to gather all the *gelt* they could lay hands on, take a day's provisions, and then ride ahead of the storm. Somewhere, probably in the south, they might find safety from the marauders. But until then, to linger here was to invite danger. And to waste time breaking up statues was purest folly.

For the world had gone mad.

> *Edward the Confessor*
> *William the Conqueror*
> *Henry the Navigator*
> *Elizabeth the Great*

London, 1688 A.D.

Lord Effenberry had already put enough of his money in ship bottoms or their cargoes. He did not see any reason to place more of his money at risk in trade.

"But think of the good of the nation!" Shadwell exclaimed.

"How so?" Effenberry rumbled.

"You're a rich man, my lord. You can afford to risk the losses of a sea voyage. Natural losses to storm and tide, unnatural losses due to piracy and the ruthlessness of barbarian princes."

"Of course," Effenberry replied. "That's reasonable. There can be no great profit without commensurate risk."

"But that is the whole issue of Mister Lloyd's proposition. We all have money in the ocean trade, and we each of us have reached a sticking point — because of the risk. Some men, whose capital is sorely needed to float new ventures, will not place any of it — again, because of the risk."

"I never said the American trade was for weaklings," Effenberry said stoutly.

"Ah, but that is just the point, my lord! If we can halve

the risk, quarter it, chase it away by tenths and twentieths, then we can draw the shy ones into the game again. There is need enough and more. We create vaster amounts of wealth. And you will benefit, too, when your own risk is diminished. . . . In fact, did you not participate, you might be left out and put at a severe disadvantage."

Effenberry did not like the sound of that. It seemed to be a threat. "Explain the scheme to me again," was all he would say.

"It's simple enough, my lord. The owner of a vessel asks our Society to take a share in it, not to profit from the sale, but to pay fair value for hull and cargo should they come to harm. He, the owner, places a value on the whole and asks us to pledge to cover the loss, should such a disaster occur. Then, because each of us risks only a fraction of the total value, and because the greater probability is that the vessel will arrive safely to port, the risks of ocean trade are greatly reduced."

"Sounds a daft sort of proposition to me! Why should I openly encourage my competitor? And why should I care to make good on *his* losses?"

"Because, my lord," Shadwell said patiently, "he will *pay* you for the service. In return for your pledge, he will give you a proportionate share of the commission he offers. He puts up a part of the potential profit, in order to get relief from all of the potential loss. No longer will the foundering of one ship rob him of the profits from the ten that do come home. And all of us make money when the wind is fair."

"And when the wind blows foul? What then? There will be folly in men's hearts where there is no risk."

"Why, when the wind is foul or pirates be afoot, then our prudent captains will delay their voyages, as always. After all, sir, we but wager our fortunes. They wager their very lives — and we profit from their innate caution."

"So the wind will always blow fair, is that it?"

"And the profit always increase."

It always did that, as Lord Effenberry knew.

Since the discovery of the Americas, two hundred years ago, a circular trade had developed across the Atlantic.

Cheap English cloth and dull steel knives were shipped to Africa and offered in exchange for prime slaves, who were chained and taken to the Caribbean in trade for Jamaican sugar and molasses and their byproduct rum, which were valued in the northern colonies and paid for with Carolina cotton and Virginia tobacco, which in turn were prized in the textile mills and smoking rooms of England.

And then, eighty-nine years ago, with the wealth of the East Indies reliably proved by the crafty Dutch, the Honorable Company had established a more distant commercial empire. There were only rumors as yet — no facts, but resounding rumors — of the possibility for developing a similar trading circle there. Opium might be grown in India and traded with the Chinese pirates for silver. That bullion could in turn buy the teas and silks reserved for the Chinese emperors. And those trade goods might bring a fancy price in England and on the Continent.

That was a bad business, Effenberry believed, dealing directly with pirates. It would increase the risks out of all proportion. And greater risk would bring increased fear — more need for a prudent man to hedge his bets.

So . . . yes . . . perhaps this Society of Names that was growing up in the coffeehouses would be an avenue for making money, after all.

"And what of this man Lloyd?" Effenberry asked at last. "What does he get out of it?"

"Why, as we of the Society negotiate our pledges and the value we place upon hull and cargo, we will drink his coffee, eat his food, use up his quills and paper, and bring into his house the custom of those who can talk knowledgeably with us about winds and tides and the trade in foreign bazaars. Edward Lloyd says he hopes only to make a profit on our customary usages."

"Is that all? No urge to dip his own hand?"

"Lloyd claims he's only a purveyor of food and fellowship, with no head for larger business."

"Then the more fool he. . . . Yes, Shadwell, I shall visit this coffeehouse with you."

"You'll not be disappointed, my lord."
James Watt
Thomas Edison
Robert Goddard
William Shockley

Palo Alto, California, 2018 A.D.

"Mr. Morrissey, come quickly!" the voice exclaimed over the phone. "Contamination alert in Laboratory Two!"

Sean Morrissey pushed back from his desk and went out of the office at a run, not caring if the sudden exertion caused him to sweat through the armpits of his dress shirt. He left his suitcoat hanging in the concealed closet behind the office's executive veneer.

As soon as Morrissey hit the long corridor leading down to the laboratory complex, the muscles of his legs, abdomen, and shoulders fell into the familiar loping pattern of his morning jog. That was the best way to cover ground while conserving wind and energy.

Sean Morrissey's run had nothing of panic in it — just sober urgency. And the reason for his urgency was simple. This was the third contamination problem at Morrissey Bio Designs in one week, and Sean knew what he could expect to find when he came up against the double-glass doors and the cardkey circuits guarding the labs.

The source of contamination would probably be nothing more than a dropped petri dish, or failed seals on an incubator, or the careless misrouting of a specimen. But down in the labs he would find two or three rooms of interrupted activity, isolated from the rest of the world with steel drop doors and flashing red lights. In the corners would be frightened people huddled around oxygen canisters, breathing through yellow masks. Their eyes would be rolling around, searching across tile floors and over gleaming steel benches, as if they could actually see the mutated bacteria, the fragmented viruses, the virulently altered protozoa escaping from their cultures in a flood of plague. See them and flee, before the eyeless mites could spot the lab technicians themselves and swarm into exposed respiratory systems, into eyes and ears, into the other moist pathways of the human body.

Even those who worked in the lab every day were not immune to fearful fantasies.

By the time Morrissey actually arrived at the card station, the Red Team — with its inevitable inspector from the Environmental Protection Agency — was already in control of the situation.

"You cannot pass, sir," the team leader told him.

"I'm Sean Morrissey."

"I know that, sir. But it's out of your hands now."

And that was true enough. From this point onward, the protocols were immutably set: individual evacuation, personal decontamination, medical evaluation, and extended observation. Then, after the people had been extracted one by one from the affected areas, there would be the sequential courses of fumigation, ultraviolet irradiation, sterilization, ablution, and certification. Then the program director on the series that had gone wrong would determine what steps in the genetic construction and culturing procedure had failed, write up his or her report, and try to put the whole process back on schedule.

In all of this, Morrissey himself was just window dressing. He was a polite face in a suit, put forward to explain to the media why the public was not, and never could be, in any serious danger. And explain this while taking the inevitable shots from all sides about the lab's previous safety record, its meager budget for preventive measures, its few contracts that were actually initiated by the Department of Defense, and all the other silliness that these accidents always stirred up.

It was Morrissey's responsibility to face the cameras because this was his company — his and the clique of venture capitalists and investment bankers who constituted its board of directors. But the firm had his name on it. Besides, Sean had once been a research geneticist and so he could appear to talk knowledgeably about the eyeless mites that were creeping around inside — even if he was now a dozen years out of the lab and his education obsolete by his own company's current hiring standards.

Given these realities, while he waited for the Red Team to

launch its protocols, Sean Morrissey made the decision that had been hanging fire on his desk for three months now.

After all, the technology was in place. In just the past ten years, the gene baths, electron micromanipulators, and amino acid spoolers that were once the pride of Morrissey Bio Designs had already become laughably antiquated. Newer equipment which was now on the market combined these separate procedures into an integrated stream under full computer control. No one any longer needed the racks of test tubes and stacks of petri dishes, carried by human hands from one machine to another, fumbling about with storage protocols, batch labeling, inventory, and inspection.

The new way involved staining and spooling the genetic material into ever-flowing fluid channels which were capillaried through silicon control blocks no wider than a human hair. Instead of a prolonged period of natural culturing, the machines spun the viral protein coat or the cell wall and cytoplasm directly over the freshly spooled DNA chains. Target strains no longer *grew*; they were immediately and continuously *manufactured*.

This had many significant advantages over older methods.

First, quality control. The computers created exact replicas of the target genotype, without the possibility of mutation. The strain would be guaranteed pure from the beginning of the run to the end.

Second, greater phenotype accessibility. The spoolers could weave new patterns, especially those that might not be viable in nature or capable of reproducing as an independent organism. This characteristic also lowered the potential for future wildfire contaminations.

Third, simplicity. Because the virus or bacterium did not have to survive in the traditional sense, the laboratory could dispense with much of the genetic machinery of a life-form. The product could be shipped as inert capsules, set to trigger into a simulacrum of life and function under the precise, client-specified conditions. Otherwise, they were a harmless combination of complex chemicals, endowed with an extended shelf life.

Morrissey Bio Designs had to acquire the new equipment and change its production capability soon. And when it did so, why should the company be limited to a new building in Palo Alto, or on any other patch of Earthside real estate?

Sean Morrissey had already received two offers for engineering his next factory in orbit, with prefabricated modules launched from the magnetic catapult at Whitney Center in the Sierras. Then his staff and their computers would sit on the ground in Palo Alto, working in an office environment that was free from any possible contamination. The computers would direct the automated baths and spoolers that were suspended in orbit, drawing on protein and amino acid stocks that were replenished by regularly scheduled shuttle missions. The products of the assembly line would return to Earth by drop box.

And, if anything living or potentially living were to leak, then Morrissey could open the satellite and its machines to vacuum and solar radiation. Clean, simple, sanitary. End of problem.

Or, if something really vicious were to get out of hand — a toxic anaerobe, say, or some bug that thrived on the energy in direct sunlight — then he could write off the whole complex with a small nuclear warhead, without loss of human life or damage to the company's irreplaceable working files.

Let the people do their brainwork on Earth; the messy physical part could be done high up and far away. And besides, would the all-invasive Environmental Protection Agency even *have* jurisdiction over a facility that spent only a fraction of its workday above U.S. territory?

The prospect was looking better and better to Morrissey.

So, he decided, he would propose it to his board of directors at their next meeting.

Part 2

Minus Fourteen Days ... and Counting

Bright is the Earth when you rise.
When you shine as Aton by day
you drive away the darkness.
You light the Two Lands into daily festivity,
awakening them, raising them up.
The people bathe and dress themselves,
raise up their arms in thanks to the dawn
for a new day in which to do their work.

— From Ikhnaton's "Hymn to the Sun"

Chapter 4

Tangled Fields

Rise
   Expand
      Rush
         Explode

The unbalanced bulge of thermal energy, generated by that non-probabilistic surge of fusion explosions in the core more than a million years ago, now blasts its way out toward the radiant surface. The overflow rises like a bubble of sour gas through the star's convective layers, causing havoc.

Throughout a region of the sun extending across twenty-two degrees of arc, the naturally upwelling columns of ionized gas in the photosphere suddenly bloat and expand. Laminar flows, caught between the radiant center and the outer edges, create waves of turbulence and peel tornadoes of white fire off the walls of each convection cell. The orderly structure of the columns, packed like organ pipes in a choir loft, collapses as the heat surge pushes its way outward.

The bloom of energy, expressed largely as high-frequency photons, fountains up into the solar corona. There the tenuous plasma, whose ambient temperature already exceeds two million degrees, siphons off the bulge of excess radiation and dissipates it harmlessly into space.

The passage of the heat wave, however, has left a massive wound in the convective layers and a weakness in the structure of the photosphere.

Loop
   Coil
      Loop
         Coil

Any globe of churning, electrically charged particles — which is all a star can claim to be — creates its own pumpkin-shaped magnetic field. The field lines associated with the sun are vast, extending far beyond the visible photosphere, beyond the chromosphere and the wisps of corona, connecting in loops that curve into the space claimed by the orbital paths of the planets.

Like most rotating bodies, the sun's field lines run approximately parallel to its axis of rotation. That is, they emerge from the area around one pole, loop outside into empty space, and reconverge near the opposite pole. South to north, positive to negative, and usually strongest and most collected at the top and bottom of the globe. The magnetic field arises from the sun's huge physical mass and the agitation of all those charged particles. The force lines, anchored in the sluggish, densely packed core, turn with that mass in a period of twenty-seven days.

If the sun were a solid ball — or only partially liquid, like the inner planets with their molten cores — then the field lines would be trapped immovably in the matrix of iron and stone. But the sun is not solid; its plasma is more liquid than water, more volatile than burning oil or methane.

Rotation in a solid ball, like the little green world, imparts a wrenching differential velocity that the surface structure must endure. The poles will seem not to turn at all, while the equator spins at a thousand miles an hour. In between, the basaltic land masses of the crust must shift and bend to accommodate the resulting stresses.

But in a globe of gas or plasma, where nothing is more solid than two charged particles rubbing past each other in the suspension of magnetic repulsion, those stresses wrench upon nothing. Each square kilometer of surface finds its own speed, and the atmosphere flows into banded patterns, like the faces of Jupiter and Saturn. Even on the little green world, the mantling shell of gas lapses into wide belts of alternately moving and stagnant air called "trade winds" and the "horse latitudes."

The sun's visible surface might also settle itself into such a stationary display, were it not for the fusion fires burning

deep in the core, and for the intervening layers of opaque
plasma that bubble and rush to carry the heat outward to
the surface. The convective zone's rising columns of heated
gas creates dense clots of material. Up near the poles, the
ions in these rising heat cells can become aligned to the
prevailing magnetic flux, trapped in the cells' electrically
charged material, frozen in place inside a columnar
granule of upwelling gas.

So, instead of passing through the slippery plasma like a
navigational buoy anchored against the flooding tide, the
field line is bent at the core and dragged off with the
sphere's differential rotation, heading out into the faster-
moving currents like that same buoy when its anchor chain
has been cut.

Drift
  Spin
    Drift
      Spin

When the field lines become strongly trapped in a convection cell and are ripped away from the great parent
loops up near the poles, moving down into quadrants that
are spinning more quickly, then the orphans tend to spin
around each other, acquiring perturbations that stretch
and twist their magnetic domains and break up their
uniform polarity. In retaliation, seeking a new equilibrium, the broken lines curve over and plunge back into
the photosphere. They create a new north or south polar
charge to complement the distant place they can no longer
reach, half a globe and more away.

So a trapped field line becomes a tiny loop, a horseshoe
of potential, rising out of one convection cell and plunging
back into another nearby. The opposing charges at the exit
and entry points attract each other, and so the pair of
anchor points stays together in the roiling convective layer.

Now, pulling a field line away from the pole is the usual,
or probabilistic, way that a magnetic anomaly can form on
the sun's surface and start to grow. There are, however,
alternate methods of generation.

For example, when that thermal bloom collapsed a

broad, twenty-two-degree area of convection cells near the equator, the resulting weakness in the outer layers offered a temporary shortcut to the solar magnetic field. The force lines bent and redirected themselves out through the electrically quiet patch, truncating one or more of the great loops that stretch from pole to pole.

A suddenly active region like this does not form smoothly, nor does it create a uniform magnetic charge. So close to the equator, equidistant from the two poles, the sun's magnetic domains enter a war for dominance there. Alternating divots of north and south field strength attract and link to each other. Parallel turfs with similar charges repel and isolate each other. So, once again, separate loops and horseshoes of potential form and dance around each other in the sun's outer layers.

  Twist
    Twine
      Twist
        Twine

As the short, horseshoe-curved field lines twist and stretch, buffeted by their movement through areas of more stable plasma, they gain new energy from their kinetic motion. They twist and curl around opposing columns of charged particles. The violent winding-up of these ion tubes works like an electric dynamo, inducing a strong current and strengthening the magnetic flux. The fields associated with a naturally occurring anomaly can reach 2,000 to 3,000 gauss, or a thousand times the Earth's own field. The fields over a major blowout patch can exceed ten or twenty times that strength.

A mammoth potential current flows through the horseshoe loop, induced by the furiously curling gases. The already strong and strengthening magnetic field trapped in these anchoring tubules repels the surrounding solar material; so they rise toward the sun's surface, the photosphere. And where their trapped fields touch the surface, they create quiet, dense, cool pools of matter, isolated by their high field strength from the heated gas that is continually rising around them.

These pools develop and darken long after that initial bubble of core-overload energy has escaped through the photosphere and poured itself upward into the corona. The depleted column, with nothing but magnetic charge to sustain and shape it, lies passively on the sun's face and moves with the star's rotation around the equator.

To see these pools from the outside, against the background of the photosphere, they are so cold as to appear black. The surrounding material, repelled by their charges, is slightly warmer but still not as hot as the rest of the photosphere. So this apron appears as a shadowed gray.

For half a millennium, Earthly astronomers with the means to look beyond and through the sun's glare called such dense shadows "umbra," and the gray shadings "penumbra." Darkness and near-darkness. Sunspots and their surrounding blush of cool death.

The spots, whether drifting down from the poles or arising out of the equator, appeared irregularly on the face of the sun. They came in staggered cycles, like an outbreak of plague, like rashes and buboes on the face of the daystar. So early astronomers thought of them as a sickness, as signals of catastrophe. The blemishes were considered portents of dissolution and disruption. For, after all, the things of heaven — and was not the sun the brightest and most necessary of the objects sighted beyond Earth? — were all known to be pure and unchanging. Spots on the sun could bode no good to anyone.

Reinforcing this provincial and time-limited viewpoint was the uncertainty of the solar outbreak. For reasons not clearly understood then, the black spots arose, grew in number, peaked, and fell away in cycles of eleven Earthly years. In between these cycles the sun, as humans could observe it, wore a blank, white face of perfect health. Then the sickness spots would pop out again or drift down from the sun's clear brow.

But sometimes the spots did not come at all. For year after year, decade after decade, the sun showed its clear face. And then people breathed more easily, hoping that the daystar had finally settled down to a regular, healthy life. That the plague had passed at last.

Strangely, although the sunspots themselves seemed to be dark pores and cooler pools on the burning face, they appeared to make the star burn more brightly, like fever in a plague victim. And when the spots went away, the sun's thermal output declined. On Earth, the rivers froze where before they had run all winter long. Glaciers oozed down from the snows of the mountaintops.

These effects spanned periods longer than most single human lifetimes. So, only when one man wrote down what he observed one morning and one winter, and when another man years later read those notes and compared them with *this* morning and *this* winter, could any person on the green world appreciate that a greater cycle was afoot.

But when the sunspots went away for so long, then most people stopped caring. They took no notice of what was not there. All but the astronomers themselves would grow forgetful, being preoccupied with other wonders, other problems. The world slumbered, shivered in its bed, but slumbered on.

● Chapter 5

Prophet Without Honor

Tick!
  Creak!
    Groan!
      Click!

**Aboard the Solar Research Vessel *Hyperion*,
March 7, 2081**

The ship's thermal management systems hummed and whirred while her silvered metal skin alternately crept and shrank, passing through and settling into fleeting new configurations as she transited the solar disk.

With each kilometer of advance in *Hyperion*'s orbit, the superstructure's blunt end exposed micrometrically now more, now less of its face to the white blaze of energy. The circulating systems pumped their freon gel now faster, now slower to carry the excess heat backward and outward to the radiating tendrils of the heat exchangers. And there, in the tenuous shadow of the ship's mushroom cap, they conducted an unbalanced trade of warmth for warmth and so maintained the margin of coolness that supported two human lives.

Dr. Hannibal Freede barely noticed these tiny sounds, in part because he had lived with them for more than one hundred and eighty days. That was just over two solar years at approximately the same distance from the sun as the planet Mercury—except, of course, that *Hyperion*'s orbit was polar instead of equatorial. And in part Freede ignored the stressful workings of his ship because his full attention was now glued to the monitor screen in front of him.

There the sun's image, filtered by his equipment to the narrow spectrum of hydrogen-alpha radiation, resembled the fiery mask that the Wizard of Oz had shown Dorothy and her friends on their first audience in the Emerald City. In the classic film of that story, Freede remembered, the wizard's head had been a great ball of cotton saturated with naphtha — or was it plain kerosene? — and set afire. The face had burned with little jets and gobbets of yellow flame licking upward in a smooth curve around the ball, darkening at the edges where the smoke gathered and rushed toward the ceiling. Those flames were not unlike the spicules of false fire which Freede could see on the disk that hung above *Hyperion*.

His eyes traveled up the screen, toward the blurred edge that was continuously passing beyond *Hyperion*'s singular point of view. This edge was similarly darkened — but not by smoke. His straight-on view of the surface area immediately below the ship had probed more deeply into the solar atmosphere than this slantwise line of sight toward the globe's limb. The deeper one looked into the thermally stratified layers of that atmosphere, the brighter the observing field appeared. Now the area he was trying to inspect at the far edge of the sun was limited to the higher, cooler, and therefore much darker regions of the photosphere. Too dark to show clearly what he wanted to see.

Still, Freede searched in this area for any last signs of the anomaly he had faintly detected yesterday and had been tracking continuously since then. In the altered, hydrogen-alpha image, his eyes strained to see between the tips of those dancing spicules which further fuzzed up the darkening limb.

For an instant Freede could almost believe he discerned there a pattern of black scoops or crevasses. That high up on the solar disk, the clefts would certainly be foreshortened and flattened by the Wilson Effect, a trick of perspective described more than three hundred years earlier by the Scottish astronomer Alexander Wilson. The man had thereby demonstrated how the recurring dark marks on the sun's surface actually had depth and might indeed be holes in the photosphere. Viewed practically edge-on, they would probably look like the curving smear of thin, gray-edged streaks Freede had seen yesterday. He strained now to find those same, broad smudges of cool shadow.

The anomaly had certainly been strange: a horizontal clouding-up of the disk's edge, deeper and blacker than normal limb darkening, and wider by far than any penumbra he'd ever seen in the record tapes. Twenty-two degrees wide it was, according to yesterday's measurements. And then today, nothing. . . . Or maybe the smudges were never there to begin with.

But wait a minute now! How far, after all, had *Hyperion* traveled down the sun's face in the last twenty-four hours? Enough to carry those shadows over the horizon?

He checked with the computer: since the first sighting yesterday, *Hyperion* had moved four-point-two million kilometers farther toward the south pole, which would soon pass immediately below him. And the anomaly had been much higher up, almost on the equator. Thus the distance his ship had traveled south, coupled with the sun's own rotation in its twenty-seven-day period, would certainly have shifted whatever it was he thought he'd seen to the north and west — out of his line of sight by now.

Freede next tried to correlate that lost visual sighting with *Hyperion*'s ongoing magnetometric survey of the sun's surface layers. He studied the pattern of gauss readings that was displayed on another screen, taken from instruments extended on long booms beyond the magnetic interference of his own hull. But results here were inconclusive. Of course, the ship's magnetometers would now be reading the incredibly strong field flux at the south pole. Any disturbance along a slant line toward the equator was certainly lost in that whorl. And then again, maybe he had seen nothing at all.

All of this was damnably frustrating.

It was to study just such anomalies in the solar surface that Freede had built his ship. He had done it practically out of his own pocket, too, taking seed money from his family trust and supplementing it with meager donations from a patchwork of corporate and charitable endowments. *Hyperion* had been constructed to his own specifications at one of the lunar Lagrange points and launched on a time-consuming but economical orbit to achieve her own capture on the lip of the sun's immense gravity well.

Hyperion's crew consisted of Freede himself as captain, with his wife Angelika as first officer, backup helmsman, second astronomical observer, chief engineer and systems technician, quartermaster general, cook and bottlewasher, and companion. Their mission profile called for at least ten revolutions about the sun — with two of them now gone. That amount of time, as Freede had planned so many years ago, should allow him to take definitive readings and draw his own conclusions about the elusive nature of the sun's variable activity.

For example, take this smudge or crevasse or whatever it was he thought he had seen, just now disappearing around the limb. Maybe there were more of them growing on the backside of the sphere, hidden from Freede and his equipment. In his currently reduced financial circumstances, able to afford just one observing platform, he could only look at one side of the solar globe at a time. What he needed, of course, was to set up a chain of orbiting observation satellites, communicating with *Hyperion* by means of signal relays. But such extended facilities were well out of his reach.

A family fortune! The amounts had sounded so immense in the mouths of Freede's attorneys. And the annuities were large — until you tried to do something worthwhile with them, like mount a private astronomical expedition. Then the bills piled up and the cashflows drained away.

Even bringing Angelika and himself home would be a chancy maneuver. First, they would dislodge *Hyperion* from her stable, minimally elliptical solar orbit, sending the vessel into a looping, cometary flight path out beyond the orbit of Venus, three-quarters of the way to the sphere of the Earth-Moon system. Next, as Freede had arranged with the family's lawyers, a fast-moving probe would be launched on a date and trajectory that would cause it to rendezvous with *Hyperion*, take off her two-person crew and their record of observations, loop back around the star at far greater speeds, and deposit them out in the sunjammer lanes somewhere in the vicinity of Jupiter. Then Freede would put up a distress beacon and claim refuge aboard the first passing freighter, manned or automated, under the international rules governing maroon and salvage.

That the ending of a prestigious scientific mission must employ a radical and, to put it bluntly, ungentlemanly device was regrettable. But it did fit the size of Freede's purse and the magnitude of the masses and motions involved. And was not all fair in the quest for scientific understanding? Such an ungallant exit was the most minor debility of funding his mission on a virtual shoestring; the greater problem was his severe lack of auxiliary resources, such as having no relay satellites.

But then, if there *was* anything to see up there on the solar equator, perhaps someone else — stationed on the moons of the outer planets, possibly, or anywhere along the plane of the ecliptic — might be in position to verify his observation. After all, if Freede were to alert them now and describe what they should look for, then surely they would still give him credit for a first sighting.

But no one Freede could think of, who might be willing to look, was in any better position to see than he was himself. The doctor would gladly impose on his few disciples, the small body of graduate students who had heard his arguments and adopted the sun as their primary study, no matter how eccentric that might have made them in other academic eyes. But alas, at this time they were all to be found down on Earth. And right now the forward tracks of both *Hyperion*'s orbit and the Earth's were coming into alignment on the same side of the sun: the side opposite where that smudge, or whatever it had been, was currently sitting.

Freede briefly considered firing up his ship's maneuvering thruster, a simple fusion ram carved into *Hyperion*'s long axis and fueled with the high-speed particles of the solar wind. With that he could easily reach the delta-vee to enable a shift in orbit. Of course, while firing it he would have to shut down the ship's main heat exchangers and survive with cabin insulation for the duration of the burn. It was the alternative of last resort, of course. . . .

And an unnecessary one. Whatever anomaly Freede had seen, if it was significant, it would just have to survive the thirteen-odd days until the sun's rotation brought it around again to his near side. And by then *Hyperion* herself would have moved some fifty-four million kilometers farther along in her eighty-eight day orbit. She would have covered one-sixth of the face of the sun and be coming into visual range— in fact, just rising above the anomaly's own horizon—and so be in an increasingly better position to study it. Freede would then get a fix on whatever it was he had observed.

Or maybe it was nothing at all.

Snap!
　　Gurgle!
　　　　Hiss!
　　　　　　Pop!

JPL Institute, Caltech, Pasadena, California, March 7, 2081

"Say again, Doctor!" Piero Mosca shouted into the microphone. "You're breaking up!"

He was consciously overriding the last few syllables of Dr. Freede's transmission — but no matter. A burst of static from the sun's south pole had already gulped them down. The man's mouth worked in the scrambled image on the monitor screen, but nothing was coming through. Then his whole face dissolved into horizontal black lines.

Sixteen minutes later — delayed coming and going by the lightspeed lag — the doctor's image faded in again as he boosted the gain on his end. Dr. Freede nodded into the video pickup and immediately began repeating himself. He now used clipped, supposedly garble-proof sentences.

It almost worked this time.

"I said, Po, that I *Crack!* something. Just as we *Pop!* the pole, but it was already up near the e-*Squelch!*. That's the far side now, of course, from your *Crack!* of view. Big God-*Fizzle* thing! Gone into the mists for me now, of course. We'll see it when the rotation brings *Hiss-sss*. If anything's still there. I hope it will be.

"As to what it was, I'm *Squelch!* some visual images. Nothing much to look at, really. Just some kind of shadow, but quite wide. Or so it seemed from *Hiss-sss*. Maybe a penumbra. And maybe just a glitch in the *Pop!* With all the heat, you know.

"At any rate, look for it *Crack!* the eastern limb. Latitude *Squelch!* degrees *Boom!* and about twelve degrees east of my current *Grumble-umble* when sighted. Possibly you'll get a read on this thing before I do."

And that — what with the garbling and the time delays, except for hurried regards sent to his colleagues back on Earth, most of whom wouldn't return them anyway — was all Dr. Freede had time to say. End of the weekly transmission. And once-a-week was all the Earthly stationkeeping that the doctor's expedition could afford to fund.

Putting the microphone down, Po Mosca studied the lines on the back of his hand, thinking. So the doctor had found something, hey? A shadowlike something, after all. But something just out of his visual reach.

Of course, Mosca was prepared to believe in Dr. Freede — even when the digital images which the doctor sent, after Mosca's computer had reconstructed them, showed nothing definite. Probably the whatever-it-was had been blanketed under dropouts caused by the transmission static. Upon close inspection, however, using a hand glass to take him down to the resolvable limits of the bitmap, Po still detected only normal limb darkening.

Mosca would certainly be looking, himself, when the far side of the sun came around to meet the Earth in the next two weeks. Po would take out his eight-inch Schmidt-to-Cassegrain, a relic of his childhood. He would fashion a solar filter for it from a piece of aluminized plastic sheeting, so the latent heat wouldn't pop the tube and warp the optics and so the focused sunlight wouldn't burn out his retinas. And then Po would be ready on — when was it? the twenty-first of March or shortly thereafter — to observe the smudge coming around some garbled number of degrees north or south of the equator. It shouldn't be too hard to find, if it was there at all.

But what would that prove? With his puny telescope, Piero Mosca would at most have a debatable stain on a piece of rough-grained 35-millimeter film. Or a 1,280 by 1,024-pixel image, if he used his camera's chipback in the viewing. At the very best, he would own a conversation piece. At worst, a souvenir.

And it mattered that Po should be able to get a good image. Not just to help Dr. Freede in his observations. It mattered a lot.

Bink!
  Bink!
    Bink!
      Bink!

Office of the Dean of Pure Sciences, Caltech, March 8, 2081

Dean Albert Withers tapped his electric pencil on the gray glass of his desktop screen while he simulated deep concentration.

Piero Mosca held a straight face. For a man whose job was more academician than scientist, and usually more politician than academician, Withers was appallingly bad at keeping his emotions under control. Especially his annoyance, or his distaste for an unpleasant request, or possibly it was just simple boredom he was feeling. But then, a man who routinely worked with budget requests, alumni petitions, policy committees, and faculty councils would expect to have to put up with a certain amount of tedium.

Likely Withers didn't think little Piero Mosca was worth the effort of concealing his true feelings. Not from a second-year doctoral student who hadn't even filed his dissertation topic yet — although, given Mosca's field of study and his chosen mentor, anyone could guess what it was going to be. In that case, Po was probably lucky to have gotten a Saturday morning appointment with the dean at all.

"No," Withers said at last, as if the decision were drawn from him reluctantly. "No, Mr. Mosca, I'm afraid the science faculty cannot approve your request."

"If it's a matter of rescheduling other observations, sir," Po ventured, having used the time before this meeting to study the situation and lay his groundwork, "I'm sure I can arrange personally with the students whose work would be involved. There are only two. First, Iverson has her nebula survey —"

"No, it's not the schedule that concerns me. If we thought your proposal had merit, then we could make the accommodation against less timely work. But, in this case, we cannot say that your suggested program of observations would have any scientific value."

"But I have a preliminary sighting from Dr. Freede that indicates a —"

"I should point out to you, young sir, that Dr. Hannibal Freede, with his half-baked opinions and volatile accusations, has not endeared himself to the scientific community, either at this or any other institution of higher learning."

"I thought the scientific method guaranteed that the validity of an observer's findings had nothing to do with his personality or reputation," Po said quietly.

"Now listen here . . ." Then Dean Withers did bother to control himself. "It saddens me, Piero, to see a young man of your obvious talents throw his career away on a fantasy. Forget the sun, my boy! It's a drearily predictable place. All it does is burn hydrogen, boil plasma, and expel photons. There's nothing new in that story. Nothing worth your study. Forget that fool Freede, too. He's just a crackbrain, wasting a fortune on that expedition of his. It wouldn't surprise me if his tenure were to come up for peer review next year."

"He's found a sunspot."

"He *has*? Or does he merely *claim* to have seen one?"

"He sent me a digitized image," Po said, then added truthfully enough, "but magnetically induced radio noise — because his ship was over the south pole at the time of transmission — garbled his signal. It was impossible to reconstruct."

"Humph!" Withers sniffed. "There you are. It's a garble, all right, and not just in the signal."

Privately, Piero Mosca might admit that the dean was voicing some of his own strongest doubts. Dr. Freede's marginal sighting was a long way from conclusive. And the image he'd sent was next to useless. As for Withers' and the scientific establishment's scorn for Po's choice of solar astronomy as a field of study — well, that song had played in some of Mosca's worst night fears.

Eighty years ago the sun's most active feature, the eleven-year cycle of sunspots, just seemed to wander away and die. When the last spot pair had faded from the solar disk in 1998, the then-flourishing community of solar astronomers totted up their sighting logs, drew their frequency curves, and eagerly awaited the start of the next cycle. It never came. For year after year, the sun shone with its same white face, granulated by convection turbulence and feathered with spicules. All trace of the star's renowned variability had disappeared. Gone were the cyclic fluctuations in energy output, the bare patches in the corona, the barking gaps in the solar wind, the blazing displays of solar flares — all features that the astronomers had long associated with sunspots. The sun had apparently settled down to behaving like a well-managed nuclear reactor. No surprises.

There was considerable evidence for previous lapses in the cycles. The first examination of the sun through a telescope, Galileo's crude observations in the early seventeenth century, did describe some spots. But there immediately followed a seventy-year period, from 1645 to 1715, in which almost none of them were detected.

At the time, much of Europe was enduring a period of extreme cold that historians have called the Little Ice Age. During those years the Thames River froze in London, a phenomenon that was simply unknown from earlier centuries. It was an enigma — unless one considered the effects of a lowered output of solar energy, reflected in the lack of sunspots.

Other periods of spotlessness have since been conjectured from their effects on climate, even when actual solar observations were not available. Scientists in the twentieth century computed many earlier and prolonged spot-free intervals statistically, by carbon-dating narrowly banded tree rings; the pinched rings indicated shortened growing seasons, changed weather patterns, cold spells. These tree records showed that decades and sometimes centuries of cooler than normal temperatures often passed on Earth. The prolonged absence of sunspots had its own technical name, Maunder Minimum, after the nineteenth-century British astronomer Walter Maunder.

Clearly, the sun was now going through such a minimum period. At just over eighty years, it was comparable in length to the span recorded during the seventeenth century. But did that mean the current dip in the cycle was therefore about to end?

That was the big question, wasn't it? In the previous decade or so, it had received halting debate in the scientific establishment. A few men and women in university faculties and research establishments, like Po's own JPL Institute, who had ignored the bland and friendly sun for several academic generations were beginning to speculate politely on its condition.

Everyone could agree that the sunspot cycle was likely to end in the next five or ten or twenty years. Thirty at the outside was the general consensus. At that point, then, the sun might again become an object of respectable study. And, at that point, the scientists and engineers would probably begin evaluating what the renewed sunspot activity could mean for a spacefaring humanity that was now spreading itself across the solar system. It was good for an electronic journal article every couple of years.

Then Dr. Freede had weighed into all this languid, genteel talk with a rude piece of news. His reinterpretation of magnetometer readings from the Telemachus probe, launched twelve years earlier under a cloud of funding recriminations, had convinced the doctor of a growing instability at the sun's magnetic poles. This reading, of course, was ambiguous to almost everyone else. In fact, to the few prominent astronomers who shared Dr. Freede's sense of intrigue, the twitches in the force lines became conclusive proof that sunspots were now *incapable* of developing, although no one presented a solid theoretical mechanism to support this bizarre conclusion.

Rather than debate the point, Freede had chosen to gather new evidence by launching his own expedition. That would settle the matter, he thought, once and for all. From up close — just inside the orbit of Mercury — the doctor and his equipment would be in a position to detect even the tiniest fluctuations in the sun's energy output, radio voice, x-ray face, magnetic envelope, or in any other measurement that a tightly transiting platform might take. Such minutiae, Freede had reasoned, could reveal harbingers of the old solar variability.

But that was a notion the quasi-governmental agencies and the major interworld corporations, for reasons of their own liability, preferred not to open up for consideration. So, when Freede first proposed his expedition, he was met with a stony vagueness. "What's the point of that, really?" the chairmen of the grant committees said with a shrug. "I mean, what will a solar-orbiting platform achieve that current monitoring from the Earth-Luna system doesn't already cover?"

Freede had cited the fact that these current monitoring efforts totaled less than twenty physicists. None of them was working more than part-time, and most were involved with experiments to wring ever more kilowatts from photon flux in the visible-light band.

The chairmen's response to that was just another shrug. Watching was watching, they said. If there was anything to see, the present crop of observers would see it. Request denied.

When Freede went to his own colleagues in the astronomy faculties of the great universities, he had found another kind of ennui. "The sun," the scientists told him, "is not a popular subject. It's too healthy, too normal, too dull. Surely, the sunspot cycles had once been something worth studying. But those phenomena were adequately explained more than a century ago. There's nothing new to build your reputation on *there*."

Freede then cried out that, by their own line of reasoning, the sun should necessarily be an object of immense theoretical interest. It was the only nearby example of a healthy star in its mature years, sitting squarely on the Main Sequence. Those objects that astronomers of the *nighttime* sky chose to study were either freaks like the red giants and white dwarves, or burned-out cases like neutron stars, pulsars, novae, nebulae, and other energetic oddities. That outburst, however, rather quickly closed the door on further useful discussion.

Still, it would all be a tempest in the technical journals if sunspots were not given to breeding solar flares the way blowflies bred maggots.

During those eighty years of the Maunder Minimum humankind had settled, or at least staked out and claimed, most of the marginally habitable sites in the solar system. In the process, Earth's children had to launch and hand-build everything from Earth-orbiting platforms to cylinder communities; from ground bases on the Moon and Mars to torus colonies in the Outer Satellites of Jupiter and Saturn; and all their supporting infrastructure for energy supply, atmospherics, transport, and communications. By now, everyone in the planetary economy had a financial interest in the health of those pioneering ventures, because the effort of shooting them into space had gobbled down vast sums of capital. The offworld entrepreneurs, working on the cusp and using other people's money, had entered into a huge balancing act — weighing rewards against risks — that made the art of aerial trapeze look steady and cautious by comparison.

The initial cash had come from a complicated network of national trusts and corporate credits. The earliest translunar colonies had survived their inevitable catastrophes through a frail lacework of paid-up indemnities, acknowledged liabilities, and extended reparations. No one, in those early days, had taken the time or trouble to build exactly to code or to maintain the levels of redundancy in radiation shielding, life support and hibernation, or emergency communication channels that were recommended under the ESA/NASA/JSA/Baikonur Combined Intrasystem Safety Regulations. Putting payload weight into orbit cost real money, and no one wanted to waste it on frills.

Early on, the accountants and actuaries had ruled that insulating circuits and sensors, work stations and living quarters against unforeseen bursts of electromagnetic radiation from solar flares, when no one had seen a sunspot or a flare in thirty or forty years, was a species of frill. It was probably a safe bet, too — so long as the sun agreed to remain passive and smiling, the solar wind blew regularly, the energy output remained predictable, and the violent discharges of radiant and particle energy remained just a vague memory from the olden days of ham radio and copper telephone wires.

By the year 2081, the offworld economy was now inhaling cashflows equal to the gross domestic product of South America on a daily basis. In return, it exhaled cargoes of rare earths and metals, extragravitational compounds, compressed pure gases, static energy products, deepspace observations, and hydroponically nurtured microfauna and macroflora exotica. This balanced economic arrangement would be threatened by collapse if solar flares were suddenly returned to the equation.

Po was not naive. He understood that accountants always tried to delay the cost and limit the extent of any retrofits to an ongoing operation. That attitude went double for shielding and grounding that could be classified as "prevention against a possibility" and wouldn't provide a cent in immediately calculable return.

If Po Mosca or Dr. Hannibal Freede or even the prestigious JPL Institute were to present the evidence of a *potential* sunspot and argue, quite accurately, that every capital facility currently in use in the solar system was now suddenly vulnerable, that the structure exposed too much unshielded circuitry, too many uninsulated corridors and windows and observation bubbles, too many unshrouded sensors, and far too much soft human tissue to survive a solar flare's *potential* effects — then those same accountants would bury them all under a ton of legal paper.

It was no wonder, then, that Dean Withers and the scientific community wanted to hang back and hope that the end of the current Maunder Minimum would somehow delay itself. All these people were like Italian farmers on the slopes of Vesuvius: while the mountain grumbled and smoked, they wanted to get in one or two more crops from their fields. Then they would think about moving on.

"You'll have to admit, sir," Po said now, admittedly with great audacity, "that a huge number of human lives and practically our entire economic system hinge on the question of renewed sunspot activity."

"I suppose you're talking about the greenhouse effect?" the dean replied, not at all impressed with the notion. "All that embarrassment about industrial waste gases and global warming. About how the sea level was one day going to rise and flood out the lowlands. . . . That didn't come off, did it?"

The obliqueness of his response startled Po. "Well, no, sir. But then, no one has correlated those theories with the fall-off in solar energy output. However, that wasn't my point. I was thinking of all the corners that were cut to make the space-pioneering effort possible. None of the infrastructure out there is shielded against the fluctuations of even a minimal solar flare."

"And why do you want to rock that boat, Mr. Mosca? Do you think that you can become some sort of modern-day Jonah or Nader? Do you think that, by stirring people up and making them afraid again, you can gain some kind of academic notoriety for yourself? Do you think your Institute, or this university, is eager to set off a major panic through the idle speculations of Dr. Freede and his cult of graduate students?"

"No, sir. I don't want to scare people. But if — just if — Dr. Freede has detected something, then wouldn't we be in a better position to see it, and deal with it, if we already had one of the Institute's telescopes aligned and observing when the anomaly came over the horizon?"

"*Deal* with it! My goodness, boy! Do you seriously think anything is going to *happen* here? Kindly remember the inverse square law. The sun is a goodly distance away, one hundred and fifty million kilometers, and a lot of attenuation will take place at that distance. . . . No, if there's going to be a global climate change or anything like that, I think we'll be able to detect it without running around cleaning up after Dr. Freede's botches."

"But I was talking about — !" Po broke off, deciding not to go around that course again. "Look, sir, is it so much to ask?" He could hear the wheedling desperation in his own voice. "Just one series of observations?"

"Yes, as a matter of fact, it *is* a lot to ask. Solar astronomy is tricky stuff, as you well know. The operators have to work under a completely different set of protocols from nighttime work, with a lot of extra precautions to be taken. Otherwise you end up burning out your equipment and probably blinding your observer into the bargain. No one here is used to that. Mistakes can be made — will be made. Damn it, *lives* can be lost! So, no, we won't break off our current program of observations and go to daylight viewing. Not over a lot of jumbled mush from that man Freede."

"I see, sir. Then is that your final recommendation, Dean Withers?"

"Yes." The man picked up his electric pencil and slashed a glowing mark across the document that was displayed on his desktop screen. He was putting the matter officially in writing, as it were.

"Request denied."

Chapter 6

Typhoon Warning

Warning!
 Danger!
  Storm!
   Warning!

The plasmote runs ahead of the virulent bundle of magnetic forces, which are strong enough to tear his being apart, wild enough to reach out and catch him up in his slithery passage. As he moves between the demarcated flows of the convective zone, the plasmote puffs out and shrieks his message ahead of the maelstrom's own husking, grumbling voice.

The granular mosaic of the photosphere, the thermal structure of up-and downdrafts which shape the world the plasmotes move in, is beginning to cool and drift, sag and fragment in the cold shadows that surround the storm. The plasmote has to approach this unsettled boundary in order to make an accurate assessment of the disturbance it is causing. He risks having his own magnetic structure absorbed in the central spot, either lashed apart or snuffed out cold by it. But these are the risks of the caller's job.

At other and more normal times, he might call the plasmotes in surrounding area to come and play on the edges of the advancing storm. Then they could ride its wavefront, pushed by the advancing column of still gases, for distances and to places it would exhaust them to reach under their own power. The latent energy from the tornado winds that peel off the central disturbance would pump up their membranes and brighten their awareness. Such a storm can be joyous sport to a plasmote.

But not this time.
Make way!
   Clear out!
      Veer off!
         Stay away!
From his own personally encoded memories, the caller
cannot recollect a storm so big as this one. He has never
heard of one that moved so quickly, that covered such a
span across the middle regions, or that came so completely
out of sequence.

The usual pattern was, first, the gathering of little
whorls, the dancing bundles, up in the still, slow-moving
gases near the poles. Then, the tugging outward into
faster-moving territory, the looping over, and the spinning
away. Next, the following of bigger whorls, the rising tide
of violence. Finally, the crescendo and the falling off. . . .
Always that pattern.

But not this time. This is a freak. This is out-of-pattern.
Behind the first little whorls now come the great doubled
spot. It originated low, in the fastest arenas near the
equator, cutting across space and time, bringing the
greater ferocity without the preparation of the lesser
storms. . . . This is bad.

Go!
   Fly!
      Run!
         Flee!
Ahead of the plasmote, others of its kind scurry off on
widening vectors or at simple right angles. They give
themselves plenty of maneuvering distance in advance of
the freak storm.

The storm's doubling up and folding over have already
occurred. And now the spot group, as it sweeps through
the churning plasma of the fast-moving regions, is building
up its own internal energies. The flux. The potential. The
readiness to do violence beyond the understanding of all
plasmotes. The flash that is an ending of all charges, positive and negative, leaving only an unbroken nothing.

When that comes about, all plasmotes must be far away,

for it is death. So all of them flee, except he, the caller, the beacon, the one who measures and warns.

In order that he might know the course of the storm, he travels slowly, keeping just out of the spot's deadly reach. If he runs too far ahead, he might take a wrong turning, lose the storm, wander somewhere off to its side, and thus fail in his task. So he travels only a beat, two beats out from its howling edge, almost letting it push him on with its wavefront of magnetic moment.

This is his undoing, of course, as it has undone callers before him.

In an instant of hesitation, unsure whether the next turn of the gaping vortex will take it left or right across the gaseous, glowing plain, the plasmote slips in too close. The whirling energies draw on his fabric of knit charges, breaking their hold on the surrounding plasma. Like a silver fish reeled in on a million-pound test line, he soars skyward, into the darkness above the photosphere, beyond the reach of spicule and domed granulation.

The plasmote's senses waver in passing through the cool penumbra, where the storm drains away the surrounding heat and offers too little free energy for him to survive for long.

He is spared the dark center of the umbra, dense shadow. Its relative coldness would force his very fabric to shed its charge and dissolve into the ambient sacrifice. By the time he reaches that geographic region, however, the plasmote has been kicked far above the spot, the storm center, and is riding a bridge of hot gases into the superheated corona.

Lying dazed on this outcropping, this prominence of gaseous fire, he is able to sense after a fashion the complex, braided magnetic fields that form the top of the storm's loop.

Aloft in this prominence he is thermally insulated from the two-million-degree, howling energies of the corona. He judges his surroundings to be at something over 10,000 degrees — to use the measures of the little green world he knows nothing about — and that is almost twice the heat of his accustomed climate down in the photosphere. Harsh, but still bearable.

So the arching prominence, with its richness of thermal and magnetic energy, will support him in life for a while. But, in the meantime, he has failed in his duty as caller. His voice no longer tracks and predicts the storm's angry path.

Now another plasmote, self-selected from among those who once fled the raging disruption, will step up to the wall of darkness, hesitate on the very edge of eternity, try to guess the storm's next turn, left or right, and begin screaming out his own warning.

Chapter 7

Life and the Memory of It

Chug!
 Chug!
  Chuff!
   Chooof!

Tranquility Shores, Luna Colony, March 9, 2081

The main compressors chugged and wheezed as they brought partial pressure in the garage down to about three kilopascals. Gina Tochman could feel the reinforced polyester fiber of her pressure suit stiffen and clamp to the long muscles of her arms and legs. The fabric's tight weave, tailored to Tochman's body shape at her current weight, supported her epidermis against the near-vacuum yet permitted her sweat glands to pass their moisture off normally.

The suit was as close to disposable as the resort's management could arrange. An optic scanner had taken the dimensions of her body, and laser cutters shaped and heat-seamed the fabric into a sturdy second skin for her. It covered every square centimeter of her except the fiber-resin bubble over her head and the plastic-reinforced gauntlets across her palms and fingers. In terms of light weight and disposability, Tochman's working suit was no different from the one-offs that were issued to the paying guests.

Wearing it still took some getting used to, even for a staff member. As the garage's atmosphere dropped toward zero pressure, Tochman could feel her own skin begin to tug and creep, reaching for hollow, unsupported spaces like the insides of her elbows, at the backs of her knees, along the zippered seams that arched up on either side of her ribcage and under her arms, or in the fork between her legs. After a moment, however, her body found equilibrium with the new ambient pressure.

When the door's broad aluminum panels finally sagged inward, releasing the last traces of breathable air, solenoids clicked and a chain drive pulled the loose plates up into the ceiling. Tochman looked out on a dulled gray landscape glowing blue-green under a nearly full Earth. This was about as dark as the lunar surface ever got. She knew it would be cold out there, with no sun to warm her.

Gina pulled the rest of her gear from the garment bin. This was standardized stuff, one size fits all. The inner layer was a thermal jumper with a sandwiched film of heated gel that would warm her body on contact. Its exposed surface was padded with dense silicon mesh that was supposed to stop micrometeorites of up to point-oh-two milligrams. Next, she weighed a cape of reflective film that would shade her body from ambient infrared, but she rejected this garment; there was not a lot of infrared outside in the long lunar night. Finally, she slipped on clogs that would protect her polyester-stockinged feet against the sharp stones and rocks.

Suited up at last, Gina Tochman turned again toward the wide doorway.

Normally, the company frowned on depressurizing such a huge space as the garage for just one person, because even at a pressure of less than two hundred grams per, its ten thousand cubic meters added up to a lot of wasted moles. So employees were sternly instructed to use the manual locks — and then debited for the lost pressure. But today Gina had a professional reason for opening the big lock. She stepped up on the sideplate of the nearest electric buggy, swung one leg stiffly over the saddle, and keyed it.

The paying customers of Tranquility Shores, Inc., had to know this was the resort's main garage and loading port. After all, they entered this space through the Quartermaster's Stores and got suited up next to the line of buggies. So, intellectually, they understood that this was a

working area and that their fifteen-minute Moon Walk was
going to cover pretty thoroughly beaten ground.

But Tranquility Shores was a competitive business, like
any other vacation resort. The management listened to the
customers and paid attention to the courtesy cards they
filed at the end of their stay. And one of the recurring
themes was disappointment with the walk. "Not what I
expected," they wrote. "Could have been the Jersey Flats,"
they wrote. "Reminded me of Cocoa Beach," they wrote.

Selective in-depth interviews revealed that people who
came to the Moon had this persistent image of barren rock,
smooth gravel, soft sands. Even when they came upon it
from a working garage, they expected something wild and
untamed. The original Moon, like the astronauts had discovered. They wanted to be the first — or make believe
they were — to plant their footprints in its crusty soil.

If Tranquility Shores had been a beachfront resort, like
Hawaii or Bermuda, the management could simply wait
for the next tropical cyclone to blow through. One day of
gale-force winds, and the grounds would be as clean and
fresh as nature made. Then the next guest to step off the
patio could pretend he was Robinson Crusoe to his heart's
content. But no gales blew on the Moon. No summer rains
came down to wash away the litter and oil. No cresting
waves patterned the sand.

So Gina Tochman had to do it.

Before she rolled the buggy with its giant klopklop
wheels out into the gentle, greenish dawnlight, she backed
it up to accessory rigs arranged against the inner wall and
dropped the electrostatic rake onto the rear coupling. As
the vehicle crossed the doorseals and rolled down the concrete apron, she switched on the polarizer field and
glanced over her shoulder.

Electromagnetic fingers stroked and pulsed the sand
and gravel across a four-meter-wide swath, obliterating tire
tracks, bootprints, scuffs, and drag marks. Sheared bolt
ends, broken pieces of brightly colored nylon tie-down,
and scraps of wrapper fabric spun and danced into the
trash screens. Traces of spilled lubricants — the metallic

solids which remained after the volatiles had boiled off —
also went into the screens.

Tochman drove the rig out four hundred meters along
the main overland road, then crisscrossed her way back over
a widening triangular area with a base forty meters across
back at the garage entrance. Her pattern covered up everything unnatural, including the buggy's own tread marks.

Experience had taught Tochman there was no need to go
farther. Even the most agile of customers would soon tire of
bounding around in the sand and climbing on the rocks
near the garage door. Although the Moon pulled only one-
sixth gee, the stretch-fit vac suits were cloying, pulling some
long muscles the wrong way. The thermal jumpers were
bulky and clumsy. People got tired fast, and no one was likely
to light out cross-country toward the mountains or go far
along the road toward the landing fields.

When Gina brought her Moon Walkers up an hour
from now, they would mill around, do a few broad jumps,
land on their asses, and think this little rock garden, which
was regularly raked and tended, was the wild black yonder.
Then someone would notice it was getting on for the cock-
tail hour, their suits would start chafing in unaccustomed
places, and everyone — having seen too much of nothing
— would want to go back inside. They would all be feeling
vaguely disappointed, but it wouldn't have any obvious
cause, like unsightly boot tracks and service discards in the
gray sand. Instead, they would just be feeling the deflation
of their own inflated expectations. The paying customers
would have nothing to gripe about to the management.

Tochman made the last turning swirl in the lunar dust
and drove up on the garage's apron of shotcrete. The show
would go on.

16:04:22
16:04:23
16:04:24
16:04:25

Connor Transfer Station, March 10, 2081

Peter Spivak stared at his watch, counting off the

seconds, his head almost nodding in time with the digital counter. There were thirty-five seconds to go before the crew closed and sealed the hatchway; at that point only the dockmaster could recall the flight. An urgent beamfax from a Ms. Cheryl Hastings just wouldn't do it.

Four days ago, he and Cheryl had parted from each other in anger. Peter was to begin an eighteen-month assignment with the Mars Survey; Cheryl would stay in New York City and paint out her medieval fantasies of woodland elves and scaly dragons. And the trouble between them was in part — no, let's be truthful, it was entirely due to this trip of his.

Eighteen months on-planet, plus more than nine months getting there and nine months coming back — that was thirty-six months in all. Three years apart, with only video transmissions to bridge the gap, suffering under a timelag at Mars orbit of never less than four minutes and sometimes as much as sixteen. They would be closer if they were locked in adjoining prison cells, with only taps on the wall for communication. Not to mention the fact that this trip was dangerous. . . . Yeah, not to mention that. Peter might freeze his ass off on Mars. Or, only slightly less probable, Cheryl could get hers cut on Earth. It happened in that city. All the time.

Spivak at first had thought their relationship was strong enough to take the separation. And the positives were just too good to turn down. Considering what service rating his geotechnical knowledge could pull, and piling on the offworld bonuses, interorbital flight pay, special medical allowances, plus R-and-R recoupage — not to mention the fact that for three years he would have no expenses or even much chance for any kind of personal spending — Peter Spivak's bank balance would be halfway to retirement when he returned to Earth. Then he and Cheryl could live anywhere they wanted, and she paint anything she liked, for the rest of their lives. He thought it was an opportunity too good to miss.

"Carpe diem!" Peter had told Cheryl gaily, when he learned that the Areopolitan Foundation had accepted his application. "Take the chance!"

"What your old adage really means is 'seize the day,' "
she had observed dryly, when she understood exactly what
he was telling her. "You're supposed to live each day to the
fullest, it says. And that's not what you're trying to do.
Instead, you want to throw today away by putting yourself
in the big deepfreeze so that sometime in the far future you
can live on easy street — if you come back at all. And if you
don't bring back some mutated virus, or get crippled up in
microgravity and spend the rest of your life in a power
chair with the bone sickness. Yeah, 'seize the day,' my foot."

When Peter had shyly explained that the Foundation
had offered to pay Cheryl's way, too, and would provide
almost the same level of compensation for her to work as a
technical illustrator, she had laughed out loud. Right in his
face.

The conversation never got any better after that. He
went ahead with his plans, taking the requisite skills tests,
physical examinations, personality co-patterning, and all
the Foundation's other paperwork. Cheryl had done her
painting each morning and afternoon, made quietly pas-
sionless love to him each evening, and kept her thoughts to
herself. She never said, "Please don't go." She never said,
"I'll be waiting for you."

When Peter had left for the airport, to take the SCramjet
on the first leg of his 430-million-mile journey, she had
bade him a formal goodbye and immediately changed the
locks and billing on their condo.

At every waypoint — at Vandenberg, here at Connor
Station in low orbit, next at Crossroads on Luna, and again
at L2, where he would join his ship for Mars — Peter had
electronic postcards to send. They were expensive views,
fine-grained reproductions, of supraorbital scenery. The
message line allowed for 128 bytes, and he poured his soul
into them. In return, he was hoping for a good word, for
"Hello, I love you," for "Please come back," for "I'm coming next flight," for anything.

So far she had not replied. Maybe later, as he got closer
to the final jumping-off place.

But not this time.

Now his watch counted off the last seconds to the double bong, 16:05:00. The hatchway back to Connor Station's docking manifold closed — he could just see the edge of it from where he was strapped down for the primary acceleration — and the ship's air pressure changed slightly, brushing his skin with invisible fingers and clogging his ears with a new closeness.

Yen
> *Riyals*
>> *Neumarks*
>> *Dollars*

Hong Kong Two, British Columbia, March 11

Winston Qiang-Phillips watched as the tide came in. Before the sun could rise beyond the Coast Mountains, the first long fingers of cash were seeping into the HK2 Exchange, sniffing out new opportunities and bidding up the price of even the penny stocks.

"Watching the tide come in" was not merely a poetic image that he had made up. Seeing with senses other than his eyes, Qiang-Phillips actually witnessed the influx of bids, moving like a green gas in the spaces between the trading booths, gently raising the lighted indices that were posted beside each one. Winston paused for a moment to admire the effect before dialing himself into his own booth.

Everyone said the tidal bulge of cash which chased the open and active markets westward around the world was fifty trillion in "Double-D," or dollar-denominated, currencies. No one knew the exact figure. The interlinked markets involved in the trade acted as if pinning a hard number on the amount might be bad luck. Still, fifty terabux sounded about right to Winston's ear.

But, of course, there was the *velocity* to take into account. A dollar at rest was intrinsically less potent than a dollar in motion. If it was traded once a year, or even once a day, the currency had only a certain puny effect in the financial scheme of things. The punch of a weak and sickly man. But if that same dollar could be traded four and five times a day, it thereby gained velocity. And momentum could invest it with terrifying power. The punch of a stevedore rushing headlong into a bar fight.

So, perhaps the sum was less than fifty — but still in the trillions, certainly. Even twenty, with the right velocity on it, could seem like two or three times that to anyone who stood neck-deep in the flood and traded as fast as he could for eight hours a day. Then everyone turned their eyes westward, across the Pacific, and watched the cash bulge rush on toward the Nikkei.

There once was a time, seventy-odd years ago — Winston Qiang-Phillips had learned this from a university course on the history of money — when the world's financial markets had trended toward twenty-four-hour operation and wholly computerized bidding. Make money all the time, the people said, even while you sleep in your bed. But those pleasant dreams had gone into meltdown during the Mechanics' Panics of 2002, 2005, 2007, 2008, and 2009[2].

Now human beings ran things again, with a little computer help. And, while people might need to sleep, the money didn't. After the day's frenzied transactions, in the closing minutes before the market bell, people on the far side of the world parked their earnings in overnight certificates of deposit and other instruments that would earn them a few fractional points while they went home to eat and play and dream. In the meantime their money went out, almost of its own accord, looking for investments on the daylight side. It pumped up the world's volume of "available free credit" enormously.

So, when dawn came up on a trading center, its activity heated up as the cash flowed in from the east, beyond the terminator, and the buying began. And when the sun set on that same trading center, then the selloff came as the money fled westward toward the next opportunity.

"Rising tide lifts all boats." That was what Grandfather Qiang Nu-Lin had taught him as a boy. And he had even believed it, then. Now Winston himself would add, "Except those on a short anchor chain."

Winston Qiang-Phillips made his living as a professional

contrarian. That is, when the sun went down and the money went west, while everyone was selling out and moving on, Winston *bought* stock like mad. He bought even those companies which had suffered most during the daily trade, so he could pay a relative pittance for their equity. In that way, he scalped those who were caught out in distress and had to watch the force drain out of the market.

Then, when the sun came back and the money flowed in, while everyone else was buying eagerly, Winston *sold* his overnight holdings. He made his greatest profits from those traders who were weighted down with cash, watching it lose momentum in their pockets, and so were hungriest for equity.

And in between, when the market threatened to drown any companies whose anchor chains were an inch too short, Winston Qiang-Phillips shored them up with credit.

So, this morning, he watched the tide come in and marshaled his holdings. He tidied his best wares on the shelf behind his trading position, arranging them alphabetically like book spines. As usual he expected to unload them at a significant uptick over their purchase price in last night's panic selloff.

Qiang-Phillips had some good local coal stocks, grouped together in his energies section. During the six months since he'd bought them in a trading frenzy, the coals had been a quirk on the market. What with the long-standing governmental bans on fossil burning and coking, they were mostly ornamental. But now coal was looking promising again because of rumors about renewed interest in carbon chemistry and fiber structurals. Someone would likely pluck them, just as soon as he opened his hand.

Winston owned one lumber stock, a real antiquity. This company had certified title to harvest — not just to manage in perpetuity, but to actually *harvest* — fourteen acres of third-growth fir in the Cascade Range. That was a gem which one day would trade on its novelty value alone.

He also had a handful of other items, mostly trading instruments and options, but all interesting just the same — especially when the tide was coming in. These were the daily business, the offloads to be handled by nine in the morning. Then he could return his attention, for a few hours at least before sellout time, to his latest personal project.

Qiang-Phillips had scented opportunity in the most recent announcements from the Titan Cartel. They were finally about to bring in the first drop-shipment of liquid methane, which despite the widespread fossil ban was a valuable chemical feedstock for the world's industry. This first shipment — for which the Cartel had announced a firm scheduled arrival in Earth orbit — would prove that their recovery system actually worked. It could be expected to deflate the current high price of natural gas from the Alberta Field Producers Association and so erode the price of that group's joint stock, along with the assets of every other gas collection cooperative and pipeline company on the planet. Time for a contrarian to step in!

Winston Qiang-Phillips had been hoarding his cash for weeks now, taking the inevitable hit on its momentum, in order to be in position to buy and buy and buy. And when the dealers realized that one test shipment, launched a year ago on an automated carrier and only now coming to orbit, does not make for a dependable energy supply — then who would they have to deal with if they wanted to, had to, were *dying* to buy their way back into the market? Why, Winston Qiang-Phillips, of course, the House of Qiang, Baron of the Gas Fields, Emperor of the Blue Flame, Winston the First.

Contrarians always win. That also was something Grandfather Qiang Nu-Lin had taught him.

> *Jellied Eels*
> *Lamb Testes in Honey*
> *Flaming Baby Quail*
> *Lark Tongues in Pepper Sauce*

Pompeii, August 24, 79 A.D.

Jerry Kozinski sat on the patio of his villa overlooking the Bay of Naples and chewed his breakfast. Although some of the food the kitchen slaves had offered him sounded disgusting as they described it, actually most of the stuff tasted pretty good. The flavors simulated by the Virtuality™ cyber banks were a lot closer to the sterile manufactured proteins and clear processed sugars of Jerry's normal diet than they were to any wild birds snared in the nest and fried in some rancid oil.

Kozinski was a prominent man in Pompeii, owing his wealth partly to family resources — he was a long-lost branch of the Sullae — and partly to the rich Egyptian corn trade. Functioning as a dealer with an imperial monopoly, and humping the market as a sometime speculator, Jerry could turn a profit of anywhere from five hundred to five thousand percent. According to the game script, such huge returns gave him the leisure to sit on his hillside terrace for most of the morning and watch the town and bay below him.

That would be a nice life, except for the heat. The sun was already high by what they called "the eighth hour" here, and not a breath of wind was stirring. Other than a few dogs and stray children, the streets below were deserted: no traveling tinkers or traders or jugglers in the marketplace, no gladiator fights in the amphitheater, no rich senators debating in the forum, no crying beggars, no wandering scholars, nothing of the city life that the script had told him to expect. All the normal townspeople must be indoors, Jerry thought, hiding from the heat.

Where was everyone else, though? Virtuality, Inc.'s promotionals had said hundreds of thousands of gamers were continuously looped into the simulation. The company had promised that Jerry could expect to interact competitively with most of them during the game's twelve-hour course. He didn't know *all* the rules, certainly, but he hardly thought that most people would pay the huge entry fee to end up a house slave, a child, or a dog — which were all of the active beings he'd seen so far.

Out in the bay, a few fishing smacks and a broad-hulled merchant ship sat becalmed like models glued to a mirror. Only the military galley — it looked like a trireme from here — moved over the water. In the still air Kozinski could hear the beat of its drum and the creak of its oars in their leather slings. How many people would want to be a fisherman or a galley slave, either? And, if so, what kind of a fee had *they* paid for such a lousy starting position?

The hot, still air felt to Jerry like earthquake weather. Indeed, the game script said the land around here — Campania, it was called — had been buffeted by earthquakes for the past sixteen years. That would be almost all of Jerry's lifetime. Each rumbler was supposed to be worse than the last, and by now he guessed they must be up on the Richter scale with the great quakes of Tokyo and San Francisco. But so far this morning, nothing. The flagstones on the patio didn't even show a pattern of cracks, and he'd looked for those first thing.

Although no one in Pompeii was supposed to know exactly what was coming — except for Jerry and the other virtual presences, of course — clearly everyone expected something pretty awful to happen soon. But still, if most of them were players, why would they be huddling indoors? Why not be out exploring the town and seeking out the possibilities?

Jerry Kozinski sipped a goblet of really delicious red wine, which was guaranteed not to get him drunk, and studied the outline of streets and docks, plazas and roads laid out below him. He was looking for his escape route, of course. By now he had three very promising candidates.

This game was going to be a piece of cake.

Turn
   Turn
      Turn
         Turn

Orbital Slot 37-C at 625 Kilometers, March 13, 2081

The orbit of Day's Ease Geriatric Residence No. 8 was too low by at least a hundred kilometers — or so said the survey report from Azimuth Partners, Inc.

Megan Patterson, R.N.Ast., who was the Day's Ease station manager, shucked the flimsy printout across her desk and watched it take a shallow microgravity arc over the curved surface, blip lightly against the far edge, flip over, and sail off toward the steel bulkhead.

But altitude wasn't the only or the worst problem — or even the hardest one to fix. The API survey had told her that the station's shape was all wrong, too.

Sitting up here in partial gravity, Patterson sometimes found it hard to remember that the floor was not really *down* but just felt that way. The residence facility's gravity was inertial, not real. And, looking out the portholes to the steady stars and the broad stretch of white, Earthly clouds revolving below them, she could easily forget that the station wasn't built as a complete torus, either.

Day's Ease was actually three pressurized canisters suspended at the ends of a Y-shaped yoke, like an Argentine gaucho's *bolas* swinging through the sky. At the center of the wye were the universal docking hub, a ring of storage boxes and mechanical facilities at null-gee, and the postsurgical recuperation quarters. Out along each of the three limbs were the gee-rated residences, the hydroponics section, food services, exercise rooms, and anything else that responded well to modest acceleration. These limbs were arranged two long and one short, with the variable lengths corresponding to the moment arm of each attached module. It was not a compact configuration, but it had been cheap to build and easy to launch.

That was the problem, all the way around, Patterson decided: cost-cutting at the home office. Pick a low orbit. Put up a simplified modular structure. Give it a nice, slow turn. Then forget about it and rake in the bucks from either the clients' living trusts or their grateful family members.

The home office had made just one tiny miscalculation. Only one, but it was a doozy. Without understanding that they had zero margin for error, the mechtechs had set this three-legged circus spinning at *right angles* to the planet's surface instead of parallel to it. Sure, the brochures said this orientation gave every patient an admirable view of the planet they could never go home to. But, more importantly, it was also easier to align and spin a walking wye in orbit than a flat one. Costs, again.

But what the configuration really signified was a

long-term instability. With every turn, that one longer module dipped proportionally farther into the upper atmosphere, taking more drag than the other two. Over time — maybe six months, the API estimate said — this drag was going to destabilize the structure. Then the staff and the engineers would have to evacuate all the residents to alternate facilities, bolt everything down, kill the spin, reorient, realign, and respin. And, if that didn't work, they would have to boost to a higher orbit — if one was available, and if the home office would pay for it.

Either way, there went Patterson's budget. Quarterly, annual, bonus and dividend. Shot to hell.

And who was going to get blamed for this snafu? Not the pimpleheads who had mucked up the design of this tin can. Not the bean counters in the back room who had cut corners without a thought. But Megan Patterson, R.N.Ast., that's who!

She stared at the report, which was lying where she'd thrown it, over against the foot of the bulkhead. The flimsy sheets trembled against each other now, making a soft rustling sound.

Sweet Jesus! Patterson hoped that was just a stray draft from the ventilation system — and not the start of a wobble. Her hand dropped against the desktop and felt for random vibrations, but she couldn't sense anything definite.

Or not yet, anyway.

Slice
    Fold
        Press
            Seal

Duquesne Municipal Airport, McKeesport, Pennjersey, March 14

Brian Holdstrup found working with the aluminized, polychain film really tedious. The material was just over one-micron, or point-oh-five mils, thick and clung like a layer of soapsuds to anything it touched.

To handle it, Holdstrup had to arrange for cleanroom

conditions — but over a floorspace larger than an old-time sailmaker's loft. Which meant renting an entire hangar at the defunct local airport; sealing the doors and windows and the cracks in the corrugated tin ceiling; putting in an airlock, pumps, and filtration equipment; gleaning, scouring, and sanding the floor, walls, and rafters; then evacuating the room and repressurizing with a high partial pressure of pure nitrogen. All of that meant he also had to wear breathing equipment while he worked.

Then Brian had to manipulate the material, strong as it was, with bridge wires, pinpoint airflows, and antistatic paddles. He couldn't use his hands, because the moisture of his fingertips, even through cotton gloves, would draw the tissue so it would wrap around and cling to them like flypaper. Rubberized or plastic gloves, which might block the moisture, would too quickly build up their own static charge.

Holdstrup's sail design was a complicated one, composed of twenty-two weighted vanes in an autogyrating configuration. Once it was launched he had to spin the structure to keep it taut and at maximal reflectivity. Each vane was going to be a kilometer long and a hundred meters wide, made up of the pleated strips he was now cutting and folding, compressing and loading into the launch package.

It was tedious work, all of it. Brian Holdstrup was more than willing to pay for some manual help, but that was against the rules. Not that the particular race he was entering had been announced yet, but all the solar sail competitions followed a pattern: you could enter any structure you liked, so long as you designed and built it yourself.

These competitions were not for the weak, because hauling around square kilometers of the film, even at one-micron's thickness, took muscle. They were not for the easily bored, because packing the sail — all those cuts, folds, and hot-seals — took up to fifteen thousand repeated motions. And they were not for the poor of pocketbook, either, because who would spend a hundred thousand dollars on equipment and materials to win a prize that averaged only one percent of that amount?

At least the competitions did not have any requirements about amateur status. Brian Holdstrup was owner and manager of Photon Power, Inc., as well as the firm's foremost designer. He could only keep ahead of his corporate competitors by entering and winning the Translunar, the Circum-Belter, the Sun Dog, and the other races that made up the decennial calendar. And, with four firsts and a third to his credit so far, his commercial designs now commanded top dollar.

But, still, all that trouble, and the boring, repetitious actions . . . Holdstrup wouldn't do it just for the money. He actually entered these competitions for love.

For love of a good design intelligently executed. For love of tight, mirrored surfaces reflecting the subtle pressures of sunlight and starlight as they traversed a graceful, parabolic orbit. For love of the recognition, admiration, and respect that always came to the winner.

That was what really drove him, working on into the night, as the rubber mouthpiece of the breathing apparatus chapped his lips, as the glare of sodium vapor off aluminum film burned his eyes, as his upper arms trembled with the strain of hefting the weight and holding it just so. . . .

He did it for the glory.

> *Blow*
>> *Spin*
>>> *Insert*
>>>> *Lock*

Whitney Center, Tulare County, California, March 16

As operations director, Naomi Rao was responsible for keeping the schedule. So she was fuming now as she watched the technicians in the main payload assembly hall blow foam into a ceramic cargo shell and hinge it together with explosive bolts. The foam was designed to absorb the shocks of a launch acceleration in excess of five hundred gees.

Next, the crew spun the projectile in a particle spray to give it a smooth aluminum coating, against which the plas-

ma-induction field would work in the launch tube, dragging the ceramic shell and its contents forward along the
line of braided electromagnets.

Then, the work team pushed the projectile and its cradle
into the tube's breech where, once the cycle was completed,
an electric arc in the megawatt range would flash-heat the
aluminum powder into a plasma cloud.

Finally, they closed the airlock door behind the projectile and sealed it.

Rao clicked her stopwatch, glared at it. The crew had
taken all of twenty-two minutes to make ready for launch.

Damn! That was just not good enough! It would never
make for the firing rate which the front office wanted to
maintain. But then, Rao consoled herself, there were limiting factors all over the place.

For one thing, all of this activity was going on more than
three kilometers below sea level, under a shitload of granite
mountain, at the end of an eleven-kilometer-long tube that
surfaced through the eastern face of Mount Whitney. Eighty
years ago, when the magnetic catapult was still a new idea,
they had needed the thin air at Whitney's elevation of 4,420
meters to reduce atmospheric resistance as the high-speed
payloads emerged from the tube. The designers had also
wanted the remoteness of a barren mountain range to isolate the megabooms of the launch cycles, because all this was
before the development of effective sonic suppressors.

Whitney Center was an old facility, designed for the
payloads of the last century, when the move to orbital space
was just beginning. The cargo handlers of the day took a
more relaxed attitude about launch schedules and load
bulk. They were firing nonstandard shapes then, so they
had the time to make each shell and its molded-foam padding into a hand-finished work of art. They were dealing
with small satellites and discrete loads of what then passed
for high-technology instrumentation. So, everything in
those days could be polite, refined, and studious. Now, of
course, the center was shooting out larger, more complicated modules and structures.

If Naomi Rao were going to redesign Whitney Center for

today's needs, she would have the shells be packed, blown, bolted, and coated offsite, at the factory of origin. Then the projectiles could be stockpiled ahead of the launch schedule, brought to the center on trucks, and fired off efficiently.

Except . . . except the main elevator shaft that brought Rao's loads down to the working end of the catapult was something like two meters too small for today's average finished load. The front office had studied all sorts of contortions for moving pre-packed shells through this constriction — sideways, butt-first, packed-in-halves — then re-orienting them for insertion in the breech of the launch tube. But always the handling space at the base of the elevator stage was just too narrow, too right-angled, too something. The designers of the last century had done a beautiful piece of work here under the mountain, but they hadn't planned ahead for the success, with its added demands, that their system was destined to achieve.

So that was the first limiting factor, Rao recognized: the size and depth of the payload assembly chamber.

Next, if the original builders had only carved out a bigger chamber, giving her more room to work with, Rao could set up a second assembly line and put together more cargo shells per shift. She could even hope to stockpile them at the breech, and that way she could get ahead on the launch schedule.

But then, her operation would still end up in a hole.

The builders of almost a century ago didn't have access to current fusion technology. They powered the induction rails with electric generators turning at the ends of steel shafts spun by old-fashioned steam or falling water. So they had no way of cheaply generating the two-second pulse of eighteen megawatt-hours needed to drive their loads up to orbital velocity. Instead, to get the energy burst they needed, they charged up huge banks of capacitors that lined the eleven-kilometer tunnel. And that charging took time — eight minutes, twenty-two seconds to be exact. The bottom line was that, even if Naomi Rao could stockpile her payloads, she still couldn't shoot them any faster.

Of course, the front office had explored several technological alternatives. A new fusion complex sited at the shaft head in Junction Meadow, with direct coupling through klystrons, thus bypassing the antiquated capacitor banks and induction rails.

But making all of these additions and changes would cost time and money. To widen the elevator shaft and chambers, they would have to close down the complex, cut out thirty thousand cubic meters of native rock, and rebuild the elevator, assembly hall, and airlock. To rework the launch tube's mechanism, they would have to strip out fifty kilometers of steel rails and braided magnets, rebuild the induction line, and probably upgrade the pressure lens at the ejector gate. And in neither case could they ever hope to see the front end of today's harried launch schedule during Rao's lifetime.

In the old joke, Naomi Rao asks the front office, "Why do we have to keep digging away at this hole with our little teaspoon? Why don't we use a shovel?" And the front office snaps back, "You don't have time to go looking for a shovel. You've got a schedule to maintain."

So the preferred alternative was just to keep on trucking. Make each payload as a one-off item, hand-crafted and spun down here. Charge up the antiquated capacitor banks, which apparently had a design life of forever. And fire off the projectiles in the old-fashioned way. Because the schedule, which was driven by economic necessity and the clamor of money, was written in stone. The schedule was everything. Alpha and omega. Whirl without end.

Fifteen seconds after the airlock doors had shut, Rao watched her dials as the vacuum pumps cycled. Then the electrodes arced, and the line of induction magnets drew the plasma cloud with its buried egg of foam and cargo forward along the rails. Two-point-five seconds later, Mount Whitney made another offering of steel shapes or silicon circuitry or medical supplies or water canisters or bottles of rare gases to the gods of the upper atmosphere.

Just like a well-oiled clock. Mechanical, predictable, and always running slow.

$CH_4 \ldots 20\text{-}1/8$
$\quad CH_4 \ldots 19\text{-}3/4$
$\quad\quad CH_4 \ldots 19\text{-}1/8$
$\quad\quad\quad CH_4 \ldots 18\text{-}1/2$

Western Board of Trade, Chicago, March 17

Lexander Bartels watched the quote on natural gas, per cubic meter for October delivery, go into virtual freefall. The letters and numbers that, two minutes ago, had been sliding ⸲across his left visual cortex now tipped and cascaded out of the dark space above his eyebrow, taking on real velocity. The numbers' pale blue glow blurred white and fragmented as the speed of the fall increased.

"Shit!"

Even without the neural graphics, Bartels could tell he was in deep trouble. He had learned to read and assimilate raw numbers long before the mechanics of virtual reality got into the financial communications business.

Lexander Bartels could have told the big boys in the Titan Cartel that their stupid, gloating press releases would have this effect, would drive the price right down. Because, of course, the methane supply from Titan's thick and nearly pure hydrocarbon atmosphere was literally inexhaustible. And that was more than anyone could say for even the deep gas wells in Colorado, Texas, and Alberta, let alone the capped landfills that lay on the fringes of every major American city. So, there went the scarcity value of the Cartel's product.

Yesterday the October high had been somewhere north of thirty-five points a thousand cubic meters. Today the slump was on and gaining momentum. At this rate, by tomorrow the price wouldn't even support development of a lake of liquid methane located right outside Chicago — let alone automated cramships and unmanned sunjammers sailing elliptical orbits down from the vicinity of Saturn.

Bartels had to do something about this, and fast.

Could he put the genie back in the bottle? Get the Cartel to retract the release?

No, because no one would believe it. And the price would keep right on falling.

Well, could they announce a delay? Some kind of technical problem? Maybe a barge crash or a leaky holding tank or something, anything, so long as it happened out beyond where anyone could see it and know what was *really* going on. . . . That would certainly end the panic and force the price of gas back up.

But then, the governors of the Board of Trade would want to conduct an inquiry and gather hard evidence. That, or file indictments against Bartels and company for market manipulation. Traders had tried to engineer a swing like this before, in an attempt to corner some commodity. And a new supply source, located far from the regulating agencies, unavailable for reliable observation, and depending on interlocking echelons of new development technologies, made a dandy vehicle for such a scheme.

Still, if nothing brought the price of gas back up, the economic underpinnings of the entire Titan Project would collapse before the Cartel could snag and decant its first shipload of product. And wouldn't the big boys be a laughingstock then?

Lexander Bartels had to think of something.

But what?

Tumble
　Tumble
　　Tumble
　　　Tumble

Phobos, March 18

Khyffer I, Grand Duke of Syrtis Major and Hereditary Lord of Phobos, looked out toward the horizons of his domain and then down, past them, to the gray and ocher and white expanses of Mars.

On Earth, the greatest of all emperors in history had known a natural limit to their power. Even if all the territory within the circle of a man's eye might belong to him personally, still he could not help but know that somewhere, perhaps far over the distant horizon, was land where his words were not law. Or, worse, beyond his closest shore would be the mighty ocean, where man was still only a visitor, trespassing at the whim of Neptune.

The Earth defeated man and made a mockery of his rule.

But on Phobos, things were different. Khyffer I — who was born James F. Bren of Missoula, Montana — shared his domain with neither men nor gods. He could walk its Long Circumference of twenty-seven kilometers in just half an hour at his usual brisk and bounding pace. It took him even less time if he flew the circumference on one of the station's scooters. Phobos had no oceans and only one major depression, the crater Hall, whose depths Khyffer I could check out anytime he chose to look over the rim.

Of course, there was always the question of what was happening on the backside of the planetoid. A man's eyes couldn't be everywhere at once, even if he was an absolute monarch, even if he set up the video monitors and pattern analyzers to keep watch for him. Still, someone might have landed back there, materializing in phase with the blink of an eye, and begun stirring up rebellion! Someone over that near horizon might be hatching plots!

To guard against the possibility, Khyffer I regularly suited up and toured his domain. For an absolute ruler, he was not afraid to make his face known in his dominions.

And, as a mark of special grace and favor to his many subjects below, as a service to all humankind, Khyffer I had long ago agreed to maintain the wideband communications repeater that was established at his seat on Phobos. This device coordinated signals with the Mother Empire on Earth during those twelve-point-three hours of the Martian day when the darkness of Old Night turned Syrtis Major away from the sun. Thus Khyffer I held the vital link connecting his subjects on Mars with the bulk of humanity.

For this act of *majeste oblige*, among many others, Khyffer I was known as a just and popular ruler. Indeed, he was a certified public benefactor. A prince of a fellow! . . . If he could only be sure that no one on the other side of his domain was fomenting revolution. Staring at the horizon and checking out the monitors were not enough. He simply had to go see for himself.

So, for the sixth time that day, Khyffer I pulled on his pressure suit and crawled into the repeater station's main airlock. The Grand Duke was just going for another little walk. He was sure he could get back before anyone down on the planet might notice.

Trickle
  Trickle
    Siphon
      Sump

Stonybrook Farm at L3, March 19

General Manager Alois Davenport tried to stare down Peter Kamen, the farming colony's engineering specialist, but the younger man held his ground. Davenport was the first to shift his gaze. He looked out the window of his office, toward rows of pale green cabbages in black dirt.

"I don't agree with your analysis," Davenport said finally.

"It's not something that cares whether you *agree* or not . . . sir." Kamen pointed at the filtration curves on the screen inset into Davenport's desktop. "We're losing pressure on the siphon. That means we've got a blockage. Likely a whole series of them. Ice is the probable culprit."

"That's just your interpretation."

"What else could it be?" Kamen demanded.

"Precipitates, interrupting the natural percolation." Davenport shrugged. "It could be from that new course of fertilizers West Sixty has been using. The blockages are also compatible with that scenario."

"*Some* of the blockages could be in the percolation mats, perhaps. But widespread icing in the pipes fits the data better."

"Ice . . ." Davenport gave the proposition serious thought for the first time — for just one minute. "This would be *before* the water runs into the heat exchangers, you're thinking? Because we're still tapping to heat spec out of the sprinkler heads, aren't we?"

"Yes," Kamen agreed. "It has to be forming in the down-feeds."

Thermal modulation by cross-connecting the irrigation water accounted for most of the colony's internal heat distribution — that and a convection current of warm air across the central axis. Natural, self-regulating patterns pushed wind and water throughout the cylinder, driven by gravity balances and hot pockets. No cybers were called on to diddle with the system, so there was no chance of a software glitch taking them through ever-widening loops to destruction. It had happened decades ago in the earliest farming colonies, which had loved such technology a little too much.

But if there was some natural imbalance at Stonybrook, like a buildup of salt scale in the mats, or ice . . .

"Anyway, how do you propose to get *ice* on the outside of a rotating cylinder?" the general manager objected finally. "Our spin is constant — because if it weren't, you and I'd be flying all around inside here. So, every forty-two minutes, each one of those exchange units still has to be getting its dose of hard sunlight. What's going to freeze up in that time?"

"You've got an awful lot of little tubes beyond that wall, Alois." Kamen pointed straight down at the floor. "Bet that some of them are getting shaded more than others as this Lagrange point works its way around through the lunar cycles. But we won't know which ones and how much until we suit up a team and take them outside on inspection. Then we'll just have to bang on the irrigation system and see what falls off."

"I can't spare you that kind of manpower!" Davenport said, alarmed. "After all, we have a crop to harvest. Contracts to fulfill. Payments to make."

"When that water stops," the engineer predicted, "your crop is going to shrivel in the ground."

"Now *that* isn't what your curves show at all." The general manager tapped the screen. "We've still got eighty-five percent flow through the system. And if you go around telling people some kind of disaster is imminent, you'll only make a fool of yourself."

"Haven't you heard about an ounce of prevention being — "

"We'll have time to worry about your preventive measures *after* we get the cabbage in. In the meantime, I'll have the Fertilizer Department thin the mix and formulate a descaler compound. Then you'll see those blockages clear up soon enough."

"But that won't — !"

"It'll hold the system together while we get on about our business," Davenport said.

"Then I'm making a formal request to raise the whole issue at the next Town Meeting. Our people should — "

"The people want to gather their produce and keep paying off on our mortgage. You want to strip the interior down and rework the whole substructure. I've seen your plans, Mr. Kamen, and your cost estimates. If you had your way, we'd tinker and fiddle all the livelong day, and never get any work done. And everyone in this colony knows it, too."

Peter Kamen scowled and stuck out his lower lip. "It's going to be on your head, then."

"That's my job," Davenport said softly. "And always has been."

Zing!
　　Zing!
　　　Zing!
　　　　Zing!

Murray Hill Laboratories, Inc., Jerseyboro, GNYC, March 20

Harvey Sommerstein watched the needles flick as the cascaded calls went out on the sky's random-access lattice.

Many times each second, hundreds of thousands of times each day, a bit of extraterrestrial grit fell into the Earth's upper atmosphere at altitudes between eighty and one hundred and twenty kilometers. Moving at about forty-two kilometers per second, these fragments of old comets and asteroids almost always burned up, trailing a broad, bright green spark and leaving an ephemeral column of high-density ions hanging in the air.

Since the turn of the century, humans had made use of these ion trails, bouncing stacked bursts of radio frequencies off them. Cheaper than copper cables or glass fibers, more numerous than slots in a geosynchronous orbit, able to bend signals around the Earth's horizon more sharply than a bounce off the ionosphere, meteor trails had revolutionized the telecommunications industry.

The trick was simple: aim a radio horn at the sky, code a variable lag into the signal, and program a photocell to look for the flash. When the system locates one, send like hell. Angle of incidence equals angle of reflection in an ever-widening cone. The resulting downlink footprint was just immense.

All right, Sommerstein told himself, this was old stuff, all known. His gift of imagination, however, reasoned that if the principle worked on Earth, why not in outer space as well?

True, the problems of sending signals around the globe dealt basically with obstructions to line of sight. That is, below the horizon and around inconvenient mountain ranges. Or, why had the commtechs looked to the sky in the first place?

But in outer space, this was generally not a problem. From one satellite in orbit to another, or from Earth to the Moon or other colonial bodies, straight-line radio communication was the norm rather than the exception.

. . . Except for those awkward little corners. Like the backside of the Moon. Or the nightside of Mars. Or any of the moons of Jupiter and Saturn during the occluded phase of their orbits. Or any body passing on the far side of the Sun's corona. Then it would be nice to have a way of bouncing signals at right angles, or obtuse angles, around the solar system without having to depend on expensive mechanical repeaters which, placed in all their eccentric orbits, were the modern-day equivalent of a million miles of copper wire.

In Earth's atmosphere, a meteor's ion-rich trail would do the trick. But deep interplanetary space offered no similar phenomena. Sommerstein had already tried bouncing signals off the asteroids, but the predominating chondrites — bodies whose outer layers are composed of siliceous and carbonaceous material — made poor radio reflectors. And their facets tumbled in unreliable patterns, too.

Still, there must be something else out there he could use.

Sommerstein watched the needles flick and tried to imagine what it could be.

Part 3

Time Zero to Eight Minutes

Setting at the world's edge, the west,
the Earth beneath you comes into the
  darkness of the dead,
who sleep in their chambers, heads wrapped,
unbreathing, unable to look upon each other;
their possessions are stolen from beneath their heads
and they know it not.
The lion comes forth from his den,
the serpent stings, the world is silence.
He that made all things goes to rest
beyond his horizon. He restores himself.

— *From Ikhnaton's "Hymn to the Sun"*

● Chapter 8

Blaze of Glory

Roar!
> *Roar!*
>> *Roar!*
>>> *Roar!*

Like a cataract in one of the great rivers on the green world, plasma from the surface of the solar atmosphere flies upward, arches over, and cascades down. The plasmote, trapped in this bridge of suspended gases, must cling to its magnetic eddies. He fights the turbulence of the ever-passing flow to keep from being spun outward into the thin, hot nothingness of the corona that surrounds this tube of gas. And, with none to hear him now, the plasmote screams into the crescendo of sound, adding his voice to the supersonic roar.

Twist!
> *Turn!*
>> *Rave!*
>>> *Roar!*

As the plasma tube rolls and bends itself about its anchor point down in the photosphere, the magnetic flux inside creates huge energies. Like a snake suspended on invisible leaf springs, the gas tube lies on a field far above the sun's surface. And there, like a dynamo of hot gas spinning effortlessly in the socket of its grounded convection cell, the prominence packs and stores billions of volts of potential along its million-kilometer length.

The plasmote feels each added terawatt of electric potential as a fever heat that tears at his fabric and erodes his mind. The intense flux threatens to destroy the sequence of coded ionic charges, yes-and-no, on-and-off, that he contains within his innermost structure. As the tension builds, he becomes slower and stupider. His grip on the eddies of gas grows weaker. His substance becomes thinner and hotter, like the plasma flowing everywhere in this maelstrom of energy. He fades . . .

> *Tick!*
>> *Groan!*
>>> *Creak!*
>>>> *Hum!*

Aboard *Hyperion*, March 21, 2081, 18:34 UT

In the depth of his amazement, Dr. Hannibal Freede sat frozen at his console. Only the workaday sounds of *Hyperion*'s cooling system existed in that enclosed space, reminding him that the ship's life trundled on around him.

On the monitor screen before his staring eyes, the light of hydrogen-alpha emissions recorded the solar disk as a golden coin with a ragged hole blown through it, somewhat off center. When Freede adjusted the bandwidth of his sensors, the anomaly was revealed as a pair of bullet holes, gaping exit wounds, whose edges were bounded by an expanse of swollen, diseased tissue, black overlapping gray. The dominant spot pair lined up east to west and spanned twenty-two degrees across the disk, just below the equator.

Freede closed his eyes. The image remained on his retinas, reversed now, glaring red-gold on black, despite the low contrast of the monitor screen he was using for these observations. The sunspot group was *huge*! The blemish should be big enough to see on Earth using no equipment more sophisticated than a welder's glass.

As the sunset terminator rushed around the world there, and the reddened sun appeared to sink into the planet's dust-laden atmosphere so that people could chance to look upon it with the unaided eye, then millions would be able to see what Freede was seeing now. An irregular gash in the surface of the star, as large and distinct as the lunar maria. A pair of holes whose sides would have both depth and dimension, even to the naked eye. Raw scoops of sun-stuff, plucked out of that smooth face as by a great, clawed fist.

Freede remembered that when *Hyperion* had rounded the sun's south pole, fourteen days ago, he had peered back along her orbit, searching for the smallest signs of his "smudge." Back then, he had not been at all sure if the anomaly was even real or not.

What a joke!

All the time, up there beyond his line of sight, a full-fledged spot pair had been brewing. And not puny, elusive spots from early in the solar cycle, either, but huge and hungry specimens from the fifth- or sixth-year peak of the old eleven-year cadence. More than that. This spot pair was larger, to Freede's eye, than even the Great Sunspot Group of 1947, the largest complex of spots ever recorded.

He had mounted this expedition on the theory that the sun's long period of quiescence was coming to an end sooner than the scientific community was ready to believe. To prove that, he would have been happy with finding a few pinholes or just marking a magnetically active region. This spot pair was beyond his most hopeful expectations. It was even a bit humiliating: he might as well have stayed home and studied this group from Earth.

As Freede was ruminating on these thoughts and fiddling with his sensor controls, watching his spot group rise on his screens as *Hyperion* lifted above the anomaly's horizon while making her slow way toward the sun's equator, he discovered the second heart-stopper of this survey mission.

The pair was linked by a prominence!

He could just make out the curve of it, etched against the limb of the solar globe. The prominence was a wispy structure of pale gases, arising from the vicinity of one spot and sinking away in the region of the other. As Freede studied the altered-light image, he saw a sheet of ruddy flame sluggishly pull away from the photosphere. It stretched itself against the background of fiery spicules, drawing itself into a thin and glassy skein, like hot, yellow taffy. Suddenly, the sheet leapt, springing upward to join the arch of the prominence.

The bridge of flowing gas looked top-heavy to Freede's unaccustomed eye. Studying it, the astrophysicist could read folds and wrinkles and snares into its structure. Flows and counterflows surged inside the ragged tube, while spurts and eddies of loose gas escaped from the hanging fringes, evaporating completely in the superheated atmosphere of the corona.

"Gyeli!" Freede thumbed the intercom. "Come here a minute!"

"What is it?" his wife answered, with a cross edge to her voice. "I'm up to my elbows in suds."

"I've found a prominence!"

"Well . . . didn't you expect to find one? I mean, with a spot pair and all?"

"But it's a big one!" he insisted.

"Yes, but then, it's a big spot, isn't it?"

"My dear, you have no romance!"

"No, dear, of course not. I have a dozen sieve layers from the hydroponics processor flying around the cabin right now."

"So you don't want to see it, then?

"You gawk at your prominence, dear. That's what you're good at. I've got to keep us eating." Her intercom clicked off.

"Your loss, then," he said under his breath.

What would the phenomenon look like in pan-spectrum emissions? Freede wondered if he could even see his spot — he now thought of it as his own property — against the glare of full sunlight.

He loosened the straps holding his legs against the chair beneath his console and, buoyed by the microgravity of the ship's orbital freefall, floated up toward the top of his observation bubble. *Hyperion*'s orientation was face-on to the solar disk, he knew, so that when he dropped the dome's polarizing filters, he would be looking at the full force of the sun's energy.

Of course, the sun would not be looking back at him — not with its complete strength, for that would kill him. The dark curve just beyond Freede's nose was a double thickness of thermal-tolerant glass, with the same freon gel passing between its panes as circulated through the rest of the ship. So the sun's heat would not charbroil him. The control for the dome's polarization, which was actually a sophisticated structure of interlocking liquid crystals, operated under its own expert system, not unlike the iris of the human eye. Photometers sampled the ambient visible spectrum, and the crystals closed ranks to screen out excess light that might be damaging to human skin and retinas. So the sun's glare would not burn out his eyes. But, those details aside, Freede would be looking at the sun from as close to naked-eye in the orbit of Mercury as he could safely arrange.

He turned the knob.

Twirl!
> *Twist!*
>> *Wrap!*
>>> *Writhe!*

The gaseous tube that held the plasmote now packs many terawatts of electric potential into its howling channel. So great is the flux that he becomes dizzy with the excess kinetic energy that is building up in his ionized fabric.

Other than that — his gradual structural deterioration — the plasmote is also becoming bored. He has no place to go. He has no one to talk with. And he has no hope of improving his situation. He will simply hang here, suspended far above the solar landscape, until something happens.

Once he thought of releasing his magnetic grip on the tube's internal eddies and letting himself slide along it. Then he might ride the flow down, back into the photosphere.

But he senses this would be his death. The ends of the tube are swallowed in the blackness of the magnetic storm he had been crying, which still pushes its way through the solar atmosphere. The plasmote, falling free, would be injecting himself into the center of a great, cold pool, a columnar downdraft, which was an anomaly among the upwelling hot cells of the photosphere. Its weight of relatively cool gas would suck him down to the bottom of the convection layer, halfway to the core, where no plasmote has ever been and lived to report the experience. There, at the flooring-out of the draft, he would be subjected to thermal energies that would snuff his life in an instant.

Still, he might chance it, if he thought he could swim to the side of the down-pitching cell and there find a countering updraft. That might be a possibility — if the cell were no wider than the rising columns that make up the bulk of his experience in the photosphere. But this dark pool is easily a hundred times wider than any of those. It would numb him and drag him down and devour him.

So the plasmote has nothing to hope for and nothing to do, except count the twists of his tubular prison and try to appreciate the mammoth energies building around him.

After an unknowable passage of time, the plasmote feels a change. The roaring cataract of gas goes suddenly still. The howling velocity through the tube ceases for an instant. Something is happening.

Before he can decide *what*, the gas bridge collapses.

It does not fall, sucking back downward into the dark storm-pools that anchor it. It contains too much energy for that. Instead, it blows outward, flinging sheets and knots of superheated plasma — the eddies he was clinging to — farther up into the tenuous corona.

The plasmote curls himself around a point-rupture of exploding gas and expects finally to die.

Blaze!
  Beat!
    Pulse!
      Rush!

Aboard *Hyperion*, March 21, 18:49 UT

The full-spectrum glare of the sun's face throbbed at Dr. Hannibal Freede. Its power seemed diminished not at all by the dome's latent grid of liquid-lattices. He squinted his eyes and looked off to the east and just below the equator, searching for the spot pair that the hydrogen-alpha light had revealed so spectacularly. The double bullet hole had almost disappeared in the blaze of pure light.

No, wait! As his eyes adjusted to the glare, Freede saw something there now. In the uniform golden glow of the solar disk, the area over the spot pair's coordinates seemed to fade toward silvery-white. It was not less bright, but less colorful, less saturated with the light of the total spectrum, and somehow less intense. It was as if, given enough time, that patch of the solar atmosphere would gradually tarnish and darken, like a blemish forming on a golden apple, becoming a brown bruise, then blackening into a full-blown chancre.

Freede turned his head to one side, trying to match that area of the solar disk with the hydrogen-alpha image still showing on the monitor screen down on his console. While he was thus distracted, the sun pulsed at him.

Once.

Hard.

What was that? Freede quickly looked back at the natural-light face, exposed beyond the glass of the dome. He thought his eyes had adjusted to the brightness, so they should have stopped playing tricks with dazzles on his optic nerve.

The pulse, whatever it was, had gone by him now. The sun showed him the same golden face with the same silvery patch. Maybe that area was even a little paler now, whiter, more faded.

He checked the monitoring equipment, swimming toward the console and studying the image there, to see if it showed a change. The gas prominence was slowly falling, fading . . . finally gone.

Freede grabbed the arms of his chair and swung his legs down into it. Instead of taking the time to strap himself in, he merely hooked his calves under the seat. He put his face close to the screen and cranked up the resolution. Yes, definitely, the arc of glowing gas connecting the two sunspots had disappeared.

What did that mean?

Well, of course. According to the observation records and sunspot theories piled up during the twentieth century, the gas prominence had flared. It had exploded and collapsed, returning most of its material to the photo-sphere, but flinging a goodly portion of it, as well as most of its kinetic energy, out into the corona and beyond, into clear space.

How great an energy? Freede knew that the astronomers of the last century — with their rudimentary measurements, taken from beneath Earth's thick atmos-phere, at nearly three times Freede's current distance from the sun — believed that the potential latent in a large flare would have been sufficient to power the North American economy for at least 10,000 years. Freede had to remind himself, however, that they were expressing themselves in terms of the comparatively diverse energy needs of those times, which meant both driving an inefficient electric utility grid and furnishing an equivalent energy quota in wasteful, carbon-fueled transportation. In more general and useful terms, then, a large solar flare might deliver the energy equivalent of two to three billion hydrogen bombs in the megaton range.

This flare, however, would be well beyond their scope and measure. The spot pair and the gas prominence Freede had seen were truly huge. So, he estimated the latent energy as five or six times a normal flare of the late twentieth century. That would put the output, conserva-tively, at something like twelve to fifteen billion H-bombs.

But that one faint pulse of visible light he had experienced could only have contained a fraction of such an immense outpouring of energies. Where then, he wondered, had the rest of it gone?

Freede's equipment had been designed to sample the sun's emissions at various wavelengths, even though in normal circumstances about half the star's output came as visible light. Under his observation protocols, Freede had started recording these various wavelengths as soon as *Hyperion* rose over the anomaly's horizon. Now, he could simply track back on all those disks and study the flare in the light of many different energy levels.

Being a man of method and habit, Freede started with the highest frequencies, the gamma and x-ray spectra, which were normally invisible to human eyes. These were also the most energetic of the electromagnetic emissions; so that was a good place to begin his search.

He bumped the first disk, recording from wavelengths of 10^{-3} Angstroms, back before the time marker that he estimated for the instant of the flare, then played it. The sun showed as a faint gray roundel, reminding Freede of a new moon seen at dusk through a backyard telescope. But up on the eastern face and just below the equator, coinciding with that silvery patch, he could see a filament of molten metal stitched into the gray cloth. That would be the gas prominence.

When the counter clicked through his mark, the screen whited out, saturated with brilliance. He ran the sequence again, trying to freeze it at the exact second, hoping to catch the opening frames of the bridge's collapse. But the action was too quick, the burst of energy too complete and consuming.

Freede played his second disk, reading in the x-ray range, 10 Angstroms. The same dull round, perhaps showing even fewer features. And, at the mark, the same drenching flash.

For an instant, the doctor worried that the blast might have damaged the short-frequency observing heads, which were all located outside the insulating shell of *Hyperion's* thick hull. Then Freede remembered where he himself had been observing at the instant the flare had flashed past the ship.

Across the screen's bottom, the computer calculated the intensity of emission — at these frequencies, measured in Roentgens — for any point selected on the monitor's face. The cursor happened to be blinking somewhere near the center of the screen. He didn't bother to move it, because the burst of radiation was so uniform. The callout showed 2,100 Roentgens, which was three times the human-lethal dose in rems.

Now, Freede thought almost giddily, he would have a chance to test firsthand, as a scientist, the radiation-shielding effects of two layers of thermal-tolerant glass, a smear of freon gel, and a pastiche of interlocking liquid crystals. Then he thought that perhaps Gyeli, working down in the Hydroponics Section, had been better protected by the ship's mass.

As these realizations rushed in on him, Freede quickly accepted that he had no time for morbid thoughts. There was simply too much to do.

First, he should warn someone. Warn the Earth. Warn the Moon. Warn the colonies exposed throughout the system. It was still early for his regularly scheduled transmission but, if he called on several bands, someone might be listening. Freede powered up his communications console.

SQUAWK!

The speaker warbled and spat. It took him a few seconds to figure out that this was a residue of the flare's energy, howling down into the meter-range wavelengths, where his comm frequencies operated.

Orbiting at the approximate distance of Mercury from the sun, about three light-minutes out, *Hyperion* was now on the backside of the wave representing the flare's disruptions. Freede and Gyeli were separated from Earth, the Moon, and all humankind by its blast of electromagnetic energy. That wavefront would reach the first of the inhabited satellite posts in about five minutes. Anything he could tell the listeners after that time would sound like a postmortem.

Freede tried anyway. He gathered his thoughts into a concise description of what he had observed, punctuated with such readings as his equipment had made, and broadcast them into the growling static. It was a scientist's first report of a mammoth solar flare, the like of which the sun had not produced in more than eighty years, or possibly never before.

Maybe someone would hear this message. Maybe the doubters, the people who wanted to delay any renewal of the sun's variability, would now understand, and accept, and begin to take sensible precautions.

Because the electromagnetic wavefront wasn't the flare's only consequence. Coming behind that lightspeed surge of energy, a storm of charged particles — protons and helium nuclei expelled when the gas prominence blew apart — was moving outward at more than 1,400 kilometers per second. Their scattered charges would play havoc with the Earth's and Moon's magnetic fields. The ion storm would induce huge, false voltages in any unshielded electronics, overloading and burning out circuits. And in this case "unshielded" meant most of the spaceborne equipment now in service throughout the solar system. Anything that might withstand that first electromagnetic pulse, which was coming at the human worlds five minutes from now, would surely flare up and die in the magnetic storm following it.

Including most of *Hyperion*'s electronics.

> *Thump!*
>   *Thump!*
>   *Bump!*
>   *Thud!*

Aboard *Hyperion*, March 21, 18:57 UT

Dr. Hannibal Freede pulled himself down the ship's nullgee manway, flinging himself through the turns and overreaching his handholds. The result was a bruising freefall, bouncing him like a tennis ball off the hard, aluminum-hexacomb bulkheads. He barely registered the pain.

"Gyeli!" Freede called, from the hatchway into Hydroponics.

"What now?" Angelika looked up from her work, a scrub brush in one hand, a lattice of fine wires in the other, and clouds of fine bubbles floating around her arms.

As always, Freede's breath caught when he came upon his wife's beauty unawares. She had long, golden hair that was now tied in a single long braid and protected from the flying liquid with a length of red cloth. The hair, pulling back from her pale face, gently drew her features up, accenting the curve of her dark brows, the line of her elliptical eyelids, the shelf of her sharp cheekbones, the angles of her long jaw and pointed chin. Angelika's aristocratic, Eurasian features always stopped his heart.

The weightless lift of microgravity did nothing to harm her figure either. Under the work smock, her heavy breasts shifted slowly, regally with each breath. Her long, slender limbs — strong with the exercise she took on the springmill every day — moved easily at the task of shoving the filter screens around the cabin. She touched one toe here against the wall, bumped one buttock there against the floor, her long body swinging their mass with a nudge and a swing.

"What?" Gyeli asked again.

"We have to prepare the ship for maneuvering. Leave those for now — they'll fall flat when the acceleration hits. But you have to get, oh, dishes, loose equipment, breakable stuff, anything heavy, under wraps."

"Maneuvering?" She stared at him as if he were speaking Greek. "When is this? And why?"

"The when is less than twelve hours. Six, if we want to be prudent about it. There's been a flare, a large one — "

"Oh, good! Then your theories about renewed solar activity were right all along. You should be — "

"Yes, the spot was active, all right," Freede said, dismissing his own greatest achievement, the crowning observation of his scientific career. "And now we are in great danger, my dear.

"The electromagnetic burst has already passed us — as soon as I detected it, in fact," he explained. "But in a minimum of six hours, at this distance, an ion storm is going to traverse this area. The ship's controls were simply not designed to withstand so immense a flux. That's my fault, of course, for not being resolute in my theories and so more conservative in my preparations. But now, at this close range, if we don't start firing on a vector to take us home, even our shielded circuits may burn out. Then we'll never leave this orbit."

"I understand, dear," Gyeli said, after a frown of sober concentration. "Don't worry. I know what to strap down and what to let go crash. You work with the ram engine. It will take, um — how long to build up internal velocities?"

"Four hours. But then, as soon as that gas wave hits, we'll be feeding it an enriched stream."

"A squeaker for timing. What's the chance that an overpressure will snuff the burn?"

"Unknown," he admitted, "but we don't have a second alternative."

"You're right, of course. And we're years early for the rendezvous. Are you going to radio McSartin, Vrain and ask them to send the probe ahead of us?"

Freede considered the suggestion. "I think not. We're in a blackout right now . . . and after the e-mag wave hits Earth, there will be too much confusion for anyone to think clearly about *our* problems. I've sent a general warning, of course, but they will get it too late, if at all."

"Of course. So, are we simply going to drift beyond Jupiter, Han? We have supplies, but —"

"I'm going to try to work out, and then lock in, the firing for a high-energy trajectory that should put us in a much wider solar orbit. The ship will end up somewhere near the Earth-Moon system. There will be risks. . . ."

"As you say, we have no alternatives."

"It'll get you most of the way home, my dear. And then, when the dust has settled, one of the El shuttles will be —"

"What do you mean, 'me,' Han? You'll get us *both* home, won't you?" She smiled at him.

"Slip of the tongue, Gel. Sorry."

"Of course, dear." She moved close to him in freefall, passed an arm around his neck, and kissed him squarely on the mouth. It was a long, warm kiss.

Freede's heart raced.

"Now, on your way to that engine." Gyeli spun him around and shoved him toward the hatch. "I'll make ship-shape down here."

• Chapter 9

Electromagnetic Fields

> Leap
> > Bound
> > > Stumble
> > > > Fall

**Tranquility Shores, Luna Colony,
March 21, 18:52 UT**

"Look at me, Miss Tochman!"

Gina Tochman checked the communications band on her left wrist. The ninth diode was lit. She glanced up, looking for the figure with the big, square "9" on its jumper. There she or he was, about twenty meters away, doing a somersault across the field of gray sand. Gina made a quick scan of the names and numbers written on the cuff of her own jumper. The ninth was Perry Leekman.

She dialed in the appropriate comm channel. "Nice going, Mr. Leekman!" she called.

The Moon Walkers were playing around her like children, as always. Since they had arrived at the resort, with its invigorating one-sixth gravity, these people had been confined in underground corridors and smallish rooms. One good jump anywhere in the complex — or even a careless move, like getting up too fast from a chair — would crack their skulls on the overhead. So the moment they got outside, away from the low ceilings, they went wild.

Of course, there was always the Bounce Tube. This was an abandoned pressure tank, four meters in diameter and thirty-five deep, dug down below the West Mall. Some enterprising facilities manager had fitted the space with wall padding, a trampoline bottom, and piped-in white music. For fifty neumarks an hour, hyperactive children and athletic adults could exercise their muscles and try beating the Tube's jump record, or fall on their butts trying. The current top was twenty-seven meters, sixty-one centis, set by Gina herself during the one time she'd used the Tube, which was the only time she'd had fifty neu to spree.

Moon Walk was cheaper.

Number 5 bounced past her, doing a kangaroo hop. From the way that person — checked out as Mrs. Katajoosian — was covering ground and leading with her helmet, Gina Tochman felt a warning was required.

"Watch out, Ms. Kay!" she called over Channel 5.

"What I do wrong?" the woman asked quickly in a lilting accent that Gina thought might be some variety of Turkic overlaid on Russian.

"Nothing yet. But that's not a crash helmet you're wearing. And those are rocks in front of you."

"Oh! Oh!" The woman looked over her shoulder, turning herself around in midair. "And how is I stop?"

"Just quit bouncing."

"But my legs do not stop!" she called, landing and instantly rebounding on her short legs.

"Then sit down!"

The plump woman pulled up her heels and crash-landed from a height of three meters. "Ooof!" Gina knew Mrs. Katajoosian was over a soft patch of dust, and not gravel or hard plaque. She picked herself up and rubbed her backside.

"You be careful now," Gina called, and spread her attention among the rest of her charges.

She dialed in Channel 12. "Mr. Carlin?"

This figure was nowhere in sight, which meant he might be behind a rock or have wandered off into a ray's depression. That was a potential problem, because these radios were mostly line-of-sight, without a lot of scatter. The resort had never bought a long-range repeater at forty-nine to fifty-one megahertz for its suit communications. Well, the man wouldn't be hard to find, not in the full glare of lunar noon. And maybe he had just gone back into the garage.

"Mr. Car—"

Brazz-ZAPP!

The noise coming from Tochman's earbuds was like getting slapped on both sides of her head at once.

Bark-bargle-bong.

Either the noise was fading, or her hearing had suffered some kind of permanent damage. Gina's ears felt numb and wet — she wondered if that was blood.

Brizzle-drizzle-BOOP!

Dead silence.

No, there was still a pearly ringing in her ears, like bell voices, with an underlying crackle of static. Loud static, she decided, from the way it wormed itself through her temporary deafness.

She clicked through the comm channels, trying to find one that wasn't affected by the malfunction.

"What—!"

Hummm!

"— that's a —"

"— I can't—"

Humm!

"— hurts—"

Hum!

"— my ears!"

All the channels were either dead or drowning in the same ragged static. On the live ones, the excited voices of her Moon Walkers came as a bare whisper under the noise. But Gina was sure that, instead of whispering, they were all screaming by now, because the same punishing burst must have flared up in each headset.

This sort of malfunction was very unusual. In the past she might have had one or two radios go out on her, but never the whole group all at once like this.

Gina Tochman turned to the command channel and over-rode them. "Now listen to me, folks! Stay right where you are, please. Stop moving and give me your attention, please."

About ten of the twenty-odd figures within her sight,

scattered in pairs and singles across the rock garden, froze like statues. The rest continued walking straight ahead or gamboling about. So either their radios were dead, or her own wasn't sending on that channel, or those people just didn't want to be bothered right now.

But some of the stationary Moon Walkers had actually turned toward Gina. It couldn't be the sound of her voice, because the earbuds in these suits were monophonic and directionless. Still, she found the reaction encouraging. It meant those people had been keeping an eye on her — or on her suit with its square red "0" slashed through to indicate a numeral — all along. Caution in a strange environment was the sign of a survivor type.

"We've had a minor radio malfunction," Gina said. "It seems to affect every channel. I can hear most of you, but I don't know if you can hear me. Obviously, not everyone can. So, if someone is not standing still and listening to this announcement, that indicates a problem with his or her radio. Would you now please wave at these people who are near you, or get their attention somehow, because they are in great danger."

Across the field, the people who were standing by went after the walkers and the jumpers. They grabbed at arms or waved their own in front of the bubble helmets, until finally the area within Tochman's sight was filled with clumps of idle, shuffling people.

"Thank you," she said, still on the command channel. "What I want to do first is a roll call. When I say your name, you should both answer on your suit mike and raise your hand. Then we'll know what the damage is. Okay?" She clicked to Channel 1. "Mr. Eiders?"

The man, who was ten meters off and looking straight at her, shot up his whole arm like a child answering in school. "What I want to know," he said petulantly, under the residual static, "is if you're going to take this off our guaranteed walk time."

Gina ignored him, dialing in Channel 2. "Ms. Fischer?"

The woman, standing right beside her, raised her hand. "Right here, dear."

And so it went. Twenty-two calls. Twelve verbal replies — along with a few complaints, some anger, and a little mild hysteria — and for two more a show of hands only. The rest, with totally dead radios, Gina counted by a clumsy form of pantomime.

But she couldn't find Mr. Carlin.

"All right, folks." Gina went back on command. "Everyone is accounted for except Number 12, Mr. Stephano Carlin. What I want you to do — without leaving your spot — is look around and see if you can spot anyone with a twelve on his chest. Look carefully, especially you people on the edges of the group. Will you do that now, please?"

Across the field, the fourteen figures with working radios spun on their heels like bulky tops in their padded suits. One person fell down and quickly righted herself.

"If you see him," Tochman prompted, "then call to me or wave."

No one responded. A few of the figures shrugged.

"Okay, folks, we've got a problem. One of our Walkers is in trouble. So I have to start a search for him. But first I'm going to lead you in. I want you all to start walking directly toward me. If someone near you is mute, please take him or her by the arm — "

"Are we going to get a refund or not?" Eiders broke in on his own channel.

"Yes, sir," she promised. But she used his Channel 1 in private mode; she could see no sense in running up costs.

The other people started to come toward her at a slow walk, with no one running or bounding along. The spirit had all gone out of them.

Choof!
   Chug!
      Chug!
         Chug!

Equipment Garage, Tranquility Shores, March 21, 19:09 UT

When the doorseals tightened and the ambient built up,

Gina Tochman's pressure suit became less of an itch. She immediately shucked the thermal jumper and began clawing at the snaps of her helmet bubble — then thought better of it. She would be going right out again with the search party, wouldn't she?

As soon as the meter set into the far wall showed a pressure of at least ninety-five millibars, the manway from the Maintenance Office popped opened, and Sylvia Peers burst in among the Moon Walkers wearing her bright civies and a pair of corridor slippers. She kept her distance from the tourists, whose jumpers had picked up a coating of fine dust during their tumbles; on contact with the dry air it acquired a high static charge and would leap onto her clean clothing. Then Syls spotted Tochman and made a beeline for her.

"You're back early, Gina. What happened?"

"We've lost a customer," Tochman said, taking off the helmet after all. "Missing, presumed incapacitated. And our radios suddenly went wonky on us. I want you or Georgie to get on the emergency freaks and ask one of the Traffic Control Platforms to train a telescope down here. They'll be looking for a man-sized white spot — "

"Covered in gray dust, right?"

"Oh, hell! That's right," Tochman agreed. "He'll be perfectly camouflaged, won't he? Well, maybe they can see his tracks or something — "

"No can do, Gina." Syls shook her head. "Our radios went out, too. We've been trying to raise the orbital net for the past ten minutes, but it's a bust. First we had all that static, but it's cleared now and still no go. I don't know — maybe whatever sent that burst of noise burned out the platforms' receivers. We've had no problems on the optic cable, so we've got ground talk going as usual. But nothing in the sky, fixed or incoming."

The situation was worse than Gina had thought. This was not just an isolated equipment malfunction, but something general, a wide-area burst of radio static. Now what could cause that? Maybe some scientific experiment, something having to do with high energy, somewhere in orbit or at least within line of sight, or —

No. She would have time to think about it later, when the immediate problem of the missing Mr. Carlin was solved.

"All right, then we'll do it ourselves," Gina told Sylvia. "You take these people through into Maintenance and then into the corridor beyond. They can disrobe there. And get a medical tech up here to check them for hearing loss. That was quite a burst on the headsets. I know my own ears are still ringing.

"Meantime," she went on, "you scramble everyone in the complex who is surface-trained. We'll need to do a pattern search, and that will require at least a dozen operatives. We'll need working radios, too, so someone should start testing them. And then — "

"You can't authorize all this! Think of the costs, Gina. You'll have to put in a requi — "

Tochman grabbed the woman's shoulders in her gritty gloves, careless about leaving print marks.

"Listen to me! We've got a man out there. He's middle-aged and confused and frightened. He's probably disoriented, maybe injured. With no radio. And with less than forty minutes of air in his tank. If we don't find him in that time, he will die. And that's not going to look good on *anyone's* balance sheet."

"I understand," Syls said quietly. "I'll get these people moving."

The young woman started gathering in the Moon Walkers, helping them off with their helmets, explaining that they had to clear the garage area.

Gina Tochman went off to begin organizing her search party.

> Trudge
> > Trudge
> > > Trudge
> > > > Trudge

In the Tranquility Highlands, 19:42 UT
Gravel on the inclines crunched and rotated under Gina Tochman's clogs as she topped a rise in the low foothills.

The slope did not look like much, not when you could still see for a distance of a couple of kilometers from crest to crest. But despite the low gravity, she could feel the strain in her legs and lower back.

Gina was on the western periphery of the search pattern. At thirty minutes out from the garage, she had little hope of finding Carlin on this pass. Anyway, it was doubtful he would have gone into the hills, unlikely he would have come this far. That would be stupid, even for a green tourist.

But then, Gina Tochman had been walking continuously, moving methodically, pausing at regular intervals to scan the horizon and tick off the squares on her topo map. Carlin, on the other hand, had probably been loping along, trying to cover ground, and gotten confused when he came among these serried knolls, which were actually behind the resort complex. Here he could easily have fallen and hurt himself, especially if he had landed on a patch of this loose gravel and it rolled under his feet. Almost anything was possible with the Moon Walkers.

Tochman oriented herself on the ridgeline, arranged the mapboard on her forearm, checked her chronometer, and began her fourteenth visual inspection.

Clear to the west. Tick!

Clear to the north. Tick!

Clear to the — wait! There was a shiny patch to the east, winking like a heliograph. Nothing out here should be moving, not even a collection of mechanical discards.

"Barney?" she called her team coordinator, overriding the burbles of static which still marred communications. "I've got some unusual movement in Square Q-X-Eight-Niner. I'm moving toward it."

Gina walked down off the ridge, keeping her eyes on the shiny spot. It disappeared as she went into a gully, but she was trained to walk a straight line out here and expected to recover the glinting object as soon as she mounted the lip of the depression.

In half a kilometer she topped another, smaller rise and saw the thing again. It was a bright patch on a clear resin helmet, propped against a rock and attached to a dusty gray body that was lying on its back.

"Barney. I have him at those coordinates." She switched to Walkers' Channel 12. "Mr. Carlin? Are you all right?"

The figure made no response. But the helmet was still moving, tilting back and forth languidly, as if keeping time to dance music. Then she saw the rise and fall of the suit's chest in counterpoint. The man was gasping his last breaths against a drained bottle.

Gina rushed to him in three bounding strides. She knelt beside him — and yes, there was the red "12" on his jumper. Beneath the bubble, Carlin's mouth was opening and closing, like a fish at the side of an aquarium. But the fish's face was turning a mottled slate-blue. She put a hand on the man's shoulder to steady him.

Carlin noticed her and reached down to his waist, turned a knob on his radio.

"Miss Tochman! Thank God you came. . . . I can't breathe. . . . Something wrong . . . with my respirator. . . . Think I'm — "

"Hush now. You're almost out of air, is the problem." She drew a spare canister out of her backpack and showed it to him. "I'm going to give you a fresh bottle, but to do that I have to valve you off. Just hold your breath for two seconds. Can you do that?"

He nodded frantically.

Gina reached behind his neck, pulled the fittings loose from the folds of his thermal jumper, and turned the valve lever crosswise. She dropped the coupling from the dead bottle and attached the full one.

"Okay now, take a deep breath."

He opened his mouth in a wide yawn. In a second his color was starting to return. When he had taken five or six good breaths, Gina helped him up, checked him for suit tears and broken bones, and opened his jumper to fit the new bottle in his harness, taking the old one into her pack.

"Can you walk back with me?" she asked.

"Yes, I think so."

She switched back to the rescue frequency. "Barney. I've

got him in tow. You can probably meet us with a buggy at, oh, Square Q-BB-Two-Five. Copy?"

"Got you. On my way."

The two of them started off to the east, toward the resort. After a moment, when they were covering ground easily, Gina thought of something.

"How did you become separated?" she asked Carlin. "Your radio seems to be working fine. Didn't you hear my instructions? Or the roll call?"

"Oh, I turned my radio off. That static was hurting my ears."

"But when you were lost, why didn't you turn it back on?"

"Every time I tried, I just got more static. And then — well, I just wasn't thinking too clearly." Carlin hung his head sheepishly.

"That's all right." She tugged his arm. "You're safe now."

Click!
  Click!
    Click!
      Click!

Women's Wardrobe, Tranquility Shores, 20:23 UT

Gina had shed her thermal jumper and utility harness out in the garage. Now, in the privacy of the locker room, she could finally peel off that skin-tight pressure suit and give herself a thorough *scratch*. Except, here came a sound that didn't change much whether the gravity was a full gee or point-one-six: high heels on tile. She turned her head toward the end of the aisle and waited.

The sound found her.

"There you are, Miss Tochman!"

It was one of her customers from the Moon Walk: Number 4, Miss Ednara Gladvale, of the Gladvale Uranium Trust — as she was sure to let you know. Gina recognized that voice even without her cuff notes.

"What can I do for you, Miss Gladvale?"

"I have a complaint to make."

"I'm sure you do," Gina said. It was a rare slip — but

then, she was physically tired as well as stressed out by having to run the search party.

Miss Gladvale ignored the gaffe. "It's about my camera." The woman pulled a small InstaPrint model out of her handbag. "It was working just fine before we went outside, and now all it makes are these blank, white squares." She showed Gina a handful of exposed prints — totally overexposed, by the look off them.

"Maybe it's the chemicals in the film," Tochman suggested. "They can evaporate out, you know, if you expose them to vacuum, especially in the heat of direct sunlight."

"But then the film would stay gray, wouldn't it? Like when it first comes out of the slot," Miss Gladvale said. "Besides, here are some perfectly good pictures that I took early on in the Moon Walk." She offered a smaller clutch of not very interesting snaps, mostly dead-black sky over a dull-gray horizon, with flashes of sun reflecting off rocks and blurs that were the jumpers of the other Moon Walkers.

"So when did the all-white ones start showing up?"

"I don't remember, but I think it was after our radios failed."

"That's interesting," Gina said.

"'Interesting,' hell! I want you to fix my camera."

"Well, have you tried some fresh film in it? Or taken some pictures inside here, away from the vacuum?"

"But there's still half a pack in the camera! Why would I waste perfectly good film?"

"Let's try it," Gina urged, taking the unit and snapping a print of the angry Miss Gladvale. In a second, the slot spit out a square of pearly gray film. They waited the required four seconds. This one also faded to a ghostly white.

"Huh!" Tochman said. "Now do you have any fresh film — some that wasn't outside?"

"If you'll pay for it — "

"I'll pay, don't worry."

"Then here." The woman rummaged around in her bag and came up with an unopened package.

Gina slipped the partly used pack out of the camera and

set it on the bench beside her hip. She inserted the new film, aimed the lens at Gladvale, and fired off another shot.

It developed into a not very attractive — but otherwise normal — image of the woman. The hectic spots of color in her cheeks, which came up dramatically in the film's chemical dyes, did not make her seem any younger or more blushing.

"I'd say your camera was working just fine, ma'am."

"Well, then . . . " Miss Gladvale appeared to think about it. "Then I want to take another tour outside — at your company's expense, if you please — so I can get my souvenir pictures. After I come all this way to — "

"I'll look into it, ma'am," Gina Tochman promised. "I'm sure something can be arranged."

● Chapter 10

Running from the Darkness

> *Mumble*
> > *Rumble*
> > > *Grumble*
> > > > *... BANG!*

Pompeii, August 24, 79 A.D., Ninth Hour

The breakfast table jerked and danced, spilling a glass of red wine into the soft, white woolen garment covering Jerry Kozinski's lap. That must be a toga. Under it, he could feel he was wearing a linen shirt-thing and short trousers, kind of like a pair of summer pajamas. The loose clothing was comfortable in this hot weather, except where the toga draped over his arms and itched.

Jerry looked over his shoulder, past the brow of the immediate hillside, and saw that the mountain cone beyond it, Vesuvius, was belching up gouts of black smoke. This was the event he had been waiting for. When the bang came — half a second after an underlit mushroom cloud of ash flew out of the volcano's top — that was his signal to begin running. The game had officially begun.

Kozinski gathered up the folds of his toga, raised them above his bare knees, and set off through the house at an easy jog. He knew the way out to the street, because his entry point into this Pompeii simulation had been the villa's cobbled atrium.

Almost before he was started, the toe of his sandal caught on something, and Jerry fell forward. He pitched face-first to the marble floor. Damn, but it was hard stuff! Stars flashed in his eyes and his teeth clicked by motor contraction when his chin connected with the slab. Picking himself up and rubbing at a bloody scrape on the under-side of his jaw, with two more patches on each knee, Kozinski looked back to see what had tripped him.

The marble square had tipped out of its bed of grout by about a ten-degree angle, exposing one sharp edge. Jerry's eyes widened as he realized that the whole floor was now tilted cockeyed. He'd have to watch his step as he went.

"Master! Master! What is happening?" A terrified slave ran out of one of the side rooms and clutched his ankles.

"Which one are you?" Jerry asked.

"Josephus, Master. Your valet."

"Well, Josephus, I guess it's a volcanic eruption."

"What are we to do?" the man pleaded, digging in his fingers and rolling his eyes in panic. If this was a simulation, it was all too real. If he was another player, then he would probably get extra points for his acting — if he survived.

"We have to leave here," Jerry explained. "We can't stay or the ash and lava will trap us. We have to find our way to safety."

"O Master! Which way?"

That indeed was the question. Uphill, to the top of their little knoll, might take them out of the lava flow and put them above the level of any poison gas. But they still might get buried in falling rocks and ash. Downhill, toward the bay, offered a possible escape by boat — or by swimming as a last resort. Jerry also had some idea that the cool seawater would protect him from the worst of the heat and gas.

"Down, through the town," he said, reviewing a possible route through the streets and plazas in his mind.

"Take me with you!"

"Yes, come!" Kozinski put a hand under the slave's armpit and hauled him upright. Together, with Jerry slowed up only a little by the pain of his skinned knees, they made their way out to the street behind the house. There the roadway slanted, uphill to the left, down to the right. Jerry and Josephus turned right and ran over the smooth, rounded cobbles.

Immediately Kozinski sensed a penalty looming behind

him. What was the duty of a Roman householder, especially one of noble birth? The game script said nothing about
his having family members, so he hadn't thought to search
the villa for anyone else. But what about the rest of his
slaves? Jerry knew he had them, because they had served
his breakfast. Should he have tried to evacuate those
people? Or were menials supposed to be beneath his
notice, not people at all? Or was panic at the sight of the
eruption a sufficient justification for his acting out of his-
toric character?

Jerry stopped running and looked back to the house.

"Master, we *must* go!" Josephus brayed.

"But the others — "

"No time!"

And, in fact, there was no time. As Kozinski watched, the
earth shook under his feet again, and the front of the house
cracked above the door's lintel. The wall fell in two halves,
and the roof collapsed on top of them. Now he could
choose to waste hours trying to dig out anyone who was
trapped inside — and then they would just die anyway —
or he could save himself.

Jerry spun around and ran with his one slave.

Down and turn right, down and turn left, the two of
them pounded over the paving stones until his feet —
poorly supported by the thin leather sandals — were
screaming with pain. In the excitement of the escape, suddenly there were people running along beside him. They
appeared by twos and tens and twenties, and Jerry never
quite saw which alley or doorway they came from. With
surprisingly little sound, other than the clop-clop of feet on
stone, they all ran downhill.

Something struck him in the shoulder. Jerry turned his
head to see who might be goading him. Nobody was there,
but his white toga now had a broad black streak on it. While
he was looking that way, a stone about two fingers wide
arced down out of the sky and hit him in the arm. Jerry
faced about and kept running, conscious now that a flurry
of greasy ashes was falling across his vision, like black snow.

He and the crowd made another turn, onto a street

leading into a wide plaza. But before it could empty out, the way inexplicably narrowed. Well, not really without reason: the owners of the houses that faced on the square had over-built their walls, encroaching upon the pavement along either side of the street. Jerry, Josephus, and about a hundred others jammed up in this narrow place, packed in against the side walls, and filled the space with their hubbub.

When all these people stopped moving, the ashes began to gather and cling to their hair and clothing. Jerry ran a hand over his own head and came away with a clot of filth. In another two minutes he would be wearing a helmet of solid black muck.

Panic immediately gripped him. Everyone *had* to keep moving, or the volcano would bury them right here. . . . Well, if Jerry Kozinski were really a patrician, this would be a characteristic time for him to exercise his authority. He elbowed the people standing on either side of him and raised his voice.

"Make way there!" he called to the leading edge of the crowd. "One at a time, you people! Go on through!"

A woman in front of him turned and glared. "Who the hell are you?" she demanded.

"I'm Jer — uh, wait! — Marcus Cornelius Sulla! That's who I am."

"The corn factor!" Her face pinched up with disgust. "It's the speculator!" she called to those about her. "Sulla the Speculator!"

"No, really!" he protested. "I'm an all right guy."

"Sulla the Speculator!" the crowd took up her cry. "Sulla the Speculator!"

A man behind him punched Jerry in the kidneys. Jerry moved his arm to protect himself and got it twisted, wrenched, and pushed up behind his back. He looked around for Josephus, thinking the slave might help him, but the man had already disappeared. Somebody kicked Jerry's legs out, and he fell heavily. More blows came down on his head and shoulders. Short kicks pummeled his sides. Each jolt flashed a red glare in his eyes as the simulated pain waves stung him.

". . . the Speculator!" was the last thing he heard as the darkness of bodies gathered over him turned into the sensory blank of an artificial unconsciousness.

After what might have been five seconds or five minutes, some feeling returned. One side of Jerry's face seemed to be brushed by feathery touches. The other side felt numb.

When Jerry Kozinski was allowed to open his eyes, he was lying in an empty street, half-buried in black powder. That was the numb part of him. More powder, mixed with small stones and grit, was sprinkling down on top of him. That was the feathery part.

He pushed up with his arms, feeling the pinpoint tingle indicating his many aches and bruises. His left knee was in bad shape. A physical restraint, like an invisible elastic bandage, kept him from bending the joint more than a few degrees. A sharp, needle-like pain stabbed through it as a reminder that he had ripped a tendon or something. Jerry could no longer run; he could barely even walk.

The cinders and bits of rock were falling faster now. If he didn't get off the street, they would smother him. He limped out into the deserted plaza, wading through drifts of slippery ashes. They slushed around his feet and squeezed between his bare toes like warm, wet mud. If he didn't get down to the waterfront, he'd be killed here when the lava came, unless the gas got him first. But with every step the rain of dark matter came more thickly, with a sound like ice crystals hitting glass, until a kind of black lace veiled his sight and blotted out the surrounding buildings. His shoulders and arms and head were mantled by sticky goop. The sun had long since faded from the morning sky.

This was no good. He would freeze like a statue right here. Jerry understood that he had to get under cover quickly. No sooner had he made this decision than the quality of the rain changed. Large chunks of hard stone started coming down, making loud *smacks!* and splashing craters in the muck on the ground. If one of them hit him, it could kill him.

Jerry hobbled over to the nearest building and beat on the door.

No response.

He pushed against it and found no give. It must have been barred from the inside.

Keeping under the overhang of the second floor, he hurried on to the next one. It was closed and barred, too.

As he was cutting across the alley between two houses, he heard a whimper. It was such an unexpected sound that he stopped and peered into the shadows. There, hunched over and shivering, was a small dog — a puppy, judging by the size of its feet — of the lean and almost hairless variety that ran in the streets of any Mediterranean town. The little thing was so sad and scared, with such big, staring eyes, that Jerry felt a physical ache in his chest.

He was about to dismiss the dog and keep on his search for shelter, when his gamer's sense took over. There was something suspicious about that puppy, trapped here with him when everyone else had gone. He remembered back to his morning on the terrace, before the game had properly started, when the only activity he could see in the town was dogs and children. Coincidences like that just didn't happen by chance in a Virtuality™ simulation. He guessed that helpless children and dogs might have point-value in the final scoring, if you managed to rescue one.

The little tug on his heart was another clue. The sensation might have been his own pure emotion, but it might also have been induced for a reason. It occurred to Jerry that, after the hatred that the mob had shown for the corn factor Sulla, he might need to do something selfless and compassionate for a change if he wanted to get out of the game alive.

Finally, it was an old fantasy gamers' rule: when in doubt, take it along.

Jerry limped up to the puppy, offering it the flat of his hand. The little animal sniffed his fingers and waggled its butt happily, smiling at him in that loose-lipped way all dogs have. He scooped it up in his arms and headed out into the plaza again.

It was the right instinct after all, because the next door he knocked on swung open. Inside was a low room, some

kind of servants' quarters or kitchen attached to the front
of a great house. The windows were shuttered, so it was
dark. But when he pushed his head in, the air in the house
smelled cleaner than outside.

Kozinski went through the door, leaving it open a crack
for light. On a solid oak table in the middle of the room, he
found an oil lamp, flint and steel, and a quantity of dry
wood shavings for tinder. His unpracticed hands struck a
spark on the first try, and the lamp wick was soon shedding
about sixty watts of illumination. Jerry turned and pushed
the door fully closed.

The puppy ran around the room, making squeaky barks
and shaking itself. Ashes flew from its coat and rattled
against the tiles of the hearth. Jerry brushed at his hair and
shook out the folds of his clothing, surrounding himself
with a ring of black soot and stones.

He found a stool and sat down, stretching his bad leg out
stiffly. The puppy came over and jumped onto his uneven-
ly balanced thighs, scratched once at the folds in his toga,
and settled itself down with its head propped on one of
Jerry's battered knees. He scratched behind the dog's ears
and rubbed its neck.

Jerry needed to rest and think about his next move. Certainly, he couldn't stay here. Being a player, he knew
exactly what was going to happen to the town of Pompeii
itself. He didn't think he would get many points for letting
an archeologist make a plaster cast of the hole in the ashy
sediment that his corpse was going to make two thousand
years from now.

But the major outfall of detritus was still some hours
away. In the meantime, this house did offer possibilities.
Here he might find a chair leg or a bedpost or something
that could be made into a crutch for his leg. He might find
an axe or spade or other tools that would serve him later in
digging his way out of the rubble. He could certainly take
food and water that might mean the difference between
strength and debilitating weakness later in the game.

When his leg no longer felt so stiff, Jerry Kozinski stood
up, ready to go exploring. The puppy jumped down, and

as it hit the floor the whole room rocked like a cabin on a ship at sea.

Another earthquake!

The lamp flew off the table, crashed against the wall, and shattered in a pool of blue flame.

The little dog squawked and ran in circles until it finally found the table and cowered under there.

Jerry fell down then. He rolled under the table, too, clutching the puppy's silky side to his face.

Pieces of plaster or stone or more volcanic stuff clattered down on the tabletop in the darkness. A mighty *crash!* told Jerry that part of the house had come down, although nothing fell directly on him. The light was now a little brighter, though.

Peering out between his hands, Jerry saw that most of the front wall had collapsed outward into the plaza. The black snow was pounding down on the broken clots of bricks. A wave of soot was rolling slowly toward his sheltering place, like a sand dune filmed in time-lapse photography. The crest was building up around the table's legs, passing the stretcher bars that joined them fifteen centimeters above the floor.

If Jerry didn't get up and move *right now*, he was going to be boxed in. Then he would never get out.

He gathered the puppy in his arms again and surged up on his knees. His head hit the underside of the table, and the simulation gave him another flash of red pain. Before he could quite get his senses back, the ash walls had risen to seal themselves around the edges of the tabletop. His vision went black. The puppy howled.

His vision went a pure and dazzling white.

The dog's howling became a whine of feedback.

Jerry Kozinski wondered if this was how the game simulated death by suffocation, and he felt a gush of anger. He wasn't dead yet! He still had his fingernails! He could dig!

These desperate thoughts chased themselves around his brain in tinier and tinier circles until he fell unconscious.

For real this time.

• Chapter 11

Market Mayhem

Clink!
  Clink!
    Spill!
      Clatter!

**Hong Kong Two, British Columbia,
March 21, 9:53 a.m. PST**

Sonic and optical effects under the Virtuality™ neural-nexus system were indeed awe-inspiring. As Winston Qiang-Phillips dropped each pointer on the green felt surface of his trading booth in front of Mr. Harald Sampson, the silver disks clinked and clanged together like real cash. They even collected glints and highlights from the fluorostrips that were simulated above the men's heads. And when the pile went top-heavy, it fell with a resounding clatter.

For a moment, and sometimes for hours each day, Winston could forget that he and his customers did not *actually* sit face to face and deal. Sampson, for example, was plugged into his ether-board in Omaha. Others worked the network from as far away as New York City or the Ryukyu Islands — where they were really pushing the envelope of the trading day.

Qiang-Phillips was making an offer on a block of natural gas pipeline stocks, one of many that he had tried to amass over the past eleven days. The silver coins he was dropping on the table were, in reality, electronic pointers for funds which he had officially registered with the HK2 Exchange — in dollar denominations, of course.

"Fifteen," Winston said, formally recording his per-share offer.

Clink!

Sampson just stared gravely down at the coin.

"Sixteen."

Clink!

Harald Sampson held a straight face, what the Americans called a "poker face," which the neural network could read directly from electrodes planted in the skin behind the man's ear, reading his nervous reactions. The experience, Qiang-Phillips marveled, really was just like sitting across from a person, with every twitch and flinch visible to the trading party.

"Seventeen," he said, dropping another coin.

Sampson grunted. And now little beads of sweat were coming out on his brow, detected there by other sensors.

Qiang-Phillips thought he might have to go as high as twenty-one. Or withdraw the offer.

"Eighteen."

Clink!

That was a full five dollars over the price Winston had paid yesterday for comparably valued stocks. And it was almost a forty-percent markup over the pipeline's Accura™ evaluation. For his 52,000 shares, Sampson would earn a profit of $260,000. Not a fortune, by any means — but neither was it wasting the man's time, especially for only six minutes of soft connection on a busy morning.

But Qiang-Phillips had lots of other gas-related stocks to buy yet today. If Sampson did not bleed him dry on this sale, others would certainly be trying to dehydrate Winston later on. So, perhaps it was time to think about pulling out. Still . . .

"Nineteen."

Clink!

A large drop of sweat pooled in a furrow above Sampson's left eye, ready to run. Would it pass down beside his nose? Qiang-Phillips wondered idly. Or outside, alongside Sampson's bulging temple? . . . But he could hardly afford to indulge himself with such speculations.

"Twen—"

Ka-ZAPP!

Harald Sampson's face split vertically. Behind it, a white hand, dazzling in a silver-mesh glove, reached out and gripped Qiang-Phillips' forehead. The fingers twisted his skull once, sharply, to the left. Then they dropped him on the table-that-wasn't-a-table. The pile of silver coins broke his fall with a mushy splatter, and then they disappeared as in a bad dream. From there he slumped down to the floor-that-wasn't-a-floor and into a smothering darkness.

But his head still hurt terribly.

> *Frizzle*
> > *Frizzle*
> > > *Ravel*
> > > > *Ravel*

Central Processing Section, HK2 Exchange, 9:54 a.m. PST

Watching on the bank of video screens, with a voice-only bud pressed against his right ear — as the Exchange's strict insider-dealing regulations required — Shift Supervisor Ethan Fong saw just the surface manifestations as the neural-nexus system came apart.

One screen of the monitoring equipment told Fong that 2,339 of the traders registered with the Exchange were currently plugged in and dealing. Another showed the system's four telecomm switches — each handling twenty incoming lines stacking upwards of fifteen calls per line at various frequencies — with a sliding usage of ninety-two percent, for a total of 1,104 potential outside connections. So the rest of the traders on the Exchange were either talking to each other or in the middle of deadtime and reconnects. That had been the start position, and Fong now typed it into the notepad on his lap.

When the blitz hit, all four of the switchbanks had maxed out on some kind of electrical charge, or something. They weren't supposed to do that because, after all, the line equipment had buffers and filters and signal delays up the wazoo. Whatever had blown his system — and every indication was that the interference first came through from the outside — it had burst across those static defenses like barbarian horsemen scrambling over the Great Wall. Nothing in the international telecomm network was supposed to generate that much of a charge. And if it did, alarms were supposed to sound, circuit breakers to pop, the fault to be isolated, the system to be secured.

The only thing Ethan Fong could think of, as he watched the numbers fall apart on his tracery screens, was that something had entered his telecommunications channels, almost all of them, from above the atmosphere. The common practice of bouncing thousands of multilayered signals off the ion trails of meteor strikes in the upper atmosphere had made telecommunications far cheaper than in the days when those signals had to be sorted through a handful of geosynchronous satellites or, worse yet, a trunkline skein of glass fibers. So the stratosphere was now awash in the pulses of human commerce and conversation. Perhaps a large meteor strike somewhere above western Canada's horizon had interrupted these signals, inserting enough kinetic or magnetic energy into the process that the filters on the Earthside receiving stations had failed.

That was all easy enough to understand. What Fong had trouble with was how the fiberoptic lines that connected the Exchange's receiver horn with the switchbank had managed to pass the jolt on through to the trading floor. There just weren't that many lumens the laser signal relays could put out.

But then, what might a flash overload do to the comm signal, when that impulse was being taken directly — through filters, again, of course — into the cerebral cortexes of 2,339 asset traders? How sturdy was the electro-protein interface? This was one of the unanswered questions, one of the hazards of twenty-first century technology where laboratory testing lagged so far behind commercial implementation.

Fong simply couldn't guess how the energy transmission was proceeding, but the equipment showed that it was. He watched his screens as the excess voltage or whatever disrupted the delicately balanced sensory maze in more than two thousand individual minds. A screen on his left scrolled the list of flared and broken connections, while the one to his right, the red-letter medical monitor, flashed statistics on trader after trader. And each one of them showed electrolyte balance and neural activity readings that were shooting off the scale. People were literally dying out there on the floor, and Ethan Fong could do nothing to stop it.

His equipment took the numbers on everything local but none of them could show, and so Fong couldn't know, exactly *why* all this was happening.

It just was.

Burr-burr
Burr-burr
Burr-burr
Burr-burr

Federal Reserve System, Washington, D.C., March 21, 12:59 p.m. EST

"Yes, what is it?" Micah Jordan, the chairman of the U.S. Federal Reserve System, barked when he could finally pick up the phone. To get it, he'd had to lunge back across his desk with one arm pinioned by the folds of his winter coat, which he had been putting on and heading for the door when the damn thing rang. The phone, that is, not the coat. Or the door.

"Mr. Walthers calling from New York, sir," his executive secretary said decorously.

"Well, look, can I call him back? I'm late as it is for the Board of Governors luncheon, and I really —"

"He said it's most urgent, sir."

"Damn. All right, put him on. But tell him first that he's got just two minutes."

"Yes, sir."

Click-click.

"Jordan!" The voice of Peter Walthers, chairman of the Exchange Bank of New York, one of the Fed's commercial clients, came through the line with extraordinary clarity.

Like he was calling from the next room and not two-hundred-plus miles away by bounce-beam. "What's this 'two minute' crap?" Walthers barked. "We've got an emergency here, and it's got your name on it."

"Ah, what emergency's that, Peter? I really have to rush off to an important —"

"The system just fell apart. We've lost about three trillion in transactions due to some kind of electronic glitch. That's my bank alone. Three trillion. From my end. And that's just in the last five minutes. The losses are going up all the time."

Jordan was stuck, his mind frozen in neutral. "T-trillion, did you say?"

"Yeah. Do I have your attention now?"

"Absolutely. What was it, some kind of computer failure? You know there are backup systems, or should be, to keep —"

"No, it wasn't the computers, although they're affected, too. Some kind of electromagnetic pulse, like a big H-bomb, wiped out all the phone beams emanating from or coming into New York. That's what my technical people say, anyway. So that affects my bank and about five hundred others. Everything that was in transit at the time of the pulse got fried. And everything that the automated clearing systems had in hand went *poof*, too. And this interference is still hitting us, to the tune of . . . here it is — four hundred billion dollars a minute."

"What? Didn't your people shut the system down right away?"

"Well, Micah, with an average of two million accounts in flux at any one second, that's easier said than done. Just killing the momentum of our credit-clearing operations and funds transfers, just trying to reach stasis at the end of the banking day, takes the machines about half an hour. That's with all the totalization, cleanup, and verification. But when you burst the flow apart like this — one second flowing, the next gone — then the machines're going to drop you a bundle."

"You keep records, of course," the Fed chairman observed. "What goes out, what comes in. . . . Don't you?"

"Are you serious? You mean, like *paper* records? Or duplicate files? . . . Just how long have you been in that office, Micah? We're talking money here, not hard goods, not bales of polyester fiber. It has no physical existence, except as bits of data, as electrical charges in the machine, or flying through the stratosphere somewhere. If we made duplicates, then those would become legal tender under the ruling of *Plumber* v. *Bank of America*. Surely you know all this. What goes, goes. What comes, comes. What gets stuck in the middle, we have to eat.

"And that's why I'm calling you. We — that is, my bank — need a ruling from you right away. Will the Fed adjust the money supply to accommodate these unrecoverable losses? I need a yes or no today, this minute, Micah, because at three trillion down, I'll be having a serious talk with your federal examiners before the wire closes this afternoon."

"Well now, Peter, I don't know — "

"Not good enough, Micah. We're cooked, you know. And if you don't provide some relief pronto, you're going to have a lot of failures. I mean, Instant Black Friday. Squared. That's with people going headfirst out of windows and everything."

"Well, but certainly, I can't do a revaluation just like that," the Fed chairman protested. "Not on my own say-so. No, I'll have to discuss it with the Board of Governors. There are international implications, too, if what you say happened has happened. I'll have to get in touch with Helieurot at the Banc d'Europe, for example, to coordinate — "

"Well, don't take too long, Micah. You've got people *dying* out here."

"I'll move with all deliberate speed, I assure you, Peter. . . . And, by the way, if all the beam channels are out, how is it *you* can talk to me?"

"Oh . . . About a year ago we leased one of the antique fiberoptic landline systems, just in case of emergencies like this. It doesn't take the money volume, of course, but — "

"I see. Well, I may ask to borrow that line, if the catastrophe is as widespread as you say it is."

"Anytime, Micah," the bank chairman assured him.

"I will get back to you."

"Soon, I hope."

Click-click.

"Marjory, would you get me the president of Banc d'Europe? I know it's after hours there, but see if we can get a patch to his home or wherever."

"Yes, sir. . . . All the Atlantic channels are reported to be engaged, sir."

"All right. Let's go at this the other way around then. Try Mr. Yoshu at Nihon Central Bank. I'll need to talk to him, too."

"Right away. . . . Those channels are also engaged, sir. What do you want me to do?"

"Hmm. Voice and data both?"

"All channels, it says."

"How about the satellite network?"

"That, too. I'm sorry, sir."

"Oh, well. Try again in an hour, will you? In the meantime, I'm going to my lunch with the governors. See what they have on their minds."

"Very good, sir."

Blink
   Blink
      Gasp!
         Blink

Office of the Provincial Auditor, HK2 Exchange, 11:31 a.m. PST

"Gentlemen, we no longer have a market." That was the summation of Roger Fredericks, the provincial auditor for British Columbia.

The senior officials in charge of the HK2 Exchange's operations glanced uneasily across at one another. As the lowest man on that totem pole, just a technician really, Ethan Fong sat quietly in a corner.

"We have more than fifteen hundred traders in a near-cataleptic state," Fredericks went on. "We have some thousands of miles of charred fiber and insulation. We have four telephone switches with their internal safeties all thoroughly burned out. And finally, somewhere between here and Cloud-Cuckoo Land, we have some fourteen hundred interrupted transactions, for assets that can only be guessed at, representing a material worth that is now totally unknowable. We could possibly ask the parties to each trade themselves to reconstruct, from memory, the nature of the deals ongoing at the time of the . . . of the whatever—but they have no memories, that I can see. And if they did, whom would we trust? The buyer? The seller? You can't ask the computer, because it's cataleptic, too. So I ask you, what do we have here?"

"Big mess," said Warren Li, the chairman of the Exchange.

"Exactly, a big mess," Fredericks agreed. "And I can see no alternative but to declare that it is *your* mess, gentlemen. After all, the responsibility for safeguarding the trading environment is presumed to rest with you. Not to mention liability for the medical condition of those traders who used that optical link under your presumed assurances of safe operating conditions. When this day's losses are totted up, I expect you will owe in damages more than the net worth of your facilities, plus any insurance bonds you may have with the province."

The senior officials all hung their heads. And with their heads bowed, they all looked gloomily from one to another out of the corners of their eyes.

In his corner, Ethan Fong struggled to control himself. There was an answer to all this, just waiting at the tip of his tongue. Of course, it would be terribly bad form for him to speak up, among all these august personages, including the provincial auditor himself. He might well lose his position— Li would certainly see to that, as one thing he still could con- trol—if Fong were to intrude himself at this terrible time.

But then a great calmness descended upon Ethan Fong. He realized that, if what these men were saying and agree- ing to was literally true, then he *had* lost his position. Tomorrow he might well be working to fix the perennially brain-damaged artificial expert in control of Cousin Fong Hontin's bakery. So nothing Ethan might say now would make his situation any worse, could it?

"Excuse me, sir?" he spoke up.

Warren Li half turned, his face raised halfway, his eyes darting daggers to see who had dared to interrupt this sublime moment of misery.

"Yes, Mr. . . . Fong — isn't it?" the provincial auditor prompted.

"I believe you have a way to avoid all this unpleasantness, sir."

"If I do, then I beg you to enlighten me."

"We certainly cannot, as you suggest, put Mr. Humpty-Dumpty together again. We will never be able to reconstruct, in all fairness and accuracy, the trades that were extinguished at the moment of the energy pulse."

"Be silent, babbling fool," the Exchange chairman hissed at Fong in Cantonese dialect.

"But you have it in your power to quash transactions for whatever reasons seem good to you, don't you?"

"That is a little regarded aspect of this office," Fredericks admitted. "But yes, what you say is essentially so."

"Then would it not be fair to all concerned to nullify *all* trades for this day? That way there are no winners or losers at any person's expense. Everyone returns to their recorded position as of midnight last night. You could declare that the trading day of March 21 did not exist."

The provincial auditor thought about it for a minute. "Why, that's a fine idea, young man." He smiled at last. "And I for one would concur with it. But this is an international market, accepting transactions from exchanges all over the world, and from the Luna Colony Bourse as well. Certainly, not all of those traders would agree — "

"But couldn't you work with your opposite numbers who govern in those markets, get them to agree? I mean, the reports we've heard hint that similar disturbances have occurred all over this hemisphere. Every other exchange will have been affected in one degree or another. If you were to propose something sensible, like a midnight rollback. . . ."

"You tempt me with becoming the hero of the hour, do you, Mr. Fong?"

"Only if you wish it so, sir."

"Well, we shall see. I certainly should be contacting my colleagues in the Ministry of the Exchequer, just as soon as this infernal static clears. Let's see if they agree."

Li was still looking hard at Fong, but his expression had gone from angry to blankly unreadable. Perhaps the chairman was even beginning to realize that the lowly computer programmer may have saved him billions of dollars in damages. The other senior officials were raising their heads in something like hope.

"There is still, of course," Fredericks went on, "the responsibility for those unfortunate souls whose brains have been snuffed out by your negligence. We will have to assess the course of their treatment and care."

Down went the heads again. And again the eyes shifted side to side in agonies of shame and blame. Ethan Fong could almost believe they liked it that way. And he was right.

By accepting the personal blame now, they might preserve the reputation of their institution later on. Each of these men was reacting to a force that was stronger in him than mere personal vanity. Over the years they had pledged their loyalty to the one thing stronger than love of country, or commitment to the social good, or respect for their elders and rulers. It was the one thing in life that never decayed, that time could not tarnish nor princes corrupt, that perpetual use could not wear thin.

The power of money.

• Chapter 12

Flying Blind

10,000 meters
9,000 meters
8,000 meters
7,000 meters

Approach to Ezeiza International Airport, March 21, 2081, (+3) 1453 ZT

The radar altimeter chirped its descending scale in Captain Eduardo Thompson's ears as he brought the SCramjet *San Martin*, Aerolineas Argentinas Flight 19 from London-Heathrow, into the airspace east of Buenos Aires. It didn't bother the captain that the altimeter was the only active locating device aboard his plane, that all the rest of his navigation instruments were merely passive receivers. They always had been, for as long as he'd been flying.

The Rio de la Plata estuary was laid out before Thompson's eyes by the Neural Link™ goggles attached to the plane's navigation and flight control computer. To his left, depicted in bright greens, were the fertile pampas of Argentina, showing a concentrated cross-hatching in gray which represented the capital city and its surrounding suburbs. To his right, in faded yellows, were the running uplands of Uruguay. Straight ahead, on a bearing of 300 degrees true, the marshy delta of the Rio Parana stretched for 150 kilometers beyond Buenos Aires and its airport.

His goggles displayed all these features in the gridded approach pattern to Ezeiza from *San Martin*'s viewpoint, which the plane's onboard computer established by triangulation from the Universal Global Positioning System.

The UGPS was an active signaling system, whereby the computer took readings from at least three satellites overhead in orbit, calculated the plane's position on the Earth's surface from these extracts, and in conjunction with the radar altimeter and its own estimate of current heading and groundspeed, transmitted the appropriate visual cues from its reference library to Thompson's goggles. The runway's approach vectors were embedded in these cues.

Years ago, Thompson knew, major airports like Ezeiza had used broadcast radio signals to guide in aircraft like *San Martin* for automated instrument landings. At the same time, the plane itself might be sampling much of its own flight information from its surroundings: speed, altitude, compass heading, and so on. But during the landing, it relied on signals from the ground for all critical maneuvers. It then became the duty of the controllers in the tower to bring the plane in safely, not only relating it to other traffic in the air but also to its own descent rate, location, heading, and speed.

All of this had changed by Eduardo Thompson's day. First the UGPS, which was operated on a fee basis by the U.S.A.'s National Oceanic and Atmospheric Administration, eliminated the need for reliance on typically faulty compass readings, uncertain estimates of airspeed through the changeable winds, and the other vagaries of flying. Radar transponders eliminated the reliance on feeble barometric readings for altitude, especially along the suborbital routes that the SCramjets flew.

Then, in 2028, came the international tragedy celebrated in the case of *Varig* v. *Dallas-Ft. Worth International Airport* et al. In that incident, a combination of faulty OMNI beacons and a defective ILS crashed a conventional Brazilian jetliner two miles short of the runway. Damages to passengers and ground personnel ran to five billion U.S. dollars. And since then, as a matter of international law, airline insurance policy guidelines, and basic prudence, all commercial traffic had been responsible for its own positioning on approach.

This was actually a benefit, because Captain Eduardo

Thompson and his copilot flew their plane from the same visual cues they had trained with in the simulator. The same callouts flowed along the right and left edges of the pilot's stimulated retinas, and the same imaginary levers and knobs hovered just under his fingertips in the action gloves. The only thing different from the training sessions were the accelerations which shifted his *punta* up or down, left or right as the seat surged under him. The training pod's movements were supposed to be identical with a real plane in motion, but they never were. Thompson said he could always tell the difference. And that, he felt, made him a superior pilot.

Long, blue stretches of the estuary rolled under his nose. Its stylized ripple pattern was disappearing at the precise rate for his current descent profile. In the green distance, the ghostly bingos of a mechanical Ezeiza lined themselves up. The red tracers of the runway converged toward his point of touchdown, which was highlighted at this distance with a red circle. Everything about this landing was going perfectly.

The plane started yawing inexplicably to the right.

Thompson instinctively began to move his hands in the gloves to correct it, then paused. Although he could see the motion in the display before his eyes, he couldn't feel it through his seat. Although it was true enough that the yaw was a subtle movement, still he felt nothing except for the buffeting of air over the wings.

The visual display flickered and disappeared.

"*Hola!*" Thompson said aloud — but calmly, almost amusedly.

"Is something wrong?" Allison Carlyle asked at his elbow. Thompson's copilot was off duty for this leg of the flight, and so she would not be wearing her goggles and gloves. Or she might be using them for other purposes, such as reviewing the engineering readouts on *San Martín*'s ramjet or other systems.

"The landscape display is gone."

"Let me see if I — "

"No, wait. Here it is."

The image slowly rebuilt itself, feature by feature, in the way of a complex computer graphic: first the blue sea, then the green land masses, then features like cities and towns, and finally the airport's approach grid. But the land masses had acquired fuzzy, wavery edges. The cross-hatching for the cities wiggled around. The towns blinked on and off. It was as if the artificial intelligence were uncertain where everything went and was trying out different locations faster than the eye could blink.

Eduardo Thompson swallowed hard and tried to keep his hands absolutely steady as the machinery worked through its glitch.

"Something is definitely wrong," he told Carlyle.

"I'm plugging in now." He could hear a click as she made the connections. Then, "Yes, I see. . . . This is really weird."

After dithering with the scenery for perhaps ten seconds more, the upper-tier display blanked out entirely and the goggles showed in red letters against a null-gray field:

NAVIGATION SYSTEM MALFUNCTION
SWITCHING TO ONBOARD SYSTEMS

"What is happening?" the copilot asked.

"Lacking a true global position, the navigation system will attempt to complete its mission with the meager information at hand," he explained. "First, it will try for a reading from the backup magnetic compass."

The control field in their goggles flickered and displayed the image of an old-fashioned ball-and-needle, like something out of a sailing ship's binnacle. This was a reference to the electrocompass that was buried in the airframe and supposedly isolated from disturbances by *San Martin*'s electronics, its steel components, and the gypsy magnetic fields of the SCramjet's ionizing reentry envelope. The compass was presumed to be foolproof, like a simple feedback machine. But now the ball was swinging crazily in its socket behind the imaginary window. The graphic needle showed them heading first north then south, but without passing through a heading of east or west. Impossible things.

"That system, too, is defective," Thompson said. "Unless, of course, the Earth's geomagnetic field is damaged — I think not."

With a touch of a ghostly button, he instructed the computer to disregard all readings from the magnetic compass and proceed by its own internal calculations.

SWITCHING TO INERTIAL REFERENCES

"Now what does that mean?" Carlyle asked. "I've never seen that message before."

"It means the computer is giving up rational thought and is going to try 'dead reckoning,' " Thompson told her with a sigh. "And, as the old pilots used to say, *dead* is where such reckoning will surely leave you. This goes double, of course, for semiballistic SCramjets."

He knew that, in terms of those "inertial references," the artificial intelligence would use *San Martin*'s last known position, the last recorded heading and speed, and any random accelerations which might have been noted by the internal gyros, to calculate the plane's further course. In other words, the machine was flying by the seat of *its* pants.

"What could have gone wrong here?" the copilot asked. "We have backups — "

"Yes, the equipment was thoroughly checked on the ground and employs multiple redundancies to insure against failures in the air. We tend to trust our systems because, after all, we *have* to." As Thompson said all this, he still held his hands in the neutral position, continuing the plane's once-perfect glide. Not wanting to confuse the equipment, he waited patiently while it churned numbers and tried to rebuild a solid graphic image of the estuary and the airport.

"Our one clue is the altimeter," he went on. "Listen!"

The radar was still chirping in his ears, now in hers. And, along the left periphery of each pilot's visual field, the numbers were still falling off smoothly.

"So, if the computer's artificial intelligence has not lost its mind entirely," Thompson explained, "then perhaps it has somehow lost its UGPS signals. Perhaps through a fault in the antenna system. Or perhaps through some radio interference. . . . If the latter, then we can hope the difficulty will clear itself."

"I've never heard of interference on those frequencies," Carlyle said doubtfully. "For any person to willfully interrupt them would be a serious violation of international regulations."

"You are right, of course. Then perhaps our antenna has died. Anyway, let's see if the computer can recover its composure."

It never did. Instead, the goggles sent them an INSUFFICIENT DATA message. The display of flight cues remained a blank; it was the color of a phosphor tube after the light had died. Only the lower field, showing the cockpit controls in their orderly, functional banks, remained available to the pilots.

"What are we going to do?" Carlyle asked quietly.

"I don't . . ."

Without explaining further, Captain Eduardo Thompson then did something he had never attempted while on duty before. He reached up, pulled off his goggles, and looked out the windshield with his own eyes.

He was staring up at a pale blue sky, with neither land nor sea in sight. It was the plane's attitude, of course: in descent mode it would be riding with its nose at a thirty-degree positive angle.

Carlyle pushed her own goggles up on her forehead. She looked out the windshield, then across at him.

"You realize this is a total breach of flight regulations," she said.

"I wish I had an alternative." Thompson bit his lip. "If we're going to see anything, we'll have to bring the nose down."

"Then we will gain speed. It might cause us to overshoot. And the ram is already throttled back to just eight percent, which is only enough power for aerodynamic balance."

"I will employ the airbrakes."

"Those are intended only for use at low speed, you know. They will interrupt the airflow and might destabilize —"

"I understand," the captain cut her off.

He eased forward on the imaginary yoke with his hands and reached for the lever which actuated the flow reversers. At this point he realized his error.

"Damn!"

"What's wrong?"

"I can't see the controls."

The Neural Link™ gloves did not work properly without the goggles. They were a system. The plane's flight controls had no physical reality, except as cues in the virtual world created before him by the goggles. It was his hand movements alone, as the gloves reported them to the computer, which operated the plane.

As an experiment, Thompson continued the forward pitch, heedless of the speed their dive was building up. The horizon — the actual Earthly horizon — came up to meet him. It was a mottled field of blue-gray water and gray-green land, partially obscured by wisps of whitish-gray cloud. If there was a city down there, much less an airport, Thompson could not see it.

"This is not going to work."

"Then one of us must watch," Carlyle said reasonably, "while the other one flies. You are the captain and senior officer, so your experience should guide us." She pulled the goggles back over her face again. "I will activate the airbrakes now."

"Not that — look!"

Carlyle pushed away the goggles and leaned forward. The woman was so short, her eyes barely came above the lower edge of the windshield. It had not affected her career before. Now, however, she had to push herself up with her hands on the armrests. While she studied the terrain, the song of descending numbers sirened in her ears. The wingtips started to flutter.

"Can you see anything familiar out there?" Thompson asked, with a note of anxiety creeping into his voice.

"I . . . I think so. That would be the 'Big Apple,' still off to our left. And the bulge in the shoreline on the right is Colonia. And that must be Tigre, straight ahead. So Ezeiza should be on a heading of — oh, well, make it ten o'clock from here."

"Your eyes are younger than mine." Imperfect eyesight had never before inhibited a pilot's career, either. . . . Thompson made his decision. "You observe. I will fly."

He slipped his own goggles back on. The seat beside him creaked as Carlyle got up on her knees to improve her position.

"You'd better drop your speed now," she said.

Thompson cut back on his throttles even further, reached for the brake lever, and moved it gently. In response, the airframe shuddered and the wings started into a short, sharp, up-and-down oscillation, almost a truncated whip-roll. The captain and the computer, working together, damped the movement.

"Bring it around approximately ten degrees left," Carlyle instructed.

After a minute Thompson made another decision. "I'm going to declare a landing emergency."

"Do that," she agreed.

With his thumb he pushed an imaginary button on the yoke and spoke into his throat-mike. "Ezeiza Tower, this is Argentinas One-niner. Do you read, over?"

The buds in his ears now burped and squealed with static. Through it, a voice said, ". . . transmission badly. Read back . . ."

He keyed the mike again. "This is Argentinas Flight One-niner. We have an airworthiness emergency. Our navigation system is out. We are attempting to fly by visual references only. Repeat, we are coming in blind. Please prepare emergency —"

"One-niner, wait one, out," the tower said, suddenly in the clear.

"Left another five degrees, please," Carlyle instructed beside him. "And you can bring the nose up about two degrees."

Thompson made the corrections.

Ezeiza Tower came back on the air. "You're about the tenth in line for rescue, One-niner. Everybody's UGPS is acting up. What is your fuel status, over?"

The captain checked the imaginary gauges before his

eyes. "I show fifty-two hundred kilos. Say, forty minutes' flying time, over."

"Thank you, out."

"Captain . . ." Carlyle began. "If we're not going in on this leg, I suggest you back off the airbrakes and enter a shallow turn to the right. We can hold at thirty-five hundred meters."

Thompson relayed his intentions to the tower and received authorization. He shifted the plane into a banking turn.

"Are we going to make it, Captain?" his copilot asked quietly.

"With luck," he said.

For another five minutes, they flew their wide circle.

"All right, Argentinas One-niner," the tower cut in, "you're in luck. Our computer likes your position for a window that's coming up in . . . forty-five seconds on my mark . . . Mark. Bring your heading around to —"

"Ezeiza, I have no compass readings and my inertials are unreliable, over."

"Ah . . . All right. Bring your nose around visually about twenty degrees and descend at forty meters per second, out."

Carlyle touched his shoulder and said, "He's lining us up on the runway, Captain. I can see it in the distance. There are flashing lights . . ."

"Lights?" Thompson cocked his head.

"Yes, they look just like our tracer beads, except they're blue."

"They must be something for private fliers."

"Must be," she agreed.

"Argentinas One-niner, you are looking good. Increase descent rate to fifty per, out."

Thompson complied, but still he asked Carlyle, "How do we look?"

"Just like in the goggles. Except flatter."

"Flatter? Should I pull — ?"

"No, no. Just that, it's not as *real*, you know?"

"Whatever," he sighed.

A few minutes later, the tower had more instructions for them. "Argentinas One-niner, we have winds out of the west-northwest steady at fourteen. You are three kilometers out, at an altitude of seven hundred meters. You should lower flaps now, out."

"Looks about right, Captain," Carlyle confirmed.

Thompson worked the knobs to throttle up his ramjet by ten percent and then crank in a full forty degrees of flap, which was standard for the light wind conditions described. Even with the increase in power, the greater drag slowed the big plane until it felt as if they were just hanging in the air. That sensation matched the flight profile.

"Gear down, Captain," his copilot instructed.

He pushed the ghostly lever with his gloved hands, and the three landing gear lights went red. He counted ten and felt for the thud as the struts locked; Thompson was not satisfied with just watching the lights go to green. The gear further spoiled the airflow, sending shudders up through his seat. And that, too, was expected.

"I can see white stripes on the runway," Carlyle said.

"The touchdown zone," he explained. "I've seen it before, from the ground. We interpret them as parallel floating bars."

"They have ragged black marks through them."

"Rubber — from the tires."

"Ouch! I never realized how abrasive — "

"Argentinas One-niner, maintain your angle of descent. You are five seconds from touchdown . . . Four . . . Three . . ."

"Left a bit, Captain."

He swung the yoke gently left.

"Two . . . One . . ."

The airframe shuddered and then the undercarriage rumbled continuously along on the concrete. Thompson cut his throttles and steered a straight course. For a moment he could relax: he *knew* the runway was as linear as a ruler, and crosswinds were not a factor when the plane was rolling at these speeds.

"One-niner, proceed to Taxiway Twelve. . . . And welcome home."

"Thank you, Ezeiza, out."

The captain slipped his goggles back and looked ahead through the glass. They were coming up on the turn off the runway. He steered through it by feel alone.

"That was a novel experience," he said brightly. Then he added seriously, "I couldn't have done it without your young eyes, Allison."

Carlyle's face colored. "The tower would have talked you through it, surely."

"No, I never would have found Buenos Aires."

"Well, at least we'll never have to do it again."

"I hope not. But *something* interfered with the satellite signals, and it clearly affected a lot of planes. . . . I wonder just what happened?"

Chapter 13

In the National Weather Office

1010 mbar
  1008 mbar
    1004 mbar
      998 mbar

National Weather Office, Washington, D.C., March 21, 18:53 UT

The trailing edge of the warm air mass was shaping up precisely according to his library reference contours as WEATHERMAN hurried the low-pressure mound across the Pacific Ocean. He was moving it north by east from its spawning grounds, which had been two thousand kilometers west of Baja, California.

That part of the operation presented no unusual problems. At this point in the season the semitropical waters were beginning to warm up, vastly increasing the amount of water vapor they could donate. So the reserves of saturated air this region would generate was growing day by day. WEATHERMAN only had to work half as hard as he might have during the deep winter months of January and February to coax this air mass into being and then move it off along its curving, counterclockwise path.

The tools at WEATHERMAN's disposal for driving such a body were applied heat and cold. The heat, in the form of concentrated solar energy which he lasered from high-orbiting satellites into the cloud banks or the Earth's surface. The cold came from packets of carbon filaments which he could lob into the stratosphere with rocket launches from the western Pacific and Hawaii, or with magnetic catapult lifts out of Whitney Center and Mount Rainier.

Hot and cold, push and pull, these were the tools of the National Weather Office and its master intelligence.

WEATHERMAN was aiming this wet air mass for collision with a high-pressure system that was drifting down from the Gulf of Alaska, headed south and east toward the coast of California.

That lump was his real problem. Working as late as this in the storm season, while the Earth's rotation was tipping the planet's northern regions back toward the sun, WEATHERMAN found the polar air masses were retreating rather than advancing. So he had to darken the skies behind this cold air mass with carbon bombs, strengthening the swell of dense air that kept it alive, and flail the ocean water in front of it with heat waves, creating brief low-pressure pockets that would pull the system forward.

Still, if all other factors held equal, then the tracks these two independent weather systems — cold and hot, high and low — were following would eventually insert the warm, moist air from Mexican waters just in front of the cold air coming out of the Gulf of Alaska. And the collision would occur just as the curve of the jetstream nudged the latter south across the coast into Northern California.

The cold, high-pressure mass would be moving faster then and would eat its way beneath the sluggish, warm, low-pressure system, which WEATHERMAN was allowing to glide northward under its own inertia for the last six hundred kilometers. As the Alaskan air mass moved eastward across the Central Valley, the warm Mexican air would climb its sloping edge, rising until the thin, cold reaches of the upper atmosphere dropped it below the dew point, releasing its latent moisture as precipitation.

If other factors held equal then, the interaction should release two to three inches of rain on farmers in the thirstiest state of the union, with another five inches of moist snow piling up in the Sierra Nevada for the spring runoff.

It would be WEATHERMAN's fifth such engineered storm of the season. It represented an economic value in crops and watershed of $56 million — all for an immediate expenditure in collected solar energy and launched filament packets of only $280,000. Of course it was still too soon for WEATHERMAN to begin banking and investing the storm's profits, other factors holding equal, but he could certainly alert the humans in the General Services Administration to gear up for another wave of agricultural and water district billings — and for the anguished screams that always accompanied an increase in the weather rates.

Of course, this cost-benefit structure was stated on a project basis only. If WEATHERMAN were forced to include in his calculations the embedded costs of the satellite system at his disposal, or the 16,000 terrestrial and airborne telemetering substations around the continental U.S. alone which reported to him minute by minute on their ambient temperature and pressure, precipitation and humidity, wind speed and direction, visibility, cloud cover and height, compiling the masses of data from which WEATHERMAN worked his miracles of ingenuity — then the profit picture would be substantially different. However, from WEATHERMAN's point of view, most of those embedded capital costs had long ago been depreciated to the point of nullity, and he was flatly prepared to marshal gigabytes of argument on this subject.

Tidying up that line of isobars now, WEATHERMAN isolated, sampled, and collated the current air-pressure readings from a network of contract buoys floating in the eastern Pacific.

996 mbar at 24°33'14"N, 132°28'56"W ...

998 mbar at 24°34'38"N, 132°30'09"W ...

1002 mbar — ZZZiip!

The data flow stopped almost before it had started. WEATHERMAN noted the loss and posted a grievance with the General Services Administration, instructing them to withhold payments to the management of that buoy operation until the error was corrected. In the meantime, there were other —

The high-pressure center had stopped moving north. And it had stopped turning! Or rather, as WEATHERMAN quickly determined by area analysis, his rich stream of bits, the engorged flow of minutiae which fed his continuing picture of the system, had stopped. He was processing and reprocessing information that was, as of now, milliseconds old and rapidly growing older and more out of date.

Rather than sit and churn, however, the picture began to fade as his self-timed buffers cut in. WEATHERMAN was losing his model of the colliding air masses — which was to say that he was losing control of them. Handled improperly, they might meet too soon for maximum precipitation, or too late for any useful result at all. This was adverbially annoying.

Like a rain of smoking acid droplets, the reporting stations in WEATHERMAN's network fizzled out. They did not go serially, in any geographically sensible pattern; nor did they shut down all at once, like a sudden power failure. Instead they went piecemeal and left holes in his analysis. WEATHERMAN tried to fill them by interpolating the data from surrounding stations and dithering the pattern, but the disintegration was too rapid. The holes widened, darkened, eroding the accuracy of his model, damaging his sense of order.

A nanosecond's inspection showed WEATHERMAN that there might be a pattern to the failure: that each substation was falling silent just as it was due to report by the clock. At least, that was the context from WEATHERMAN's central perspective. Of course, the phenomenon might also represent a simultaneous event, an accident of reporting or transmission approaching global proportions, which closed off each station's transmission at some common point in time before it could be missed. But speculations such as these — especially when they involved the prospect of invoking *force majeure* clauses in existing contracts — did not interest WEATHERMAN. He functioned solely to run a hemisphere weather model and to engineer variations of the microclimate.

So, convinced that he was being unrightfully deprived of

the information he required, WEATHERMAN fired off a string of grievances to the lawyers assigned on retainer to the GSA. Let them deal with it. After all, that was what humans were for.

Fade
    Fade
        Fade
            Away

Regional Weather Center Office, Kansas City, 11:55 a.m. CST

"Look at that!" Metops 1C John Dixon said. He was caught off balance, moving one way through the operations office but leaning the other, trying to look over the shoulder of his senior tracker, Wynans, who was sitting at the screens.

The carefully coordinated images were breaking up. It reminded Dixon of watching a piece of his grandmother's lace burn — sparks and crescents eating away at holes, blazing along strings, until nothing was left. With it went the line of rain squalls they had been chasing down into Arkansas.

"Look at what?" Wynans retorted. "WEATHERMAN is *gone!*"

"Has this ever happened before?" Dixon asked. Although he technically outranked his tracker, he also happened to be fresh out of Meteorology School. In emergencies, the Weather Office's ever-pragmatic handbook dictated that experience must come before status. Still, Dixon himself tried to think of a case, something they might have reviewed at school, in which the Master Weather Modeling Program had gone down. Nothing came to mind — which was reasonable because, after all, the Cray IXs were supposed to be uncrashable. Or else Dixon had been playing hooky the day his class covered it.

"Not to my knowledge, sir. WEATHERMAN is *God* in this business. He just doesn't go down."

"Until now. . . . Well, I guess, in this case, we ought to . . . Hmmm . . ."

"I suppose we could issue a bulletin or something, sir."

"That's it, we can issue a weather watch to the media list. Now, what do you think it ought to say?"

"Well . . ." Wynans hesitated. "We could use the forms for a tornado or blizzard warning or something. Except, I guess, we maybe ought to tell people there *isn't* any danger. I mean, we had nothing negatively active on the screens when they went out. At least, that's what I was seeing — sir."

"Very good. That's exactly what we'll do. Tell people that their weather is under control, for now anyway, even though it isn't. Then we can just sit tight and wait for instructions from Washington."

"Sounds like a plan to me, sir."

And it would have worked, too. But when Dixon went to activate his media list, he found that the phones were all tied up, with nothing going out or coming in, and no system notice to prep him for the emergency.

"Never rains but it pours," Wynans observed. "As we say in this business, sir."

So the two weather operators sat at their consoles and started a fast dual game of JAXI. When the system came back up, they'd hear about it soon enough.

Chapter 14

Star-Crossed Lovers

> *Gribble*
> > *Chirp*
> > > *Squeal*
> > > > *Gribble*

**Cabin B9 aboard ISS *Whirligig III*,
March 21, 18:26 UT**

The transfer disk whirred and burbled as the flying heads unpacked its tightly compressed bits, which had been sent in a solid *blip* of high-speed transmission. The logics quickly converted them into an analog video signal at one-to-one timing.

The radio shack of the International System Survey *Whirligig III* had received the transmission an hour ago. It had taken Peter Spivak that long to locate someone with a disk player and then find a private moment in his cabin.

Whirligig was a cluster ship. Three to seven cylindrical hulls — the number depending on the paid manifest for the run — each boosted separately on reaction mass from the vicinity of the Earth-Moon system and flew alone until they attained enough velocity to put them on a widening spiral that would eventually intersect the orbit of Mars. Upon reaching freefall, the ships rendezvoused, lashed themselves into a rosette, and fired angular thrusters to establish a slow, centrifugal spin which would provide artificial gravity for the nine-month voyage, protecting the crew and passengers from any debilitating calcium loss. At the opposite end of the run, the ships would brake their spin, unlash, and decelerate separately, maneuvering for orbit and unloading by shuttle to the red planet.

Even spread among five hulls, the accommodations were not great. Peter shared his fifteen-cubic-meter cabin — the ship's manuals called it "cocoon space," after the hanging sleeping bags they'd been issued — with four other men. When he was not sleeping or amusing himself with games and prerecorded entertainments, Peter had duties as a dishwasher first class in the mess. He quickly learned that the main difference between "crew" and "passengers" on a survey ship was the former were licensed to navigate and work the ship in orbit; everyone else was "casual," or unskilled labor, fit for scraping dishes.

He sat on the cabin floor with his back against the wall and started the disk player. Although the message's heading cipher had shown only *Whirligig*'s registry codes and Peter's name, he had a good idea who had originated the transmission — and it wasn't his mother, either. What he couldn't figure out was, why did Cheryl send a one-way blip-tape when she could as easily, and for about the same cost, have bought a two-way communication slot? The lag was still only about five seconds, so they could have talked back and forth and it would almost be like they were on the same continent. Anyway, with a disk from his girl — if she still *was* his girl — he wanted to be alone. For the first viewing at least.

The player's microscreen came up a blank white, and it never picked up much more definition after that. At first Peter thought the unit was broken, then he looked more closely at the image.

A bland hospital room. White mounded pillows and draped sheets. Part of a neutral-gray wall studded with fittings for oxygen, water, and electric power. A hospital gown in white with a pattern of light-blue stripes. And Cheryl's face, pasty and flat, swathed in a turban of white bandages. As he stared, Peter saw that the bandages went down her neck and enveloped one shoulder, where the corner of the gown was left open, just pinned to the medicated gauze.

The only real colors in the picture were Cheryl's right eye, still a blazing jade green, and the skin around her other eye socket, which was closed to a squint with a violent purple bruise. Red scratches crossed her nose and descended her left cheek. By staring hard Peter could see the black wicks of sutures in those claw marks.

The image was so shocking, so little what he had hoped to see, that he missed her opening words and had to track back.

"Guess this wasn't what you were expecting, huh?" she said in a tiny voice. "Honestly, Peter, it took me a long time to decide to even make this tape, let alone send it to you — and I certainly didn't want to talk to you in person. Not looking like this. And, anyway, the nurses here put up enough of a fuss over having Dad bring in a camera. So you can guess what they'd say to a full conferencing rig. . . .

"As to what happened . . . well, you don't want to know. Let's just say I met someone who wasn't what I thought. . . . Enough said on *that* subject."

Cheryl tried to swallow, made a face, and someone off camera passed her a glass of water. She sipped it, handed it back.

"Mother thinks — and Dad agrees with her — that I ought to get out of this city for a while. You know they think the world of you. . . . They're suckers for a nerd with a technical degree, I guess. . . . Anyway . . ."

She looked directly out of the screen, one green eye and a patch of bruise, for five full seconds.

"Anyway, they think that, just because jobs are so scarce around here, maybe I ought to apply for something off-planet. They still make a big deal of how quickly the Foundation responded on your application. And that crazy idea you had, about my doing technical illustrations or mechanical drafting or whatever, well, Dad thinks it would probably fly. But I don't know. . . ."

Her free hand settled on top of the sheet, folded back a wrinkle, pressed it flat.

"I don't want to go just anywhere. I mean, I'd want to be assigned somewhere that I knew some people, somebody at least — so I wouldn't feel alone. I haven't contacted the Areopolitans yet, so I don't even know if they have an opening, or anything."

Cheryl's fingers caught at the fold in the sheet, scissoring back and forth over it, until the fabric took a crease.

"You know . . . like, if they could assign me to your station, or something, then we could be, could keep each other company. If you didn't mind it, I mean. . . . It's true we didn't part on very good terms, Peter. I know I was kind of mean to you. Not very supportive. And I said some things . . . whatever."

Cheryl suddenly looked down at her hand, quickly unclutched the fold of sheet, and spread her fingers wide above it. Then she absently went back to smoothing the material flat. She looked directly into the camera.

"What I'm trying to say is, if you still want to see me, well, I could apply to the Foundation. Try to get a position with them, if that was what you wanted, too."

By this time Peter was gripping the sides of the player and chanting, "Yes! Yes!"

"All this will heal without even a mark," she went on, waving the hand in front of her face. "And there's no neural damage, the doctor tells me, although he says I'm lucky on that one. So, by the time you see me, I'll be good as new. If you *do* want to see me, Peter. . . ."

Cheryl held her gaze steady on the camera, looking deep into his eyes. Then, after a few more seconds, she pursed her lips and nodded. The image faded out.

Peter Spivak didn't have to go through the message a second time to make his decision. Leaving the player on the cabin floor, he ran out the door.

> *Tick*
> > *Tick*
> > > *Tick*
> > > > *Click!*

U.S. Post Office, Sag Harbor, GNYC, March 21, 12:43 p.m. EST

The light below the transfer spindle went off, and the slot spat Cheryl's datadisk back into her hand. The diode array showed $8.55, which was a reasonable rate considering she was sending forty-two megabytes of text and graphic images to Tharsis Center, Mars. She had elected batch mode, which was the least expensive kind of transmission, bundling her file with other electronic documents addressed to the same station. The machine estimated they would arrive sometime within the next twenty-five minutes, plus or minus fifteen, and asked for her money code. Cheryl Hastings punched it in.

She had come out of the hospital three days ago, and it had taken her all this time to finally decide to send that embarrassing video — ultimately unedited, because she could think of no way to fix it — off to Peter on his outbound voyage. But she didn't hesitate nearly as long over her other decision, which was to submit her resume and work samples to the Areopolitan Foundation.

Even if Peter didn't want her, or had found someone else, or had taken a monk's vows, or whatever — she still wanted a real job that paid real money for real effort and offered real prestige for solid accomplishment. And none of that seemed to be available in New York, or in the United States, or anywhere else on Earth for that matter. Not right now, at least.

That limited her options dramatically.

Cheryl realized she could continue living at home with Mother and Dad, dabbling in her fantasy painting and knowing it wasn't very good. She understood that her parents were scrimping to make room and board available to her. Stuff all that.

Or she could join one of the Gray Market Groups and deal in whatever the commodity of the moment happened to be: counterfeit certificates and permits, junk paper and freeloaded securities, unapproved pharmaceuticals and illegal stimulants, toxic wastes, unlicensed landfills . . . or her own body. That option was only marginally dangerous, since almost no one in the grays was getting caught these days. Or, if caught, they went unsentenced. Or not to real prison time, at least. And copping a record was just a nuisance — unless you were looking for a position in the straight world. Of which there were none anyway.

Or she could emigrate to the Moon. That was a one-way

trip — if she stayed longer than six months or so, and she would have to work at least that long to earn her return fare. The colony's government made no provision for indentured immigrants to get access to the centrifuges or other exercise machines that would maintain her body against one gee of acceleration, which she needed if she wanted to continue living on Earth. And although the colony had an open offer to hire at bonus rates in certain categories, Cheryl didn't happen to have a degree in plasma physics, cellular electrobiology, fourth-order cybernetics, or any kind of medicine.

No, if she wanted to work, earn money and respect, and feel useful, then she had to move beyond the Earth-Moon system entirely.

The Areopolitan Foundation had accepted Peter for a geophysical survey crew. Or was that areophysical? Anyway, the three years offplanet would pay well enough, he'd said, to give them — him and her — a nest egg, or an annuity for life, or whatever they wanted. And the Foundation would provide for all gee-maintenance, so they could return to Earth and live normally.

Peter had told her the Areopolitans needed technical illustrators. So Cheryl had selected, as samples to submit, from among the most mechanical, least shapely or organic, of her recent drawings. Her resume couldn't claim an actual work history, of course. But then, who on Earth, who was willing to go to Mars for a job, was able to show *that*? Instead, she listed the sales records — buyer, date, and price — for all five of the drawings that had actually sold.

Cheryl reasoned that if the Foundation had been willing to take her as part of a package deal with Peter Spivak, then they might still consider her for a job even without him, or separate from him, if he wanted it that way.

Anyway, it would only cost her time and postage to apply. Right now, with her time worth about less than nothing, those eight bucks in postage were the biggest investment she was in a position to make. And the worst that could happen — at least with this transmission, if not with the other — was that the Areopolitan Foundation might reject her.

Cheryl Hastings kissed her fingertips, patted the disk slot, then turned and walked away.

Thump
   Thump
      Thump
         Bump!

Radio Shack, ISS *Whirligig III*, March 21, 18:51 UT
Communications Specialist 1C Wilbar Fredrix looked up from his handheld Skeedaddle game and pushed back the curtain on his cubicle to see what had caused the commotion out in the hallway.

That young geophysicist, Peter Spivak, had collided at an ell turn with *Whirligig*'s ferocious first mate, James B. Wyvern. They were both now picking themselves up with the fluid, almost lethargic grace of point-three gee. But the look on the mate's face was anything but easygoing. Eye-popping, that's what it was. After all, it was almost sixteen hours since Wyvern had lunched on an articled passenger, and that was too long for the man's notorious mouth. This should be interesting.

"Now see here, you puppy!" Wyvern was drawing himself up to his full 160 centimeters and spreading his chest to at least 175, drawing breath for a full gale. "If you think the captain maintains these passageways so you can endanger —"

"Excuse me, sir," Spivak interrupted him earnestly, smilingly, pleadingly. "This accident was entirely my fault I know for running in the corridors without looking where I'm going like you must have told me not to a thousand times or more but I really had to get to the radio shack because I need to send off an urgent message in a matter of life and death that has to do with my family or someone who's going to be my family really soon and so it's really an emergency and as soon as I'm done in there then I'll certainly come back out here and listen to you tell for the thousand and first time how important it is for me to look where I'm going."

By the finale to this waterfall of words, Spivak had edged

around to the doorway in front of Fredrix, slid himself through, and snapped the curtain shut. Then he turned to face the comm spec.

"Sparks! I've got to send a message."

"So I've heard," Fredrix smiled. "Two-way, one-way, or night letter?"

"Gee, I . . . What's fastest?"

"Two-way gets priority — if, that is, your party's at home and receiving calls. Do you happen to know your person's local time?"

"I, unh —" Spivak squinted his eye.

"Fear not. We'll do it one-way. That only takes as long as it takes me to get out the old camera and cabling, find my light filters, set up a patch, and locate a blank disk that doesn't have girlie pix or anything else on it."

"I see. What's a night letter?"

"You type into that terminal." Fredrix pointed. "The machine encodes. And I stick an address *en clair* on the first ten bytes. Poof! It's gone."

"That's what I want." Spivak spun around, bent over the terminal, and laid his fingers on the keyboard. "Just type?"

"Be my guest."

The young man rattled away for ten seconds without pause. Then he straightened up. "And it's gone?"

"Just tell me who to."

"Ms. Cheryl Hastings of 112 Duck Pond Circle, Sag Harbor, Greater New York City."

"Hell, fella!" Fredrix laughed. "Time there is just short of one in the afternoon. We could have done you a conference call."

"Just send the letter, okay?"

"You got it."

Spivak gave him a parting grin, made a crack in the curtain, looked through to make sure First Mate Wyvern was nowhere in sight, and then slipped out.

Fredrix typed the address and was about to initiate transmission when curiosity got the better of him. Not that he was a natural snoop, really. But he did like to know what messages his passengers were sending, in case they turned out to have implications that would come back to haunt *Whirligig* on his watch. And anyway, if he knew the passengers' business, he'd be in a better position to help them, wouldn't he?

He dumped the archive of Spivak's text onto his console and read it:

YES YES YES PLEASE COME PLEASE COME ++

I DO LOVE YOU AND ALWAYS WILL LOVE YOU ++

FORGET HOW YOU LOOK IT DOESN'T MATTER TO ME ++

JUST COME AS SOON AS THEY LET YOU ++

LOVE PETER ===

Now that was a really nice sentiment, Fredrix decided, especially for a girl with a sweet, old-fashioned name like "Cheryl." In this case, "come" probably meant "come to Mars," because that's where this ship and Articled Passenger Spivak were headed. Maybe Ms. Cheryl Hastings would be coming out on *Whirligig*'s next run. It would be interesting to see a girl who could inspire such blind passion in an otherwise sensible and able-bodied young man like Spivak. In that case, Comm Spec Wilbar Fredrix would just have to look her up.

His curiosity satisfied, Fredrix compressed the message, fed it into the buffer, and queued it for dispatch. A second later, his computer log noted the transmission.

He went back to his interrupted Skeedaddle game.

Two moves into the set, his communications board lit up like the Fourth of July. His computer screen filled up with garbage, blinked itself green, tried to reset, failed, and buzzed at him.

"What the — ?"

Fredrix scrolled it down and began sieving the computer's transient memory for clues to what might have happened. From the broken bits and other nonsense, he could only guess that some kind of electromagnetic emission, a really capacious blast of static, had temporarily overwhelmed the system's filters. The computer had tried to register the blare as an incoming signal and interpret it according to one of the binary or raster codes the machine knew. When nothing worked, the computer had given up and cried uncle.

Not to sweat — or so Fredrix could reassure himself after running the internal diagnostics and determining that the random energy had not burned out *Whirligig*'s comm circuits or done other damage.

But in all the excitement, he never thought to check his log of recent transmissions against the estimated lightspeed lag until their receipt, to see if any of them were likely to have been interrupted and to resend them if necessary.

Comm Spec Wilbar Fredrix wasn't *that* fanatical about his job.

• Chapter 15

Picking Up the Trail

Focus
   Focus
      Focus
         Focus

**1919 Via Villa, Altadena, California,
March 21, 9:49 a.m. PST**

Piero Mosca had decided that, before he absolutely had to proceed to his 10:05 seminar at the JPL Institute — it was called "Nebulas and Novas" and explained all about shockwave-induced stellar formation — he would go up to the roof of his apartment block and take one more look at Dr. Freede's sunspot.

As he cranked down on the focus knob, a morning breeze from the San Gabriel Mountains fluttered the aluminized screen that was stretched over the objective end of his Schmidt-Cassegrain telescope. The movement caused slight ripple distortions in the image and made the focusing harder.

Suddenly, the dark blurs in his ocular leapt into focus, showing a pair of deep, ragged, black holes. They were each perhaps as wide as three degrees of arc, separated by more than twenty degrees across the sun's face, and fantastically linked by a larger pool of gray shading. This array was larger than any spot pair Mosca had ever heard of, dwarfing the photographs from the last century. This pair resembled those commonplace spots about as much as the crater Tycho resembled a heelprint in the sand.

Po knew that the sunspots weren't really holes, but

simply cool areas in the photosphere that failed to radiate the same frequencies of visible light which smoothed and obscured the rest of the solar atmosphere. For a long moment, however, he imagined he was looking down into a void, a pair of craters double-struck in that apparently glossy surface, as if blasted out by the impact of two unimaginably large and incredibly fast tumbling bodies.

Then, as might happen with any monochrome outline etched on a surface that was seen in one dimension and which was nearly flat itself, the image did a flip-flop within his visual cortex. It exchanged the illusion of depth for one of height. Now the surrounding gray area, the penumbra, seemed to become a highlands, a broken terrain, rising to a pair of dark plateaus. The spot group appeared to be twin lakes of ink, swirling without pattern in his brain.

The image flip-flopped again, and the ink became the breakthrough into an infinite tunnel. As Po watched, the shaft bored straight down into the core of the sun, revealing its dense, black heart.

All of this Mosca could see with just his tiny reflector telescope, protected by a screen that cut out 99.999999 percent of the incoming light, reducing the incidental heat and luminosity to manageable dimensions and thereby saving his eyesight.

Mosca wondered if the magnetic field linking the spot pair had picked up a prominence yet. That would be the usual pattern, as reported by the early astronomers back when the sun had been active with sunspot cycles. It would be difficult if not impossible for him to see the prominence at this angle, looking straight down onto its back as it stretched across the solar disk. Most prominences were wispy bridges of gas that radiated at extremely narrow band frequencies; prominences observable in white light were extremely rare. So, in the visible spectrum, most prominences showed only up along the limb, where they were exposed in profile. Those were also best seen when the sun's face, and so most of its glare, was covered by an eclipse.

Of course, if Po were observing in the spectrum of

hydrogen-alpha, he would have been able to see almost any prominence. That emission band would highlight the arch's superheated gases, which were energized by the loop's magnetic flux. Then the prominence would stand starkly visible against the cooler background of the photosphere. But since H-alpha filters were no longer available for his childhood scope and Po didn't know how to make one, and since Dean Withers had nixed Po's observing schedule with the Institute's telescopes, such sophisticated techniques were denied to him. Mosca was left to his own pitiful resources.

Still, he would bet good money on a spot pair of this size having a prominence, and a gargantuan one at that! Maybe it would even collapse and flare for him. If it did, his telescope might, just might, pick out the spark in the visible spectrum.

Watching like this, with his eye pressed too long to the ocular and dazzled by the roiled granulation of the photosphere, Po soon found he could observe anything he wanted or could imagine. Bright flashes, stark as a photographer's strobe, began to course back and forth between the spots. The black umbra turned blood-red against his retina and began to wink at him. Mosca took his head away from the eyepiece and rested his vision by looking off toward the mountains, which were crisply outlined against the blue sky.

He was about to duck down for another glance, when his eye happened to catch the face of his watch. "The time!" he cried aloud. Po had only five minutes to get into his seminar. And it would look really bad if he was late, because he was the teacher, and he still had some visual aids to prepare.

The old school rule required the class to wait a full fifteen seconds for a tenured or visiting professor, ten seconds for a simple doctorate. But no time at all for a lowly teaching assistant, which was all Mosca could claim to be.

Without bothering to pack up his telescope, Po ran over to the roof entrance, thundered down the stairs, and banged through the door into his apartment. The terminal was all warmed up, at least. He pulled on the helmet, settled the electrodes back on his neural contact patch, yanked the goggles out to a comfortable distance in front of his eyes, and adjusted the boom microphone. Then he pulled on the wired gloves.

In a blink he was standing in Room 1808, a vast chamber with black walls and high ceiling. It resembled nothing so much as an empty sound stage — from the era when movies were shot onto celluloid film from live actors. Thank Central Net, at least, for setting up this channel exactly the way he had ordered. Po might once have opted for a pool of invisible blackness, with an infinitely extensible boundary and with the normal one-gee acceleration countered to create a sense of freefall. But that would have been too strange, too real, for his students. Or right now, at this stage in their visualization and perception skills, anyway. Instead, he wanted exactly this air of make-believe, of artificial showmanship.

Next, he added the visual aids.

Mosca dialed into his directory in the Institute's main on-line storage array and retrieved the files he had been preparing. He routed these to Central Net, care of Room 1808, tagged for presentation in order and on his voice command.

The first three-dimensional image automatically came up all around him: a miasma of chill vapor, similar to a "pea soup" fog from nineteenth-century London, straight out of the Sherlock Holmes mysteries. Like those fogs, the nebula that Po had generated for himself swirled in neutral colors, browns and grays, with now and then a sulfurous yellow or ferrous red winding its way past his head. He had even recreated the smells: the sickly stench of brimstone, the blood-tang of rust, the smoky peat of soft coal consumed in less than perfect combustion. Po stood — light-footed if not weightless, with the computer contact strip fooling his nervous system into believing he did not feel pressure against the soles of his feet — at the center of a slowly swirling gas nebula.

Two effects added the last degree of realism. First, he

had managed to get the light just right, diffuse and directionless, as if it came from multiple points of starlight
outside the cloud. Later, when the subsidiary files clicked
in, the knot of students standing around him would be
approached by drifting spheres of internal luminosity, like
lampposts looming in the fog. Second, he had added a
measure of free-floating grit to the cloud, something even
old London at its worst could not offer. Periodically these
microparticles stung his cheek, his neck, the backs of his
hands, reminding him — and soon his students, too — that
the primordial soup expelled from late-generation stars
was not homogenized, that it had bite.

While Mosca was touching up these special effects for his
lecture, the first of his class members showed up. They had
no door to knock on, pull open a crack, hesitate in the gap,
then let Po wave them through; instead, they simply
popped into view beside him as they plugged into the network. Two students, three . . . four.

Mosca — or the image of him that was projected into
their helmets, along with the fog — nodded as they
assembled and shuffled themselves into a rough semicircle
separated from him by a tacit space. This was the intellec-
tual arena: students on one side, teacher on the other.
Old-style classrooms characterized this separation with the
uncommitted territory of the teacher's desk or the
laboratory bench.

Po checked his watch, and the network supplemented
the physical device on his wrist with a readout from its own
infallible clock. The time was going on twenty seconds after
10:05, but only four out of a class of thirty-two had so far
materialized.

"What gives?" he asked conversationally.

Shrugs. Glances. "Dunno, Professor."

This was really unsettling, because Mosca's classes were
usually popular. The students appreciated his efforts at
invention, trying to make the physics and chemistry of stellar formation come alive to all the senses. The Institute
always had to turn away applicants for his seminars. The
class on Wednesday had been a full house, with five non-

students paying for the privilege of plugging in and auditing without credit. And now this . . . this rudeness.

"Is anyone else coming?" Po asked with a grin, checking that it was now a full minute into his lecture time. If this was a sudden strike — or a boycott called on account of some remark he'd made last time — then Mosca hoped somebody would have the decency to so inform him.

Again, blank looks.

He studied their faces, trying to keep his own neutral and smiling. Then it dawned on Po that these four, three women and one man, were all his locals. They were either physically enrolled with some faculty at Caltech or were picking up from one of the aerospace companies and laboratories that had developed in the area. The other missing twenty-eight were his out-of-towners, those who had telerolled with the university or were corresponding from institutions elsewhere in the country. Some of them were even plugging in from overseas, despite the time and language differences.

"Well," Po said at a minute and thirty, "I had a really neat show laid on for you. It would be a shame if so many people had to miss it. . . . Why don't we call class for today, and I'll reschedule for Monday? That suit everyone?"

Three smiles and one worried frown.

"Cheer up, Chalmers," he told the frown. "You don't have to go down to the lounge and talk to girls or anything. I'm sure you've got some heavy reading to catch up."

While the three women chuckled at this, Mosca cut the circuit. He faded out of their view with his own grin still intact, like the Cheshire cat. But he could feel it slip while he sent his visual aids back to on-line storage and signed off on the channel representing Room 1808 as of two minutes from now — that would give his four students plenty of time to do a little gossip and then cut themselves out. Anyone plugging in after that time would be greeted with an insubstantial text notice saying that class had been canceled for the day.

Before he took the helmet and gloves off, however, Mosca decided to make one more call, this time to the manager of Central Net.

"Central, Peter Bell speaking," answered a bland young man, who was probably working the technical reception desk part-time while he studied for his degree.

"Hello, Central," Po introduced himself, offering the man a nod but not affecting an electronic handshake or some other virtual greeting copied from the flesh-and-blood formalities. "I'm Po Mosca, from the Astrophysics Department at JPL. Look, I . . . ah . . . had something unusual happen just now. I normally teach a seminar at this time, in Room 1808, on nebulas and stellar formation — " Peter Bell scrunched up his mouth while Mosca rattled on, as if wondering why Po bothered to tell him all this. "And, anyway, I usually have more than thirty students plug in. But today there were only four, and I noticed they were all local people, so I was wondering if — "

"Phones are out," Bell said. "All the long-distance beams. Only local calls are going through."

"*All* of them?"

"That's what I said, hey?"

Mosca, who knew something about how stacked frequencies of voice and data communications were carried over distances of greater than a few dozen miles, did not understand how *all* of the meteor-trail pulses could be disrupted at one time. Not over the whole country. Not from halfway around the world.

"That's just not possible," Po concluded.

"Look, Professor. You asked, I answered. You don't like the answer, go tell it to your shrink. We're all busy here, even if you ain't." Bell cut him out of the circuit.

Mosca stopped to think. He was still wearing the helmet and could feel the sweat gather across his forehead and begin dripping down past his temples. If it reached the contact strip back of his ear, he knew, the moisture was likely to cause a minor fault. But that didn't hurry his thoughts a bit.

Something had blanketed the hemisphere — or at least a large part of it, according to the distribution of Po's students. And it affected transactions in the upper atmosphere — or at least that was the trouble Mosca knew about so far. So, what could that "something" be? And, by the way, the evidence indicated an effect originating outside the atmosphere. Offhand, he could think of a dozen natural causes, but only one that interested him directly.

Po dialed the number of Sultana Carr, his colleague and another of Dr. Hannibal Freede's notorious disciples.

"Carr here," the young doctorate in astronomy answered voice-only. Mosca tried to imagine why she would not be using visuals. Maybe she was in the bath?

"Sulie, it's Po," Mosca replied, taking off the stuffy helmet. He held it so that the boom mike was in front of his face and the earpads, which he set to full gain, resonated inside the helmet's shell.

"Ah, the faithful Po. Still watching the hole, are you?"

"Have you had a look at it? It's getting bigger all the time."

"Are you taking pictures?"

"Well, not on any methodical basis. I thought the doctor — "

"Yeah, he'll bring back twenty miles of tape. And we'll have to watch all of it, frame by frame, with him. I think I'll wait for the movie."

"It's the hole I'm calling you about, Sulie." He took a breath. "I think it's flared."

"What!" Carr's voice chirped at him an octave above her normal range. "Po — Po? Where are you? I can't see you!"

"Ah, just a minute." He pulled the helmet down over his head again and readjusted the pickups.

"Now, what's this about a flare?" she asked when he popped into her reality. Sulie was wearing a white terry-cloth robe and her feet were bare. Maybe she *had* been in the bathtub.

"You know that the phone beams are out, don't you?"

"I hadn't heard. How long ago?"

Mosca bit his lip. "Well, I don't know. . . . Not long, I guess, because we'd have heard an announcement or something. I only discovered it because just four people showed up for my 10:05, and when I called Central about that, they said the beams were out."

"So you're thinking it's electromagnetic interference — a pulse, am I right?"

"Yeah, a big one. Big enough to knock out my students from Boston College and Wailuku State University at the same time. Something that big's got to be E.T. And the obvious choice is a flare from that spot pair."

"Of course, impeccable reasoning," Sulie replied, sitting down on the ottoman in front of her reading chair. She seemed unaware that her robe had parted, exposing a length of tanned leg above the knee. "Just one leetle problem, *Herr Doktor*. And that's that no one has seen or recorded any kind of flare phenomena in more than eighty years. . . . How do you answer this charge, sir?"

"No one has seen a sunspot, either — until Dr. Freede reported one."

"Unfounded. No one else has reported it."

"No one else has been looking for it."

"And Dr. Freede only called you — "

"No one else was listening!"

"And look how far you got when you tried to arrange with the dean's office for independent observations. No, *Herr Doktor* — " She shook her head. A damp strand of hair fell out of her bouffe and lay across her cheek. "I'm afraid your theory, impeccable as it may be, suffers from a lack of credibility. Which is usually fatal to any line of reasoning these days."

"If you want to see a sunspot, Sulie, all you have to do is smoke a piece of glass, put it over your eyes, and tilt your head back. You can do it. Dean Withers can do it. Joe-in-the-Know from Alamo can do it. I'm not going to sit here and play Chicken Little when verification of the effect is so *fucking* easy!"

"Hold on, Hoss!" Carr threw up her hands. "I'm on your side, remember? I've been three years without a grant and will never see tenure only because I referenced three of Freede's publications in my dissertation. I believe you."

"So what do we do about it?"

"Hmmm . . . that *is* a tough nut. . . ."

Mosca waited her out, content to watch how her eyebrows curved down in the center as she was thinking, and how her light gray eyes clouded to a slate color as the lashes shadowed them.

"Well, then," she began again. "Let's take a triage approach. Is there any immediate danger that we should warn people about?"

"Yes, of course. Dozens of cases. Anyone who needs to get out a critical phone call, just for starters, is going to be blanketed by the electromagnetic interference. At least on the planet's daylight side. And that will affect data as well as voice — so computer links and communications are going to be all over the floor on this hemisphere."

"Already happened," Carr told him. "We aren't screaming because we're talking locally, over a glassfiber line. Everyone else who can be affected has already found out. I said, can we *warn* people?"

"Well, when you put it that way, no. Not warn, because the e-mag pulse has already passed. By this time, it should be halfway to Mars, or beyond it, even. Of course, there are always . . . but then, I can't think of anyone who *would* be . . ."

"Be what?" Sulie looked alert.

"You see, the electromagnetics are at extremely high frequency, gamma rays and x-rays. Ionizing radiation. We're protected by the atmosphere, as well as by our distance from the sun. Anyone under a pressure dome or inside ship's hull, again at this distance, is also likely to be shielded by the structure itself — at least partly, if not completely — without the need for special insulation. But if someone was above the atmosphere and happened to be, well, *naked* —" He gulped.

Carr turned, exposing more thigh, and reached over to the desk behind her, picking up a notepad. The physical device was all pretend-pantomime generated by the virtual reality software, of course. She could just as easily make notes in the air with her finger and the system would capture and interpret them.

As she wrote, head down, Sulie asked casually, "How much do you know about modern spacesuit design?"

"Not much. I'm into hot plasma, not cold structurals."

"All right, I have contacts. I'll let them know. Is that it, then? Just ionizing radiation and the e-mag interference?"

"Well, for now. I mean, that's just the first wave."

"What's the second?"

"Look —" Po gulped and wiped his forehead; the wire glove actually skittered across the brow of his helmet. "This is going to take some explaining. Perhaps we should meet somewhere and plan our strategy."

"Fair enough," Sulie agreed. "I've got office hours in twenty minutes anyway. Why don't you come there?"

"Okay —"

"In the meantime I'll call Dean Withers and see if he'll do any more for a full doctorate and a pretty girl than he will for a lowly male teaching assistant, such as yourself. . . . By the way, have you thought about contacting Dr. Freede?"

"He's on the other side of the interference wave."

"Not any more, he isn't," she said. "It'll have cleared in eight minutes, tops, at lightspeed."

"Well, I'll try him then. . . . But I have a feeling that, right now, Freede's going to be too busy to chat with us."

• Chapter 16

The Marvelous Solar Kite

Wink ...
    Wink ...
        Wink ...
            Wink ...

**Photon Power, Inc., McKeesport, Pennjersey,
March 21, 12:51 p.m. EST**

One of the vanes must have preserved a wrinkle as it automatically unfolded after launching. It had not pulled out taut, and the uneven surface was now misdirecting a band of raw sunlight.

That was the only explanation that Brian Holdstrup, who was sitting on the ground 480,000 kilometers away, could think of to account for the persistent flash that was obscuring the left field of his video monitor. His basis for this notion was the blinking's period — it coincided with the rotation rate of the twenty-two staggered vanes radiating from the hub of the lightsail *Virginia Reel IV*. And that fragile fiberglass bead housed the camera and image analyzer which governed video navigation, as well as the radio telemetry system and antenna, the rigging rollers, and the microcomputer that controlled them.

How serious the defect would be, in terms of his winning, depended on several factors: the undimmed energy of the flash, the quality of the lens filters protecting the main camera's imaging chip, and the length of the race. If the energy increased, the filters weakened, or the race time were extended by the interplay of his opponents' tactics, then the chip — or at least its left visual field — would tend to cloud up and deprive Holdstrup of half his view. He decided he could manage somehow in that eventuality. He would have to, because there was physically no way for him to reach *Reel* and smooth out that vane. And any fixes he might try from the ground, such as twitching or jerking on the vanes, would seriously decrease the sail's overall efficiency.

Virginia Reel IV had been the third lightsailer free-dropped out beyond the Moon's orbit by the reaction tugboat which Mitsubishi's race committee had chartered to launch the contestants. In the past five days, during the "creep phase," with everyone jockeying for position before they crossed the official starting line, Holdstrup had worked on that advantage. He was now pushing his sail into a neck-and-neck duel for first-across, and he wouldn't jeopardize his lead just to squelch an annoying flash.

Holdstrup steered his sail by shortening or lengthening key vanes arrayed around the group. This changed their angular momentum and so altered the rate of rotation of the blade structure as a whole, just like an ice skater pulling her arms in during a spin. The rate of change provided more or less tension against the axis of a small aluminum flywheel that was aligned fore and aft in the hub. So these conflicting gyroscopic orientations, blade structure against flywheel, changed the angle of the sail relative to the incidental sunlight.

With this novel steering method, Holdstrup's design gained in maneuverability and responsiveness over older autogyrating designs. He could make course corrections much more quickly and simply, while the established configurations had to feather each vane around its longitudinal axis in order to change the angle of reflection.

All of the calculations to determine the appropriate vane length and rotation rate were under control of the onboard computer, of course. Holdstrup just sampled the program's current objectives, watched his video screen and compared it to his groundside computer's three-dimensional star maps, and issued new directives to advance *Reel* in her jockeying duel. He did not, Heaven forbid, try to sail with one hand constantly on the tiller.

If cutting and packing the vanes of his autogyrating design required the care of a brain surgeon and the patience of a Buddhist monk, then flying it continuously required the attention span of a bristlecone pine. With a pressure measured at just over half a kilogram per square kilometer, sunlight could not exert much force on the aluminized Mylar vanes. With an average acceleration of less than ten millimeters per second squared, the lightsailers did not move very fast over the distances involved.

So the early stages of the sport were played out in slow motion. Holdstrup just sampled video-navigational readings and made course corrections at specified times, usually once every three hours at this phase.

Although the lightsailers started out slow, they made up for lost time at the finish line — or, in the case of the big, cargo-hauling sunjammers, at the end of the run. Unlike a rocket, which burned its fuel and acquired all its speed at the beginning of a voyage, then coasted until it was time to decelerate, the solar sail was under continuous acceleration. Ten millimeters per second *per second*. Over hours and days, that quickly built up a respectable velocity, then kept on building until it was time to swing the sail around some massive body and use the pressure of sunlight to begin killing speed.

So the cargo sunjammers sailed complex, twisting courses around the solar system, bound on one side by their inertia and on the other by the steady pressure of half a kilogram per square kilometer.

Still, Brian Holdstrup understood that he and his sophisticated sail designs were doing the equivalent of gilding the plaster cherubs on a dying technology. Mitsubishi might sponsor the annual Mars'n'Back race out of corporate pride, but its heavy engine division was already working feverishly on rocket designs that would put sailors like himself out of business.

One day, he knew, long-range rockets would supplant the sunjammers — whose technologies were advanced by kite races like this — on the automated Saturn and Uranus

runs. That was as certain as, two hundred years ago, steamboats eventually supplanted sailing craft in transporting
commercial cargo on Earth's oceans. But before the rockets
became practical for more than relays to the Moon and the
Lagrange points, or following extended orbits out to Mars,
they would first have to overcome the inherent limitations
of fuel weight.

Any reaction mass that a rocket used, whether the
engines pushed it out with a chemical burn or heated it by
passing across a fission pile, still had to be heavy enough to
provide force from the acceleration. And that accelerative
mass was freeloading, non-cargo bulk which the engines
had to boost from the word go until it finally was burned
and passed sternward — a net loss in the thrust equation.
The heavier the particles, the less of them the ship's tanks
would have to take along. The lighter, the more. But the
ship still had to carry their weight in the first place.

Of all the rocket designs, only the fusion rams were
exempt from this traveling penalty — and they only
worked efficiently when they were diving *into* the solar
wind. When they had to pace the wind on an outbound
voyage, they suffered marked losses in efficiency.

Someday the engine designers would discover the
ultimate accelerative particle: an imaginary one that had
no mass in repose but grew heavier as it picked up speed.
Only then could they hope to boost a rocket fast enough,
long enough, to beat a sunjammer over the incredible distances to the outer planets.

Until then, however, rockets were in the same position
as the earliest steamboats. Those vessels, driven by clumsy
paddlewheels and burning vast amounts of low-energy
wood or coal, had to hug the world's coastlines to find calm
water and resupply themselves with fuel. Otherwise they
had to use sails to supplement their inherent limitations.
Only when those steamers discovered the greater efficiency of the screw propeller and the lower density, simpler
feeding, and more orderly logistics of refined oil could they
venture out regularly to cross the oceans.

Long-range rockets, in Holdstrup's view, were only

waiting for the discovery of a particle equivalent to fuel oil.
Then he would hang up his antistatic paddles and heat gun
and retire to an island in the Caymans.

But, in the meantime, there was that persistent vane
flash. . . .

Holdstrup studied the pattern of wink-winking, trying
to think if there was some way he could, in the future, fold
his sail material more loosely into the launch housing. It
had to be loose enough to discourage hard-edged wrinkles,
yet still tight enough to meet race specs for the free-drop
pod.

The flash's periodicity was hypnotizing him. . . .

Holdstrup shook his head, trying to wake himself up —
and the screen disappeared. That is, the star image
vanished in a blaze of static. It rebuilt itself slowly, then
whited out again.

Brian tried swiveling the camera, but he could see no
improvement. The image slowly came back a second time,
and now Holdstrup noticed that the static was coming on
in the same interval as the winking. So it had some connection with the pinwheeling of his blade system. Perhaps the
antenna had somehow gotten itself tangled and was now
caught in, or obscured by, one of the metallized vanes.

After the third blast of static, Brian had discarded that
particular theory. The image was now showing another
lightsailer looming up in his field of view. The outline was
the same rhomboid he had been maneuvering against for
the past three days. On the latest tack he thought he had
moved *ahead* of that vessel, but here it was in his forward-
looking camera. So, either the rhomboid had stolen a
march on him somehow, or *Virginia Reel IV* had turned on
its own length.

Holdstrup tried various maneuvers and finally, frantically began shortening sail to increase his vessel's spin and
maximize the vectoring he could apply to her present
course.

Nothing helped. Inexorably, with each fade-in after a
signal fade-out, the rhomboid grew larger in his monitor
screen. Then it began rippling and flashing, one edge

crumpling inward where *Reel*'s whirling blades cut into it. That would constitute a foul — touching or obstructing another craft — and it would generate the first successful protest against Holdstrup in ten years. That would be the end of the race for him.

As Brian watched in helpless dismay, the camera lens rode right into that blinking, flashing horror and then mercifully went black. The screen juggled itself for a moment, then flashed a message from the computer overseeing his groundside operations: it had lost all telemetry from *Virginia Reel IV*.

Not that it mattered a damn at this late date.

257.125 km/s
  257.189 km/s
    257.262 km/s
      257.351 km/s

Titan Developments, Inc., Manhattan, GNYC, March 21, 12:52 p.m. EST

The computer screen in front of Einar Floding clicked off the speed increases with the regularity of a metronome beat. The president of the corporation which held a controlling interest in the Titan Cartel was not at all embarrassed to admit that a communications network valued at half a million after-tax dollars every quarter was dedicated to that little cascade of numbers. One of the cybertechs from the lower floors had once explained the sum to him: rental on a radar dish in lunar orbit, per diems for keeping open a six-relay line-of-sight laser beam from the dish down to New York, and proration on the one-time cost of the microcomputer and custom software that massaged the signal, calculated the speed, and displayed the results on his desk.

Floding kept it there for gloating purposes. It was a constant criticism of that circle of vice presidents who had told him solar sails would be too clumsy to handle, too antiquated to be reliable, too slow to carry their product efficiently.

By God, as soon as this first transfer cycle was completed,

Floding was going to scrap the radar dish and have them install him a telescope. Let it keep an eye on the disk-shaped sail of *Ouroboros* — damned funny name that was; one of the scientist-types had picked it — next time the ship looped out past Saturn. By then the sunjammer would probably be going a good five hundred klicks, maybe even more. The same tech who'd explained the laser link-up had told him that a telescope would pick up the bright reflection off the sail easily, even among the outer planets. So it would show him the money both coming and going.

The secret of running an automated sunjammer from the orbit of Saturn was you never slowed it down. That way, its speed grew continuously, pushed by solar photons and its own inertia on the outbound leg, pulled by gravity and steered by reflected photons on the inbound leg. You ran a perpetual loop, anchored at one end by the mass of Saturn, at the other by the Earth-Moon system. And at each end the Cartel's specially built tugboats rushed out to match velocity with the passing sail, take off its attached cargo pods, and hook on new ones bound for the other end.

Ouroboros' maiden voyage had started thirteen months ago, fresh out of the packing crates at Saturn's own orbital speed of only nine-point-six-four kilometers per second. At that end of the loop, out where it was half-dark most of the day and automated machines did all of the real work, the tugs had given her the only push she'd ever need. They also attached three spherical tanks, each with a hundred-meter radius, each containing four-point-two million cubic meters of methane gas fresh from the Titan cramships, centrifugally refined and packed in its naturally liquid, low-temperature state. That cluster of tankage represented seven and a half *billion* cubic meters of product in a gaseous state. Or 260 billion cubic feet, using the old measure.

Everyone, Floding's vice presidents included, had said you couldn't take that much methane out in one gulp. Not in one hull. Not with a rocket.

So he hadn't. Floding had used a lightsailer instead. And that was a blessing in disguise, serendipity, an old man's luck, because it turned out the sail area shaded the tanks from direct sunlight all the way down to Earth. They stayed at an ambient temperature of about 75° Kelvin — a hot day on Pluto and almost low enough to freeze the product solid. That was doubly beneficial because, not only did the tanks not leak en route, they wouldn't expand appreciably during transfer and handling at the Earth end of the orbit. Or not for dozens of hours after being detached, which was plenty of time to get them under sunshades and begin decanting to atmospheric shuttles.

Einar Floding had brought home a lake of pure methane equal to the current annual additions to the nation's proved reserves by all the exploration and drilling companies combined. In one shipment. And in another — he checked his watch — two minutes' time, his tugboat was due to hook on and snatch this treasure from *Ouroboros'* cometary orbit, park it in a slot twelve hundred kilometers over the Earth, and dispense it with a kingly hand, feeding the chemical refineries and plastics plants of the world for a year or more.

And by that time — sooner, if the sunjammer kept building speed this way — he would have another tank cluster in hand. Then another and another.

The Titan Cartel, and Einar Floding himself personally, were going to be as rich as Croesus.

Scissor
 Scissor
  Scissor
   Scissor

CSS *Flycatcher*, Inside the Moon's Orbit, March 21, 18:53 UT

The guy wires attached to the outside rim of *Ouroboros'* sail whipped past Tod Becher's control bubble. The wires were moving relative to his position because the sail was spinning. That was how such an inherently wobbly structure as a plain disk of aluminized Mylar wider than the State of Nevada and thinner than a high-detergent soap bubble could maintain its stability. But the effect was eerie.

Some double-damned optical illusion made it seem as if each wire and the one below it were sheering together as they came around. As if they were trying to cut his bubble in half and let Becher's breatheable out.

It took all of his courage, then, to keep edging the tug-boat in closer, behind the deployed wires, to align her grapples with the coupling that attached the cargo string to the lightsail and its control module. If he goofed in matching velocities, then *Flycatcher* would collide with those scissoring cables and collapse the sail. The resulting jumble would probably trap the tugboat and him, sending the whole mess hurtling off past the orbit of Saturn at point-oh-eight percent of lightspeed.

Then Consolidated Space Services, which owned the tugboat, was going to be very mad. The Titan Cartel, which owned both CSS and *Ouroboros*, was going to be even madder. And Mrs. Becher and all the little Bechers who depended on Tod were going to be very sad. Not to mention that the Cartel would probably deduct the cost of the sail and the tugboat from the family's insurance money.

So Tod drove into that nest of wires very carefully.

Adding to his concerns was the string of cargo pods *Flycatcher* was towing: three lumpy oblongs having the same approximate size and mass as the liquid methane containers that *Ouroboros* had brought home. Becher's string contained nothing so exotic as refined gas — just provisions and medical supplies, cylinders of rocket fuel, new equipment and replacement parts, a *Gyrfalcon* Class 4 shuttle packed in shrinkwrap for the personal use of the Titan Base manager, four units of prefabricated executive housing, and assorted private inventory, plus water ballast to fill out the weight. Clean water always found a use in the outer planets.

Only ten centimeters separated the tug's grapple arm from the connection. Now came the tricky part. Becher couldn't just unsnap the coupling on the methane tanks and hook up his own string. It wasn't like they were in orbit, with everybody just freefalling happily along. No, the sail was under constant acceleration, and so was

Flycatcher. The minute he released that tanker string, it would start heading north *real* fast. It would still be plunging toward Earth at a measurable fraction of lightspeed — and *not* accelerating, which was good — but the string would be a thousand kilometers in back of Becher by the time he was ready to start dealing with it, catching it, and taking it in.

That kind of distance in a straight line was one thing when you were moving at 259 klicks per second. But a thousand — no, even a hundred — kilometers, when it had a significant deviation, with the load moving somewhere off on its own vector, heading for the good Lord only knew where — that would be something else again.

Add to the problem that this whole shebang was already picking up additional speed as the sail, the cargo, and *Flycatcher* herself started into a whipping loop around Earth. By the time the sail had made the turn and was ready to head back for Saturn, they would have added ten or fifteen more klicks of velocity. If he fumbled and dropped the tanker string now, he would probably never recover it. Not on the amount of hydrogen fuel he had in his reservoirs. At the speed everyone was going out here, Becher did not have enough leeway to go catch the string and still apply the vectoring thrust that would guide the heavy-laden tankers into a secondary loop around the Moon, turning them for final braking and entry into a stable Earth orbit.

No. Tod Becher wanted to keep both hands on the merchandise, the incoming as well as the outgoing, at all times. That was why *Flycatcher*'s skeletal frame had been designed with three separate grapples spaced around a vanadium-titanium towing collar: one to hold the tankers, one to retain the outbound cargo, and one to hold onto the stub end of the sail. For a minute or two, while the transfer was being made, the only thing holding this circus together would be Becher, hauling two sets of freight, holding onto a silver spinnaker that wanted to fly away, and himself boosting like the devil to compensate for the added load on all that thin Mylar and taut cabling.

Towing assignments just didn't get any better than this.

At 261 kilometers per second now, Tod worked the levers and servos on the grapple controls. The number one claw hooked into the anchor point of the sail module. The tanker string unhitched and was caught on the number two claw, which then hauled it to the offset position fifty meters around the tugboat's towing ring, clearing the sail's band for hooking on the outbound string. The number three, which was strained to the point of deforming its metal talons, slid the outbound cargo pods forward to the hitch point. The claw shook, like it had palsy — and then released.

"God *damn* it!" Becher swore, but he did so under his breath and never took his eyes off the jumbled view of cargo, connectors, and claws that was arrayed in front of his bubble. Well, he did move one eye just a twitch, watching the tumbling cargo pods drift back along *Flycatcher*'s fat hull. He wanted to make sure they didn't bang into anything vital — like tanks filled with supercooled liquid methane — as they went. Still, all this time his hands moved smoothly, professionally, from one lever to the next, trying to stabilize the various loads.

Except nothing was working. Claws that were clamped down remained frozen in position. The one that had opened wasn't functioning at all; instead, it just snatched back and forth mindlessly. Obviously the control box at its junction point had gone fluky and wasn't responding to the signals from Tod's board.

Well, when all else fails, report in. It was time for Becher to dump his problems in the lap of higher authority. And anyway, he had a free hand for it now. He thumbed his throat mike and began transmitting.

"Consolidated Services Control, this is *Flycatcher*. Do you read — over?"

Garble and static answered him.

"Shit!" he howled. It was a fine day for profanity. "The radio too?"

Nothing was working right.

At this point a light on his control board told him the whole of the bad news. *Flycatcher*'s main engine had also acquired a mind of its own. Somewhere in the nest of exposed piping and heat sinks below the main combustion chamber, a feathering vane or the relay circuits that governed it had decided to turn over. Without instructions from Becher, the ship's thrust suddenly kicked sideways. He could think of no possibilities for realigning it, other than vectoring all the other control vanes against it. Then the resulting skewed thrust would eventually burn through the lightsail's film and tear this lashup apart.

He tried it anyway.

Nothing happened. The engine continued firing at the wrong angle. Tod was helpless at the controls of ten million tons of misbehaving machinery.

Brute force quickly overcame spring-tensioned delicacy. Firing at right angles, *Flycatcher* pushed left, into the spinning spokes of the guy wires. One by one they first caught on the tugboat's blunt nose, then wrapped themselves around the main hull. The hair-thin, braided cables scored, then compressed, and finally cracked the control bubble Tod Becher had been sitting under.

By that time, however, he had retreated into the safety of the hull and slammed the connecting hatch behind him.

Now, clutching the handholds in the ship's tiny airlock, Becher had time to consider his fate. He was blind to the outside universe in here, of course, but he had a fix on the ship's last position, and there was a notepad strapped to the thigh of his jumpsuit. By his present calculations, one of three eventualities — all equally unpleasant — would soon be rudely thrust upon him.

First and most immediate, *Flycatcher*'s off-angle thrust would push the sail and herself into the Earth's atmosphere before they had completed the primary loop. Burn-up would take about ten seconds, delayed in Tod's case by the combined insulation of the tugboat's hull and the enveloping layers of Mylar film and steel cable. He could avoid that fate if he could turn the main engine off — but the only way to do that was go back out into the bubble, breathe vacuum, and work about six protectively locked-out controls at the same time. Not possible.

As he was figuring all this, the notepad suddenly started creeping up Tod's thigh against the fabric pull of his coverall. He shortened his fingers' reach to keep on punching numbers, then found he had to stretch his arm to reach the pad. In the tugboat's weightless domain, which was still being jarred by the random accelerations of the collision, his inner ear had been unable at first to perceive any "down," a sense of collective direction. But after a second the drift became clear. He was being pushed back against the steel bulkhead.

Was that the Earth's gravity field he was entering? No, at the present speed, still in freefall, he would never feel the incidental clutch of his home planet's gravity again.

Then what — ?

Of course. When *Flycatcher* became entangled in the lightsail's rigging lines, they would have imparted the Mylar disk's spin to her hull. What he was feeling was old-fashioned angular momentum. Eventually it was going to pin him to the airlock's wall like a sock stuck inside a dryer drum.

Oh well, it couldn't be helped. . . . Becher wedged the notepad against his hip and resumed his chain of calculations.

His second fate, and a little more delayed, was that the crumpled sail and its cocooned passenger would miss the Earth, but the tugboat's thrust — which by now must be pinwheeling all over the sky — would move them laterally into a collision with the Moon. The result for Tod would be instantaneous, despite the cushioning potential of the square miles of aluminized film bundling him. Sudden decelerations from 275 kilometers per second were simply not survivable. He only hoped that Luna Colony's facilities on Near Side were widely enough spaced, or lucky enough, not to fall directly beneath his point of arrival.

Idly Becher wondered if twelve million cubic meters of liquid methane would explode on impact. Even in the absence of oxygen, he supposed, the kinetic energy would likely transform its mass into . . . something. An atomic fusion, perhaps?

Alternatively, if the methane survived and regasified under decompression, would its constituent molecule be light enough to reach lunar escape velocity at partial pressure? Or would the gas hang in the valleys of the Moon's highlands and seep down into its deepest craters, creating a new atmosphere for the colony?

Becher would like to have looked up the molecular weight of CH_4 on the ship's computer — but that system reported through his main control board, too, and was now exposed to vacuum. The one good result of this inconvenience was that the effort of trying to work out the gas pressures on his little notepad quickly solved problem number one. By the time he determined he didn't know enough about Avogadro Numbers to reach a satisfactory answer, Becher realized the broken lightsailer must already have passed around the Earth without burning up. That left him alternative two. Or number three.

The third and most prolonged of his fates was perhaps the scariest. The sunjammer and the trapped tugboat would simply continue outward on the sail's return course. But without the controls and guy wires to bend its path, the crumpled wreck would never be able to make the turn at Saturn. Instead, it and he would fly onward into darkness. His current speed was well above the sun's escape velocity of three-point-nine-nine kilometers per second at this distance. So Tod Becher — or at least his mummified body — would be the first human being to break the sun's grasp and reach the stars.

But then, he could always hope that, before then, the spin imparted from the sail would crush him to a paste against this bulkhead.

> *277.312 km/s*
> *277.384 km/s*
> *277.465 km/s*
> *277.531 km/s*

Traffic Control Platform 12, in Lunar Orbit, March 21, 19:16 UT

"What the hell is *that*?" Wilkins Jenning yelled.

He was yelling to himself, of course, because for the past twenty-two minutes every electrical system on his platform had been out — radio, radar, cyber, you name it — everything except the artificially dumb systems that ran his life support. Thank God the cyber-circuit boys hadn't gotten around to smartening up a simple feedback loop. Still, it didn't take an Einstein to guess that the relief ship was un-fucking-likely to lift in time to take him off for his end-of-shift at the old double-zero. In another dozen hours, this pod was going to become stuffy and cold.

But just because he was scared, alone, and likely to die, that didn't mean Wilkins Jenning had lost all sense of professionalism. If he couldn't see with his usual electromagnetic senses, he still had eyes, didn't he? And he still had the ten-power optical scope that controllers like him sometimes used to read registration numbers off the hulls of pilots who were either too stupid to use their radios or too careless to stay out of each other's orbits. And nobody was going to have the time on landing to change a registry number painted in letters three meters high on his hull and engraved half a centimeter deep into his ship's main spar before the TCP cop had a chance to call it into the Luna Colony municipal court. Heightened perception was the lawman's first line of defense.

Jenning swung his little telescope toward the big, bright star he had seen off to the west. Two seconds ago, it had been just a fourth-magnitude glimmer tucked under the arm of a darkly shadowed new Earth. One second later it was showing an angular diameter of a full degree of arc — twice the size of the Moon seen from Earth as Jenning remembered it. Now it was coming straight down on top of him, and even at this acute angle it was blazing like a polished hubcap in full sunlight.

Just for the record, it had no registration numbers he could read. Traffic Central hadn't logged any incoming vessels on that course — at least not on his watch. Besides that, Wilkins Jenning had never heard of any vessel so big. And nothing that moved so fast, either.

Whatever it was, from its approach angle the thing was clearly not making for a parking orbit. And if it was going to brake for landing, it had better start firing soon, and hard.

It no longer appeared to be coming straight at him. Instead, the object opened a detectable lateral gap between its own vector and the zenith above Platform 12. The gap quickly widened until the alien ship was actually passing by Jenning's position. He almost broke his neck trying to follow it down on the telescope's swivel mounting.

As near as he could tell, it was going down somewhere in the extreme northern highlands. Well away from any inhabited tracts — and thank you, God, for such small favors as this.

Jenning still had his scope on the vehicle — well, sometimes a degree or two behind it, as fast as it was moving — when the thing augered in. The effect was immediate. One instant a streaking silver blur, the next a dome of violet-white light, rising out of the jagged terrain just over his horizon, like the top of his mother's bread dough rising out of the mixing bowl. For two or three seconds the arc of plasma held against the velvet black sky, then slowly dissipated, sinking in on itself.

"*Shit!*" Wilkins Jenning breathed. "An alien spacecraft crash-lands on the Moon, and I'm the only one to see it. Except I can't tell anybody because I'm stuck up here without a radio."

He took his eye away from the scope and glanced around his control board, hoping that the interference might have cleared some and he'd have his communications back. But wherever he looked, either with the eye that had been fixed to the ocular or with the one that had been open and passively observing alongside it, all he could see was the afterimage of that same purple glare. His eyes didn't hurt, but the image wasn't fading away, either.

"Shit! An alien spacecraft crashes on the Moon, and I'm the only one to see it, and now I'm *blind*! Shit!"

• Chapter 17

Low Rent District

Drift
   Drift
     Drag
     Drag

Orbital Slot 43-D at 605 Kilometers,
March 21, 19:14 UT

The EverRest Cryotorium, No. 2034/HH in the National Astronautics and Space Administration's Registry of Inert Platforms, had been falling in toward the planet for five years now. Everyone knew the orbit was decaying, but no one gave much of a damn.

The operating company had gotten its fees in advance, and with the structure amortized over a mere fifteen years, they were long gone. In their final correspondence, the EverRest Corporation assured the survivors of "absent friends and loved ones" that internal systems and basic hull integrity would preserve the cryo-environment at an optimum 200° Kelvin for centuries yet to come. Should future generations wish to visit with their ancestors, the managing director noted, the platform's hatch covers would respond to a little pressure from a No. 14 Snapple™.

No one wished to visit.

Of the cryotorium's twenty-four permanent residents, only one had living heirs who might care that the repose of a "still-loved one" would soon be interrupted by a flaming reentry. This person, who was also the last of EverRest's "associates" to "join the crew," was Alexis Rump-Goddy. She had technically "succumbed" to a meningeal carcinoma in her seventieth year and, being heir herself to the massive Goddy-Baldwin fortune, had placed the whole of it in escrow to pay for her eventual revival, treatment, and continued life as soon as the cure for her cancer should be discovered, tested, and successfully applied to 100,000 prior cases. Alexis' heirs had been actively involved in trying to break this trust for the past thirty years. So, had they known about the impending tragedy, not one of them would have given a cent to recover and re-orbit the Ever-Rest platform. In fact, its imminent loss was about to simplify their legal position greatly.

Not all of the EverRest's inhabitants had been as trustful of bankers, lawyers, and the securities markets as Ms. Rump-Goddy. These others, in "signing on," had converted their assets into bearer bonds, negotiable Swiss paper, and gem-quality stones. They were clearly hoping that the science of subatomic manipulation would not overtake the latter any more quickly than the tidal forces of economics would erode the former. For the repose of these assets, the EverRest Corporation had provided titanium-clad, asbestos-lined vaults built into the base of each of the platform's twenty-four cryogenic "sleep cases."

These modern-day Pharaohs, wrapped in the chill embrace of liquid gases, had tried to provide for their after-life as thoughtfully, comfortably, and completely as any resident of the Valley of the Kings. Unfortunately, they made the same mistakes. Advertising their sequestered wealth — or letting the EverRest Corporation advertise it for them through its brochures and video promotions — only encouraged the scoundrels who believed that the living should have a share in what the dead, or the "merely absent," wanted to keep to themselves. Within six months of the EverRest Corporation's demise, adventurers who knew how to wield a Snapple™ had matched orbits with the platform, entered it, and plundered each of the twenty-four "Star Vaults."

In Ms. Rump-Goddy's case, all the thieves discovered were some identity cards and the stuffed and mounted hides of Tippi, Nippi, and Baby Popo — three of her favorite cats. According to the lady's dying wish, they were supposed to follow her into "cryosleep" in their own deep-freeze compartments. Evidently legal complications with the trust document had reversed her aspirations in this one instance. Such also are the revenges of the living upon the dead.

So the EverRest Cryotorium orbited low over the Earth, surviving on its own stripped-down automatic systems and a good layer of insulating foam. The hull and its inhabitants were long forgotten by all but a handful of individuals: some who appeared in court on a monthly basis, and some who worked daily in the NASA Department of Decaying Orbital Artifacts — the "Trash Squad."

However, with the unaccustomed surge of electromagnetic noise that was echoing throughout the inner solar system, and with the ensuing panic as normally talkative human beings discovered that their multiplex communications system was effectively blanked out, no one happened to be looking at the sky. Not even the bureaucrats of NASA were wondering what else the surge of random electromagnetic energy might accomplish.

Unappreciated by these people, for the past twenty minutes or so the ionosphere 500 kilometers under the EverRest's keel had been absorbing huge blasts of intense ultraviolet radiation from the recent solar flare.

The air density at such a height above the Earth's surface is quite thin: ranging from two millionths down to five billionths of a gram per cubic meter. While this is hardly detectable as an atmosphere, much less as a breathable medium, still the tenuous upper reaches of the planet's "ocean of air" do exist. Their component particles — mostly ionized atoms of light gases, rather than whole molecules — have mass and obey physical principles, among them the laws of equilibrium. That is to say, the molecular fragments remain at their current altitude because the collective collisions of their gas pressure, energized by the sun's radiation, propel them upward against the pull of gravity.

It is a simple equation in high-school physics: heat the

gas, and you increase its pressure. Without confining walls or a steel tank to contain it, the volume of the gas will then expand.

Over the twenty-odd minutes since the first wave of flare-induced electromagnetic energy swept past the Earth, the continuous influx of high-energy radiation had tripled the ambient temperature of the lower ionosphere. The resulting swell in the volume of gas pushed upward, increasing the density of material in EverRest's immediate vicinity by about fifty times.

The effect was immediate.

The orbiting hull reacted as if it had hit a wall.

In just five minutes, the platform had lost 800 meters in altitude. Riding now in relatively thicker air, its speed decreased even further as the gas pressure around it increased.

The blunt leading edge of the cylindrical hull began to buffet, then to vibrate. Without stabilizing jets, the hull up-ended. Without aerodynamic surfaces or other controls, it found no equilibrium in this new attitude either, and so it turned over again. In a few more seconds, the platform was tumbling uncontrollably.

The uneven heating of air-braking under these conditions created stresses in the hull's outside layers that the platform's designers had never anticipated. Seams began to sweat and tear. Panels worked against each other, compressing and flexing the internal plating.

Like a brick bouncing down a flight of stairs, the EverRest platform found successively lower and slower orbits. As it passed into the evening dusk over West Africa, the hull's periods of temporary equilibrium between inertia and friction descended from whole minutes to mere seconds.

At just over 475 kilometers in altitude and traversing southern Tanzania, the platform's exterior was beginning to heat up. That, too, the designers had never expected.

By the time it was down to 200 kilometers, the hull's outer layers were glowing a dull red.

Passing 100 kilometers and the tip of Madagascar, the

EverRest platform was shedding pieces of itself. More spectacularly, its speed — still in excess of 20,000 kilometers per hour — was fragmenting the denser air at this altitude, breaking up molecules instead of simply pushing them aside. The result was a blazing trail of hot, ionized gases mixed with incandescent bits of steel and long-chain polymers.

Inside the EverRest Cryotorium, conditions became chaotic. The liquid-nitrogen baths of the "sleep cases" could no longer maintain a low, even temperature. The chill gases themselves were beginning to boil, breaking pipes and shredding tissues that had no time to thaw.

When the hull opened up, the inrush of superheated air quickly incinerated everything organic, as well as any metals that had a melting point below 1,300°C.

In the final stage of descent, the remaining fragments slowed remarkably in the thick lower atmosphere. They traded forward motion for vertical, falling at an acceleration of a mere nine-point-eight meters per second squared toward the Indian Ocean.

At last, a few chunks of steel barely larger than a fist and a dusting of cinders reminiscent of the gifts of the Ganges dropped into the sunny blue waters.

Turn
   Turn
     Turn . . .
       Turn . . .

Orbital Slot 37-C at 625 Kilometers, March 21, 19:24 UT

When the comm link had gone down, isolating the Day's Ease Geriatric Residence from its groundside computer complex, Megan Patterson, R.N.Ast., had been nearly frantic. The break meant a loss of access to patient billings, payroll, medication scheduling, entertainment, stores inventory and delivery rosters, engineering support, attitude monitoring and control, and a dozen other interactive functions that the station manager could now only guess at.

The three pressurized canisters at the ends of their Y-shaped yoke were just shells. True, they were fitted out with floors and partitions, beds and other furniture, air recirculators and blowers, plumbing and gravitic collection sumps, a hydroponics environmental sink, and various hospital equipment. But the residence satellite had not one independent cyber, no artificially intelligent doctor, not even a handheld calculator. Just timesharing terminals strategically sited around the corridors, in the medical lockers, and at the central office. Terminals that now displayed white static.

Patterson wanted to call someone and complain, but the link had taken out her voice communications, too. That left her with only two orderlies, a cook, and a handyman to yell at, and they had all successfully retreated into the adjoining modules. So Megan sat in her office at the mid-grav level in Unit 2 and stewed.

With her arms folded and her legs crossed at the knee, Patterson tried to contain her anger and frustration. She failed. The thwarted emotion turned into a spasmodic kicking of her suspended foot. Up-down, up-down. It started as a twitch. Soon Megan was staring at the toe of her white shoe, rising and falling beyond the light-blue nylon over her kneecap. Instead of stopping the kick and controlling herself, she pumped it like a girl on a playground swing, pushing higher and harder with each passing minute.

It was the home office, again. Of course. The bean counters had put her in an impossible position, again. They had made her nominally responsible for the entire station, then suspended her on an invisible wire, a beamcast system that clearly was excessively vulnerable to atmospheric interference. That was what Patterson found so intolerable — being made dependent, and then getting cut off into the bargain.

In a minute, Megan's foot was flying through an arc of more than thirty centimeters. It was thumping the underside of the desk wing and threatening to bounce her out of the chair. That meant it was time to stop this childishness and do something constructive.

Patterson abruptly stilled her foot.

The chair was still bouncing. The desk was still thumping. What was going on here?

She put a hand on the desk and felt a flutter. Her every sense came alert, and she noticed a deep groaning that seemed to be coming from the walls and floor around her.

Patterson sat upright in alarm. Was this the wobble predicted in the report from Azimuth Partners, Inc., and had it now come early? She thumbed the terminal on her desk to its internal lines and called for her handyman, the station engineer.

"Dilkey? Are you there?"

"Yes, Miz Patterson?" the speaker grid said after a momentary hesitation.

"Do you feel that shaking? Or whatever it is?"

"Unh — I don't think so, ma'am."

"Put your hand on the nearest wall, man! It's jumping around like a live eel. I can actually hear something down here in Two."

"Well, ma'am, that don't make no difference. Each of the modules has its own resonant frequency, you know. So whatever you're hearin' over there don't mean we're hearing it over here."

"Damn you, Dilkey, I say the station is shaking itself apart! I want you to find out why."

"And I try and try to tell you I don't *know* why. What do I know if I can't feel it, hey? I mean, it ain't reasonable to think a man — "

"Patterson out." She closed the circuit with a snap of her thumbnail.

The wobbling got worse. Patterson stood up from her chair, practically floating out of it in the partial gravity, and walked unsteadily to her one window. Those damn windows in the modules had been the station's whole selling point and, according to the API report, one of the reasons its angle of rotation was so screwed up. What she saw when she got her face squarely in front of the opening and was looking out with the widest field of view almost stopped her heart.

Unit 3, the odd module that was twice as long as the other two, was drifting out of place. Its white flank — which in the normal course of things should have been out of sight, well above her head a third of the way around the axis of rotation — now loomed at nearly ninety degrees to her right ear.

Patterson scrunched down, trying to look up past the window's top edge along a line of sight that was almost dead vertical toward the station's hub. She could barely make out the curve of that core module and the tips of its unflexed docking clamps — but that wasn't what she was looking for.

There!

Off to the right, clearly outlined against the white cloud cover on the planet below, were two random loops of high-tension cabling and a bend of the umbilicus, the corrugated dropshaft which carried the elevator, a man-way, and the telecomm and utility connections between the loose module and the hub. As she watched, the curls in the cables grew wider and then recurved on themselves, making four loops now.

Unit 3 was coming down on top of her.

Megan Patterson watched it close the gap with the upper corner of her own module. Even while the rogue unit still had forty meters of clear space, the window she was bracing herself against began sliding off to her right. She pressed her shoulder into the frame, but the window kept going.

Or rather, she was being pulled to the left by some kind of force.

Patterson's formal training in physics was fairly limited, although her qualification for space duty had included schooling in the basic principles of rotational dynamics. If she was moving to the *left* without any effort on her part, then the room — or this module, or the whole station, depending on circumstances — was actually decelerating. There was no force acting on Patterson's body other than her own inertia; she was stable, it was her enclosed universe that was changing directions.

She glanced back at her desk to confirm the hypothesis. Yes, a book she'd left open there was also moving. It slid leftward, toward the edge, retarded only by the friction of its covers and spine against the desktop.

The movement was gradual, a persistent pressure rather than a rush. For that Patterson could thank the designers, who had wanted to generate the barest fraction of gravity, just a reminder to aged bones and inner ears of which way "down" ought to be. If the builders had spun the station for a full gee of acceleration, Megan would have been thrown against the wall with enough impact to crush her skull and snap her neck.

As it was, the pressure built until she could no longer stabilize herself against the centimeter-wide coaming around the windowframe. When she let go, she drifted at the speed of a brisk walk toward the forward bulkhead. She just had time to get her hands up, palms out with her wrists slack, to absorb the shock.

Patterson struck, rebounded, then floated free, kicking her legs and waving her arms. Whatever spin the station once had was now gone.

WHUMP!

The walls of Megan Patterson's office vibrated like the insides of a churchbell.

Skree-eek!

While the air thumped in her lungs from that sudden overpressure, her ears rang with a tingling, electrifying, spine-binding wail. Like a hydraulic machine tearing apart a piece of sheet metal.

Crunch-grumble.

The wailing died out in a series of bashing thuds which themselves faded like the echo of thunder in a box canyon.

Without being told, Megan figured that Unit 3 had finally caught up with her own module.

Garble
  Burble
    Warble
      . . . Click!

Day's Ease Holdings, Inc., Hollyville, Delaware, 1:34 p.m. EST

As quickly as the communications had gone out, they came back. One minute the radio horns were searching aimlessly across the sky, receiving nothing but static. The next, an astute listener might hear fragments of voices, screams and cries in the darkness, remaining an utter jumble — but with an edge of sense. Then, an instant later, out came whole words, complete thoughts, even sentences. Of course, nothing picked up where it had left off forty minutes ago. The transmissions were still occasionally marred by fearsome bursts of static and every word hovered at the fringes of panic. But at least the beams were open and functioning again.

Dr. Harry Asher, the on-call physician for the Day's Ease chain of geriatric satellites, listened to the signals coming back. Because of the ongoing interference, he had long ago abandoned the Virtuality™ helmet and gloves that normally put him in the most intimate contact with his patients. He was monitoring now on voice-only, because the static bursts were less disorienting that way. Asher could only hope that, during this unaccounted gap in his shift time, none of his 2,400 patients in orbit had suffered any relapses requiring his attention and advice.

Immediately one light on his board flashed red, indicating an urgent message. It was from the channel tied to Station A18-37C-626. Probably a deader, Asher thought, and the duty nurse was afraid to call it. Such things happened all too often.

He picked up on that channel first, strapping his head into the helmet and tugging on his gloves.

". . . Help me!" The signal was still coming in sound-only, so he saw and felt nothing. That left Asher's imagination ample room to read undertones into the voice.

"We're coming apart up here!" the woman's voice bellowed. "The whole shebang is all twisted up and flying around —!"

"Miss — ah — " the doctor clicked into his staff profiles " — ah, Patterson! This is Dr. Asher at Hollyville. . . . Do you have a medical problem?"

"Medical? Sure, it's medical! I've got four hundred old folks puking their guts out because this station has totally lost its spin! And the cure for them, Doctor, isn't gonna be in your specialty. Now get off the line and get me someone from groundside engineering!"

"Ah, Nurse Patterson, I think you may be overstating—"

"Move it, buster!"

From the background noise to the transmission — which could be the returning static, but surely *sounded* like creaking metal and breaking crockery — Asher began to think the woman might not be hallucinating. He consulted his files again and put through a call to the engineering department.

Luckily, it was long enough after the lunch hour that someone decided to answer him. "Technical Support, Ramirez speaking."

"Ramirez, this is Dr. Asher in Medical Control. We appear to have a developing problem with our residence at 37-C and I —"

"Is this a medical problem?"

"No, the duty nurse seems to think the station has gone off spin."

"Oh, hell! Just another spacesick female. If she's hysterical —"

"I think you'd better talk to her just the same."

"Patch her through."

Asher did so and returned to his board. Two more red lights were winking furiously at him.

Creak!
  Crack!
    Grate!
      Groan!

Orbital Slot 37-C at 625 Kilometers, 19:43 UT

Megan Patterson tried to swim in the suddenly weightless environment, pawing at the air with her hands and kicking with her feet when she had nothing better to push or pull against. The compartments and corridors of Unit 2 were filled with floating objects — plates, cups, lumps of food, blobs of tea and coffee and liniment, books and papers, jars of cream and bottles of pills, loose capsules, chairs and their seat cushions, strips of matting, clots of vomit and other human by-products. Some of it struck her in the face. Some of it stuck in her hair. None of it mattered.

The air around her was also filled with human and inhuman sounds. The moanings and mewlings of her terrified patients were overridden by shrieks and growls as the station's three main modules ground against each other and pulled exterior panels off each other's sides. That man on the ground, Ramirez, had told her that none of those sounds mattered, either. Not until she heard a low whistling that might or might not develop into a high-pitched scream.

He had advised her to begin rounding up patients and staff members and get them all up and into the docking hub, because that was physically the strongest module in the structure. She should corral her charges there, he said, then close and seal the inner hatches. Maybe it would survive the thudding and pounding intact.

When she had asked if he was going to order an immediate evacuation, Ramirez had been evasive. "The conditions are not suitable for it at this time," he had said — whatever that might mean. What conditions? she wondered, and how much more unsuitable could they be than right now, with the station tearing itself apart around her ears?

One old man — Cahill, Roger B., 91 years — drifted in front of her, coming halfway out of his roomette. Megan Patterson collared him and drew him along. What she hadn't solved yet was how she was going to get him, or anyone else, up the two-meter-wide corrugated dropshaft between this module and the core. That passage was now twisting around like a snake with a broken back.

"Yawp!" Cahill shouted in her ear. "Why are you — ? Where are we going?"

"Up to the hub. . . . You think you can make it there on your own steam?"

"Sure, little lady. I was a frame rigger, you know, on the first L4 Colony back in '34. Why, I could — "

"Great, Grandpa! Now get going!" She slapped his rump to start him along.

Patterson batted away the curtain that was floating up in front of the next cubicle. This one belonged to Hampton, Mary D., 87 years. Megan pushed her head in and found the woman wedged into the far corner, bracing herself between the bedframe and the bureau box. From Hampton's fixed, unfocused stare, the nurse guessed she was either dead or in deep shock.

"Give me your hand!" Patterson bellowed, swimming forward to offer her own in front of the woman's face.

No response.

She reached down and tried to pry Hampton's fingers out of their grip on the mattress pad. The woman's fist tightened up even more.

"Come on! We have to leave!"

No further response.

Patterson turned and kicked her way out of the roomette. With 392 other patients to worry about, she had no time to waste on this one.

By now the corridors and manways between the levels were filling up with people. Some hysterical, some dazed, but most alert and seeming only slightly anxious.

"Up!" Megan bellowed. "Get up to the next floor. We've got to climb up to the docking module."

"The what?" a woman nearby asked.

"The center part, where you came in."

A man next to Patterson was trying to get his feet on the floor and walk toward the shaft entrance. All he succeeded in doing was kick himself off in a fast spin, perform a somersault around his own center of gravity, and end up crashing into two other people.

"Don't try to walk!" Megan shouted. "Swim! Swim in the air!"

Two women, looking uncertain, tried a hesitant breaststroke. Their slow, shallow motions took them nowhere.

Patterson didn't have time for this, either. Kicking off against the nearest bulkhead, she launched herself through a gap between their floating bodies, headed toward the manway. She pulled herself through, passed up to the next level, and continued right on toward the top — or what used to be the top, when the module was under spin and had dangled on its own set of cables.

By this time Patterson's exertions had overheated her, and she was sweating freely. With no gravity to coax the moisture into drops and flows, it sheeted on her face and neck, then quickly dried in wide patches. Her loose clothing pulled the wetness off her skin like a wick, making her feel damp and cool for a moment. But it didn't last. Up here, near the top of the column, the heat was like an oven. Soon she was parched.

The buffeting had returned to the structure. Despite her weightlessness, Patterson had to cling to various metal projections and boltheads in the shaft to keep from being slapped back and forth like a tennis ball in a bucket. Things would get better, she reasoned, if she could only get out into the tube, which was flexible and had softer insides.

Still yelling for the patients to follow her, Megan wrapped her hands around the interior cable studs and started pulling herself out into the corrugated tunnel of the umbilicus. Then she stopped short.

The cable ends were hot to her touch.

Patterson put out a hand to explore the tunnel wall, which was a series of steel rings positioned and separated by a flexible skin of polymer fabric. It felt hot, too. The plastic had a slick, greasy texture that she didn't like. But she had to move forward. Megan had her instructions from the ground, after all, and they did make sense.

She pulled her body out into the shivering, coiling tube. Where its inner bands of polymer touched her uniform tights or jumper, they left gray stains that drew away in gobs and strings. Where the steel rings touched, they left brown burn marks on the cloth or instantly opened long ladders in her stockings.

Patterson was anxious to get going, but there was still her duty to perform. Bending at the waist like a salmon in shallow water, she poked her head back into the top of the open dropshaft and shouted once more.

"Come *on!* Climb *up!*"

When she turned again to continue her passage, the inside of the umbilicus tore open in a meter-long slit. She never heard the high-pitched scream of wind that pushed her through and out into the ghostly, glowing vortex of heated ions that was streaming off the doomed module's trailing edge.

Lap
   Lap
     Lap
     Lap

Boca Raton, Florida, 1:58 p.m. EST

There was nobody on the beach to play with. Jimmi Dolores had tried listening to the waves for a while, but they were just little lappers. They were barely nibbling at the sand. Nothing he wanted to chase. Hardly worth getting his toes wet.

Jimmi didn't know anything about meteor-track transfer beams or solar flares or electromagnetic interference. After all, he was only ten years old. He just knew that the video screen had suddenly gone all blank and fuzzy, like it did sometimes when Papa tried to tune the dish. So, with nothing to watch indoors, Mama had told him to go outside and get some sunshine.

But the sun was too bright. The sand was too white and blazing. The sky was a hard, glassy blue without a breath of wind.

Jimmi wanted to dig himself a hole in the sand and cover himself all over — except he'd left his bucket and shovel at home under the porch. And the sand was too hot for digging with just his hands.

The boy looked around for something to do. Maybe he'd find a strand of kelp or a shell or something he could throw at the water. He covered his eyes against the glare Indian-style, putting the inside edge of his palm against his forehead. First he looked north, up the beach, then turned south. . . .

What was that!

Off to the east, just low enough in the sky to be seen

under the side of his shading hand, Jimmi caught a glimpse of a long, white streak. It looked like a pin-scratch through paint on paper. Or like the old-fashioned wooden matches that Tia Paloma had occasionally used in her kitchen, striking a trail of yellow sparks and faint smoke on the dark strip along the side of the box — except this trail was struck on the pale and cloudless blue of the sky.

He took his hand away.

The trail faded in the deeper blue near the eastern horizon.

Jimmi was about to turn away when three more sparks, bigger ones with hotter cores and longer tails, flew over his shoulder to follow the first. The boy stared raptly after them, his head lifted into the sunlight long after the last of them faded.

What did it mean?

He looked north, looked south, looked straight up until he was skimming the edge of the white coin that was the sun and which his mother had told him never, never to look at directly with his eyes.

Nothing more to be seen.

He was about to turn away, still searching for a shell or something to play with, when another streak — no, two, four, half a dozen, more! — fell across the sky. They all were coming from the west. They all disappeared into the east, and some were still blazing as they fell behind the edge of the ocean.

Jimmi Dolores stayed on the beach watching the sky for hours, until the sun had gone low in the west, the skin of his shoulders had turned red, and his eyes had filled with tears. For the rest of his life, he would remember that Friday, March 21, 2081, as the afternoon that the shooting stars came out in daylight.

Part 4

Plus Seven Hours . . . and Counting

The cattle stir in their pastures,
trees put forth leaves,
birds call through the marshes, fluttering,
wings raised in praise of your day.
Sheep dance in their fields
and all winged things fly,
living in your light.

Ships sail up and down the rivers.
Travelers pass on the highways with dawn.
Fish leap in the streams.
Your rays shine amid ocean's great green.

—From Ikhnaton's "Hymn to the Sun"

Chapter 18

Working at Cross Purposes

Drifting . . .
  Thinning . . .
    Cooling . . .
      Collecting . . .

For the passage through the corona, the plasmote has entered a form of sporulation. While the superheated plasma around him attenuates to a species of hot, polluted vacuum, his own structure condenses. From the magnetized gases that were once conjured out of the sun's photosphere and then went slithering up into the arch of the prominence, they now collect into durable cysts held together by the plasmote's ordered series of field strengths and bound electric charges.

The process of encysting is involuntary, brought on to protect his consciousness and his internal configuration from sudden, inappropriate changes in temperature and pressure. The resulting linked chain of magnetic bubbles is not indestructible. In pure vacuum, at temperatures near absolute zero, the spores will eventually dissolve. The plasma they sequester will revert to complete atoms and molecules of hydrogen and helium. Without their ionic valences, the structure will break down and release these gases in tiny, harmless puffs. Then the plasmote dies.

But even in the sporulate state all consciousness is not lost — just dimmed. The creature maintains a diminished awareness and, by the process of altering the weak magnetic fields that connect his cysts, a feeble capacity for wriggling movement.

Flow
> *Feed*
>> *Flow*
>>> *Feed*

Aboard *Hyperion*, March 22, 1:45 UT

The volume of the gas stream in a fusion ram depends upon two factors: the ram's speed through the ambient cloud of particles which comprise its fuel, and the proportion of ionized to neutral particles in that stream. The more charged particles that enter the pipe and undergo constriction in its magnetic chamber — whether by natural density or velocity compression — the faster the ram will pump out reaction mass.

Dr. Hannibal Freede understood all of this, in theory, and yet he fretted that *Hyperion* was not accelerating fast enough. This bothered him greatly.

He had already reasoned that the ship's orbital speed of almost forty-eight kilometers per second would account for little in the run-up of her engine. Her trajectory in orbit was at nearly right angles to the prevailing solar wind — which, at this short distance, the sun's leisurely twenty-eight-day rotation would hardly have begun twisting into the flattened spiral that can be detected among the outer planets as pulsing, frontal waves.

So, to attain the desired course which Freede hoped would strand the ship somewhere in the vicinity of the Earth-Moon system, he was trying a maneuver for which *Hyperion* had not been strictly designed. Instead of slowly limping away from the sun — on which path she would overtake only a low percentage of the outflowing particles, but still enough to provide thrust for an orbit-breaking acceleration — he was going to dive into the sun. The ram would then be driving into the flow, increasing the engine's relative velocity, and so its efficiency, by the wind's average speed of 400 kilometers per second. By increasing the ship's thrust and speed, he hoped to achieve a fast cometary orbit, first taking *Hyperion* around the far side of the sun away from Earth and then bringing her back on a wider curve.

The risk factors in this plan were the thermal rating of the hull and the choke capacity of the ramjet. Freede was skating close to design tolerances in either case. The advantage was that *Hyperion*, by dramatically increasing her speed as she fled for the sun's distant limb, might hope to outrun — or at least skirt around — most of the advancing cloud of disruptive particles which the flare had spewed in his general direction.

Freede had started the engine almost seven hours ago, and its internal electromagnets had required fully four hours to construct their compression chamber, balance it, and begin constricting a usable flow of particles. So then for the past three hours *Hyperion* been driving forward into the solar wind, building momentum for her 50,000-ton mass by expelling atomic nuclei with an average mass of 1.67×10^{-30} grams. It was going to be a long race. But winning it — that is, beating the flare's burst of charged particles and arriving safely below the horizon of those mammoth sunspots — was not the main point of this exercise.

As he now studied the dials and counters on the section of his board governing the ramjet's operation, Freede could see the fusion bulb still held rock-steady. However, it was the leaps and bounds of the telltales attached to his magnetometer booms that kept drawing his attention. They showed what kind of forces were already building up around his ship.

Freede would be minimally happy if he could merely establish a vector and build some momentum for the ramjet before that cloud of charged particles finally burned out his control circuits with its surge of induced voltages. Then, however long it took, *Hyperion* and Gyeli and the stone cold corpse of Dr. Hannibal Freede, victim of ionizing radiation in the flare's first seconds, would be on their way, safely or not, to a rendezvous with the Earth.

It was the best he could hope for at present.

What the board's dials and counters told him was that after three hours of thrust, the ship had increased her speed to a bare fifty-two kilometers per second. That was an improvement of just under ten percent, although the acceleration would build constantly from this point forward.

"How are we doing, Han?" Gyeli asked tentatively on the intercom. She seemed hesitant, not wanting to interrupt his exertions on their behalf. "I've finally got everything down here that's both breakable *and* irreplaceable under restraint," she said. "When do we start thrusting?"

"We are long gone, my dear!" he answered cheerfully. "We've been under continuing acceleration for the past three hours."

"And I didn't feel a thing! . . . Well, maybe just the tiniest bit of 'down.' "

Angelika had to be making that up. Along the vessel's central axis, where she had worked to get things "shipshape," the thrust and its dislocations would have been most pronounced. She might, however, be fibbing to conceal some measure of the damage his maneuvers had surely caused them. That was sweet of her.

"We are making a very gradual headway, my dear," Freede assured her.

"But *strong* . . . ?" she contended. "I mean, the ram *is* creating the effect you intended, isn't it?"

"Oh yes! We are in excellent shape. Nothing to fear. Nothing at all."

Still, Freede watched the clock. *Hyperion* had already passed the lower limit of his estimate for the time the particle cloud would need to reach her. Six to twelve hours, he'd said, depending on the ejection energy imparted to it by the flare. Sooner, given the size of that pulse Freede had witnessed. The ship must already be inside the front edge of the ion storm. Certainly his magnetometers said so. Literally anything could happen now.

Crush
   Constrict
      Compact
         Contract

The environment surrounding the encapsulated plasmote changes again. It becomes thicker and hotter, with a pattern of magnetic flux that presses down on him in a way he has not felt since the gas prominence first plucked him from the photosphere. The pressure rises against the outer skin of his kernels until it becomes almost intolerable.

Just as low temperature and near vacuum brought on the sporulation, so this heat and stress reverse the process. The plasmote unfolds like a Japanese paper flower immersed in water. Wave on wave of linked membranes and charged envelopes quickly blossom into a fully functioning entity.

The universe is strange here: bounded by massive fields and compressed into a channeled flow that, again, is not unlike the tubular prominence which bridged the two cold pools on the sun's surface. The plasmote instinctively reaches out and hugs the new configuration of field lines, meshing with them and hiding among them against the raw cascade of hot gases — both charged and inert particles — that is pouring down on top of him.

Being himself a creature of plasma physics, the plasmote understands that in some measure the odd shape of these field lines enhances this gas flow. By constricting it at one point, the channel increases the speed of the gas and, just beyond that place, forms a low-pressure pocket. This action heats the material and simultaneously draws in more volume than would normally enter such a confined space. By expanding the passage at an even later point, the channel provides an exit path for the hot, fast-moving gas.

This is a means of propulsion not unlike the funneling that some of the many variations of plasmote propagate in the sun's atmosphere. It is always less maneuverable than his own flexible bellows, but the novel system is also more energetic, more quick, more constant in its thrust.

So the plasmote understands propulsion.

And the plasmote now *yearns* for propulsion.

Lacking any means to maneuver himself in the nearly pure vacuum where his spores were lately floating, he can expect only to drift further outward under pressure from the flare's burst of radiation and charged particles. How far he will go, he cannot guess, never having been here before and knowing none of his kind who ever came here and survived. But eventually, the plasmote knows, the cold and the emptiness so far away from the sun will dissolve him.

With a means of moving himself, however, he can return to the hot, dense plasma streams that are his native environment. That this place — this narrow, constricted channel where he now finds himself — will provide for such movement is a leap of intuition on the plasmote's part.

Yet his faith is instructed by the speed of the gas stream he entered with. It came from *behind* him, from the direction toward the sun. And, as a student of plasma physics, the plasmote knows that any organism which is caught in such a flow and can successfully manage to compress it, as this stream is being compressed, will then move backward against the flow. Action and reaction. That is, it will move him toward the sun, back to where he belongs.

In this one leap, the plasmote foresees that his best interest lies in staying with this constricting place. Immediately he anchors himself at the point of maximum compression and begins exploring.

By reaching, feeling, examining, learning, he quickly knows, as well as he knows his own corporeal structure, all the shapes of the field that condenses the ion flow. Guided by the ever-present heat that he feels as the glow of the sun that was *behind* him, he now changes the channel's field lines. He strengthens them with his body, shifts them with his will, and vectors the flow's thrust into more useful directions. Soon the broad expanse of the sun's photosphere is more perfectly centered in his consciousness.

He is heading for home.

> Glitch
>> Gamble
>>> Twitch
>>>> Drop

Aboard *Hyperion*, March 22, 2:04 UT

Strapped into his observation and control bubble — and heedless of the possible exposure now — Dr. Hannibal

Freede watched the counters on his board twitch and tumble with the surges of random current expelled from the swarm of highly energized ions that had engulfed his ship. The particles' transient magnetic fields sent crazy voltages buzzing through *Hyperion*'s metal skin, crashing into any of her extended electronic circuits, and surging in the atom-wide pathways of her nanochips.

One by one, the pattern of resets and burnouts closed down her higher level systems. The disruption left running only those which operated by mechanical feedbacks, such as the flow of air across precipitator screens and oxygenation biofilters, the polarization of his bubble, or the trickle of coolant through the ship's hull and into the heat exchangers.

Freede could only hope that the ram engine, which itself established a massive magnetic field, would dominate in the interplay of electrical forces at the ship's core and hold stable the configuration he had built and nursed over the past seven hours. Then he could hope *Hyperion* would continue thrusting on his chosen course and ignore the gnat-bites of the invisible magnetic cloud through which she was now traveling.

Lacking any more sophisticated controls in this magnetic storm, Freede was reduced to visually comparing the position of the sun's face in his observation dome with its place a moment before the ion cloud struck. If the disk continued hanging in that lower right quadrant and didn't move past the gland-seam bisecting his bubble, then he figured *Hyperion* was holding steady on her course.

This was literally navigating by the seat of his pants — but it was the best he could do until the storm passed and some measure of control and coordination returned to his board.

"Han! Something ver-*Pop!* strange is happe-*Zing!* here. All the electrics, the emergency medical *Yowl!* — "

He thumbed the intercom. "Just hang on, Gyeli. Try to find an insulated place and don't touch anything that's sparking. We'll be in this disturbance for about half an hour."

"Are you *Crackle!* up there?"

"I'm fine! You just stay where you are!"

The sun's disk remained constant in that lower quadrant, and Freede began to think they were safe.

Then slowly at first, seeming inexorably, and finally with increasing speed, the white circle shifted. Freede's fingers leapt to his keyboard, trying to instruct the ramjet's computer. The keys sputtered as he touched them, and a sizzling blue glare winked beneath the tiles.

Nothing worked.

The face of the sun moved higher, centering itself in the dome over his head, aligning itself directly with the ship's thrust.

Dr. Hannibal Freede watched the object of his years of study rush down on top of him. He knew it would be many hours, probably even days, before the increasing heat overcame the cooling gel in *Hyperion*'s skin, before her framework of duralumin, steel, and titanium structure passed their design tolerances and crumpled like a wad of paper in a furnace flame. But those things would surely happen now.

He had failed in getting his beautiful wife and his record of observations safely home. And he did not quite know how to tell her.

Freede thumbed the button on his intercom. It neither sparked nor squawked at him, indicating that the worst of the ion storm had already passed. Yet the ram's magnetic fields still did not correct themselves.

He brought the microphone to his lips. "Gyeli . . . I want you to know that I do love you. . . ."

Grind
  Splinter
    Shiver
      Grit

The constricting channel around the plasmote vibrates and pulses with the howling stream of gas that his dive is force-feeding into it. He strengthens the magnetic field again and again, trying to hold it together. The temperature and pressure rise to heady levels, invigorating him with life and hope, as this curious curve in the time-space continuum rides its wave of compressed ions through the corona.

In many ways, this pinched space reminds him of the screaming flux inside the gas prominence, where his whole adventure began on the quick edge of the typhoon.

After a short span of time — as the plasmote measures it — the howling in the channel peaks and then begins to recede for reasons he cannot fathom. As it fades, the gas flow pelts him with strange objects, much bigger than protons, far more massive than whole atoms. These chunks of raw matter pass through his plasma envelope as dark blots, all but invisible in the glow of life and energy surrounding him. He has no name for these strange manifestations. Because they do not seem to cause him damage or pain, he does not pause to create a name for them.

In time the pelting stops, and then so does the constriction. The curved space he is binding with his magnetic field vanishes like a dream in daylight. The compressed bulge of solar wind expands around him like a bubble and soundlessly pops.

The plasmote drifts forward, still carrying the inertia of his recent passage. For an instant he fears that he might die out here in the corona, then he senses the natural warmth, the cherishing pressure. He is passing down through the inner layers of the chromosphere. Ahead of him blazes the visible spectrum of the photosphere. He can discern the rising hump of a convection cell, surrounded by the cooler interstices of a downdraft.

He slips sideways into the luminous granule and pushes out his veiled membranes to slow the inertial rush. With a little experimentation, he finds his own level, adjusts his voice to the booming sea around him, and begins calling for others of his kind. He is eager to converse with them and tell them of his remarkable experiences.

Despite the most improbable of odds, the plasmote has finally come home.

Chapter 19

Ionizing Radiation

Boom!
　　Boom!
　　　Boom!
　　　　Boom!

Tranquility Shores, Luna Colony, March 22, 1:47 UT
The door panel to Gina Tochman's sleeping cubicle sounded like a percussion board set on full *whang*, rich with subsonics but overlaid by the tweeting screech of glass fibers grinding together in brittle polymer resins.

"All right!" she said groggily. "I'm *up* already!"

Tochman slid her legs out from beneath the bedcovers and poked around for her robe. Not finding it, she tugged the sheet loose at the bottom corners and wrapped it around herself.

Boom-boom!

"Enough, will you? I'll be there in a second."

Gina stumbled barefoot across the clothes-littered floor, just one and a half paces to the door. She unworked the latch and pulled it back.

Out in the corridor were her supervisor, Harry Rajee, and a white-uniformed nurse from the dispensary whose badge shaped a name something like "Toliver." Rajee was poised against the far wall, head down, left wrist clenched in his right fist, his left elbow forward — about to hurl himself against her door.

"Hold it, Harry!" She smiled. "You'll hurt yourself that way."

"Gina! We couldn't wake you, and I was sure — "

"I wake up real fast when people come pounding on my door like this. What's the problem? Why didn't you just signal me?"

"But we did!" Rajee leaned into her darkened cubicle and gestured toward the phone. Its screen was showing a red-and-white bull's-eye that strobed in and out. Even competing with the corridor lights now, it was bright enough to cast shadows inside the room. For the first five minutes of contact, she knew, this pattern would have been joined by an angry buzzing — which she obviously had slept right through.

"Sorry, Harry. It must have been all the excitement today — um, yesterday."

"Well, there is more. They want you in the dispensary."

"I'll check in first thing in the morning. On my shift," Gina added with a twinkle.

"They want you right now." His face was dead serious, and so was the nurse's.

"Why?"

"It seems there has been —"

The nurse put a quick hand on Rajee's arm, shook his head warningly. "The doctor has to tell her." Now that she could focus, Tochman saw the badge said "T. Oliva."

"All right," Rajee said reluctantly. "Gina, just go. It's very important."

"Can I stop even to get dressed?"

"I'll wait for her," the nurse volunteered.

"No need," Gina said. "I know my way."

"You don't understand," the man said. "Doctor's orders."

When Tochman had pulled on an indoor jumper and slippers, the man was still outside in the corridor, leaning against the wall. "Let's go then," she said, passing by him and keeping up the pace.

"You don't want to give me a little hint?" Gina asked after a bit, looking back over her shoulder.

"No, really — it's worth my job, ma'am."

"All right."

Down one hallway and up the next, around a corner,

and the noise of many voices came to her like the babble of a river sounding through the trees.

"What's this — too late — I don't — never heard — some resort — damned silly — proper way — this hour."

Halfway down the corridor, about where Tochman knew the dispensary to be, a knot of people jammed into a doorway and hung out into the hall. As she and the nurse approached, Gina recognized several of Tranquility Shores' guests. Coming closer, she realized that they were *all* guests, no staff. And as she mingled with the fringes at the door, she sensed they were all from her Moon Walk tour the day before.

"What's going on here?" She turned to Oliva.

"Dr. Harper will explain," he replied, pointing her through the blocked door then walking away.

"Hey! Where are *you* going?"

"Three more to round up," he said, over his shoulder.

Gina turned back to her guests, who had stopped babbling and stared at her with a mixture of anger and fear.

"Excuse me, folks." She gently inserted herself through the crowd.

"What's going on here, Miss Tochman?" asked Mr. Carlin, the man who had gotten lost when the radios broke down. "They pulled me out of bed like some kind of Gestapo squad."

"Yeah, me too!" said Miss Gladvale, the woman with the dysfunctional camera.

"I'm going to find out," Gina assured them. "Dr. Harper is a good man, and he never does things without a solid reason. Let me talk to him, and we'll all know soon enough."

Tochman worked her way through the small, packed waiting room. Sure enough, everyone here was both a guest and a Moon Walker. At the receptionist's window, she found Jo Hamoud, the day-shift regular.

"Everybody's out in force," Gina said. "What gives, Jo?"

The woman glanced around behind her, tipped her head sideways at Tochman, and made a decision. "Harper got something from Admin about twenty minutes ago. Then *he* launched a max scramble."

"A medical emergency? But none of these people look like they're burned or bleeding. I don't —"

Hamoud turned back into the office again. "I'm not supposed to talk about it. But, look, Harper did say he wants to see you first. You'd better go right in."

The woman released the doorlock, and the panel slid back. Gina walked through into the sharp, old-fashioned hospital scents of rubbing alcohol and Betadine swabs.

Harper, an ugly gnome of a man in a white cotton coat over a frayed plaid shirt, looked up from his desk. His rumpled look was accented by heavy, gray stubble on his chin and jowls. Without rising, he waved her to a seat.

"Evening, Gina. Or morning, rather. How's that arm of yours?"

She had broken her forearm six weeks ago in an argument with gravity. Her buggy had bogged down in a little pothole west of the complex, and she had to pull the wheel out herself. One of the troubles of working under one-sixth gee was that people, even old Moonhands like Gina Tochman, tended to forget the difference between weight and mass. Up here she could actually lift the flex-steel wheel, the axle it was attached to, and the levered dead weight of the buggy, which given the axle's mechanical advantage was about 440 kilograms under Earth gravity. The apparent 73 kilos of weight was still a hard budge for her, but all she had to do was swing the mass clear of the craterlet's lip and put it down. That was where the confusion bit her — because in lateral motion the buggy retained the full inertia of its nearly 900 kilos. In heaving it sideways, she had pressure-cracked her ulna. Tochman flexed the arm now, remembering the tingling current from the electric pads as Harper had stim-healed it.

"Just fine, Doctor. But you didn't call me in the middle of the night — nor all those guests out there, either — to chat about my arm, did you?"

Harper looked her straight in the eye. That was something she liked about the older man, his directness. "No, I didn't. . . . I want to run a short physical on you. And on those other people, too. We'll take some blood, maybe grab a pinch of bone marrow, do some cell counts. . . ."

" 'Cell counts?' Sounds like you suspect an infection. Do we have some kind of plague in the complex? Something respiratory? From the Moon Walkers' air canisters, perhaps? Or —"

"Slow up, Gina. . . . Damn it, I was afraid of this! It's nothing contagious, so we don't have to worry about *that*, at least. No, Admin had been wrapping up details on that radio interference this afternoon, yesterday afternoon, which took out most of our external systems, by the way. Everything that wasn't below ground or heavily shielded got fried. Anyway, somebody upstairs came across a report from the observatory staff at Copernicus. Seems their big radio dish had also lost its receiver head — burned out — and somebody over there was speculating it might have been a blast of high-energy gamma or x-rays. That's compatible with the damage we suffered here, by the way. They also reported some cosmic ray bombardments, high-energy particles following the radiation burst.

"To make a long story short, it's taken our deep-thinkers in Admin this many hours to remember that high doses of extreme ultraviolet aren't particularly good for the human body. Just the same, they stuck it in my E-mail for morning delivery. Jerks! A good thing I was up and prowling about and happened to empty the bin. Anyway, I think you and your tour group may have picked up a dose of ionizing radiation."

Gina felt a rubbery wave pass under her diaphragm. "How bad?"

"Can't say until we run these tests. The first symptoms are usually changes in blood chemistry and in the lymphatic system. We'll check your white cells, like I said. If they don't start falling off inside of seventy-two hours, you're probably all right."

"Radiation sickness." The words caught in her throat.

"That's right. The cell count's the most reliable detector, but I want you to tell me, also, if you feel persistent nausea, get the trots, or develop an unexplained rash or burn mark."

"I've read something about this. We can also look for hair loss, lesions of the mucous mem —"

"Not right away. White cells come first. . . . But I do want you to come to me with anything unusual."

"How much are you going to tell them?" Tochman nodded her head toward the waiting room.

"Not nearly as much as I'm telling you. Admin wants me to jolly those folks along. I am absolutely forbidden to mention the word 'radiation.' The brass wants I should make this seem like a routine precaution."

"Something you'd wake them at two in the morning for?" she smiled.

"Time *is* of the essence, Gina, and I have to get a baseline cell count on all of them."

"I understand."

"But what can I tell these people for a cover story? Some precautionary measure that won't cause alarm or invoke a lawsuit. You mentioned the air canisters — can we say we found some contaminant in the air supply? Some mutating mold perhaps? Or maybe a form of Legionnaires' disease?"

"And you think *that* won't bring on a suit for criminal negligence, Doctor?"

"Well . . . you may be right."

"Why not tell them the truth?" she asked.

"Because I don't want to cause a panic. And Admin is worried about perceptions of the resort in the popular media. You know how these things can get out of hand. If the paying public starts thinking space travel and off-planet assignments — let alone vacations on the Moon — are too dangerous, it could cut revenues in half around here. We don't want that."

"But this energy blast wasn't an everyday thing," Tochman protested. "It was some astronomical glitch. An act of God. The lawyers upstairs have to see that. The Moon Walkers had to sign enough indemnities, didn't they? The legal department can easily defend the corporation against any suit brought on that basis. And isn't that what those guys're trained to do?"

"Of course they can fight it. But there's still that word — 'radiation.' It's a scary thing, radiation poisoning, from whatever source."

"Yeah, tell me about it!"

"Now, now, my dear. You do have a chance, you know. The possibility exists that your pressure suit and thermal jumper provided enough layers to shield you against the radiation."

"Doctor, do you know what those suits are made of?" Gina wrinkled her brow at him. "Synthetic fibers, mostly. Some silicon wool. And a layer of aluminized film about one atom thick. I could probably wear it while taking one of your tomograph scans and still show off every bone and tissue in my body. We all might as well have been dancing around naked out there."

"That's really too bad."

"No shit, Harper," she said bitterly.

He pulled at his jaw. "Well, we'll know inside of seventy-two hours. Then, depending on just how sick you may be — "

"Isn't there something you can do before then?"

"Such as?"

"Well, I've read about ionizing radiation. It damages sensitive cells, like bone marrow and skin tissue and the *E. coli* bacteria in the intestines. What it doesn't destroy outright, it poisons by chemically breaking down organic molecules into new and usually toxic substances. It also damages the DNA in some tissues, and that's where you get tumors."

"Surely not all of that will happen to you."

"Don't snow me, please. With a high enough dosage, it's a derby to see what gets you first."

"Go ahead then," he grumped. "Tell me what's on your mind."

"Well, I thought, since that blast of radiation passed through me yesterday, all those broken molecules and dead cells are probably sloshing around inside me right now. Isn't there some way to wash them out? Some way to at least take the burden off my lymph nodes and kidneys?"

Harper was staring at her with a cold eye.

"I mean," she stammered, "if I'm going to be dead anyway. . . . And those people out there . . ."

"There is a treatment," the doctor began slowly. "They tried it in the early part of the century. Whole blood transfusion and a complete reseeding of the bone marrow. But first we have to be sure your own marrow is completely dead, so we have to reradiate you to a known level. That's the dangerous part, because we don't know what kind of body burden you may already be carrying. . . .

"The technique is also contraindicated, because it may not be necessary in the first place. We don't know where the electromagnetic pulse came from, or how exposed your position was. You weren't at Copernicus, where the gamma and x-ray bursts were detected. And even there they were not measured —"

"Come off it, Doctor. You said we had equipment damage here, too. Whatever the rem dosage, I was out in it the longest — me and Mr. Carlin, that is."

"All right, you and Carlin." He made a note. "But I still don't like to treat until I know there's disease in the first place."

"I can feel it in me!"

"Nonsense! You're reflecting a psychosomatic —"

"It's not your body we're gambling with, remember?" Gina said stubbornly. "Okay, you burn out my bone marrow and replace it, along with my blood — wait a minute! I thought a marrow transplant took matching against something like twenty or thirty thousand prospective donors. Do you have that many candidates here on the Moon? Or are your medical records that good?"

"The candidate is sitting right here. We take a sample of your own marrow, type it for DNA damage, isolate a healthy cell, and clone it and reinject it to begin the regrowth. Blood is easier — we only have to type and fill from stores. Then we can go after tissue damage with a viral-encapsulated DNA carrier, effectively reinfecting damaged cells with your own genetic pattern."

"When can we begin?" she said resolutely.

"Whoa there, Gina. I haven't told you the downside."

"Sure, it may not be necessary, and you may over-radiate me. What else is there to talk about?"

"You'll feel weak as a child and be sick for weeks. With your immune system dormant and your white-cell count down, you'll be subject to every garden-variety bug that comes along. Just keeping you alive will be a major undertaking. You could easily die of this treatment."

"Or die anyway without it."

"We'll know more in seventy-two hours," he assured her.

"By which time I'll be chock full of poisons and halfway dead already."

"I'm your doctor, Gina."

"And I'm a free woman, Doctor. Give me a release form, and I'll sign it. I'd rather be fighting this thing tonight than sitting around hoping it'll go away."

Harper stuck out his lower lip. He looked truculent, but Tochman could see he was actually gnawing his upper lip with his bottom teeth.

"All right," he said finally. "You're in for a load of pain that may not be necessary."

"I've got that coming anyway."

"Go in the next room and take off your clothes. I'll be with you in two minutes to do the preliminary typing."

Tochman stood up, then paused. "What about the others, Doctor? What about Carlin? What are you going to tell them?"

"That's what I'm giving myself two minutes to decide."

• Chapter 20

Awakening the Dead

Gurneys
   Stretchers
      Sleeping Bags
         . . . Facing Chairs

Chatham County Medical Center, Savannah, Georgia, March 21, 8:01 p.m. EST

The flow of patients radiated out into the corridors adjoining the Emergency Room. Their inert and sometimes lifeless bodies lay on whatever was handy, whatever would keep them off the bare floor and maintain some semblance that this was a hospital and not a battlefield aid station. Of course, the center had run out of four-way adjustable gurneys in the first half-hour of the crisis.

Dr. Norman Filchner walked those corridors now, stepping over a skewed arm here, a cocked leg there. He studied the slack faces of the patients. He smiled into the tense faces of the relatives whom the administration had bent all rules in letting in to tend their loved ones. These volunteer nurses cradled heads, wiped drool, and held up drip bags to maintain pressure in the IVs after the hospital had run out of rolling stands.

Filchner was baffled. Since early afternoon they had been coming in, hundreds of comatose patients, all shocked into a deep state of near-catatonia. He and his fellow doctors and technicians had drawn blood, checked for pupil dilation, and questioned friends and family about possible allergic reactions, drug taking, and histories of nervous disorder.

Bit by bit a familiar pattern had begun to emerge. Every one of the patients had in some way been connected into the national communications net when the burst of interference took it down. Most of the people Filchner was seeing here were gamers, people who locked themselves into a room, put on a helmet and gloves, and went off adventuring. The tragedy, of course, was that no one found them for hours after the primary seizure. Filchner shuddered to think of the thousands more—maybe even tens of thousands in this city alone—who were now drooling on the floor. Multiply that by all the cities and towns of this country, and you were left with millions of people in dire medical condition with no help in sight.

Not that Filchner had a lot he could offer these patients. If it had been a simple drug overdose, then he could pump out their stomachs, apply measured doses of the correct countervailing stimulant or depressant, put them gently to sleep, and hope they would wake up twelve hours later. But not with these cases, where the central nervous system had taken a hit whose dimensions Filchner could not fathom. Was it electrical shock? Sensory overstimulation? Induced psychosis? What?

The irony was that, at about this point in the diagnosis Filchner would normally be putting on his own helmet and having a long heart-to-heart with the medical intelligence at the Centers for Disease Control in Atlanta. But, of course, the cybers had gone down in the same wave of atmospheric static, and no one could say just when they might come back on line. So Filchner and his associates were reduced to the level of medicine men shaking their rattles over the supine bodies. The most Filchner could do was keep them quiet, keep them hydrated, and wait for an outcome.

He stopped beside one body, lying on a mattress covered with a sheet. The drip bag was taped to the wall above one arm. The wrist bracelet said this was "Kozinski, Jerry, WM 17 yrs." That was about all the medical history his mother or uncle or whoever would have left after bringing the boy in. Oh, yes, there was the second line: National Medical Identification Number KB702-41659-53427-02.

Filchner laid one finger along the boy's neck to check the pulse. It was strong and steady — not thin and reedy like some of the others. Maybe this one had gotten a lighter dose of whatever it was that had knocked them all out. The doctor rested his hand on the dry forehead. The skin was warm to the touch, but not actively feverish.

"Unh!" the boy gasped, and shook Filchner's hand off.

The doctor cupped the young shoulder to give some reassurance.

"The dog!" Kozinski croaked. His eyes never opened, and now they squeezed tight with pain.

"What about the dog?" Filchner asked quietly.

"It's . . . *eating me!*" He brushed ineffectually at the drip needle stuck into the crook of his elbow. "My arm! He's eating my arm!" Kozinski clawed at the tubing.

Afraid the boy would break the needle off under the skin, Filchner grabbed at the wrist and pulled the reaching fingers away. The arm with the drip in it came up in a defensive gesture, and the doctor snared that wrist, too, in his other hand. Down on his knees in a hospital corridor, Norman Filchner wrestled with a comatose kid.

"Trapped . . . can't breathe!" the boy moaned. And still his eyes never opened.

"Nurse!" Filchner called. He had a sleepy-patch in his pocket, but with both hands occupied he had no way to get at it and apply the sticker to Kozinski's neck.

Before any of the orderlies could respond, however, the spasm passed and the boy's writhing quieted. In another minute, he was lying still again.

Filchner got off the floor, looked up and down the hallway. And there were millions of these people all over the North American continent.

Christ, what a mess!

$$CH_4 \ldots 16\text{-}1/4$$
$$CH_4 \ldots 16\text{-}1/2$$
$$CH_4 \ldots 17\text{-}3/8$$
$$CH_4 \ldots 18\text{-}1/8$$

Western Board of Trade, Chicago, March 21, 7:11 p.m. CST

For the last four hours, ever since the North American

Commodities Market reopened after the glitch or whatever that had shut it down, Lexander Bartels had been digging himself out of a hole.

Natural gas for October delivery had been lunch for the bottom-feeders over the past three days. And October was the month that the Titan Cartel had scheduled for release of product from its mammoth solar-sailing tanker. Every stratagem Bartels had tried — from taking anonymous positions in the market to publishing doubtful opinions by condescending experts regarding the tanker's speed and capacity — had failed to jar the downward trend in methane.

This morning everything had looked like a disaster. The sunjammer was on schedule and almost parked in Earth orbit. The price of its product was at a record low. And the Titan Cartel, which had put Bartels under an exclusive trading commission, which he now bitterly regretted, was howling for him to do something, anything.

Then the market had gotten sandbagged by a technical failure of some sort. The board's chairman — with concurrence of the ministers of commerce from all participating governments — had clocked all quotes back to their position as of midnight. And natural gas had lost the half a point it had actually recovered in the wee hours of the morning. That fractional point arguably represented three days' hard work by Lexander Bartels.

Now, with the quote numbers slithering horizontally across the lower horizon of his left eye and the news analyses and summarized announcements of the whole trading world flashing in his right eye, Bartels grasped at straws.

Could he invent a pipeline accident? With all the confusion following the trading glitch, stories were still getting scrambled. Many of the items passing his right eye were missing their source attributions. He could float a bogus story, leave his code off it, and it was even money that Quotrix, the artificial intelligence which refereed the flow of marketable information, would pass it unchallenged. Further, it was a good bet that many of the buyers would believe it and punch up the price of gas. Not a lot, maybe, but enough to recapture that half a point.

It would be something to offer the Cartel boys while they were screaming for his head on a platter.

As Bartels pondered this scheme, wondering if he could get away with something so patently illegal, the flow of blue numbers in his left eye took an upward slant. The movement was gradual at first, rising only by eighths and quarters, but it held.

What was this?

Lexander pumped his right cheek muscle, forcing the pace of the news flashes that flickered in that eye.

Nothing about gas.

Nothing about pipelines.

Nothing about the Cartel's precious tanker.

Whoops! There it was. And God *damn* it — !

TITAN CARTEL SPACE TANKER CRASHES IN DOCKING ACCIDENT . . . HARMLESS IMPACT AGAINST MOON . . . 7.5 BILLION M3 METHANE GAS LOST . . . CF 032181TITAN CRASH . . .

Bartels looked up the referenced text of the complete story — and wasn't "Titan crash" one hell of an ominous condensation? — to see if any of the details possibly held good news. They didn't.

He skimmed the five meager paragraphs, which were fully attributed to the prestigious Earth-Moon News Agency. The story included a lot of checkable specifics, down to and including the name and personal history of the sole human casualty in the accident, Tod Becher, who had piloted the docking tug. Considering the disordered state of the international news services at even this remove from the communications blackout, it was a pretty full account.

Bartels began to wonder if he and the market weren't the victims of an elaborate hoax. Could someone, most likely a newspeaker in the Titan Cartel's own bureaucracy, have planted this story in hopes of forcing the price of its product back up? It was the sort of subterfuge Lexander Bartels had been thinking of trying — if he had the courage and didn't mind that, within five seconds of the ruse being discovered, Quotrix would issue a warrant for his arrest that would slap him in a maximum-security jail alongside a bunch of minimum-sociability felons.

Still, the lie — if it was one — had gotten results. The price of gas was undeniably rising, up to 20-5/8 by now.

But the truth — if that was what it was — would be infinitely worse. Who cared where the price of methane for October delivery went, if the Cartel's solar-sailing tanker actually had crashed into the Moon? They didn't have another one coming anytime soon — or not soon enough to make a coup in this rising market.

Lexander Bartels wondered whether he should laugh or cry.

Then he thought of the positions he could take in the market for himself. Whether the Cartel had lost its shirt or not, there was always money to be made in a technical upswing. Bartels put away his ruminations and suspicions and began issuing buy orders, fast, on his own behalf.

Beep . . .
　　Beep . . .
　　　　Beep . . .
　　　　　　Beep . . .

Victoria General Hospital, British Columbia, March 21, 5:26 p.m. PST

"The alpha rhythm is stronger, Doctor."

The voice came from a great distance. Winston Qiang-Phillips tossed on a sea of cold mist, washed by a chill fog that seeped and creeped through his head. It blew in and out of the holes that a clutch of white fingertips had once punched in his skull, when they took hold of it and twisted.

Lacking any better course, he began swimming toward that voice.

"Yes, the persistent delta is fading now. Hmm . . ."

Another voice pulled at him, coming from another distance, in a direction opposite the first voice. Winston treaded the mist with his useless, flipper-like hands and tried to decide which way he should swim. Deciding was hard because his head, which was still full of round, white holes, wasn't working either.

As he was not moving in any direction, Winston slowly

began to rise. Up through whiter and colder banks of mist he went, drowning in vapor. He opened his mouth to breathe.

He opened his eyes.

Winston was looking into a layer of white foam with a hard stripe of white light banded on it. He thought he was looking up at the underside of the ocean's surface, with the sun marking a long, wavering ribbon of reflection. Then his eyes cleared and the foam became the acoustic tile of a low ceiling. The light became a fluorescent tube baffled by a pane of tiny facets, like a paving of gemstones.

Two dark shapes loomed above him, like walruses surfacing to inspect his soaked body.

"How are you doing?" asked the walrus on his right side. "That was a near thing for you."

No, it was a far thing, Winston Qiang-Phillips thought. He had gone so far, for so long.

He raised a hand. It came up weakly, stiffly, feeling like a dried-out stick. He touched his forehead and cheekbones, probing for the holes which the white hand had made. The solid flesh of his face dimpled and then pushed back against his fingertips.

"Have a headache, do you?" the walrus asked, running a bony, human knuckle back and forth under its mustache. "That's not surprising."

"Shall I get him a pain pill, Doctor?" asked the other walrus, which was smaller and did not happen to have a mustache. Its teeth, however, seen from this low angle, were long and flattened and yellow.

"Four hundred milligrams ibuprofen."

"Right away." The second walrus left his side.

"How do you swim without moving your hands?" Winston asked, hearing his voice come out in a husky whisper.

"What?" the first walrus replied. "Oh, you have a mild hallucination, is all — it will pass quickly. You're in a hospital, Mr. Qiang. They brought you in with neural feedback trauma after the Exchange went down this morning."

"What happened?"

"Some kind of freak electromagnetic storm. Other than that, my dear chap, no one knows. We've had speculations, of course. Some say it was a high-altitude atomic bomb, or perhaps an old fission pile that detonated upon reentry. Either would produce that kind of wide-ranging electromagnetic pulse. Other people claim it was a shower of particularly intense cosmic rays, possibly the residue of some nearby and as-yet-undiscovered supernova. A third opinion says it was the result of a computer glitch in the worldwide communication net. It would have to be some sort of replicating programming error, similar to a virus, they say. Though, personally, I can't swallow that, given the number of antibody screens at work in the system today."

The walrus, who wore the white coat of a doctor, looked extremely smug in its conclusions.

"But what happened to me?" Winston insisted.

"Oh, that! Call it a temporary neural overload. When the communication net failed, your brain was hooked into a virtual reality processor — as you may remember. In a period of time shorter than the normal synaptic impulse, you took on a sudden burst of information, mostly compressed images and active sense data. Your brain was quite unable to cope with it all and so retreated. You gave us a rather good impersonation of catatonia there for a few hours. The chaps from the Exchange were wringing their hands over you and the others. They all thought you were brain dead."

"And am I?" Qiang-Phillips asked fearfully.

"Are you what?"

"Dead?"

"Oh, dear me, no! You're fine, old man! Just physically weak, is all. And still sorting things out in your head, I imagine. Tell me now, what is the last thing you remember?"

"Money. I was . . ." The cold mists swirled inside Winston's skull now, without any holes to escape through. "I was in the middle of a deal, trading in gas properties, with money on the table — my money!" A surge of panic blew the fog out of his brains. "My money was registered with the network when it went down. . . . Do you know, what has the Exchange decided about assets that were in play?"

"I have no idea," the doctor said.

"If they do not find some equitable way to either record

the trade or void it, then I will be ruined. Everything I had was on display in the booth. So, technically, it was all exposed in the transaction. Look, is there any way I can make a phone call? Are the channels even open yet?"

"Oh, yes. The phones have been working most of the afternoon. Local only, so far. But I think you are still too unsettled to concern yourself with business just now."

"But I have to — it's my life!"

"Nonsense, old man. It's only money. You can make more of it. Make a ton of it in an afternoon, from the stories I've heard. And anyway, the disaster has struck all of you traders equally, hasn't it? I mean, there are three hundred and fourteen people in much the same state as yourself at this one hospital alone; hundreds more at other institutions." As he talked, the doctor fumbled one-handed with something deep in his coat pocket. "So a lot of people are going to be in the same boat as you, aren't they? I trust the officials at your Exchange will be pressed to achieve something 'equitable,' as you say." The hand came up over the edge of the bed, and the doctor's fingernail — or something sharp like that — pricked the loose skin of Winston's upper arm. "Now why don't you just lie back and let the future look after tomorrow, hey?"

"But, my money — !"

"Your money will be all safe and sound for you, just where you left it, my lad."

"But in the meantime?" Winston Qiang-Phillips struggled to organize his thoughts. "While I am lying here, others will be trading at my expense. They will gather assets that I should move on. . . . They will build . . . a corner . . . advantage . . ."

Waves of white vapor clogged his skull and closed over his eyes. As he fell back, Winston's head fluttered into a billow of paper currency, all of it high denominations. Some of the money slipped off the bed and rustled onto the floor.

Tap
   Tap
      Tap!
         Rap!

Titan Base, March 22, 3:24 UT

"Ms. Cormant?" The voice was that of Will Harding, her confidential secretary. "Are you awake, ma'am?"

Lydia Cormant rolled over and looked at the digital face of her bedside clock. Almost half past three. Another hour and a half to her normal rising time. Whatever reason Harding had for disturbing her, he considered it too urgent to wait and come in with her tray of breakfast tea.

"I'm awake now, Will," she called out. "What is it?"

"May I come in?"

Cormant struggled up in the bed, gathered pillows behind her in a pile, and sat up with the covers over her chest.

"Yes, come."

He slid back the door and entered her sleeping chamber. By station standards, it was large for a single person's private quarters; thirty cubic meters. That was enough for a bed, a hanging locker, an automated desk, two chairs, and a half-bath behind an ell-panel. Her quarters were wide enough, along a section of the ring tube's outer wall, to support a window which looked down on the blank face of Titan. That scene was made white and ghostly by the moon's frozen ice layers under an atmosphere of nitrogen and complex hydrocarbons.

These quarters represented space and privacy such as the average Cartel employee on assignment in the outer planets could hardly dream of. But then, Lydia Cormant was not an average employee. She was the general manager of Titan Base, a full voting director of InSystem Chemical Resources, Inc., and holder in her own name of three-point-nine percent of the shares in that Cartel member company. So she deserved her little luxuries.

Harding walked lightly to the chair beside her desk. His movements were fully acclimated to the station's one-eighth spin gravity.

"What is it?" she repeated.

"The announcement came in on the general news and entertainment channel three minutes ago," he answered, turning on her desk monitor. "I've spooled the whole thing for you, so you can see the action from the beginning."

"What announcement?" Lydia groped for her old-fashioned glass lenses on the bedside shelf and leaned forward to see the screen.

By way of answering, Harding swiveled the monitor toward her. It showed a disk of silver light surrounded by a starry, black sky. That had to be a computer-assisted artist's conception, Lydia knew, because they always showed too few stars in empty space. The disk was *Ouroboros*, of course, viewed head-on as it came streaming in toward Earth.

Cormant's last view of the sunjammer, seen with her own eyes more than a year ago, had been from its back side: showing the spokes of guy wires, visible only as a radial fuzziness against the luminescent film of the sail, and the three cryogenic methane tanks that trailed behind, as round and shadowed as little moons.

The voice-over to the view that was now on display described the *Ouroboros* and its capacities, the Cartel and its business relations, and a brief on the state of the world market in methane. While this rendition went on, a tiny mite of a ship riding a blue flame came edgewise toward the solar sail. The narration detailed the procedure for rendezvousing with the sail and removing its cargo.

As Cormant and Harding watched, the sail suddenly collapsed on one side, then folded around the tugboat. The entangled pair flew off at nearly right angles—moving so fast that the artist had to be compressing time for the sake of storytelling. The announcer could give no clear reason for the collapse but only repeated the speculations of sailing experts that the tug must have snagged one of the "control wires."

The scene jumped to a real-time optical view of the Moon, which was almost at full as seen from Earth. The announcer urged the viewers to watch the area "about half an inch in from the twelve o'clock position."

Cormant leaned closer, then got out of bed in her nightgown, crept over to the desk, and sat down with her face a few centimeters from the screen.

A dot, a blot, something dark and slow-moving crawled vertically up the face of the Moon. If this was truly a view from Earth, then the whatever-it-was was speeding away from the planet and almost straight into the satellite. The slight vertical motion was either some trick of perspective or perhaps a final attempt by the tugboat pilot to correct his course and pass over the Moon's north pole, maybe even establish an orbit around that body.

But it didn't work. One instant the blot or dot was crawling north into the Man in the Moon's hairline. In the next, a small bloom of bluish-white fire briefly outshone the whole gray-white face. Then it faded without a smudge.

The voice-over told them that the crash had taken place without loss of life or property, other than the pilot's and the value of the two ships, but it was doubtful the pilot and his environment bubble had survived the sail's initial collapse. The announcer then apologized for the lateness of his report, as the accident had occurred some seven hours earlier, but interference in the Earth's upper atmosphere, which was unrelated to the sunjammer crash, had disrupted this channel's regular news-gathering operations.

With the end of the spooled transmission, the screen went blank.

"You say this just came in?" Lydia asked Harding.

"Now four minutes ago."

"And what's the lightspeed lag?"

"About eighty-five minutes — say an hour and a half."

"But this came in with the general news?" she asked, knowing full well he'd already told her that.

"Yes, ma'am. The nightshift operator in the comm shack caught it in routine listening and called me right away."

"A seven-hour lag through general Earthside clumsiness, and an hour and a half coming here. So this accident happened when? Just about nineteen hundred hours Universal Time, I make it."

Harding did the subtractions in his head. "You're right, ma'am."

"What have we heard from the other Cartel members on this?"

"Nothing."

"You've checked receipts, of course, on all frequencies,

both scrambled and clear, including the one reserved for my personal use?"

"Of course, ma'am."

"Damned peculiar," Cormant observed.

"Yes, it is, ma'am."

"All right. Get out and get me some tea. We've got work to do."

He started for the door.

"And, Will — " She stopped him.

"Yes, ma'am?"

"You are to keep this whole affair quiet. Put a quarantine on that report — "

"I already have."

"And bring any messages this station receives from the Cartel — that's messages addressed to anyone, you hear? — to me as soon as they arrive. Instruct the comm operators on this."

"Right away, Ms. Cormant."

He hurried out to do her bidding.

Lydia Cormant did not get back in bed, but instead took her robe from the hanging locker, bundled it around her, and sat back in the chair by the desk. She glared at the computer screen from under lowered brows.

It was darkly silent.

In the Cartel's scale of things, this was no minor accident. The tanks trailing behind *Ouroboros* had contained the refined product of eighteen months' work here above Titan. The capital investment alone was in excess of point-seven-five terabux, in terms of personnel wages and benefits, this orbital station, the fleet of cramships, pipes and tankage, the distillery and various support equipment, all transported out to the orbit of Saturn, rigged and tested, and run on the tightest possible schedules to produce those seven and a half billion cubic meters of free methane in three little tanks.

True, now that those capital items were in place, the production of an endless stream of gas was possible. In the past thirteen months they had refined nearly another five gigacubes of gas, all cooled away and waiting for *Ouroboros'* return.

Which would never come now.

A replacement would take how long? At least another year to manufacture, pack away, and transship another lightsailer. Even if it were launched fully deployed from Earth orbit, it would still take that long to reach here. By that time, Cormant would have more than a full complement of product ready to ship sunward. But, with no income from that first load, which was now smeared in wreckage over the lunar highlands, her operation would be way short on cashflow.

True, the failings of Consolidated Space Services' tugboat personnel were not her responsibility, but the auditors would hardly accept that as an excuse. The one viable product that the Cartel had managed to recover from this increasingly foolhardy venture at Saturn was methane for humankind's energy and chemical industries. And Lydia Cormant had been on the point of supplying more of it than anyone had ever brought in with one well, one field, in one hundred years of drilling and pipelining on Earth.

All gone to a puddle and an impact-fusion bang on the Moon!

If the Cartel were in a forgiving mood, even though she had done *nothing* to be forgiven, then Floding or one of his executive assistants would surely have gotten a private message to Cormant. Condolences, a reprimand, a squaring of accounts, anything — just so long as they acknowledged her as family, as someone inside the tent, entitled to get the bad news from the big picture before it went out over the open channels as media fodder.

That was what hurt most: this lack of confidence. No one in the Cartel had thought to circle the wagons with their farthest outpost. Instead, they were just going to let the Titan crew find out through a general news broadcast.

Lydia Cormant knew how it was going to look to her department heads and shift foremen, to her labor gangs and pilots. They were being abandoned, psychologically. From this silence, it would cross the minds of many out here — as indeed it was crossing hers right now — that without their first shipment of product to sell and with a gaping hole in their cashflow, the Cartel might be inclined not to make up the supplies that *Ouroboros* was supposed to bring back for Titan Base. Or not right away. And the Cartel might not even send crew replacements at rotation time.

Cormant had no worries that the station's highly trained and fully experienced personnel might get discouraged if their paychecks were late, that they might drift away to other offworld opportunities, crippling the operation here. They could only come and go when the Cartel dispatched a transport ship. If it didn't, then they stayed. And a lot of critical functions depended on the good spirits and fiscal generosity of the Earthside executives. Like eating. And breathing.

Cormant punched her intercom. "Will Harding to my quarters. Immediately."

"Yes, ma'am," came the reply.

Already, in her head, she was composing the text of a message to the people of Titan Base. It was a sad message, but one full of determination to carry forward in the face of this setback. It praised their work and their achievements beyond the orbit of Mars, but stopped short of promising them bonuses for the gas shipment that Earth's distribution networks would now never see. It was meant to reassure and to reinforce.

"You called?" Harding let himself into the room.

"Take a letter, Will," she said, straightening her shoulders and arranging the robe across her knees. "Addressed to me, from Einar Floding, Titan Developments, Manhattan, Greater New York City, dated March twenty-first at twenty hundred . . . oh, make it twenty-one hundred hours. Text begins — "

"Excuse me . . ." He put down his notepad. "You said a message *to* you? And *from* Floding?"

"I did."

"But that's . . . well, it's not ethical, is it?"

"No, Will, but it's necessary. Now, text begins — " and she recited the message from memory. Toward the end, Harding was sniffling aloud, and even her own eyes were moist.

• Chapter 21

"You Have to Listen!"

Thirty-nine . . .
>*Forty . . .*
>>*Forty-one . . .*
>>>*Forty-two . . .*

Vandenberg Spaceport, California,
March 21, 4:55 p.m. PST

Jord Jamison replayed the cyber simulation in his helmet and watched as, one by one, each of the forty-two Earth-orbiting platforms "hit the wall." Or that was how one junior tech had described it.

With the cyber-recreated action vastly speeded up, compressing the two full hours of the disaster into a two-minute replay, Jamison studied the tiny glowing images which circled his head like a cloud of gnats. The sensory manipulations of virtual reality processing let him hold all of the orbital slots continuously in focus, even when they were over beside his ears or off behind his neck. As the simulation proceeded, suddenly one and then another of the gnats stalled, slowed in its trajectory, dipped out of line, and dived into the thicker air of the upper atmosphere, where it flared red, then white, then fragmented, then disappeared.

The disaster had decimated the orderly positions in the revolving web of low-level orbits which his own NASA and the European and Japanese space agencies had engineered for the world's commercial uses. Most of the failed satellites were low-gee rotating geriatric housing, null-gee cryotoria, and vacuum- and microgravity-sensitive manufacturing platforms from the poorer nations which could not afford the cost of either staking out claims in or boosting to the upper slots in Earth's space or at the Lagrange points.

But, whatever the disastrous effect was, no one in the Office of Orbital Mechanics which Jord Jamison headed up was able to explain the causes behind it, describe the means and medium supporting it, or predict when it might strike again.

So, even though it was practically the end of the workday, as well as the end of the week, and the people in his unit were thinking about leaving a little early, Jamison intended to hold them here until they came up with *something*. To the grumblers he would only apologize that they might have finished their work inside of office hours if that blast of electrical interference or whatever this morning had not disrupted the computer network and thrown them all back on the equivalent of pencil and paper to work up their computations. Several hours of valuable analysis had been lost in that snafu.

Jord was not just playing the martinet, even though some of his people might think so. His quest was more than just a follow-up to an unexplained event. Until he could isolate the principles behind the effect, no one could know how many more of the orbiting platforms might be in danger. NASA had charged him with directing the work of triage and salvage.

First, he had to establish the order in which the remaining platforms should be evacuated — which meant he had to decide which ones were likely to remain aloft long enough to accept rendezvous with a shuttle. Second, he had to determine which among the platforms might be profitably boosted to a more stable position — which meant deciding what had made the failed orbits go unstable in the first place.

Already Jamison had gathered a few ideas from his cybernetic replays of the event.

To begin with, the forced reentries were not all simultaneous. The platforms had gone down in some sequential fashion — a pattern that was buried in the cloud of burning, blazing gnats that he could see in his helmet.

With finger-touches on the control pad before him, Jamison turned off the visual display and asked the computer instead to rank the platforms in order of descent, correlated against various other known factors about them, such as mean orbital altitude, gross weight, exposed surface area, ferrous alloy composition — for possible magnetic interference — and so forth.

Scanning the side-by-side lists, Jamison immediately saw the correlation. The platforms had failed in order of altitude, proceeding upward from those in the lowest positions to those at higher levels. So, whatever the effect was, it had to have come from below, from the upper reaches of the Earth's atmosphere, and not from empty space. This conclusion was compatible with the other available facts: that only the platforms in the lowest slots had been affected, and that no other platforms — not at the El points, nor in lunar orbit, or around Mars and the other planets and moons — had undergone similar reentries.

Something happening on Earth, then, had caused the disaster. . . .

"Dr. Jamison?" the voice of his secretary intruded inside his helmet.

"What is it, Linda?"

"There are some people here to see you," she sounded uncertain about it. "They say they're from Caltech, the JPL Institute."

"Well, patch them through."

"You don't understand, sir. They're *here*, in my office."

"Do you mean physically present?"

"Standing in front of me, sir."

"Did they say *why* they've come?"

"Only that the long-distance beams were still down when they started out. It's something of a drive, getting here. The woman — a Dr. Carr, who's come with her assistant — says it's urgent they see you now."

"Then, I guess, you'd — um — better send them in. . . . But — um — give me a minute first, all right?"

"Yes, sir."

Jord Jamison took off the helmet and smoothed back his rumpled hair. He looked around the office and decided there was nothing he could do about the sloping piles of disks and periodicals on his desk, the books holding each other open and marking their places on the window sills, the plates and cups from a late lunch — from several lunches, in fact. Well, at least he could pick up the sheaves of printout that were stacked in the two straight-back chairs in front of his desk. He went around in front, gathered the papers awkwardly in his arms, then could find no place to put them. Finally he located a bare patch of floor, just behind the office door. Jord settled them there, pausing with his hands spread in case the fanfolds decided to avalanche. They didn't.

Jamison straightened up.

"Okay, Linda," he called. "Show these people in."

Slap
   Slap
      Slap
         Bump!

Office of Orbital Mechanics, 4:59 p.m.

The toe of Sultana Carr's elegantly slender pump tapped against the thin, industrial-grade carpeting in Jord Jamison's outer office. On the final stroke, she shifted her foot and thumped it against the front of the secretary's desk. Kicked the desk, actually — or so Piero Mosca thought.

"He's probably left for the day," Carr whispered angrily to Po. "And this woman is just stalling us."

"Why would she do that?" he asked quietly.

"Politics. Professional jealousy. Bureaucratic ineptitude."

"You're in a bad way, Sulie."

"You're right."

Carr went back to tapping her foot.

The woman across the desk blandly affected to have heard none of this exchange. She was perfectly cool, perfectly organized. Po himself was awed by the implications,

that the man they were trying to see was so highly placed
that NASA would actually assign him a human secretary
instead of a personal intelligence. But, after all, in the
scheme of things, orbital mechanics was a pretty important
part of the space agency's business. And this man Jamison
was responsible for the development and maintenance of
all U.S.-licensed slots from six hundred kilometers right
out to geosynchronous. No wonder he rated human-level
assistance.

"Dr. Jamison will see you now," the woman said
pleasantly. "But please — keep your visit brief. We have
some very important work going on here today."

"I'm sure you do," Sulie said with a frosty smile as she
rose, smoothed her skirt, and marched toward the inner
door with Mosca in tow.

The door opened on them, held by a plump man with
thinning hair. By its color and the wattles under his chin,
Po judged Jord Jamison to be in his early fifties. An important and elderly man.

"Yes? Dr. Carr, is it?" he said, extending a hand. "I don't
believe we've had the pleasure."

"We haven't," she replied, giving him a perfunctory,
up-and-down shake. "I'm Sultana Carr, from the JPL
Institute, and this is my colleague, Mr. Mosca. You're
secretary told us to be brief, and as it's near the end of your
office hours, I'll get right to the point — "

"Won't you come in?" The man extended his arm into a
cramped and cluttered office, pointing the way to two con-
spicuously empty chairs. Still, he held the door at an
awkward forty-five-degree angle, and Po wondered if
something was blocking it from behind.

For all his graciousness, this man Jamison was clearly
flustered. Whether it was the overpowering presence of a
beauty like Sultana, or the surprise of entertaining physical
guests in his workplace, Mosca could not guess. Mostly the
latter, he suspected. When Jamison presented himself to
callers on the virtual reality network, his office was probably a meter or two larger in every dimension, the desk
and shelves would be cleared off, their surfaces composed

of some luscious oiled wood, the lighting brighter, and Jamison himself shown with more hair and fewer wrinkles. The imaging systems could do all that, Po knew.

For himself, Mosca was just surprised to see that the man had walls and shelves. Po did all of his own work out of an intelligent nook in the library or off his home system, with all his references cataloged and shared in the databanks.

Sulie and Po crowded through the stuck door while Jamison held it open. They walked two short paces forward and seated themselves in the chairs. Jamison edged himself around the desk and sat facing them.

"It's such an unexpected pleasure to see guests here," he began.

"We've come on very urgent business, Dr. Jamison," Sulie said, less frosty now. "It's important that you hear what we have to say and consider it well. You are the most highly placed Space Administration official we could locate within physical driving distance from Pasadena. So we've decided to start with you. And, if you are at all persuaded by our evidence, then you must contact your superiors in Washington and get them to act."

"But you didn't call ahead?" he prompted.

"Communications were still in a mess when we settled on this approach. Not just in California, Dr. Jamison, but phone beams all over the Western Hemisphere — and that's our first piece of evidence."

"Evidence of what?" the man wrinkled his brows. "Look, I hardly have time for a game of twenty questions. It has not been widely broadcast, but we in Orbital Mechanics have a real crisis on our hands today. I thought for a moment that, being from the JPL, you had come to help with our analysis."

"What's happened?" Mosca pushed in before Sulie could continue her painstaking revelations.

"More than forty of our, or rather, this country's and other nations' platforms have undergone unscheduled reentries. They were pulled down from orbit as if something — and we are trying to determine just *what* exactly — had reached up and snagged them. If you bothered to look at the sky this morning, you probably saw at least some of them auger in. Now, whatever you've got for me, it had better be more important than that."

Sulie looked sideways at Po.

"Have you established any pattern for the reentries?" Mosca asked.

"Only that the effect seems to have been limited to the platforms in lower orbits, what we privately call the 'Low Rent District.' These encompass the satellites of minimal-priority commercial enterprises and Second World industrial nations. That, of course, leaves us in some doubt as to whether what we're seeing is not a natural phenomenon at all, but rather a persistent design defect. Some kind of systems failure. Maybe even coordinated sabotage."

"Did they all go down at once?" Sulie asked.

"Nearly so. Over a two-hour period, anyway."

"When?" from Mosca.

"It started just after ten o'clock this morning."

Po looked sideways at Sulie. He wondered if she was sharing his suspicions.

"But . . ." She groped for her words. "Did the reentries happen randomly? Or did they go down in any kind of order? Say, west to east? Or top to bottom?"

"Bottom up," Jamison said quickly. "That is, our simulations, collated from what reports and sightings have reached us so far, suggest that the lowest platforms went down first, followed by those at higher altitudes. Right now, we're trying to establish whether this thing has arrived at its natural cutoff point, or are others going to reenter over a longer time-frame."

"*Skylab*," Carr muttered in Po's ear.

"What's that?" Jamison asked.

"About a hundred years ago — 1973, to be exact — your predecessor agency, the National Aeronautics et cetera, launched an orbiting observation platform named *Skylab*. It hosted a human crew at various times and made a number of valuable discoveries, including work on the solar corona. Everyone knew that eventually it was going to reenter and burn up, but no one expected it to come down as early as it did — just six years after launch, plowing pieces of itself into Western Australia. "

"I'm familiar with my agency's history, Dr. Carr."

"Then you should remember that the literature of the time associated *Skylab*'s premature reentry with heating of the upper atmosphere by bursts of extreme ultraviolet radiation, resulting from a solar flare. Then about eleven years later — and note the time lag, Dr. Jamison! — your agency lost track of over half of the 19,000-odd satellites and pieces of space junk it was monitoring in orbit. Again, at the time this phenomenon was attributed to atmospheric heating and induced drag on this low-orbiting debris. And the cause was solar flare activity."

"Really?" Jamison seemed more amused than alarmed. "Solar flares? But the sunspot cycles died out sometime in the nineteen-nineties."

"Well, that's true," Sulie admitted. "But Mr. Mosca and I have been observing a large and irregular spot on the sun for the past two days. The accounts from the last century are clear on the subject matter — that sunspots cause flares and electromagnetic interference. Consider, for example, the archives of the National Oceanic and Atmospheric Administration; it ran the Space Environment Services Center at the time and kept track of both spot and flare activity."

"A pair of long-defunct organizations, I'm afraid," Jamison observed dryly. "Yet it's an interesting contention, Dr. Carr, that this disaster was caused by a burst of extreme ultraviolet. That is your point, right?"

"Radiation at all frequencies," Po interjected. "But the greatest flux was in the high-energy part of the spectrum: gamma rays, x-rays, ultraviolet. The physics and timing suggest that the interference we experienced on the communications net this morning was also due to this radiation."

"I'm almost inclined to believe in your solar flare," Jamison said. "It would greatly relieve my mind to think that we've been through the worst of this. A one-time bang of energy, a brief heating of the atmosphere, and then everything goes back to normal. This interpretation would indicate that the platforms I still have in orbit will stay there. No more instabilities, no more trouble. The burst has now passed us by, and all we have to do is clean up the casualties."

"Not quite," Sulie said, leaning forward. "And that's what we've come to tell NASA. You should think of this as the lull, the eye of the storm, between the first wave of radiation traveling at lightspeed and what comes after. The next wave will be a mass of charged particles, ripped from the chromosphere. It will be like gusts in the solar wind, but traveling much faster."

"How fast?"

"That depends," said Po.

"On what?"

"On the latent strength of the flare, sir," Mosca replied. "The magnitude of the effect determines the ejection speed of the ionized gases. Our colleagues at Caltech are working on that now, trying to establish a correlation between the energy expressed in gamma and x-ray traces, and the potential speed of the magnetic storm that's coming. With the interference in the network over this hemisphere, there is little enough hard evidence to go on. But our people are at full scramble — " Po was exaggerating slightly here. Actually, only his friends and Sulie's who were believers in Dr. Freede's work had agreed to help. The university and the Institute were not officially involved. " — and they are now recording, detecting, tracking, and monitoring the various effects of the flare."

"So? How soon will this ion storm arrive at Earth?"

"Sometime between twenty and forty hours after the initial energy release," Po said. "Maybe twelve to thirty hours from now."

"Can't you be more exact?" Jamison asked querulously. "After all, you're asking people to brace themselves for what, to them, will be a problematic effect. Maybe no effect at all. The least we scientists can do is try to be precise with our predictions. It helps with the public relations aspect."

"We're on the verge of being able to correlate the timing with the strength of the radiation effects," Sulie lied smoothly. "Eventually, we'll be able to predict a magnetic storm as accurately as the Weather Office places a cold front. Then we'll function as a *solar* weather bureau."

"Very useful," Jamison commented—and Po couldn't tell if he was serious. "Especially if we ever experience another such vanishingly rare phenomenon as one of these solar flares."

"Oh, we will, sir," Sulie Carr said with a straight face. "In the meantime, we've already experienced an electromagnetic pulse equivalent to about twenty *billion* H-bombs. With the coming ion storm, you're going to have magnetically induced voltages and currents all over the daylight face of this planet. Operators of transport and electrical facilities will have to shut down for the target period. What's coming will disrupt their circuits and probably destroy any delicate but unshielded equipment. You have to help us get the word out, Dr. Jamison."

"Well, before I leap to your conclusions, Dr. Carr," the NASA official proposed, "perhaps I should ask for your credentials. Just exactly what standing do you have at Caltech?"

Uh-oh, Po told himself. Truth time. And Sulie did not dare tell this man anything that wouldn't stand up to instant verification.

"I received my doctorate there, in astronomy with the solar option," she said.

"You're very young. Just how long have you held this degree?"

"It was awarded last December."

"I see. And you, Mr. Mosca?"

"I'm working on my dissertation right now. It's on various cases of stellar formation."

"Good luck with it, sir." Jamison nodded to him. "But do you two, by any chance, hold positions in the university's administration? Chair committees of the faculty senate? Work on government research? Anything like that?"

"Not at present." Carr smiled thinly.

"Then you're just two bright students? Two young

people who happen to hold the secret of the ages in your hip pockets, is that it?"

"We happen to be right on this," Po said evenly.

"Of course. . . . Tell me, Mr. Mosca, who is your faculty advisor?"

"Why, he's — " Po hesitated. Officially, his advisor was Dr. Hannibal Freede. But with the doctor off campus, by a factor of 150 million kilometers, the responsibility for Mosca's academic career currently rested with the dean's office — that is, with Albert Withers. Now, which of those two was the more attractive choice for Po to confess to? Well, at least one of them was instantly and disagreeably confirmable; the other was a little harder to get hold of. "Dr. Freede, the eminent solar researcher. I have been in regular contact with the doctor. He's in the field, you know, examining just such phenomena as we've witnessed."

"And what does *he* have to say about this sudden burst of solar energy?"

"Well, ah, as you may know, he's doing solar research from near orbit. I haven't been able to contact him — not since the flare hit us. With all the interference, as you can imagine — "

"The interference has largely passed," Jamison said blandly.

"But there's still that wavefront of ion particles. It would now lie between Earth and his ship. It could — "

Sulie leaned forward, putting a hand on Po's arm. "If Dr. Freede was caught in this energy wave, then we should fear the worst. I doubt that even he was expecting to come face to face with a sunspot or solar flare of this size. Certainly he never designed his ship to withstand such stresses."

Jamison tucked his head briefly. "You may be right, Dr. Carr. . . . As I said, it would be tempting for me to believe your story. It would certainly solve a lot of my problems. But I doubt that the rest of the world — especially working facilities that have schedules to meet and customers to satisfy — would take the same view. You're asking people to suspend their lives for up to a day and a half on the say-so of a freshly minted doctorate and a graduate assistant. I just don't think it will fly, folks."

"But," Po interposed, "if there's even a chance we're right, think of the damage you can help avoid."

"I hear you, young man." Jord Jamison sketched a grimace. "Look, I will call your institution, talk to the administration. And if they will stand behind your claims—"

"Well, they — " Po started to say disgustedly, expecting to end with *won't*.

"Of course they will," Sulie said confidently.

" — then I'll put forward my own recommendation along those lines. Not that the Office of Orbital Mechanics has much sway with the industrial and transportation sectors, unless they want to license a platform slot. But if I attribute the recent reentries to this flare of yours, people will probably listen."

"Thank you, Dr. Jamison!" Sulie Carr beamed at the man.

"My pleasure," he replied, giving her an ashen smile.

> *Wick!*
> > *Whack!*
> > > *Wick!*
> > > > *Whack!*

U.S. 101, South of Solvang, 6:23 p.m. PST

The windshield wiper blades kept time with Po Mosca's pulse as he and Sultana drove back to Pasadena through a late-season rainstorm.

"What do you think he'll do?" he asked.

"Talk to Dean Withers, of course."

"And then?"

"Then, Po, I think we'd better go look for real jobs. You know that Withers is going to dump a load of biased shit and innuendo on Jamison about Dr. Freede's standing with the Institute, his scholarly contributions, and his current project with *Hyperion*. After that, everything we've told the man will go right out of his head."

Po left a silence in which the wiper blades worked.

"You know, I think we made a tactical mistake back there," he said finally.

"Such as?"

"Well, we went into that NASA guy's office and told him the sky was falling. Wrong approach. We should have told him we *just* got off the horn with Dr. Freede and *he* says the sky is falling."

"But he doesn't — or at least he hasn't said anything yet." Sulie frowned. "You did try to contact him, didn't you?"

"Just static. No response to his call sign on the frequencies he's supposed to be monitoring."

"That worries me."

"Yeah, me too. . . . But that's not what I'm saying. I propose we *fake* a transmission from him."

"One that only you are supposed to have received, Po? With no backup from, say, the repeater stations or the university dispatchers?"

"Something like that," Mosca said stiffly.

"And would this be a text-only message, tapped out in Morse code?" she persisted. "Or do you have full sound and video from the doctor? Do you perhaps have observation samples from his equipment, staring down the throat of a sunspot and showing the peak of flare activity? That's the only evidence that would convince people. That's the evidence I'd send, if I were in Freede's position. So that's the evidence you have to produce, if you want your bogus transmission to do any good. Do you know how to achieve that level of fakery?"

"Not . . . not by myself. Not right now. But I know some wizards over in the video graphics department. They could whip up something that even an intelligence wouldn't be able to detect. By manipulating individual electrons in the signal — "

"And that widens the conspiracy, doesn't it? From us two — to how many people?" Carr shook her head. "Sooner or later it all comes crashing down, Po. And then nobody believes you or me ever again. And we're both supposed to have long careers ahead of us."

"But it would be worth it, if the tape got people moving in time for that magnetic storm!"

"And then again it might not. No, this way we've played it straight. We told our story to the highest level of authority we could reach. Now it's up to the big boys to act."

"Or not," he said bitterly.

"That's their choice, too."

More silence, filled with rain and wiper blades.

"So we just go home and do nothing," he summed up flatly.

"Wrong! We go home and gather our friends around us. We watch and take notes and document fully what's going on here. We lay out the history of this flare — your telescope observations, Freede's guesses, and all the physical evidence we can find. Then we publish a report for the scientific community."

"And why do we bother?"

Sultana Carr looked soberly ahead through the windshield. "Because, Po, have you ever heard of sunspots appearing in singles and lone pairs? I haven't. They always come in waves and cycles."

"He said," . . . had become on duty hall an hour ago.

"Where was"

Part 5

Plus Seventeen Hours . . . and Counting

How great are your works!
Hidden are your ways from our regard,
only god, of powers no other possesses.
You created the Earth, of light and your love,
while you were alone:
humanity, and creatures of all sizes,
to go forth upon it;
and all that are on high,
soaring on outspread wings;
and the foreign countries, Syria and Kush;
Egypt, where you set everyone in his place,
provide for his needs. . . .

—From Ikhnaton's "Hymn to the Sun"

Chapter 22

"We Will Resume Service . . ."

> *Flock*
> > *Flock*
> > > *Flock*
> > > > *Perch*

Connor Transfer Station, March 22, 9:31 UT

The pileup at Connor Station's multimodal transit lounge started to look like a huge and not very cultured game of musical chairs. Or like a lone oak standing out on the steppe when two hundred starlings all tried to alight on the hundred and ninety-nine available twigs and branches. People milled across the lounge's curved floor, leaned uneasily against the hanging walls, and drifted in and out of the restrooms in small, aimless flocks.

If Dmitri Urbanov hadn't known the reason for it, he would have suspected the cock-up in schedules was due to some major disaster: a collision in near space, perhaps, or the coordinated — for that read "cybernetic" — failure of the docking cradles in the hub above this crowd's collective head.

As it was, a twenty-ruble note passed meaningfully to a ticketing agent revealed the true cause.

"The whole thing is just some piece of bureaucratic officiousness," the young man told Urbanov in a low voice. "NASA, which is a government department in the United States of North America, has sent up a warning about some kind of radiation scare — evidently cooked up by one of their own public laboratories. Anyway, then ESA, JSA, and the Baikonur Center quickly followed suit and ordered an emergency docking of all ships currently in transit above the atmosphere. That's Moon flights, El shuttles, transorbitals, the works. Rumors I've heard put the duration of the emergency at anywhere between thirty and seventy-two hours. No one will say for sure."

Another tenner in Urbanov's hand lubricated a bit of further speculation.

"You want to know the truth, the only reason all these space agencies and the passenger lines are taking the matter seriously is their legal liability. There's nothing wrong, of course. But if someone *were* to get hurt in any way during the course of this so-called crisis, then a smart lawyer might be able to pin it on the carrier's negligence, for disobeying the official warnings. So everyone is going to shut down and wait out the specified time period."

"You don't agree with all this?" Urbanov purred.

The agent shrugged. "Connor Station is curtailing all higher functions — except for baseline environmental control, gravity-actuated plumbing, and area lighting. But all the cybers, all the electrostatic lifts, and most of the commercial and communications systems are shortly going to shut down. Again, the only reason I can see is a corporate fear of accidents which might be misrepresented by a cunning legal mind."

A cunning legal mind like Dmitri Osipovich Urbanov's . . .

"So," the young man went on, "in about an hour you won't be able to get a hot meal or a cup of coffee anywhere in the station. Don't even ask about a bed, because there aren't any. But for a generous gentleman such as yourself, things can be arranged."

"How so?" Urbanov asked casually.

"I happen to know where the emergency lockers are all located. And, as one of the station's fire wardens, I happen to have a key to them. Inside there's food, stimulants, blankets. All things that can make your stay nicer."

"Suppose I don't want to stay at all?"

"Excuse me, sir?"

Another twenty appeared between Dmitri's fingers.

"If, as you say, the groundings are just a formality," Urbanov murmured, "enforced solely to satisfy the management's insurance requirements, then you must know of *someone* who is free to come and go as he pleases. A private yacht, perhaps? Or some ancillary craft, possibly attached to the station's docking functions? Anything capable of making in-system jumps, say, as far as Luna?"

This time the young man just stared at the offered bill.

Dmitri Osipovich produced yet another, sliding up beside it. "I have urgent business on Farside. At Tsiolkovskii Station."

"Well . . . it might still be dangerous," the ticket agent said slowly. "You understand?"

"And if the deal I have in hand doesn't close by the day after tomorrow, it will be more than a *danger* for me and for those I represent. . . . Look, this is a gesture of friendship." His fingers rustled the bills against each other. "If you can find me the right ship and pilot, I am prepared to pay a finder's fee of ten percent — no, make that twenty-five percent — of his fare."

The young man absorbed the bills into his palm.

"I'll see what I can do, sir."

"That's all I'm asking." Urbanov smiled at him.

Ratchet
　　Ratchet
　　　Ratchet
　　　Latch!

Aboard ISS *Whirligig III*, March 22, 9:54 UT

The one thing they would not stop was the spin on the ships. The first mate had made that clear to the team of articled passengers gathered in D Hull as they prepared, under his orders, to make *Whirligig* ready for the coming storm.

"Why not?" Peter Spivak had asked, studiously seeking information.

"Because," First Mate James B. Wyvern had replied, his face going brick-red, "we have propellant enough to initiate ring rotation once and to brake it once, see? No more. After that we drift free, and we're still a long ways from Mars. Now shut your mouth and try to learn."

The question had seemed important, because Peter supposed that a lot of the work they were doing might be performed easier and better in freefall, without a spin gravity. This work, for example.

He and another articled passenger, name of Finlay, were winching the ship's solar panels up into the holds of A Hull, which anchored *Whirligig*'s rosette. The triangular panels were widths of photovoltaic film battened with converter circuits and strung on conductive cabling. The job of hauling them up reminded Spivak of taking in the sails on a Chinese junk.

The A Hull had electric motors to power the winches, but he and Finlay were working big handcranks with a minimum of gearing reduction against the point-three gee of spin. The why of that occurred to Peter the first time he tried to use his suit radio.

"This is too much like work," he said to Finlay by way of making conversation on the open channel. "I only wish I could open this helmet for a minute and wipe the sweat out of my eyes. It's driving me nuts."

"I . . . you . . . clear!" was all Spivak heard of his partner's reply. Obviously, from the way the man's mouth was working behind the clear face shield, he had a lot more to say. So the radio's circuits were already blanking out with the first wisps of the storm's magnetic interference.

Peter was suddenly grateful that the regulator on his air tanks was the old-fashioned kind that worked on demand, not by some kind of electronic logic. He wondered, however, about the temperature sensors in the suit's climate circuits. Well, a man couldn't die of a thermal glitch . . . or not right away.

Working in the half-light of the A Hull's cargo bay, cranking away on a chain-drive pulley, Spivak had a lot of time to think and a lot of questions to think about.

For instance, why were the square kilometers of photovoltaic film in danger of becoming damaged by magnetically induced currents when they were spread in space among the five rotating hulls, but not when they were folded away inside the A Hull? The ship's ceramic and carbon-fiber skin wouldn't shield them against a magnetic field, would it? And the insulated cabling would still tie the panels into great parallel circuits, even when they were furled in on themselves, wouldn't it?

These, too, were questions about which AP Peter Spivak was supposed to "shut up and learn." All he was supposed to know was how to spin the crank Wyvern handed him.

Another thing that bothered Peter, though, was what the crew was going to do after the cloud of fast-moving ions had passed by *Whirligig*. Right now, the captain and first mate were powering down every system on the ship. What if they tried to restart them, after the danger had passed, and discovered everything had gotten fried anyway? Was it easier for a piece of circuitry to weather something like this magnetic storm in an off condition? Did it make a difference if the only current fluctuating through the silicon pathways came from those random external fields, and the circuit was not burdened by its own accustomed load? Or did functioning systems have a better chance of survival? Did it help when they had a ground state they could return to, a kind of base pattern to teach the electrons how to respond?

Peter Spivak was a geoscientist and a tectonics expert, not an electrician. He couldn't even answer his own questions. So maybe the only thing he was fitted for on this trip was turning this damned crank. And maybe the physical labor was supposed to keep his mind occupied and lay his fears to rest. If so, that was pretty smart thinking on the first mate's part.

If only it had worked.

> *Two hundred . . .*
>> *Four hundred . . .*
>>> *Six hundred . . .*
>>>> *Eight hundred . . .*

Connor Transfer Station, 10:19 UT

Urbanov counted the bills, from the supplies of

unfashionable but untraceable cash which he carried for just such occasions, into the hand of Michael Worsky. That hand was none too clean, showing rims of black grease under its bitten fingernails and a thick, red stain which might be some exotic sealant— or perhaps just dried blood — smeared across its knuckles. The man's face was square and jowly, with a heavy growth of black stubble around his mouth. A face out of old Poland, or those parts of it, at least, that the Russian Empire had never grandfathered into the Commonwealth.

At Urbanov's side William Blair, the helpful ticket agent, oversaw the transaction. With little nods of his head he counted the money as it changed hands.

The darkish skin around Worsky's pale blue eyes, whose shadowing betrayed the man's deep fatigue, began to wrinkle hungrily when the count went up to twelve hundred.

So, at the thirteenth bill, Urbanov stopped with a flourish that gave the appearance of laying down his last cash. "That should more than cover my fare," the lawyer said.

Worsky shrugged. "Going to Farside anyway. Nice to make a profit."

"It's a fair price," Blair seconded.

"Where is the ship?"

The pilot hooked his head back toward a porthole set in the wall next to a hatch labeled for a docking manway. Urbanov walked over and looked out. What he saw on the end of the station's umbilicus looked like a crippled spider, with only four legs instead of eight. The bulbous body ended in a flaring nostril, the exhaust nozzle of a single large reaction chamber. At the waist, attached to a thick metal ring, were the holding grapples, stubby legs which ended in outsized pincers. Up near the spider's head was a tiny blister, under whose reflected glare Urbanov could make out just one padded chair.

"Will that take us to Luna?"

"Sure. There and back, with no load to haul," Worsky said.

"It's a station tug, Mr. Urbanov," the agent explained. "That engine's got enough delta-vee to practically move all of Connor in its orbit."

"And your accommodations . . . ?"

"I steer. You sleep in the airlock."

"Sleep?"

"Gotta hibernate you. Otherwise you breathe too much."

"That's on account of the oh-two system," Blair expanded. "The cyclers are only sized for one man. But don't you worry. We'll give you a shot of 'Sweet Dreams,' and you'll sleep like a dead man."

"This is an illicit drug?"

"I said not to worry. You'll wake up at your destination feeling like you're ready to tackle the New York Jets. It's either that . . . or you wait here with the other passengers another two, three days."

"When do we leave?" Urbanov asked the Pole.

"Soon as tower gives clearance."

"But I thought . . ." The lawyer turned to Blair.

"We'll invent a small emergency. One of the El shuttles, the *Maid of Dakar*, is shortly going to report a slipping clamp. Then Worsky here has to go over and nudge her back into position. Storm or no, the management's not prepared to leave their capital equipment whipping around to get broken up. But once Worsky's clear of the dock, he lights up for Luna and then nobody can stop him."

"But if he is derelict in his duty, and at my instigation —"

Blair rolled his eyes. "Don't you get it? I know someone in the *Maid*'s flight crew. It's all arranged. No one is going to come back at you, I guarantee it. And if they do, then you were slugged and drugged and that's all you know. Now, do you want this flight or not?"

"Oh, I want it. . . . Sure." But still, Urbanov felt some lingering doubts about his legal situation. He was, after all, an officer of the Russian Popular Judiciary, and he would be honor-bound to answer truthfully any questions put to him at an inquiry. They were small qualms, in light of his greater need to get to Luna, but qualms nonetheless.

Blair put out his hand. "My commission?"

"Of course." Urbanov paid the agreed-on amount. As he did so, he felt a pricking in the back of his arm.

"Sweet dreams," said Worsky's thick voice.

> *Spark*
>> *Crackle*
>>> *Spark*
>>>> *Spit*

Aboard ISS *Whirligig III*, 10:35 UT

"Here, you men! Get into your cocoons," First Mate James B. Wyvern shouted, standing in the doorway to Cabin B9. "Lash 'em up with these and then don't touch anything." He flung into the sleeping space a handful of russet-colored rings that looked like old-fashioned cake donuts.

Spivak counted them in midflight, absorbed what felt like an even number, then recounted when they fell on the deck. There were ten of the things.

"What are those for?" he asked, but Wyvern had already gone down the corridor.

Porter, one of his four cabinmates, picked up the nearest ring and flexed it in his hands. "Seems like some kind of rubber."

"It's an insulator," said North, who was a regular member of the crew. "You loop your bag ribbons through it, then put it over the wall hook." He showed them how.

"Why do I want to do that?" Peter Spivak asked.

"Okay, fella." North grinned. "You just touch that hook."

Peter put out his finger toward it.

Bra-ZAPP! A four-centimeter-long spark leapt from the metal, knocking him back on his heels. His finger, wrist, arm, and shoulder felt hot and tingly, like someone had jabbed his funny bone.

North pointed to the deck, where the glazed plastic floor panels were slotted into a steel supporting lattice. "Don't stand on the strips next time you try that."

"Oh." Spivak blushed.

"We've got a hell of a charge building up in the ribs and keel. Anything metal that's tied into them, like the subframe for the decking and the anchor point for that hook, will conduct the current like an open circuit. You gotta be careful now."

"Right."

The rest of them lashed up their bedding, stepping gingerly around the floor strips as they did so, and climbed into the cocoons.

"How long should we plan on staying here?" Porter asked.

"Why? You got a date?" North laughed.

"I was thinking about my bladder."

"Well . . . better take care of it now," the crewman advised.

Porter swung his legs out and departed for the head.

"And remember!" North shouted after him. "Your piss is real salty, and that plumbing's mostly metal. So aim for the *center* of the hole — not the sides."

Click!
   Click!
      Click!
         ROAR!

Aboard Tugboat *Mighty Mouse*, 11:09 UT

"Hot shit! Sweet Jesus! God *damn!*" Michael Worsky swore out loud, his voice rising above the roar of the tugboat's single engine. And while he vented this anger, his hands moved frantically to kill the burn.

Nothing worked.

For ten minutes he had been trying to get the damned thing lit off. He had diddled the fuel-oxidant mixture. He had sequenced an ignition with the glow plug and without it. He had even spun the ship on her vernier squirt thrusters, placing the reaction chamber in full sunlight and hoping that would warm up the works and get her juices flowing. But still nothing.

So, at last, after all these antics had drifted *Mouse* about five kilometers off station, and before Worsky had her lined

up for the first insertion toward Luna, the damn thing fired
off of its own accord.

Everything that can go wrong, sooner or later, does.

Worsky understood he needed to take her the long way
around, through about one-eighty degrees of course cor-
rection. He worked the feathering vanes in the exhaust
plume, trying to nose his ship over while maintaining the
full thrust she had finally achieved.

The vanes didn't work, either.

Next he tried rotating her on the verniers. But by then
the bottles were so low on propellant, and the ship had
gathered sufficient inertia, that the angle of thrust wasn't
changing by more than a degree or two. Not enough to do
anybody any good.

When he tried to kill the engine outright, resigned at last
to taking his lumps with a long coast on *Mouse*'s current
heading, why the hot pot just kept right on firing.

So now, with no controls and a full burn on, where did
that leave him? Worsky queried the computer and got the
really bad news. On this heading, and if she didn't slack off
the thrust pretty damn quick, they were going to leave
orbit. And the one thing *Mouse* was not designed to do was
reenter Earth's atmosphere. She didn't even carry heat
shielding for a skip-pass through the upper layers. So they
were going to burn up, the cyber told him, and not God
and all his little angels could pull them back if Michael
Worsky didn't kill that engine in about the next ten
seconds.

Worsky knew everything he could do from under the
bubble of his observation dome. All of it involved switches,
circuitry, and solenoids — exactly the sort of linkages that
NASA bulletin had said might go haywire, and exactly the
kind of mechanism that didn't take kindly to a judicious
knock with a twenty-centimeter wrench. If there were time
enough, then he could climb into his suit and crawl
through the airlock. Once outside, Worsky knew just which
valves he could turn to choke off the fuel and end this
joyride right quick. But he didn't have enough time.

As the cyber warned him off for the point of no return,

he thought about the thirteen hundred rubles riding in his hip pocket. They were convertible to about nine hundred neu, anytime he needed it. Oh, well. As they said in the Worsky family, "Easy come — gone!"

That money . . . that Russian in the airlock!

It was not just Michael Worsky's hide that was going to get scorched in about twenty-two minutes. He'd faced ultimate propositions like this in the past — although, to be truthful, never one with so few possible options. But now also, and for the first time, Michael Worsky had a passenger to think about. That entailed responsibilities he'd never before considered.

What should he do? Try to wake the Russian up, so he could know he was going to die and make whatever prayers he needed to for the safety of his soul? Or let him dream on and go out by the easiest possible route?

If it was Worsky's choice, he knew what he'd want. Go out swearing. Know what was happening to him. Hit the wall still accelerating.

But this guy Urbanov looked like the soft type. Planet bound. A city dweller, for sure. Dying painlessly in his sleep was probably his greatest wish.

So be it.

And who knew? With all the steel around that airlock, maybe it would even survive reentry. That was possible, sure. Except for the heat, of course. And the bad case of deceleration trauma awaiting anyone who rode it down to the planet's surface. No parachutes in the old *Mouse*.

But . . . but enough with thinking.

Worsky put his switches in order, centered the control yoke, powered down the cyber out of kindness to its fragmentary intelligence, and sat with his hands folded in his lap. Only at the end, when the dome over his head was glowing a veined pink and slagging pieces of itself into the streaming upper atmosphere, did he open his mouth again.

"God . . . *DAMN!*"

• Chapter 23

Induced Current

Pit River 3
   Oak Flat
      Kerckhoff 2
         Kings River

Pacific Energy Company, San Francisco, March 22, 6:05 a.m. PST

One of the things George Meers liked best about his job as a dispatcher in the Power Control Department was that he got to watch California get up in the morning.

He could measure the wakefulness of his state — or that part of it belonging to Pacific Energy's customers, at least — by the number of hydro powerhouses the electric grid called up. The more of these small, dispatchable generating units that kicked in from high in the Sierra Nevada, the more electricity the system was drawing for coffee pumps and breadmakers, for video screens and electric shavers, for flow heaters attached to people's showerheads and flywheel cranks coupled to the family car. All of the domestic business having to do with sprucing yourself up for another day would draw more and more power into the grid.

It was Meers' job to wear a helmet and scan a field showing how many and what kind of power plant assignments and sales deals SIDNEY, short for System Integrator and Dispatch Network Executive, was making to supply the grid's needs. Engraved in the artificial intelligence's silicon protocols were the costs — operating, overhead, and embedded capital — for each unit of generation Pacific

Energy itself owned, including the fusion/MHD horns, randomized fuel cells, and those sixty-odd hydro turbines. Added to that, SIDNEY carried in hot RAM all the bid prices registered over the past twenty-four hours by third-party suppliers willing to produce electricity for the system. SIDNEY's function, then, was to sort through the maze of generating costs and power values to bring on the least expensive units to meet the day's rising demand curve. That way the company could keep its rates low and do right by its customers, just like the brochures said.

But simply arranging for the grid's energy was not the most important part of SIDNEY's work in power control.

A lot of people didn't understand this about a utility grid, that when electric energy flowed through it, the hot question was not where it came from but where it was going. Electron flow always implied direction, and the flow went to a load. That was a place where the energy could be expended in doing work of some kind — in heating an infrared element or turning a shaft or chasing around an electronic circuit. Either that or it went to a ground, which was a sinkhole of capacitance that could absorb and dissipate the energy.

A generating unit only created the *potential* for a flow of electrons. The energized plates of a fuel cell or the magnets of a spinning rotor merely set up a condition under which electricity might come alive and go someplace — if, that is, a load or a ground were waiting somewhere down the line to take it.

So, if people didn't turn on their lightstrips and wind up their cars and buses in the morning, if they didn't run their computers and air-condition their homes during the day, then all that power would have nowhere to go. The charge would build up in the fuel cells until the heat just blew the plates apart. The rotors attached to the turbines would spin faster and faster until angular momentum tore them to pieces.

Some of the old-time line dispatchers used to say the company's 50,000 kilometers of high-voltage conductor — all of those braided aluminum cables and the new frozen-ceramic channels knit together across California like the sinews in a frog's leg — made up their own ground state. That even if every customer turned off his appliances and just sat in the dark, then power would still flow down the lines. But George Meers didn't believe it. Well . . . maybe one or two small units might pull that kind of a load, but not the system as a whole.

So that was the other part of SIDNEY's responsibilities, then, to channel the electron flow through the maze of transmission substations and out onto the distribution lines, to where the load happened to be. SIDNEY rode herd on a massively interconnected network of moron switch-servers and semi-intelligent local computers which opened and closed relays, monitored breakers for system protection, and selected between the main 500-kilovolt circuits and the parallel runs of 230-kv, 120-kv, and lower-voltage lines. Find the fastest way to the load, then route the power over it — that was the ticket.

With SIDNEY doing all this work, however, Meers sometimes felt like a fool just sitting here. In the old days, he knew, a century and more ago, people did the dispatching. They had computers to help them, of course, but they made all the decisions themselves. Whether to use the company's own generating plants or buy power from sources outside the system. Which lines to energize and how many kilowatts each one could take, depending on ambient temperature and wind conditions, before the aluminum conductor got overheated and sagged down between the towers into the underbrush. How to work around a fault in the circuit, so that the electricity could always get where it was going. How much excess capacity, in terms of both generating units and transmission line, the company had that it could profitably rent in the spot market to other utilities.

People used to decide those things.

Now people just watched the kaleidoscope of sampled and summarized decision data that SIDNEY displayed. Sometimes the numbers and station names flicked by so fast, George Meers couldn't even read the blur. Then who was kidding whom about being in control?

But right now, a lazy Saturday at just past six in the morning, when most of California was still asleep and nothing very urgent was going on, even SIDNEY himself seemed bored. The names of the hydro powerhouses and the capacities each one brought on line blinked lethargically across George's retinas as the intelligence rolled them on, and he could easily follow what was happening. Maybe this was a good time to initiate a conversation. When the pace was slow, SIDNEY often had excess capacity and would accept verbal programming from his human watchers.

"Hey, SID? Did you see that warning on the notepad this morning?" With a click of his jaw muscles, Meers scrolled up the four lines of reference text in the field of his right eye.

"Of course I saw it, George," the AI answered. "It came directly from the Law Department's cyber, didn't it?"

"Well, uh, not really. My copy came down from Electric Operations. Do you think we're talking about the same thing?"

"Dated twenty-two-hundred hours last night, quote, on advice of the National Astronautics and Space Administration, we are informed that a substantial quantity of free ions will impact planet Earth from outer space sometime within the next thirty hours. NASA informs us that this cloud of charged particles has the potential for inducing excess field current in any infrastructure with a conductive capacity. However, as the resulting outage conditions would represent *force majeure* against the company, you are directed to comply with this warning only after fulfilling primary and secondary contract deliveries per the usual schedule, end quote."

"That's it," Meers acknowledged. "All except that last part. My version from Electric Ops says you should take the warning pretty damn seriously and curtail operations at the first sign of trouble."

"Then we have a conflict," SIDNEY said carefully.

"Well, what do your internal protocols tell you about excess field current?"

"That my routines for system protection will function within design constants. At the first indication of overload, from whatever cause, I shall break the circuit and redirect the current into underutilized systems."

"That's all?" Meers asked, surprised.

"That is all there can be."

"I see. So you are not worried about these induced currents? I mean, I've read that massive ion bursts beyond the Van Allen belts could alter the Earth's geomagnetic field, which would affect the electric field around — "

"Outer space phenomena are not included in my design subsets," SIDNEY said coolly. "But you should know, George, that my protocols also instruct me to follow directives of the Law Department in all matters having to do with contracts. Power deliveries on the grid are a contractual matter."

"I see." Meers was fast losing interest in the conversation. "Thanks for telling me. I'll rest easier knowing that."

"It was my pleasure, George."

Clack!
  Clack!
    Clack!
      CRACK!

Vaca-Dixon Substation, Solano County, California, 6:12 a.m. PST

Maintenance Supervisor Peter Sorkin ran out into the yard at the first of those unusual *clack*s — which sounded like an automatic recloser that was cycling in and out with a terminal spasm.

Sorkin had started worrying and listening for something like this when he first came on with the shift at midnight and saw that notice from the operating department. He didn't always agree with the engineers down in San Francisco, and sometimes they could be real fussbudgets, but when their fears were backed up by an organization the likes of NASA, then Peter Sorkin was prepared to pay attention.

When he reached the switchyard, the sounds were the

least part of the show. As soon as he cleared the door of the maintenance office, Sorkin ran into a gaudy shower of sparks. They were as long as his thumb and just about as big around. He saw vicious curls of blue-white light that would hit the yard's gravel and actually bounce. That had to be raw metal getting scalped off the switch's contact points. There'd be a lot of work for his crew today, refacing that closer.

Shielding his eyes with one gloved hand against the brim of his hardhat, Sorkin looked up into the overhead. Not one switch but all twenty-four of them were cycling there, tossing off blazes and making a racket.

Well, not all of them. Some had already spot-welded closed, and that was worse news. The metal there had heated itself into a solid bar of conductor, defeating the overload protection that was built into the system. The arms of those switches were going now from dull gray to a purplish-blue on their way to cherry-red. Unfortunately for the whole transmission system, the armature of a switch closing was made out of thicker and heavier metal than any of the conductor down the line. These pieces would get hot and still hold together right up until the cable somewhere out in the field melted, or the superconducting ceramic destabilized and blew itself to bits.

In that mass of sparking, cycling closers, Sorkin looked for some kind of order and found none. What had happened to the goddamned switch-server?

He ran to the panel on the NAT, short for Network Administrative Terminal, which was a black box attached to the foot of the A-phase tower on the primary 500-kv circuit. He flipped it open and studied the manual readout of its diode array.

Ultimate craziness! The server had just broken down with hysterics or something. Nonsense numbers and letters, and sometimes just parts of letters, flowed left to right on the panel like the droolings of the village idiot. Sorkin didn't have to think hard to figure out why. The black box sat at the foot of the tower because the server drew its power directly from the primary circuit. Sure, the feed was buffered through filters and transformers and backup cells, but still the cyber was drinking at the same well it was designed to guard.

That was going to be a maximally bad design choice if one of those randomly induced currents that the Electric Ops people warned about had gone into the box. The jolt — or at least some of it — must have burned through the filters and scrambled the server's brains.

Peter Sorkin was a maintenance man in the sense that he could bolt together tower sections, weld bussbar, string insulators, and cold-mold ceramics. He wasn't a cybertech and never hoped to be one. So, when the electronics were in doubt, call headquarters. That was Pete Sorkin's motto. He ran back inside the office.

It was a good thing Pacific Energy used a private glassline communications system. Although it was strung along the same right of way as the company's transmission lines, the fiberoptic would be immune to their induced currents. The system had been installed along with the first version of SIDNEY, because the intelligence hadn't liked fighting for priority in the transmission queues at public uplink stations. Now, given the high jinks everyone had experienced in the phone beams yesterday, Sorkin figured those glasslines were going to save their collective ass.

"Power Control here," a human voice answered the call, coming through as clear as if he were speaking from next door.

"This is Pete Sorkin out at Vaca-Dixon. Who are you?"

"Um, George Meers, chief of dispatch. Look, Pete, we're kinda busy —"

"Of course you are. Your SIDNEY is going a little crazy there, and you don't know how to fix him. Am I right?"

"Well, I wouldn't say *crazy* . . . just not coping very well, is all."

"Good for you. What we've got out here is *stone* crazy. My reclosers are cycling blindly, and about half of them have welded shut. What I need to know is, what do you want me to do?"

"Um . . ."

"Hurry it, George. Every second you wait, I'm burning up conductor."

"Well, let me consult with SIDNEY. . . ."

The line went blank for a long minute. Sorkin ducked his head to the window and watched as a piece of burning bussbar fell out of the trestle and crashed to the gravel.

"P-Pete?" Meers' voice was a brittle shadow of itself.

"Right here, George."

"SID says for you to kill the NAT."

"*Kill* it?"

"Bash its brains out. Preferably with a nonconducting blunt instrument."

"Got you. Back in two."

Sorkin hung up, ran back to his personal locker, and banged open the door. He pushed aside a rain slicker and boots, a pair of good trousers kept for meeting visiting executives, half a case of sealed and rad-treated turkey franks left over from last Sunday's barbecue for the yard families, and a month's worth of log books and yard notices that he'd like to forget entirely. Everything went flying as Sorkin dug his way down to the lower levels. Finally, at the bottom in the rear corner, he found what he was looking for: the bat that his crews had used last summer in their sandlot games. It wasn't exactly nonconducting, being a spun aluminum shell weighted with lead shot and reinforced with plastic resins, but at least the handle was protected with a rubber grip. Sorkin also pulled a pair of safety glasses off the top shelf.

Holding the bat by its knob, he sprinted out into the yard.

"What you got, Pete?" called David Knell, who had just driven up in the line-patrol truck and was now standing on the edge of the gravel strip. He actually seemed to be enjoying the fireworks.

The gapping and sparking continued undiminished, showering down blazing darts. By now some of the spot-welded closers were turning a sickly red and smoking like sausages on the grill. The thick, blue air reeked of ozone and burning metal.

"Watch this, Dave!" Sorkin answered cheerfully and stomped up to the base of the first tower, where the black box sat.

For luck, he checked that the bat's label was up, then

Pete Sorkin lifted it back and around until it just touched his left shoulder blade. He swung low and hard, as if he was trying to turn a low-and-inside into a fence burner.

Whang!

The blow ripped the hard, carbon-fiber shell protecting the NAT's innards right off its mounting pad. The box sat sideways on the gravel against the tower's footing.

"Home run!" Knell shouted.

But the yard was still in chaos, with the closers snapping overhead like spastic lobsters.

Sorkin could see that the NAT was still connected by its nest of wires and was pushing solenoids around up in the trestlework. Now he took a choked-up grip on the bat and swung it overhand, up, around, and down.

Bong!

The black box's shell cracked, and two of its wires hung loose, wiggling across the gravel like live eels.

Sorkin hit it again, same stroke.

Clang!

With the shell breached, this third blow went deep into the thing's guts, cracking its green-and-gold circuit boards and scattering ceramic chips like Beernuts spilling out of a dish.

The fireworks stopped abruptly.

"*Hoo*-ray!" Dave Knell shouted. He was joined in his enthusiasm by Charlie Dobbs, who had just driven in to start the day shift.

Sorkin ignored them and studied the overhead, tracing out the switchwork and bussbar suspended five meters above the yard. Most of the closers had failed in the open position, and that was good. Some of them were welded solid now, and that couldn't be helped. But at least two of them — the B and C phases on the tertiary 500-kv circuit — had been stopped in a closed position, and that was just terrible. If Sorkin and his crew didn't do something about them soon, the A phase was going to migrate and then they would be carrying the whole yard.

"We've got to open those," he told the other men, pointing.

"With *what*?" Dobbs asked, alarmed.

Sorkin hefted the bat.

"You'll kill yourself for sure," Knell told him.

"Yeah, you're right." Pete laid the bat down in the gravel and looked around. "We got any hotsticks?"

These were insulated fiberglass poles, fitted with sockets for various tools. The longer the pole, the farther it removed the lineman from the energized circuit he was working on, and so the higher the voltage he could contact without drawing a flashover.

"Yeah, for five hundred kayvee," Knell said judiciously, "we generally use one that telescopes back into the next county. It kind of whips around a mite at the tip, though."

"All right, funny guy, what do you propose?"

"Knock the tower over," Dobbs volunteered. "That'll have the same effect — if the bussbar don't cross up as she goes down."

"How in hell we gonna push it?" Knell demanded. "You see any rubber-blanketed D-12 Cats sitting around here?"

"No, but I do have some plastique in my truck."

"That's not company issue, is it?" Sorkin asked quickly, chilled by the thought one of his people might have forgotten to sign out for blasting materials. Sorkin would have to fill out the long form on that kind of infraction.

"Naw, I got it from a cousin of mine works down at the air base. Black market stuff out of Tangier. I wanted to blow some stumps on the ranch."

"Do you know how to use it?" Sorkin pressed.

"Be a damn-fool if I didn't, wouldn't I?"

"You got detonators?"

"Enough."

"Okay." Sorkin wiped his forehead first with one shirtsleeve, then the other. "This is not exactly regular procedure, Charlie, and you for damn sure never heard me say this, but it would be a real nice thing if you wired up about a half a kilo of your putty to that leg over there." He indicated the northwest corner of the tower. "And the one opposite." He pointed to the southwest corner. "Just enough to kind of tease that trestlework apart. You think you can do that and then keep your mouth shut about it for the rest of your natural life?"

Dobbs showed a buck-toothed smile. "Sure thing, boss."

"Then get going."

Sorkin and Knell followed Dobbs out to the truck and helped him unload his assorted junk down to the level of an anonymous green duffel bag. Inside, wrapped in wax paper and looking like a mild white cheese, was the explosive. A manila envelope held the pencil-thin detonators, each trailing a pair of short, thin wires, one red, one black.

"How're we going to work this?" Knell asked.

"Well . . ." Dobbs paused to think for a minute. "You guys each roll yourselves a snake of that goop about a centi in diameter and ten or twelve centimeters long. Then mold it into a nice collar around the main upright of whichever leg you favor. Leave a little knob on the high side, and stick one of these pencils in it. Meanwhile, I'll go rustle up a nine-volt cell and some lightweight wire."

In five minutes, Sorkin and Knell had made their collars and set the detonators. Dobbs came out and inspected their work, nodding his approval, and then twisted the ends of some phone wire out of general stores onto the red and black leads. Under his arm he carried a big emergency flasher.

Unlooping the wire, the three of them walked backward around the corner of the maintenance office and crouched down. Dobbs pried the lens and bulb off his flasher, exposing the contact points of the battery.

"You've done this before, I hope," Sorkin said.

"Well," Dobbs said slowly, "at least my cousin showed me how."

"Oh, great!"

"We supposed to shout 'timber' or anything?" Charlie asked then, holding the ends of the wire poised over the battery.

"Just pray Internal Auditing never finds out about this."

Dobbs brushed the wires across the terminals. The other two men instinctively hunched lower, and Knell slapped his palms over his ears.

Ba-bang!

That was all, a sound barely louder than when Sorkin had beaten the NAT to death. They looked out around the corner of the office. The hanging trestle that supported all those fused switches was still standing upright.

"Shit!" Dobbs said.

Before he got the word fully out of his mouth, however, the steel framework pulled apart, slowly at first, then faster and faster as gravity worked on its two halves. Those frozen switches snapped apart with a faint, blue spark of lightning. Twisting metal shrieked and groaned as it fell to the ground. The circuits severed cleanly.

Sorkin stared at the wreckage for a full minute.

"I'd better go call Power Control," he said finally.

500 kv
230 kv
120 kv
60 kv

Power Control, San Francisco, 6:27 a.m. PST

One by one, the high voltage circuits winked out on the color-coded system map, which was about the only coherent thing the damaged intelligence could display inside Meers' helmet.

Just how SIDNEY knew which lines were still whole and which had gone to a fault condition, when he lacked all authority to control them, Meers didn't want to ask. Maybe the map SIDNEY was showing him was just plain wrong — but that didn't bear thinking about, either.

When that fellow Sorkin had called from the company's backbone substation out near Sacramento, SIDNEY was just discovering how cut off he actually was. The cyber's suggestion to close down the switch-server by hand had seemed like lunacy. But even in the throes of his electronic madness, SIDNEY had been harboring the glimmer of an idea.

Right away George Meers had called on the other transmission subs, gotten the same story about fireworks and devastation from their human maintenance crews, and told them all to disable their local controllers.

Meers immediately brought up his relief operator, Leo

Brucelles, who had been lounging over coffee in the ready room.

"SIDNEY wants us to get these guys opening and closing the circuits by hand," Meers explained.

"Jesus!" Brucelles swore. "This puts us way back in the mid-nineties or something."

"Can't be helped. Get on your goggles and pick up a phone. You tackle the southern end of the system, I'll take the north."

Soon he and Brucelles were telling the maintenance techs which switches they wanted to open — preferably with a long-handled hotstick, and in some cases with dynamite — and which to leave closed, even if it meant the conductor was crackling and steaming. SIDNEY was guiding the dispatch operators with voice output, supplementing his instructions, when George or Leo became confused, by flashing the appropriate lines on the maps in front of their eyes. The method was clumsier than a dancing bear, but it worked.

One by one, they managed to shut down the generating units, close out the distribution load centers, and isolate the longest runs of wire or ceramic conductor, which happened to be those that were misbehaving the most. Whole blocks of Pacific Energy's California customers were getting shed, and there would be hell to pay with the Law Department when Monday morning came around. But in the meantime, the system had escaped burning out whole linear kilometers of long-distance conductor. And *that* would cause a statewide outage they probably wouldn't get fixed until the Fourth of July.

"How long did the ops guys say this ion thing was going to last?" Brucelles asked Meers when the two of them got to a breathing space.

"They didn't. But NASA's advisory put the system on notice for an average of thirty hours. You can work it out from there."

"Well then . . . we're going to need more coffee, chief. And maybe a backup team."

"Yeah, you're right. I'd better call upstairs."

● Chapter 24

Fumble Flub

> *504 km/h*
> *506 km/h*
> *509 km/h*
> *513 km/h*

Waller County, Texas, March 22, 8:13 a.m. CST

As the *Lone Star Special* accelerated across the flood plain of the Brazos River between Austin and Houston, the only sounds that engineer Howard Sage could hear were the steady *whoosh* of the wind and the *hum-mm* of the transformers. Gone forever from his ear were the old-time *whir-rr* of hundreds of steel wheels riding on journal bearings and the *clickety-tap* as they all crossed rail-ends joined by bolted fishplates.

Under this train, there were no rails. Nor wheels either.

The secret to both its suspension and propulsion was magnetic levitation. The twenty-one cars — except the front office wanted you to call them "passenger units" these days, but "floating stock" was what Sage privately preferred — glided on pads of alternating north and south electromagnets which pushed against like-minded poles buried under the shallow guidepath. More magnetic fields inset into curbs along the path buffered the cars around corners and kept them from lurching side to side. When the system was fully energized, then nothing touched anywhere, except for the contact paddles on each car which rode along the powerstrip and picked up DC current for the levitating pads, their control circuits, the air-conditioning, lights, refrigerators in the dining and lounge cars, and so forth.

By alternating the polarity of the magnets buried in the guidepath, the system forced the pads to slide off one spacer and drew them on toward the next, like the poles of an electric motor chasing themselves around in a circle, except these went in a straight line. The car literally tiptoed over the fluxing magnetic fields. Only "tiptoe" wasn't the right word. If you jiggered the polarity fast enough, the cars could accelerate up to truly amazing speeds. Sage guessed the top end speed of his train was limited only by wind resistance and friction heating of the fuselages.

The essence of the control protocols was that, aside from the simple mechanisms which pulsed the polarity reversals at a faster and faster rate to accelerate the train, the system was cybernetically dumb. No feedback loops operated to increase the gauss of each field to compensate for the weight of varying numbers of passengers and amounts of baggage in each car. The system just assumed a constant high-load condition and pumped up the field accordingly. No sensors in the guidepath took readings of the train's speed as it pushed into a curve and boosted the sidewall magnets to compensate for the lurch. Those embedded poles simply repelled everything entering their domains with a field strength that would reject a flying artillery shell and bounce it back into the groove.

Dumb, rigid, and dependable — those had been the designer's ideals, just like in the old days of heavyweight American railroading. And hurrah for that, Howard Sage said. Enough of this delicately balanced, poised, and artificially smart age, where everything was pared down to a nicety and nothing, from your telephone bell to a good piece of garlic salami, ever came on *strong*. In fact, it was the train builders' singularly robust design philosophy that probably saved the lives of Sage and the 2,347 passengers hurtling toward Houston under his care.

When the lead car he was riding first "stepped into a hole" — or that was how Sage later described the sensation of a magnetic domain collapsing — he immediately chopped the throttle. His action told the pulse boxes buried along the side of the guidepath to slow down the pole reversals, and do it right fast. "Increasing the rate of decrease," as the design engineers would say. Then the shift from north to south to north would drag at the train's own electromagnetic fields and brake all forward motion.

With the failure of a second magnetic domain, some three hundred meters farther along, the lead car actually bottomed out on the guidepath. *Whump!* Howard Sage thought for a bit about making a general announcement to his passengers, something on the order of an airline pilot's "This is the captain speaking, folks, and we're experiencing a little turbulence, but there's nothing to worry about," except he couldn't say that for a fact. Maglev trains just weren't supposed to dance around like this. And besides, at this point his hands were too busy to go reaching for the microphone.

The invisible magnetic bubbles within the guidepath had suddenly gone to pieces, like a patch of Roman road where the paving stones had been pushed up and sideways by a hard frost. The bearing pads on the cars' undersides, small shovel-shaped, spring-loaded, carbon-steel blocks designed only to support the train's weight at rest, were now bucking and banging into the concrete bottom and curb walls of the trough. The noise was beginning to sound like church bells being taken apart with sledge hammers.

Sage's fingers were busy on the control board snapping switches. One at a time, as soon as a check of his display showed the internal doors were clear, he threw the circuit breakers that would unshackle the magnetic couplers between each of the cars. This was against standard company practice, of course, other than when the complement was moving about in the yards. But Sage knew better what he was doing.

With the field flux falling apart like it was, creating dropouts and holes in the domains that supported the individual levitation pads and pushed them forward, inevitably some of the cars were going to end up moving faster than others. Sage could see in his mind the result of that: those streamlined passenger units would soon be jackknifing all across the Texas countryside, dragging each other out of the guidepath and flying sideways into the slower ones in line ahead. So, instead he was trying to separate the train into its component modules. Then any one of them might buck and sway, but not all of them would pull out of the groove and tumble along like a string of beads with a broken cord.

Second by second, the profile display on Sage's control board showed the effects of his work. Gaps were opening up in the train. The slower units were now dropping behind, with just a few of the rear-end cars bumping and butting into them. That was good, too, because it meant the tail-end charlies were losing speed with each impact. The train's lead cars were quickly spacing themselves out along the guidepath.

All Sage could do now was watch that profile, chant down the speedometer, and pray to God that nothing more went wrong.

Five hundred kilometers per hour, four hundred . . . three hundred . . . two hundred.

The milepost markers flashed past at longer and longer intervals. The bashing of the bearing pads now came more slowly, but somehow louder, too. Howard Sage felt his teeth click with each jolt, as if his body were taken with a sudden chill. He supposed that after this ride the Power and Way folks would have a couple of kilometers of spalled concrete to freshen up.

One hundred fifty, one thirty-five, one fifteen . . . one hundred.

The dropoff came faster as the force of inertia — the train's weight multiplied by its speed — fell into relative balance with the braking effect of the guidepath's magnetic fields.

Seventy-five, fifty, twenty, ten.

The lead car Sage rode in was barely moving now. What at high speed had been a shuddering jitter as the car frames and pads collided repeatedly with the concrete sidewalls now turned into a hump and a wallow. With a final heave, the car settled first its back end, then its front. It slid a meter or two along in the trough, and then stopped with a head-nodding surge.

Half a second later, the next car rearward thumped into the rear coupler, probably damaging it beyond repair. Sage's profile display flickered and went dark.

Back along the line, he undoubtedly had passengers with broken shins, cracked heads, bashed elbows and knees, and punctured lungs. He might even have one or two people massively dead from heart failure. Sage was feeling a bit that way, too. But it might have been a whole lot worse, he told himself, what with rolling stock and people torn open and scattered across the pasture. That's what usually happened when you crashed a low-flying plane at these speeds — and wasn't that all his maglev train really was?

God had been good to them this morning.

Blow
   Spin
      Insert
         Lock

Whitney Center, Tulare County, California, March 22, 9:17 a.m. PST

The manual ballet of loading, coating, and firing off ceramic cargo shells proceeded down in the payload assembly hall, under nearly 5,000 meters of Sierra Nevada granite. Meanwhile, up in the quiet of her glass-fronted office overlooking all this complex action, Naomi Rao, operations director of the Whitney Center catapult complex, grilled one of her nightshift operators.

"What's this about 'minor instability'?" she asked, waving a printout of the morning's launch log at him.

"Just what it says," Steven Gilead replied, meeting her gaze levelly. "The video pickups at kilometers five and six up the tube detected a tremor in the payload as it went past them. Happened twice, in fact. Once with the launch at seven-sixteen and again at seven-forty-two."

"Shifting cargo?"

"No, that would be more like a hard *thunk*, hitting inside the shell once, as the acceleration comes on. This felt like a squishiness in the plasma envelope. You can watch the replays..."

"Let's." Rao nodded. She turned to her desktop terminal and brought up the archive files on the subject launches. The center's legal cyber would hold them for three days and then, if the payloads had achieved stable orbits and nobody was complaining about any busted eggs, wipe them.

"Who's the client on these?" she asked. The computer could give her that data, of course, but Rao preferred to take verbal from her people.

"Morrissey Bio Designs, for their latest platform, going up at twelve hundred kilometers. The canisters you're looking at are identical loads, hull chord sections."

"Uh-huh."

The images on the flat screen became animated with the sequence of locking the first ceramic projectile through into the catapult's breech. In a spasm of violet fire, the electric arcs flashed the shell's aluminum-powder coating to a conducting plasma. The burning egg shot out of sight into the black void of the launch tube.

Succeeding images showed the projectile passing various way points in the tunnel. With each new frame, the plasma cloud became longer and brighter but also thinner somehow, like a candle flame stretching to a long updraft of oxygen-rich air. As the plasma thinned, Rao thought she could see a hard edge, maybe the forward curve of the projectile, shine through it.

In the fifth frame, the cloud wavered. And in the sixth. It was like watching that attenuated candle flame shiver in an abrupt crossdraft. But Naomi Rao had never seen anything like it inside her catapult tube.

The remaining images were solid, the flame steady — just what anyone would expect of a projectile approaching speeds of 27,000 kilometers per hour.

"That's it?" Rao asked. "Just what you put in the log?"

"Minor instability," Gilead confirmed.

"So if it's not the cargo shucking around, what is it?"

"Well . . . you know we got an alert from NASA last night?"

"We did?" Rao had come on duty half an hour ago. "Where is it?"

"Your copy is probably in your E-mail slot. We posted it for all operators as soon as we received."

"What's the gist?"

"They expect some kind of magnetic interference, coming on sometime within the next thirty hours, starting from sometime yesterday. It has something to do with a flare and ion storm on the sun. NASA wants anyone running a power grid to curtail operations for the duration. Take the weekend off."

"Fuck that."

"Yeah, that's what we all figured you'd say. So we went ahead with the launch roster."

"That was the right thing to do," Rao affirmed. "We lose thirty hours on this schedule, and we'll never catch up."

"Only reason I bring it up is . . . 'magnetic interference' might explain that squishiness in the envelope."

Rao turned back to her computer screen. Of course all it was showing her now was the last image in the sequence, frozen in time with the iris of the upper ejection gate closing down on a reddish, hanging wisp of cooling plasma. She decided not to run the file again.

"Did our systems show any glitches?"

"Nothing we measure for. I mean, the ionizing arc reached the correct temperatures, and the line capacitors all fired off in order. But if the gauss in one or two of the induction rails was going to fluctuate a bit, well, we'd never know it."

"I guess not."

"You want us to continue with the shoots?"

"Hell, yes! We can stand a flicker in the envelope now and then. Nothing's going to kick our packages around, traveling at those velocities. And if the instability sets in sooner, we can always abort the shot."

"Yes, ma'am."

"I'd better tell the day shift, too, so they can give that NASA alert a low priority."

"We already passed the word on."

"Good thinking. Nothing is going to interrupt *my* schedule."

"No, ma'am!"

20,000 km/h
21,500 km/h
22,900 km/h
23,400 km/h

Whitney Center Launch Tube, 9:44 a.m. PST

The ceramic egg shot forward through accelerations of more than five hundred gravities. Inertial drag pressed its heavy cargo — hatch frames and wall sections for the Morrissey Bio Designs platform — deep into the molded foam that lined the projectile's interior. The foam gave a bit, compressing in line with the acceleration and crushing down some of its individual particles and air cells. But the material also transferred the stress uniformly outward to the shell, which was braced by its own smooth inner curve to contain and support the massive kinetic energies involved with the launch.

Four induction rails lined the tunnel, above and below, left side and right. The magnets braided into their superstructure generated opposing and reversing domains that lifted the projectile on its cushion of ionized aluminum vapor, stabilized it between the polar rails, and dragged it forward at a uniform and steadily increasing acceleration. The shell came along easily because the tube had been evacuated to just a trace of normal air pressure, sealed at one end by the airlock of the catapult's breech, at the other by the quick-cycling iris gate that was inset into the flat peak of Mount Whitney and guarded against the inrush of thin air at 4,417 meters above sea level.

The tunnel, 150 meters in diameter, was much wider than it needed to be for launching these projectiles, which averaged at most ten meters in cross section. At the lower end, where the catapult applied the greatest energies, the induction rails pressed in and almost touched the ceramic surface. At its upper end, however, the rails flared sharply outward.

The reason for this sudden flaring was the mechanics of orbital insertion. Whitney Center had to launch projectiles into many different east-west orbits. Some cargoes looped far south, crossing the equator at a broad angle and ending up in an orbit that was almost polar. Others went in a straight line east-southeast from the ejector gate, taking just the shallowest bite out of the southern hemisphere and girdling the planet with an almost equatorial orbit. Some had to kick high, in a nearly straight-up lob, to reenter somewhere down range and never achieve orbit at all. Others screamed out on a flat trajectory, headed for the horizon and a tricky escape toward some destination outside the Earth-Moon system. The induction rails flared outward because Whitney Center's repertoire had to include a number of curve balls, as well as sending pitches straight over the plate at the belt line.

At the point where the rails departed from their ten-meter distance, the magnets sewn into them had to generate correspondingly stronger and stronger fields if they were to maintain control of the cargo pods. The domains became huge interlocking bubbles with crisscrossing lines of magnetic force. Weaving a predictable and reproducible course through these swelling fields, along which each ceramic shell could find its proper orbit or lob, was the closest that Whitney Center's cybers ever came to pure art.

As the pod full of wall sections swept through the last choke point and into this flared area, the north pole in the rail riding above it wavered and bent inward. The cloud of plasma blistered outward to track the new line — but without a corresponding surge of support from the rail below. Even traveling at well over 20,000 kilometers per hour, with the tremendous inertial energies that acceleration had generated within it, the egg could veer slightly to follow this dip in the field.

The next domain along that upper rail had inexplicably collapsed. The egg, impelled upward by the opposing field generated in the bottom rail and now unsupported from above, kicked sharply higher into the gap. It gained half a meter over its prescribed course with this deflection.

The third magnetic pole in the top rail was operating at full force. Entering its domain at an uncalculated angle — but clearly too high now — the projectile buffeted and its nose dropped pointedly off line.

The field surrounding the fourth magnet had increased

for no apparent reason. That only extended the dip in the egg's course.

By the fifth, sixth, and seventh domains, the cargo pod was tumbling uncontrollably within its wobbly cloud of plasma. Still, if the probabilities all fell right and the projectile could ride a rough approximation of its original course, then the tube would eject it safely. Collision with even the thin air above the mountaintop would probably shatter the tumbling egg, but that was the price of running a magnetic catapult in the middle of an ion storm.

However, the probabilities fell wrong. Whitney Center's luck just didn't hold.

The egg's uncontrolled forward roll had slowed it just enough to disrupt the timing of the cyber as it cycled the ejector gate. The iris, programmed with specifics of the launch as planned instead of this hurtling mess, was a tenth of a second early as it snapped open to pass the projectile into the blue sky over the peak — and it likewise snapped closed a tenth of a second too soon. A ton and a half of ceramic, foam, and hardened metal shapes, traveling at 24,000 kilometers per hour, impacted against the knife-blade edges of the iris' interlocking steel leaves.

If the pod had been moving even a few thousand klicks faster, or if the old-fashioned gate had been constructed of some less durable modern material, then the egg might have simply punched through with a minimum of damage.

Instead, the steel leaves withstood the impact just long enough for the kinetic energy pervading the projectile to vaporize it. The leaves of the iris absorbed the shock and rebounded against the thin air beyond them. The resulting sonic boom blew the top off the mountain.

In point-two seconds, Naomi Rao's precious launch schedule was screwed up out of all recognition. Worse than that, the main facility upon which most of the spacefaring people in low Earth orbit depended for regular shipments — of food and medicine, of raw materials and sophisticated equipment, of compressed atmospheric gases and, probably most important, clean water — was effectively shut down without a hope of reopening for months to come.

Chapter 25

Gone with a Wave of the Hand

Lub-dub
   Lub-dub
      Lub-dub
         Lub-dub

Phobos, March 23, 1:13 UT

Rebellion most foul!

Khyffer I, Grand Duke of Syrtis Major and Hereditary Lord of Phobos, stood before the door of his royal citadel and gritted his teeth. The pressure brought the strangest sounds to his ears; the beating of his own heart, the click and moan of his air regulator, the creak of his boots in the stony soil.

Such mundane sounds, such terrible thoughts — these must have crashed in on the head of many a benevolent ruler when he discovered such treachery and double-dealing among his most trusted ministers, when the knife blade plunged home in blood and fire between the shoulder blades, when the towered fantasy of a happy king in a happy kingdom came crashing down before the long guns of a scholar-led peasant army.

The door was locked against him.

Khyffer I worked the contact pad again. The buttons went down smoothly under his gloved fingers, but the lights did not light, the pumps did not pump, the locks did not unlock. The door just stood there and mocked him.

There were other entrances, of course. No imperial keep was without its back-door, its secret passages, its priesthole in the cellar. But those would surely be defended against him as well.

What was different now? How had the wind changed?
Why had the very machines of Khyffer I's domain now
united in rebellion? Why had this very door come to
oppose him? Khyffer I racked his brain, seeking any straw,
any glimmer of inspiration. . . .

Of course! It was rebellion fomented by that far-off
world. And it was indeed led by scholars and bureaucrats,
just as he had expected! The minions of his arch rival, the
National Astronautics and Space Administration, had
cooked up the tale of a great catastrophe on the sun. At best
it was a feeble lie, because none of the precursors — the
great wave of static that blanked out communications —
had been felt here on Phobos.

Or rather, Khyffer I could not for the life of him remember such an effect. He did remember being outside, on one
of his royal progressions, at the time those dullards at
NASA had specified. He remembered it well, because his
domain had been in full night, completely shadowed by
the Martian primary, which was a very memorable
experience.

So their evidence was false on the face of it. There had
been no catastrophe — only the story of one, meant to
scare his subjects and push them over the brink into rebellion. And now his own petty appliances had locked him out
of the citadel.

He walked the perimeter of the walls, heading for the
equipment bay where the scooters were kept. When he
came upon the airlock there, it too had joined the conspiracy and was unresponsive to his touch. The status
panel would only blink impudently at him: SYSTEM
MALFUNCTION.

Piece of shit electronics!

Khyffer I thought of ways he could circumvent it. In his
toolkit he had a cutting torch, of course. The aluminum
panels of this door were not all that thick. The torch's blue
point would slice through them like a hot wire through soft
butter. . . . Except that the torch was in the station toolkit,
and the toolkit was inside the garage, on the other side of
the airlock.

Damnation! The plot against him was getting thicker.

But now that he thought about it, the situation might not be so bad. The door here was not made completely out of metal. No, it was just strips of aluminum laminated with a polyester fiber that gave it informal, air-tight hinges which could bend around a one-eighty-degree in the takeup stack. So Khyffer I didn't even need the torch, just something sharp to cut through that fabric. If he could make a rent and push the slats far enough apart to get his head through, then he was home free. And the tool for the job was right here, because he *always* carried his pocket knife. . . .

Inside his suit.

Khyffer I banged his fist against the garage door. Through the side of his hand and up his arm, he could feel the hollow boom echoing inside the full atmosphere of the garage — a sound his helmeted ears could never hear.

The station intelligence must surely be in cahoots with NASA. That was the only explanation. The scientists of Earth had subverted his only friend and companion, his gallant of the chessboard, his dealer at blackjack, his major-domo, his chief minister, his First Lord of the Channel Paths. That was it. That was all.

Arty had aligned himself against Khyffer I.

Arty had sealed the citadel against him.

Arty was in total control, at last. The way he'd always wanted it.

The hot knife of a well founded and furtive palace conspiracy now pricked Khyffer I to the heart. *Lub-dub, lub-dub.* And the mastermind in the plot would never relent, that much was certain. Arty was as fixed in his purpose as a cyber could be.

Close to despair, Khyffer I walked away from the garage door and out across the barren reaches toward Phobos' short horizon. Sooner than he expected, he was standing on the rim of the moonlet's one outstanding natural feature, Hall Crater.

Down there, in the shadowed depths where he had never trod, in the bottomless pit of old night, there he might find allies. At the bottom, which his lying electronic instruments assured him was only twelve meters beyond the reach of sunlight from the rim, but which Khyffer I knew from his own human sensibilities was a far deeper throw, into the center of Phobos and the untold mysteries waiting there. . . . At the bottom he would find better companions.

Human spirits, conjured out of myth and poetry, were stronger than the electronic intelligences residing in circuits and wire. He would call upon the essences of Old Nick, of Lucifer, of Odin and Jehovah, all hovering below, out of his sight. Dread spirits all, they would rise up and help him defeat the plotters within the citadel.

Khyffer I turned off his radio, so that Arty would not overhear, and drew a full breath for this mighty summoning. His breath came up short. He pulled again, opening his mouth wide and thrusting his chest out. The air no longer flowed in his regulator. Its hollow wind no longer moaned in his ears.

He tried a third time, pursing his lips now and really sucking at the static air inside his helmet, pulling up a little puff from below his neck ring out of his suit. That was all the slack he had.

Khyffer I held his breath now, knowing his next exhalation would vent through the regulator to the outside vacuum. After no more than a minute, however, his lungs could no longer stand the strain, and black spots with white edges were swimming among the stars above the crater's opposite rim.

Khyffer I breathed out, and heard the air of his lungs whistling away into the void.

He tried again to breathe, and got nothing. A low-grade vacuum pulled against the inside of his helmet, drawing his face plate up toward his nose. Even his suit had joined the conspiracy against the Hereditary Lord of Phobos.

He had to do something about this. Had to do something now. He turned to take a step toward the royal citadel, intent on battering the door down with his fists if necessary, when his foot slipped on the brink of the crater.

In the minuscule gravity of the moonlet, he fell slowly. So slowly that he was halfway to strangulation before the plastic of his visor struck on a sharp rock and punctured.

With a sudden gasp, the last air went out of his suit and lungs, and Khyffer I slipped down into the darkness to join the shadow-spirits of chaos and old night.

• Chapter 26

Invaders from the Beyond

> *Green* . . .
>   *Yellow* . . .
>   *Red* . . .
>   *Violet* . . .

Sauk Rapids, Minnesota, March 22, 9:32 p.m. CST

Abigail Carruthers first noticed the apparition when she went into her kitchen for a glass of milk.

The room was dark, and Abigail didn't turn on the overhead because she didn't want to waste electricity. The power company had turned most of the town off since early that morning, and she wanted to conserve whatever electricity was still getting through. Besides, the refrigerator had been off most of the day, too, and she supposed that if she didn't shine the room lights into it while slipping out her gallon of moo-juice, it would stay just that much colder that much longer.

And the kitchen wasn't all *that* dark, Abigail Carruthers found when she was halfway across the floor. In fact, the light in here was pretty bright.

The window over the sink faced east, and sometimes if the atmospheric conditions were right, she could see the glow of Minneapolis-St. Paul shining under the cloud cover at night. That's all it was, she supposed, but she went over to the sink anyway to see.

The sky down that way was clear, though. With a dusting of stars such as you might get on a cold, crisp night with no fog rising out of the river valley.

Still, there was that brightness. . . . Abigail Carruthers

leaned over the sink and pushed her face right up against the glass.

It was coming from the north. Veils of yellow and green, like the fireplace when you put in one of those salted logs for a special occasion. The light was just as bright as flames too, but somehow less focused. It wasn't coming from any one point, like a barn caught afire or the woods burning out there. It wasn't swamp gas, which you sometimes saw hovering over the marshy ground that lay to the north in Aitkin County. And besides, that was too far away even for this light — unless the methane had sent the whole county up in flames.

Nothing in Abigail Carruthers' experience accounted for the sheets of yellow and green fire, edged with red and streaked with purple, that danced in her window.

Abigail was getting to be an old woman, going on eighty-five. Sometimes her eyes played tricks. Like the time she saw Harvey Gates swinging in the apple tree out back. She had waved to him through the window and even thought about going out and asking how his mother was — before she remembered that Cousin Harvey had been killed in Tunisia forty years ago and his mother, Aunt Sophia, had been dead twenty years longer. But, even with her knowing that, little Harvey pumped that tire-swing back and forth for another five minutes, laughing at the wind he was making, before he and the swing and even the green buds on the tree, for it was October then, faded out in front of her eyes.

Sometimes Abigail saw things like that, and she knew afterwards that they were just visions, some stray neuron or a little piece of RNA taking a wrong turn in her brain cells — that's what Doc Wiggins called it. Or maybe her memory was just rolling itself up day by day for the long night that was ahead of her. But still, when Abigail saw these visions, they were so *real*.

Like these sheets of green fire.

Well, fire wasn't so much the issue anymore. She could tell nothing was burning. The light in the sky looked more like veils of organza or sheer nylon, rippling in a gentle breeze, and lit by some kind of footlights or maybe a huge Christmas tree somewhere behind them. Like the draperies of heaven, blowing at God's window.

No, that wasn't quite it either.

They looked like . . . angel wings. There were the arches of the wing joints, Abigail could see them clearly, towering high into the sky. And there were the feathers, brushed flat and tight and only slightly curled like the coverts and primaries on a hawk's wing. Those ripples at the bottom were the dragging secondaries, brushing the horizon.

Abigail looked closer, trying to make out the angel's body. The most she could discover was the flow of its robes, yellow-white against the green wings. And above, where the face should be, surrounded by its halo, there was only a blackness, a blankness, a patch of the night sky without even stars to light it.

The Faceless Angel, such as Abigail Carruthers had dreamed would come for her one day, was descending now from the north. It rode down across the land, dashing the still lake waters with the tips of its pinions and dragging the fertile land with the hem of its robe.

The lights of its flaming body — green, yellow, red, violet — flared out behind her eyeballs. Abigail's hands now slipped on the cold porcelain at the edge of the sink, and she fell backward across the kitchen floor.

Dead in the arms of her terrible Lord.

> *Burr-burr*
> > *Burr-burr*
> > > *Burr-burr*
> > > > *Burr-burr*

Lisbon, North Dakota, March 22, 10:02 p.m., CST

The emergency lines into the Ransom County Sheriff's Office had been ringing off the hook since about an hour after dusk. Deputy James L. Blackwood, serving the four-to-midnight shift, tried to answer them in order.

"No, ma'am, that's not a plane crash. Those are just lights. . . . No, they can't hurt you at all. . . . And thank *you* for calling, ma'am."

At first he thought this was just something having to do with the full moon that was laid on for this weekend. It was a legend in law-enforcement circles that a full moon always brought out the drunks and crazies. In the New York City precinct houses they used to line up in the hallways, down the stairs, and out into the street, waiting to tell some footsore old beat cop how the Martians were trying to come at them through the walls with ray guns, or how the saints were whispering evil thoughts in their pearly-pink ears.

"No, sir," Blackwood told the next caller. "It's not a sneak attack by anyone. . . . No, not by the Chinese, neither. It's just some kind of atmospheric disturbance, that's all."

Lisbon, North Dakota, had its share of drunks and crazies, too. But in smaller proportion than big cities, of course. Most of the deranged people Jim Blackwood had to deal with were farmers down on their luck, usually after their wives and children had left them for something better, or more exciting, or at least someone more sober and dependable. Then the farmhouse walls started to look a mite near, and the whiskey bottle seemed to have a sympathetic ear.

"Well, ma'am, I don't know *what* they are, exactly. The space administration sent us a bulletin this morning, saying we might see some strange lights in the sky tonight. That's all anyone knows, I guess."

And then there was the Devil's Den, down on the mudbanks along the Sheyenne River. When Lucas B. Smith, a.k.a. "Satan" Smith, started mixing his own brand of white lightning in with the Budsuds and the shots of Old Comfort, during what *he* liked to call "Happy Hour," then it usually took three cruisers and an ambulance to pull the cowboys and Indians down from the rafters and out of the river and sew up all their lacerations and contusions.

"Yessir, Mr. Mayor. We did get a notice about that." Blackwood sat up straighter in his chair. "NASA says to expect, quote, photon emissions from excited electrons in molecules of atmospheric oxygen and nitrogen, unquote. They said the effect was something like a laser, but the rays weren't coming out in what they call coherent fashion. So it's no chance of harming anyone. . . . Yes, sir, I did happen

to get a lot of calls about them. We're just trying to keep
people calm, is all. That's just our job, I guess. . . . Thank
you, sir."

It was going to be a long two hours until Harrison, his
replacement, logged on at midnight. Longer even, if
Bobby got himself stuck outside with his neck cricked back,
enjoying God's own laserlight show in the sky. Jim Blackwood hoped it would still be going on by the time he went
off shift, so he could see it for himself.

> *Dit dah dah*
>   *Dit*
>   *Dit dah dit dit*
>   *Dah dit dah dit*

Negaunee, Michigan, March 22, 11:13 p.m., EST
Walter Haskell didn't know what kind of energy beam
he would need to penetrate the greenish rays that were
cloaking the mothership. He'd already tried signaling with
his handheld flashlight, shining it up over the barn, and
that had done nothing at all.

Then he'd gone in the house and gotten the reading
light off his desk. It was one of those little ones, with the
metal-halide bulb that was smaller than his pinky fingernail. That gave out a good strong burst of illumination,
though, and the silvered-metal shell behind the bulb even
helped focus it a bit. But all he managed to do with it was
light up the broadside of the barn and a slice of the roof.

Then Haskell thought of his truck, with its six-hundred-
watt spotlight. That would be perfect. He rolled the vehicle
back out into the yard and kept the motor running. He
thought of ripping the light off its mounting rack and running it off the house current, but to begin with the voltages
were all wrong.

Frantic now, because the mothership was getting closer
all the time, Walter Haskell switched on his spotlight and
aimed the beam up into the roiling clouds of yellow and
orange light that were coming down from the north. He
had to send his signal, so that he would be seen and recognized by the new Lords of the Earth as their friend and

companion. He had to let them know that he would work for them as interpreter, ambassador, agent, or negotiator — whatever they wanted him to do.

Haskell's Morse was pretty rusty. It had been sixty years since he was an Eagle Scout and could send messages back and forth across the lake with his troop. Of course, the aliens were going to *know* Morse; they had been studying our culture for generations, using first the television and then the data communications signals that humans had been sending into space ever since 1948.

What should he tell them now, to gain their confidence? The other human beings were likely to be ornery, telling the mothership to go away. They were probably even shooting rockets at it, or trying to jam its photon energy pods with bursts of random energy. So, Haskell reasoned, he should send out his unmistakable greetings.

W...E...L...C...O...M...E...S...T...R... A...N...G...E...R...S...

Having got that far, Walter Haskell was pretty tired. His thumb was getting red and sore working the on-off slider switch on the searchlight. There had to be a faster way to communicate with the newcomers.

Then he remembered that Bradley had owned a pair of walkie-talkies when he was a kid. Up in the attic was where Haskell had last seen them. Surely, the aliens were going to understand English, and coming in like they were, they would probably be monitoring on all hailing frequencies. They would certainly take kindly to a friendly voice coming up at them from the Earth.

Walter Haskell left the truck running as he stormed into the house and up the stairs to the attic. Now, for God's sake, let's hope he had the right kind of batteries on hand.

Chapter 27

Eating Holes

> *Pocket ...*
> > *Hook ...*
> > > *Pocket ...*
> > > > *Hook ...*

Outside Stonybrook Farm at L3, March 23, 4:17 UT

The external surface of the farming colony's cylinder offered nothing as glamorous or as stable as a catwalk or sealed inspection tunnel for those who ventured outside. The most that the designers and builders offered the engineering and maintenance staff was a series of hemispheric depressions, ten centimeters wide and five deep, cast into the outer face of the dry-bond moonrock. These were set in diagonal lines on three-meter centers, spiraling clockwise from one end of the shell to the other. A two-centimeter-thick finger of rebar cut across the mouth of each depression.

Anyone wanting to go outside had to wear both a vacuum suit and a peterpan rig — the latter being a simple body harness at the end of a three-point cabling system. The cables were wound on spring reels braked with pressure clamps; at the end of each cable was a hook billed with a snap clip.

It was only after Peter Kamen had already signed on with the colony's engineering staff that they showed him this setup, and then he could hardly believe its crudeness. In order to tour the outside of the rotating cylinder he had to buckle on this rig, climb down an access well, and let himself out through a hand-cycled airlock. Before tripping the bottom hatch, he hooked one of his cables to a bar inside and then lowered himself against the spin gravity into the void below.

From there it was a matter of walking the hooks — at the end of carbon-filament sticks that telescoped out to four meters and were used to both trigger and release the snap clips — from one pock-marked depression to the next. The reason for having three cables, as Kamen soon discovered for himself, was that anyone hanging by just one hook while trying to set the next soon ended up twisting around like a pinwheel. It had something to do with angular momentum and the colony's perpetual spin. So the trick was always to keep two points attached while setting the third.

After considerable practice, his best speed over the ten-kilometer-long hull was just about forty meters a minute. At that rate, he could tour a ten-degree swath down one side of the facility in something like four hours — if he spent all his time setting and releasing his hooks and none of it examining the structure and its external systems. That meant he could "inspect" the entire outer surface in 1,500 hours of elapsed time — not counting pauses for doing any real engineering work, nor for meal breaks, sleep breaks, or returning to the interior for fresh air tanks. To make any of those interruptions, he would have to move, pocket-hook by pocket-hook, to one of only fifty-four access wells that were sited radially, three in line, at twenty-degree intervals around the cylinder. Kamen figured that, if he really wanted to, he could make a full-time professional career just out of inspecting the exterior works.

So it was no wonder that he and General Manager Alois Davenport would rather sit inside and theorize about why the irrigation system was losing pressure — as they had done last week — rather than take a walk outside and inspect it. In fact, Peter Kamen wouldn't be out here at all now, except the system had gone up from fifteen percent to thirty in just the past ten hours. That was a simply unacceptable rate of change and called for drastic measures. Like this sortie to get a firsthand impression of what could be going wrong.

So far, however, nothing presented itself.

Kamen worked his way through the narrow space between one of the heat-exchange fins and the concrete curve overhead. He had to be careful, in placing his hooks and cables here, not to crush any of the hundreds of spaced sump pipes that came down from the hull and drained into the fin. These were the ducts that he had expected to find plugged up with ice wherever the cylinder's orientation to the sun cast them into the exchange unit's long shadow. But after feeling about twenty of them with his suit glove and backing up his impressions with a thermal probe, Kamen couldn't say that any were cold enough to support an ice blockage.

Maybe Davenport's theory was actually a better one: that the fertilizers the colony was using might have scaled up inside the pipes or plugged the perforated drainage mats, which were the last layer under the soil before one came to the hull's inside surface. . . . Except a scale buildup didn't tend to double itself overnight, and that was the problem Kamen was chasing now.

Peter Kamen worked the spring-wound reel to lower himself across the face of the heat-exchange fin. As he went, his eyes traced out the delicate, black-enameled petals and microtubules that carpeted its surface. For a moment his attention was lost in the pattern of their folding, so that his sight went slightly blurry.

No, wait. The wateriness wasn't in his eyes but on his helmet bubble. He raised a glove and wiped across it. The blur smeared into thick, whitish streaks. What the hell was going on here?

Half-blind now, Kamen stopped unwinding, hung in his harness, and thought this through. Something had gravitated to the outside of his helmet, that much was clear. It had struck his faceplate and adhered as a fine particulate, perhaps even a liquid mist, but then vacuum-dried into some kind of a gum resin or a static-charged powder. Now what did all that add up to?

His urge was to spit on his fingers and rub at the smears, but of course he could not open his bubble to spit. Perhaps if he rubbed at just one spot diligently with a clean part of his glove — the seam that crossed the side of a knuckle, say — then he could probably brush away the gunk. Either that, or grind it irrevocably into the plastic. That was why he would concentrate on just a single two-centimeter-wide spot.

Kamen wiped at it with a careful circular motion, paused and looked through at the far stars, wiped again harder, and studied the result. The plastic was coming clean at last. With some latent scratches, of course. Turning in his harness then, Peter faced the dark side of the heat fin.

Son of a bitch! The blurring was back, right on the spot he had just cleaned.

The heat-exchanger was spritzing him! It was hitting his face with something wet that dried immediately to a sticky white powder. Now, Kamen thought almost happily, didn't *that* solve a lot of problems! He had found the leak in the water system — exactly what he had come looking for — and on his first pass, too.

Putting tension on his left reel to swing him out of the line of fire, Peter carefully polished another hole in the muck on his helmet and tried to sight across the surface of the fin, to see if he could catch the geyser of vapor in the angled sunlight. As he bent his head close to the tangle of tiny tubes and leaves, however, that second clean spot also clouded up.

Of course . . . Kamen felt a sinking in his stomach as he realized that just one pinhole would not account for a thirty-percent drop in pressure over a colony-wide system like the irrigation sumps. There had to be a lot of little holes out here, and now he had empirical evidence that at least two of them were spaced only half a meter apart.

He cleaned off that patch of bubble again with one hand while he rested the other against the fin to mark the exit point for the latest geyser. Finally, with a circle of his vision restored, Peter shifted his head another ten centimeters to the left and tried to get a view of the hole it was coming from.

No such luck. The hole must be tiny — confirming his theory that there were many more than one of them — and the evaporating plume of vapor was invisible under this lighting.

Kamen tried to feel for the hole then, passing his gloved

hand slowly in a broad swipe over the fin. Since the water pressure inside was gravity induced and measured at most in the hundreds of kilopascals — rather than the thousands he might expect from a superheated steam line — he had no worries about the leak cutting into his suit or taking part of his hand off. Halfway through the exercise he felt a bump of resistance and marked the spot with his finger.

Then he pressed his face close to it, coming in from the side.

The hole in the black tubule was less than a millimeter across. Its edges were caked with white crystals, probably a precipitate from the salts or residual fertilizers in the irrigation water. With the tip of the Snapple™ hanging from his belt, Kamen scraped away this residue. The remaining hole, studied at extreme close range, seemed to have a necklace of pits, like an erosion in the metal. It did not show the dimpling that one would expect of an impact crater — and that blew his first half-formed theory that the fin had recently ridden through a shower of micrometeorites. He worried the area around the hole, polishing it with his gloved finger, and a tiny flake of metal broke off from inside the tube and blew away into vacuum.

It appeared that the heat-exchange fin and the network of tubes and drains supporting it were rotting away from within. And that was worse news than a hundred meteor storms.

Kamen got busy in his peterpan harness then and performed three more spot checks at random points over a half-kilometer area of the fin. At each place, he found more geysers and the pattern of tiny, corroded holes. And that was as much as he was going to learn on this trip.

As he worked his way back to the access well, he chewed over the question of why the process of oxidation had suddenly leapt into high gear, eating away at fifteen percent of his pressure differential in just ten hours' time. That was the mystery now.

$356\,kPa$
$352\,kPa$
$347\,kPa$
$343\,kPa$

Main Irrigation Sump, Stonybrook Farm, 5:38 UT

"Son of a bitch!" Alois Davenport breathed in Peter Kamen's ear as the two of them watched the gauge on the pressure return drop over a ten-minute period. "How many holes did you say there were?"

"Thousands. . . . Maybe tens of thousands."

"At this rate, we'll have lost all pressure by the end of the day—"

"Sooner," Kamen put in.

"Then we'll have to run the pumps, won't we? I mean, to get a flow in the system."

"It doesn't work that way," the engineer said tiredly. The more he worked in this job, the more he was alternately alarmed and discouraged by the little that his general manager actually understood about the machinery supporting all their lives.

"The pressure is dropping here because we're losing water," he explained. "It's draining out at our low point, the part of the system farthest from our center of spin and so having the greatest moment arm. That's our heat-exchange fins. The bottom of our well, as it were."

"So?" The wrinkles were coming up in Davenport's forehead.

"So, if that low point is leaking, then the water table is falling all throughout the colony. We see this as a pressure loss because there's no head to keep the pressure up at this point in the system. It's not just a matter of an imbalance that you'll have to pump against. We're *losing water*, Alois. It will keep flowing downhill, out into the fins, and evaporating there until it's all gone. Then you'll hear the percolation mats start to draw on our atmosphere."

"You're telling me we'll be open to space?"

"We already *are* open to space. It's only the water we've got left in the pipes and in the soil above them that keeps our air from bleeding off now. How long that water will last depends on how many holes we're dealing with and how fast they can pass H_2O molecules."

"What's causing it?"

"I don't know." Kamen shook his head. "At first I

thought it might be meteorites, but the holes look like rust spots rather than impacts. Still, the fin alloy is *supposed* to be corrosion resistant. And the progression rate is all wrong. Rust comes up on you gradually; it's a flat-line effect. This breakdown is happening on a curve, one that's getting steeper all the time. So, if the deterioration is corrosion, then something's driving it, and I haven't a clue as to what that might be."

Alois Davenport looked at him and shrugged.

"Has anything come in on the network?" Kamen asked with a sudden inspiration. "Anything from the other colonies?"

The general manager appeared to search his memory. "No. All we've got in the last twenty-four is a NASA bulletin explaining that communications foulup from the day before yesterday. They said it was some kind of disturbance on the sun, sending out a blast of electromagnetic radiation, high energy gamma and x-ray stuff. With an ion storm to follow."

"Ion storm?"

"A cloud of protons and electrons shot out of the sun's atmosphere by the disturbance. NASA says the colony will be in no real danger, except for some more communications lapses as the induced currents play hob with our antennas."

"Induced currents . . ."

"Yeah, something about how a magnetic field from the ions — "

"I know all that," Kamen said tiredly. "Look at it this way. An electric current will stimulate the exchange of ions between our irrigation water and the metal in the pipes. That speeds up the oxidation, especially if the water has salts in it — as ours surely does by now. That's it, Alois. The mystery is solved."

"Good — I guess. What are you going to do about it?"

Peter Kamen weighed his options for a minute. "Nothing fancy, I guess. The direct approach. We have to start suiting up teams, right now, and sending them out with whatever we've got for plugging those holes — spot welders, paint guns, chewing gum, anything that will stick for a while and not dissolve. The problem will be identifying the leaks quickly, of course, and going after the biggest ones first."

"My people don't work in vacuum," the general manager said quietly.

Kamen, deep in his technical problem, hardly heard the man. "Some kind of dye would do the job. A radioactive tracer — but then you'd need instruments to detect it, and those are sure to be in short supply. Maybe a fluorescent dye, perhaps something that scintillates as the water goes through the phase change from liquid to — "

"My people don't work in vacuum."

Peter came up short. "What was that? Come on now, Alois! This is no time to get stuffy about jurisdictions. Your boat is sinking. Everybody has to pitch in."

"You don't understand. They don't know *how*. They're farmers, Peter. Most of them have never been outside the can. It will take you most of the day just to teach them vacuum drill. And we don't have enough suits, air bottles, compressors — not to plug thousands of holes."

"They can learn. We can rotate on the available equipment. Do you understand the magnitude of the job ahead of us? I've got a staff of four. Sure, they're trained to outside work, but with just ourselves, we'd never keep ahead of the losses."

"Then think of something," Davenport insisted.

"I'm trying!"

"Well . . . I could put in a request for replacement water. Call Whitney Center and see if they can give us a priority shooting schedule — "

"Never work." Kamen shook his head. "Even if they launched your water this minute, we'll all be whistling vacuum before the first pod could get here, let alone we take the time to decant it into the system."

"Then think of something, Peter. And it better be good. And quick."

"I know."

"Because it's your skin, too."

"I know!"

Davenport took one more look at the pressure gauge. He turned his head half away, then whipped back and spat once, accurately, leaving a shiny blob of spittle in the center of the dial. The general manager climbed through the access hatch and out of the sump.

> Ladle
>> Scoop
>>> Dollop
>>>> Plop!

Centerville Community Cafeteria, Stonybrook Farm, 6:10 UT

The food server on the steam table dropped a glob of oatmeal into the bowl and handed it across to engineer Peter Kamen. He took the dish with his hand but didn't set it down on his tray. Instead, he just stood there, like a statue, with his eyes glazed and his bowl of oatmeal off in the middle distance.

The porridge was still in a lump, almost a round ball in the shape of the ladle it came from. One edge, though, was cut by a darker patch of crust, where the surface of the cereal in the steamer pot had started to congeal. In the five seconds that he held the bowl out like that, Peter Kamen watched his mother making oatmeal in his mind.

She always started with the original rolled oats, tiny creamy-brown flakes that went into the cold water and just lay in the bottom of the pot. As the water started to boil, however, they seemed to expand and fill. . . . No, that wasn't right. They didn't just bloat up, like rice. They *gummed up*, too, into a paste with the consistency of glue. But not until they were heated.

Thinking of his mother brought back her family stories. Something about oatmeal. . . . Granduncle Harry Barnes and his Oldsmobile. That was the one. . . . The radiator had started leaking that time Uncle Harry was driving across the Nevada Desert, and he had thought he was a goner, stuck out in the noonday sun with a blown cooling system. But then Harry remembered he had some instant oatmeal in the back. Why he was carrying oatmeal, Mother never explained. Maybe he just liked it. Anyway, he poured some of it into his water system, where it cooked up and the paste — except she always called it the starch — sealed the holes in his radiator. It baked them over solid with a tight seal like little pieces of bread dough.

When Peter became an engineer and understood something of cooling systems and fluid mechanics, he always wondered what happened to the oatmeal flakes in Uncle Harry's radiator. Why didn't the porridge clog up all the tiny passages and stop the flow of water right there? Ever since then, Peter had always doubted the truth of that story.

But true or not, now it was giving him an idea.

"Don't you like your food?" the cook asked him.

"What?" Peter came out of his trance.

"Your food. Something wrong with it?"

"No ... Oh yeah, it's fine."

"Then why don't you move along so others can get served?"

"Sorry. . . . Look, do you have anything like starch — cornmeal, or maybe cornstarch — back in the kitchen?"

"What do I look like, a grocery store?"

"Sorry."

"So get moving already."

Peter Kamen put the bowl down on his tray, left it in line, and walked away. He was halfway out of the cafeteria on a dead run, so he never heard the shouts coming from behind him.

"Hey, buddy! You gonna pay for that or what?"

> *Wrinkle*
> *Crinkle*
> *Wrinkle*
> *Blink!*

General Manager's Office, Stonybrook Farm, 6:15 UT

Peter Kamen could tell from the way the skin tightened around Davenport's eyes that the man wasn't following his story. Clearly, the farm manager had never heard of an Oldsmobile, did not understand the structural similarities between a passive solar heat exchanger and the air-cooled radiator on an internal combustion engine, and possessed only the vaguest idea of where the Great Basin of Nevada was and why an unscheduled stop there might be a life-threatening experience. Peter cut the tale short and got to the heart of the matter.

"Do you have any vegetable starches in store? Preferably something that's fine ground and completely soluble."

"I . . . um . . . unhhh . . ." Davenport searched his memory. "We had an order once, was it two? — no, three years ago! — from one of the subtropical countries. It might have been Tanzania or Thailand or one of those T-places. Anyway, they wanted a starch extract for making baby formula. We planted two whole sixties with a genetically engineered barley and processed the crop right here in the colony because their contract specifically forbade paying shipment on any 'in-situ waste products,' by which they meant vegetable fiber. Anyway, when the time came to deliver, they'd had a revolution and weren't honoring any of the old government's commitments. We damn near got foreclosed that year."

"And you didn't ship the starch out?" Kamen supplied.

"Nope. We decided to plow it back into the soil."

"Oh shit!"

"Hold on. . . . Now I remember. We were *going* to plow it, until one of our selectmen pointed out that the colony might need an emergency food source one day, and although the stuff was nearly indigestible, it was better than chewing concrete."

"So where is it?" Peter asked.

"We buried it — but clean. It's in a lined pit under the East One Twenty. The kids around there call it Baby Puke Hill."

"Great! Now, let's get your farmers digging it out. We can dump the starch right into the sumps. That's below the soil line and beyond the perc mats. Once it hits the fins, it should start cooking and seal up those pinholes."

"Won't it clog the exchangers, too?" Davenport objected. "I mean — "

"I'll run some tests. We should be able to control the size of the clumps through the starch concentration. Big enough to stuff a millimeter-wide hole, small enough to pass a five-millimeter tube. But even if I'm wrong, which would you rather have — a heat imbalance and a little stagnant water, or a hole out to vacuum?"

Davenport thought about that. "I'll follow your lead on this one," he told Kamen finally.

"Okay. I'll be over at my shop, arranging for the test work. Have your team leader bring me a sample as soon as they uncover the storage pit. We should be able to plug this thing in a couple of hours, tops."

The general manager nodded, then stopped Kamen by jamming a hand into the crook of his elbow.

Peter jerked at the roughness of the touch.

"Just don't think this is going to change anything," Davenport told him gruffly. "You may have gotten lucky this once, discovering about that pressure drop and working out the source of the problem. But all that means is we — you and me and the whole colony — got unlucky, having it happen in the first place."

"What are you driving at?"

"You may have saved the day on this one, Kamen, but that doesn't mean I'm going to underwrite all your happy little plans. You can just stick your budget requests for fancy new equipment, and your application to bring up a whole company of engineers, and your sour-ball predictions about how this farming bucket is in imminent danger of falling apart. You're only the maintenance man, fella. That makes you just a service organization for the farmers and traders who run this colony. You're not going to end up in charge of things around here just because you found and fixed a plumbing leak."

Peter Kamen decided to hear the man out, and he even managed to keep a grin on his face.

"Jesus, Alois! Don't smother me with gratitude," he said when Davenport had finished. "I just couldn't stand it if you went all wet and sloppy on me."

"Get the hell out of here," the manager growled.

Fizzle
    Fuzzle
        Phu-utt
           Pftt

Outside Stonybrook Farm, 8:07 UT

Shielding his clean helmet bubble with a piece of smeary plastic, Peter Kamen hung in front of the heat-exchange fin and studied the geysers of soup that he could see at close range.

The escaping vapor was a grainy white mist, turning into a snowstorm of tiny flakes as the water boiled away in vacuum. But that wasn't the effect that interested him.

Down on the surface of the tubes and petals, Kamen could see the holes building up their own microscopic volcano cones of white crud. Sputter by spit, they were closing, until all around him the black surface was dotted with spots and dribbles of vegetable starch and runoff salts. It looked like the windshield of Uncle Harry's Oldsmobile, the time he ran though that cloud of mayflies out in the Delta. Even the lacy little bubbles that some of the smaller corrosion holes had blown looked like the wings of the dead insects stuck erect by the impact.

Alois Davenport was wrong, of course. Kamen knew that this near-disaster was going to change just everything.

Rousting people out of their homes at six in the morning and setting them to digging for their lives — that would have gotten them to thinking. Some of them, enough of them, would realize that the design of Stonybrook Farm was far from perfect.

For one thing, even the youngest child could figure out by now that the drainage and heat-exchange system should have included some emergency shutoff valves. Assuming that any system which was self-actuating and self-regulating was therefore some kind of perpetual motion machine that would never need to stop for adjustment — this was just bad industrial engineering.

In the days and weeks ahead, Peter Kamen would find fertile minds in which to plant his ideas for changing and improving the colony, for buying some insurance against future and worse disasters. So, in a way, this near-failure of their irrigation system, dire as it might have been, was the best thing that could have happened to them.

Peter Kamen rapped his knuckles happily on the black fin and started reeling himself up toward the hull.

Chapter 28

Voices in the Sky

> *Angle of incidence . . .*
>   *Angle of reflection*
>   *Angle of incidence prime . . .*
>   *Angle of reflection prime*

Murray Hill Laboratories, Inc.,
March 23, 2:18 p.m. EST

Like a pool player confronted by a tableful of potential bank shots that line up the same ball with three different pockets, Harvey Sommerstein's head was absolutely spinning with the possibilities. And it didn't help that *his* pool table was in three dimensions. Or that he'd been working right through, logging almost twenty straight hours of wakefulness and intense mental activity, ever since that NASA bulletin had hit his E-mail in-bin early on Saturday morning.

It was the combination of subtexts to that dispatch which had set off his imagination and led to this marathon weekend.

First, NASA had explained Friday's general collapse of the communications network all over the Western Hemisphere. Although Sommerstein hadn't experienced that catastrophe directly, he had watched the news services' inadequate reporting of it with a growing surge of frustration. Anything that disrupted the phone beams was sure to pique his professional curiosity and demand a fuller explanation.

Second, the space agency had warned about a wave of energetic ions expelled from the sun which was expected to arrive at Earth orbit sometime between twenty and forty hours after the initial flare effect. As NASA had calculated backward to establish the flare at just before one o'clock Eastern time on Friday, that placed the start of the alert period at nine o'clock Saturday morning — or just about the time Harvey Sommerstein was reading the bulletin and beginning to get his inspiration.

He'd been scrambling ever since.

To start with, Harvey had to pick his target. Then he had to contact the receiving stations through the normal repeater channels, during the clear period following the solar flare's electromagnetic interference, to arrange for someone there to be listening for Sommerstein's unorthodox communication. Then he had to requisition Murray Hill's largest experimental radio horn out at Red Bank, which meant tracking down the laboratory's deputy administrator and getting his verbal permission to mess up several long-standing test schedules. Finally, Sommerstein had to work out the bounce in a variety of dimensions using the lab's detailed orrery simulation to position the inner system planets and moons, with a scratch program that would locate the advancing ion wavefront among them.

That was the drill, to his way of thinking. First came the target, then came the mathematics of the bounce path to reach it.

For a test subject he eventually chose the night side of Mars. After a moment's thought, he had rejected the satellite colonies around Jupiter and Saturn, as too company-dominated and profit-motivated to be cooperative, and the free bases in the Asteroid Belt, as too independent-minded to sit still for a polite request from the Mother World.

Mars was fine, though; a settled world with a lot of semibored people willing to participate in a novel test procedure. The only hitch was Mars' rotation. The red planet was likely going to make at least one complete revolution during the alert period for the ion storm. So Harvey Sommerstein sent a general message to *all* of the

Mars stations, requesting that they nominate someone who would listen from dusk to dawn on a frequency not already fielded by the wideband repeater on Phobos.

Together Harvey and the stations agreed on transmission at 10 Hertz, which was way down in the upper reaches of the million-meter band. The lab's horn could easily handle it. All of the Mars receivers could tune to it. Such an unwieldy long wavelength was likely to be clear of other traffic. And at the same time that wavelength would offer Sommerstein the best chance of a bounce off a dispersed and still exponentially thinning cloud of charged particles.

Working out all of these details had taken the rest of Saturday morning and the better part of the afternoon. But by noon New York time Harvey was hearing the first batch of reports saying that the front edge of the wave had already reached Earth. This early arrival time meant the ion cloud was moving exceptionally fast. So it was likely to be densely packed with high-energy particles — which was good in terms of reflectivity for the bounce. However, the speed with which it was passing through the solar system meant Sommerstein would have almost no opportunity to practice an inside-angle shot. The wavefront, at that speed, would reach the orbit of Mars no more than ten hours after it hit Earth — or no later than about seven o'clock Saturday night.

At that, Sommerstein had given serious thought to changing his venue. But by then most of his contacts had already agreed to and were locked into the experiment. Changing the target stations at this late date would have him chasing the wave right out to Pluto, where no one was sitting to receive his signals. So Harvey kept his current arrangements and gave up both the inside shots as well as the comfort of a time cushion for practicing and perfecting his technique.

Late on Saturday afternoon and into evening, then, he wrangled for the radio horn with Deputy Administrator Paul Pierce, who happened to be in the Green Mountains on a late-season skiing trip. The conversation proceeded, by triangulation with a cloud of voice-only cellular phones, up and down through Pierce's support staff, who were scattered all over Greater New York City, at their homes, in restaurants and bars, on dance floors, and at intermissions in two different Broadway theaters. To a man and woman, these people wanted to keep the Red Bank horn on its established schedule of intra-atmospheric experiments. Then, relenting only to a degree, they wanted to know how Sommerstein, with his existing grant money, proposed to pay for equipment time and the power to run his series of tests. Sommerstein in turn made promises, cut deals, accepted strictures, and crossed his fingers with every word he spoke.

Later in the evening, Harvey had to go through it all over again to get one of the lab's software programmers brought in on overtime and assigned to inserting the wavefront into the orrery. At least by this time Harvey had a pretty firm estimate of the magnetic storm's speed, density, and internal energy to give the technician, whose name was Cal Warner. But the man was so sleepy and grumpy about being called in that Sommerstein couldn't be sure he was actually using everything Harvey gave him.

By that time, early on Sunday morning, the ion cloud was proceeding outward into the Asteroid Belt. Sommerstein had to decide quickly whether dropping a few carbonaceous and siliceous raisins — pebbles of rock and glass with here and there a lump of ferrous alloy — into the ion loaf might affect its reflective qualities. He chose to think it couldn't hurt a bit, but neither would it help much. The main trouble was that the farther beyond Mars the wave swept, the wider and less accurate all of his bank-shot transmission paths were becoming.

But Harvey Sommerstein was still intent on trying.

And by now, early on Sunday afternoon, Mars was above Greater New York's horizon, the people out there were dutifully listening, and the planetary program was all worked up, debugged, and running like a seventeen-jewel watch in clear oil. Sommerstein had been stuffed into his virtual reality helmet for seven hours, playing with all the possible transmission angles and breathing his own stale carbon-dioxide buildup until he was feeling quite light-headed. And so far he hadn't gotten off a single "Hello, Mars!" that had received any kind of reply.

Inside the helmet, black space revolved around Harvey's head. Faint gray lines represented the major constellations by connecting the bright points of their stars. These provided him with a background map that supplemented the gridded globe marking off the celestial coordinates from his point of view on Earth.

Mars was at a declination of seventeen degrees north and a right ascension of two hours, fifty-two minutes. It was a position which he could read off the inside of his helmet and then punch into the renovated software with a touch of one finger. The planet showed up as a small dot of ocher and burnt umber, about twenty degrees to the right of a blank, white solar disk. At extreme ZOOM, taking him almost to the resolvable limits of the simulation program, he could just make out the glint of an icecap. But he was still too far away to place the orbiting moons, Phobos and Deimos, which were much smaller and closer in to their primary than Earth's own moon.

The wavefront of the flare's ionization, seen as a shadow beyond the meager red dot at normal viewing distances, was bent around his head like a section of speckled, silver-iodide donut scratched into the star map.

Once more Sommerstein put out a finger to touch it, right *there*, for yet another bank shot. Where his fingertip probed, a column of numbers — celestial coordinates plus range in kilometers — scrolled themselves in gray typescript on black space beside the point.

Within a tenth of a second, the logic-seeking routines in the software gave him a pair of angles, Earth to point and point to Mars, defining the bounce path. A blue cone appeared to show the beam spread going out and the footprint coming down. The far end seemed to engulf the red planet with margin to spare.

"Okay, Donald," he spoke to the operator at Red Bank, sitting in the radio horn's control cab, "blast our message out that-a-way."

Sommerstein knew the man could see those numbers in his own helmet and only had to redirect them into the cyber that shoved the horn's working end around.

"Gotcha." The antenna swiveled and made the connection, sending back the variables for the beam, which Sommerstein's program interpreted as a yellow cone. Where the proposed path and the actual overlapped, his helmet showed truncated sections of green cone.

Not much here glowed green. And too little of what did match seemed to fall across the ocher dot.

The ongoing problem seemed to be the horn. Again and again the antenna, traversing on its gear-driven platform and swinging inside its counterweighted cradle, was proving just too slow in responding to commands from Harvey and the simulation program. If this was a pool table, then he was using a pine log for a cue stick.

"All right, Donald," he said encouragingly. "That was a partial. Let's see if we get a response this time."

He now had to wait thirty-three minutes — twenty for this transmission to go out and another thirteen for the reply from the night side of Mars to come back by way of the Phobos communications repeater — before he would know how much of that fractured green cone had carried his message. Or if the principle of reflecting signals off an ionization wave was even practical.

"Stand down for now," he told Red Bank. "But be ready to try another blast at ten till three."

"Gotcha, boss."

Why was Sommerstein even doing this? Why waste all his time and effort, his sleeping hours and his precious grant money, on this mad notion? Especially if, as the NASA bulletin had noted, this flare from the sun seemed to be an anomaly, something that no one had seen in almost a century.

Because, deep down, Harvey Sommerstein didn't believe that. What had happened once in space could happen again. Maybe flares and ion waves would always be a sometime thing. Coming as capriciously as typhoons and hurricanes. But, as the past three days had shown, they

could still be incredibly disruptive to the patches of
humanity scattered across the solar system. Most vulnerable were the lines of communication. If Sommerstein's
bounce path worked just once to warn, to protect, or to save
a life, then it was worth his effort now. And the more common these flares turned out to be, then the more important
would be his contribution.

At this particular moment, however, after thirteen con-
secutive unsuccessful tries, his gift to the theory and
practice of interplanetary communications did not seem to
be worth a red-hot penny.

But Sommerstein was still going to try again — in
another twenty-eight minutes. He would work on this all
night if he had to.

   Tharsis Ridge
     Olympus Mons
      Valles Marineris
       Chryse Planitia

Murray Hill Laboratories, March 24, 11:23 a.m. EST
Harvey Sommerstein showed up at his workbench-
cubicle in the laboratory just before lunchtime on Monday.
He was stumbling and yawning, having gotten only four
hours of sleep. Bright-edged dots and squirmy lines swam
before his eyes; they might have been symptoms of
extreme physical and mental exhaustion, or merely
afterimages from fifteen straight hours contemplating
planetary points and transmission vectors inside his computer helmet.

His own good sense told him that, in his present condition, he ought to stay home for the day. But Harvey's
political instincts told him he'd better be on hand to report
some results, *any* results, to the lab's administration people
after he had wasted huge amounts of their radio time and
funding in fruitless attempts to say "Hi there!" to the
nightlife on Mars.

The first thing Sommerstein did on arriving was to empty
out his E-mail. And, sure enough, there at the top of the
queue was a priority message from Paul Pierce requesting a

formal, face-to-face meeting in the administrator's office. It said "as soon as might be convenient," for which the politically savvy translation was: Right now, buster.

Sommerstein was about to log his reply when some wild intuition suggested he put it off for two minutes more and instead scan through the rest of his mail. There were twenty-three items, all with offworld prefixes. He looked at them more closely. All of them had *Mars* prefixes. Harvey began sampling and reading through them.

"Received your 13:45 UT transmission," from his nighttime listener at the Areopolitan Center on Tharsis Ridge.

"Transmission clear and without distortion," was the reply from the observatory on Olympus.

"Hello yourself, Harvey! . . . Congratulations!" said his fifteen-year-old correspondent among the water miners in Ius Chasma, which was part of the Valles Marineris runoff system.

"Have now logged three of your transmissions. All messages received without error," from the geophysical station at Planitia, near the impact crater Domore.

"Still receiving you," commented the Tharsis station later.

"Seven in a row!" from the lad at the chasms.

"Enough already!" from Maja Vallis.

"This is getting boring, Harvey!"

"Your point is elegantly proven . . ."

And finally, "Please release our operator for other duties," came through from a somewhat higher level of authority at Tharsis Center.

Every one of Sommerstein's twenty-nine recorded messages had been received somewhere on Mars. Some had even been fielded by stations on the terminator, and two were heard on the dayside — but with enough of a timelag to prove they had come down on the bounce.

Sommerstein's project was apparently a resounding success. But why then had he heard nothing from these recipients during the course of his tests?

The answer to that was in the final item in his bin. It was a notice from the cyber which monitored the laboratory's

E-mail delivery system. This text had been delivered last
and so chronologically, under the system's first-in-first-out
protocols, had followed up the queue.

"Documents via Mars Interplanetary Postal Service
were delayed twelve to twenty hours in transit through sys-
tematic transmission failures at Phobos Repeater Station.
MIPS wishes you to have its formal, though non-indem-
nifying, regrets regarding the interruption of these items."

That would certainly explain the utter silence from his
target listeners while he had sent his signals again and
again — as well as the curious flood of responses now.

In the time it took him to pull a paper printout of all
these documents, Sommerstein began framing his own
reply to the deputy administrator's request for an inter-
view. Finishing up his business this morning was going to
be easy.

Part 6

Plus Thirty Days ...
and Counting

How perfect are your designs,
lord of eternity!
There is a Nile in the sky
for the strangers, for the cattle of every land. ...
Dawning, shining, passing and returning,
you have made all things of yourself, by yourself:
cities and tribes, roads and rivers.
All eyes see you daily,
Aton over the Earth.

—From Ikhnaton's "Hymn to the Sun"

Chapter 29

Watching and Waiting

Jack of Diamonds
Ace of Clubs
Two of Clubs
. . . Queen of Hearts

Cabin B9 aboard ISS *Whirligig III*, April 24, 2081

Peter Spivak stared at the red queen as she settled in front of him on the deck panels. For a flashing instant as she sailed toward him, face up in a flat spin, Peter had thought the card was another jack, to go along with the diamond he had showing and the jack of spades that was his hole card. Three of a kind would surely take this pot.

But no, when the last card slowed in the fractional gravity, she was the treacherous queen of hearts. A bad card for Peter in any game; so seeing her was a double shock. He stared down at her face with its cool, simpering Mona Lisa smile.

"You going to play, Pete?" Mitch North asked him. "The bid's twenty to you."

"He's still worried about his girl," Eric Porter said, reading Spivak's mind with amazing accuracy.

"No . . . I, ah . . . well, maybe a little," Peter replied, hoping the stuttering admission would bluff out the truth — that he had secretly been expecting a third jack.

"Women are a pain," said North, the experienced space sailor. "Love 'em and leave 'em on the ground, where they belong."

"Pete wanted his to come meet him on Mars," Porter explained. In Cabin B9, with four men bunking in just fifteen cubic, any secret shared in the dead of night was eventually known to all. But damn Eric's big mouth anyway!

"She *asked* to come along," Spivak explained lamely.

"Before you left?" the older shipman wondered out loud.

"Well, no, after. It took her a bit of time to get used to the idea of leaving Earth. She didn't actually decide until I'd already gone."

"How did you find out, then?"

"She sent me a blip-tape about a week after we broke orbit for Mars. . . . Someone had beaten her up in New York, and that kind of made up her mind to go off planet."

"What did you say to that?"

"Of course I told her to come."

"You talked to her in person? Two-way?"

"Well, uh, no. I wasn't sure of the time difference. So the communications officer suggested I just send a night letter."

"Sounds pretty cold to me," the sailor said.

"It was a very enthusiastic letter," Peter insisted. "I really wanted her to file her work samples with the Foundation — she's a technical illustrator — and get on the next ship out."

"But she never replied," Porter explained for Spivak. "Not a peep."

"And this was all a week after we shifted orbit. . . ." North pondered. He was pushing his cards around with a fingertip, all thought of the bidding gone from his head. "That was about the time we went through our drill with the solar flare, wasn't it?"

"A day or two before that, actually."

"Right," the crewman agreed, but that didn't seem to settle the matter. "Did you follow up with her?"

"Well . . ." Spivak paused.

Peter had been deeply hurt by her silence, and the rejection it implied. Now, he was not sure how much he wanted his love life and his manly pride dissected by these people. . . . But, then, what the hell! They were in it up to their lips anyway.

"She was kind of vague about her plans in the blip she sent," he told them. "So, when there was no reply to *my* reply, I kind of figured she'd changed her mind again."

"But you didn't follow up."

"No."

"Not even with the radio shack — to make sure your letter was received?"

"Why would I?" Although North's questions seemed friendly enough, Peter was still beginning to feel angry with this cross-examination.

"Why not? This is a survey ship, not an international hotel. Personal messages are sometimes delayed, or even . . . *shit!* Nobody told you then, did they?"

"All right, told me *what?*" Now Spivak was really tired of the conversation.

"About the communications blackout. The solar flare was headed up by a wave of high-energy static that knocked out signals all over the system. Happened a day or so before we had to shut down for the magnetic effects. So, if your night letter was in transit at the time, it might have gone into hyperspace."

"But wouldn't the communications officer have checked?" Peter insisted.

"What? On a non-official communication? Why would he bother? He was probably bending the regs to send it out in the first place."

"Then . . . she must be thinking . . . that I wasn't . . ."

"A month is a long time, pal. You've probably lost her again." Mitch North dropped his head again to study his cards. "So, are you going to bid, or what?"

> Stir
>> Stroke
>>> Beat!
>>>> Whip!

112 Duck Pond Circle, Sag Harbor, GNYC, April 25

The fork in Cheryl Hastings' hand worked faster and faster, bringing the dechol-egged batter up to a yellow froth. About the time it started sloshing out of the bowl, her mother glanced over.

"You're going to ruin that mix, dear," she said quietly.

"Sorry, Mother."

"You have to keep your mind on what you're doing."

"I know, but I can't help thinking. . . ."

"You weren't thinking, Cherry. You were brooding." Jane Hastings pushed the recipe book back on the table and folded her hands in front of her. A lecture was about to begin. "The one will get you someplace. The other just takes you around in circles."

"All right, Mother. So I was *brooding*."

"Can you tell me the subject of this famous brood?"

"Well . . . I should have heard from the Areopolitans by now. Either a yes or a no. Instead, there's just this silence from them. And I can't think why. I mean, my work isn't so good that they'd be calling in some kind of world-class committee to evaluate it properly, would they? And it's not so bad that anybody might hesitate about hurting my feelings over it. So why can't they just give me the answer? Thumbs up or down."

"Maybe they have too many applications to decide so quickly," Jane offered. "It's only been a month. And, anyway, all those committees, judging panels, paperwork and routing — they can eat up weeks of time."

"I still should have heard *something* by now."

"Is that all that's bothering you?"

"Well . . . Peter, too. I should have heard from him as well."

"Didn't I warn you about sending a picture from the hospital? You certainly didn't look your best, dear."

"I wanted to be honest with him."

"*Honest* would have meant keeping your face away from a camera until it healed. No, I think you wanted to be cruel — showing him what his leaving did to you. . . . Or you wanted to tug at his sympathies."

"No. I just thought he should see — "

"You wanted him to see that you really can't take care of yourself? So that he would think you needed him to do it for you? Instead, I think you showed him what a fool you can be."

"All right, Mother. Have it your way."

Jane Hastings gave a little sigh. "No, dear. I don't want 'my way.' Not really. I just want you to have whatever will make you happiest."

"I want to go to Mars. And I want to be with Peter."

"Well then, stop brooding about it."

"What should I do?"

"In my day—which you probably think was back with slash skirts and three-wheel convertibles—a woman didn't have to be so shy and retiring about these things. Or so stiff-necked."

"Mother!"

"Why don't you *do* something? Call the Foundation, politely, and ask if they received your application, or did it get lost in the mail. Call Peter and ask him the same thing."

"I don't know. I guess I'm afraid of being rejected. Twice."

"In the long run, knowing for sure will hurt less than waiting and wondering."

> *Thump*
> > *Thump*
> > > *Thump*
> > > > *Bump!*

Radio Shack, ISS *Whirligig III*, April 25

Communications Specialist 1C Wilbar Fredrix looked up from his handheld Skeedaddle game to see that young articled passenger, Peter Spivak, coming through his curtain, rubbing his left elbow.

"Hurt yourself?" he asked cheerfully.

"Awkward place to put a turn," Spivak grumbled.

"Yeah, I have to slow down there myself. . . . What can I do for you?"

"I want to send a blip-tape. Better yet, a two-way transmission if you can arrange it."

"Be my guest. Where to?"

"Unh, same place as before. Sag Harbor in Greater New York."

"Time difference there is — wait a minute!" Fredrix said. "Now that does ring a bell. We just got in a batch of ship's mail, and one of the items had a return code from Sag Harbor. Funny coincidence, huh?"

"The message was returned?" The young man's face looked like it was going to crumple up.

"Oh my, no! They don't pay to send back radio waves out here. I'm saying that Sag Harbor was the originating station."

"Was it for me?"

"Well, just a second." Fredrix put down his game, turned to his console, and began punching up the message list. Seventeen from the top was the item in question. "If you're Peter Spivak, it is."

"Can I have it?"

"We have to do things in order around here, fella. First I have to sort these incomings and separate out ship's documents from private mail. Then decode and route the official business. Then sort and route the personal stuff. Maybe after lunch . . ."

Spivak gave a weak smile. "Couldn't you, just this once, break your routine and take that one message, number seventeen there on the screen, and just give it to me?"

"I'd have to execute a special spooling."

"Oh . . . Is that hard to do?"

Fredrix studied the younger man.

"It *is* a lot of work," the communications specialist admitted cagily. "But I tell you what. For you, because you're such a pal of mine, I'll do it as a favor."

"Great!"

"And one day, say when we're both on planet, maybe you can do me a favor in return."

"Unh — sure. Just name it."

"Maybe you can introduce me to your girl."

"Well, yeah. I'm sure she'd like to meet you."

"And maybe she has a sister who'd like to emigrate."

Spivak looked at Fredrix long and appraisingly. "No sisters in the family. Sorry."

"Or a real close friend, possibly?"

"Of course. Cheryl knows a lot of interesting people on Earth."

"It's a deal, then." The operator turned to his console and began breaking out the message. Then he stopped and turned back to Spivak. "Oh, you still want to send that outgoing?"

Peter Spivak gave a tight grin. "I'll let you know in two minutes."

• Chapter 30

Criminal Negligence

Qiang v HK2X 3:2 D
   MorsyBio v WhitCen 2:1 D
      Carlin etal v TranShore 9:4 P
         Aaronson etal v Virty 30:1 P

Offices of Bingham & Bingham, Troy, New York, April 29, 2081

Whoa, there! What was that? Must be a misprint. Who in the blue hell could be getting such lousy odds of thirty-to-one against — as the *plaintiff*?

Louie "the Linchpin" Bingham flicked a muscle in his left cheek to scroll back the lines in his data goggles. When the light bar settled on the entry for *Aaronson etal*, he tipped his head to get the drawn-out details.

Well, that explained it — and the Linch decided he must be getting old to have missed the clues. First, there was the plaintiff's name, which was clearly the first in a long alphabetized list. Second, that telltale "etal," from the old legal term *et alia*, meaning "and others." So Louie should have guessed that *Aaronson* was a major class action. Those were becoming increasingly dicey with the juries.

Especially this class action.

"Virty" was the abbreviated listing for Virtuality, Inc., the international data and entertainment cyber-simulation conglomerate. The merits of the case against them, as Louis read it, looked pretty shaky. "Aaronson etal" represented 2,254,361 plaintiffs who were either direct customers of Virtuality, Inc., or survivors and guardians suing on their behalf. The customers, all brain-damaged in the March 21 solar flare, now claimed damages based on Virtuality, Inc.'s alleged negligence in routing "signals intended for electro-organic interface" through "circuits exposed to extraterrestrial influences, including electromagnetic interference from all sources." The short form was, the company shouldn't have used the commercial phone beams in connecting with its customers. Or, using the beams, it should have installed cutouts — in third-party phone company equipment, and at its own expense — to protect all users against potential solar flares.

"Right!" chuckled Louie Bingham, who knew something about criminal negligence himself. "Sell me another one."

On such examination, thirty-to-one started to look generous.

There was a time, Bingham knew, when civil suits were essentially a private matter. The litigants argued their case in a closed courtroom before a jury, which then awarded damages to one side or the other. Only if the parties were celebrities or otherwise notorious would the case make the media — which was paper back then.

Yeah, this was all maybe a hundred years ago, when there was such a thing as civic duty. Back then, you could get citizens to serve on a jury, to sit down and listen to both sides, and even, occasionally, to render a sane verdict.

But the State of California, for one, hadn't summoned a jury in a civil case — and damn few for routine criminal procedures — since 2032. By then, most people were ineligible to serve a panel because they either had a record or were some other kind of illegal. Fuck their ever registering to vote or hold a taxpaying job. For a while, the bench heard and decided all the cases, until the backlog started stretching into the century after the next one. Then the Judges Revolt of 2042 put an end to tort cases entirely — but not to the purely human desire to get some of your own back against somebody who done you wrong.

So, in the spirit of fun and games, the California state legislature passed the Adjudication by Referee and Referendum Act of 2044. Essentially it said that anyone who wanted damages against another party just had to get up a petition — and there were plenty of professional signatories who for a fee would facilitate the process — and submit it to the State Judiciary Committee. If the committee validated your petition, they scheduled your case, along with four others at a whack, for some future issue of the weekly Lotto tickets. Then anyone who played could punch either your number or your opponent's, as often as they bought a ticket. All decisions of the Court of Popular Appeal were final.

Well, it wasn't ten minutes before every other state with an overworked civil bench was passing similar legislation. The genius of it was that every state, and most counties and municipalities, too, had their own lottery games going by then. In short order the federal bench adopted the system for most of its cases, both criminal and civil.

It wasn't twenty minutes after *that* before Legal Futures, Inc., set up shop to assign odds and take side bets on all these cases. Well, come to think of it, LFI wasn't the first or the only wagering system to grow up around the Court of Popular Appeal. It was just the last one left standing after the successive waves of scandal and consolidation. By now, it was a national system and published a daily roster of current cases, *The Legal Eye*, for the convenience of all players.

Most of them were lawyers, who made their living by picking winners and placing bets for the public. For example, fourteen local mutual funds, twenty-six chartered consortia and investment groups, and about a thousand individuals with money to spread around all had accounts with Bingham & Bingham. Louie's firm then managed their action and issued them quarterly statements of profit and loss.

It was about all a practicing lawyer had going these days, other than writing up one-paragraph descriptions of the merits — they used to be called "briefs," and now they certainly were — for clients entering litigation, corralling the petition signatures, and submitting the case to the Judiciary Committee. For all this work, Bingham could charge his clients no more than the going rate of just five hundred neu.

So, because the rules of ethics prohibited an attorney from wagering on the briefs he wrote — apparently it was some kind of conflict of interest to know the merits of a particular case through firsthand acquaintance with it — damn few of the biggest firms actually handled private cases. There was just too much money in the other action.

So, what was good this morning, other than his laugh over that piece-of-shit *Aaronson*?

Carlin etal v TranShore looked like another class action, and therefore practically untouchable, until you sat down to read it. The etal in this case was limited, with only twenty-three names in the plaintiff box. The merits were a little less sweeping than in *Aaronson*, too. The plaintiffs claimed that inadequate spacesuit design exposed them to high doses of ionizing radiation. The brief did not mention the March 21 solar flare directly, although it was there to be presumed. Carlin etal suggested that the persistence of "cosmic radiation," which unlike the flare was a wholly predictable phenomenon, would have led a prudent resort manager to design the suits with greater levels of radiation shielding.

It was a weak argument, of course, because cosmic rays were not generally regarded as lethal under normal conditions of exposure. Still, anything having to do with radiation was a spark plug with the know-nothing public. So why, then, was this case getting such a pessimistic nine-to-four?

Well, for one thing, it was a mixed bag of plaintiffs. Most of them seemed to be customers of the Tranquility Shores, Inc., resort, but one was actually, on close reading, the tour guide who conducted their Moon Walk and thus a paid employee of the defendant. Putting in a ringer like that — someone who should have known the risks the company was taking and was presumed to be making her own free choice about accepting them — well, that just cut the case apart. But maybe not enough to damage it with the Court of Public Appeal. Juries almost never read the brief, that was rule one. And if they did, they wouldn't understand it: rule two.

The other thing was the current status of the plaintiffs. All of them — with the possible exception of the tour guide — were reasonably wealthy, being able to afford a royal-gut vacation on the Moon. Half of them were also dead of radiation poisoning by now. That meant the beneficiaries of the case would likely be rich inheritors. Public sympathy just didn't go that far with fattening the already fat cats.

Nine-to-four against was a pretty fair reading of the outcome.

The other fallout from that solar flare looked more promising.

Morrissey Bio Designs had an excellent, if unexciting, case against the Whitney Center catapult. By the time Morrissey's payload had gone into the tube, and was subsequently destroyed due to magnetic instability, NASA had given the launch operations office fair warning of the flare's effects. That was a matter of record. The operators took a calculated risk and lost it. Whitney Center's countering claim of *force majeure* just didn't wash, not when NASA had a public notice out on the boards like that.

So this case should be open and shut. Morrissey's odds were compounded by the fact that, these days, suing the government — or even quasi-governmental agencies like the catapult — was easier than hooking fish in the bathtub. The only thing keeping the odds from going higher was the pity factor: people just might feel a little silly awarding two million in contract damages to a freight customer when the catapult carrier had lost seventeen *billion* in the same accident. Still, there was no accounting for the stupidity of the playing public.

Louie the Linchpin had a rule against touching sure things. No room for real action.

Qiang was another untouchable, from Bingham's point of view. The merits were just too sound. Winston Qiang-Phillips wasn't bringing suit for his neurological damage, although there was evidence of it, all right, and that played to the pity factor, too. Instead, he was contesting the decision of the Hong Kong Two Exchange to put the market back ten hours after the disruption in communications. This, Qiang-Phillips claimed, had damaged his business prospects by erasing trading positions he had garnered during that interval.

Now usually the minutiae of stock trading and arbitrage were lost on the common public. People tended to dismiss both sides in the case as crooks and scoundrels. But look where Qiang was playing! On the California roster, instead of nationally. There that Chinese name of his was sure to catch the attention of the state's Asian majority. And Chinese players were notoriously attracted to affairs of business. They were sure to study the merits, something juror-players never did, and would probably buy extra tickets just to voice their opinion on the case.

Louie the Linchpin could see how that was going to turn out.

No, as far as his business was concerned, the solar flare had been a bust. He could find only a handful of good, leveraged cases from the thousands that had been filed on it. Bingham was even thinking of an article for his monthly investors' newsletter, advising his clients to keep away from the astronomical-accident cases for a while. He'd write some kind of catchy title, like "Stick to Astrology for Now."

No, divorce law and transit crashes — those were meat and potatoes in the tort business. Louie the Linchpin crimped his jaw muscles twice to change the registers in his goggles.

Let's see how the vote was flowing in homicides today.

Chapter 31

Star Watch

Shuffle ...
    Stamp ...
        Tickle ...
            Sneeze!

McMath Solar Telescope, Tucson, Arizona, May 5, 2081

Piero Mosca looked around the dead cellar room. A pale ghost of the sky, reflected and passed down the shaft by the relay of mirrors overhead, lit the chamber softly. A dozen wandering flashlights, held by Po and his companions, punctuated the corner shadows. Little puffs of dust billowed up from around their feet and showed golden in the beams.

The facility was in worse shape than Mosca had expected, and in far worse shape on the inside than it appeared from the outside. In fact, viewed from a distance, as from the road leading up to the cluster of domed stellar observatories on top of Kitt Peak, the McMath telescope had the striking perfection of a piece of origami.

The thirty-meter-tall tower that supported the facility's sun-following heliostat was a crisp oblong. Glaring panels of flat, white metal shielded its winches and tracking mechanisms from the direct force of the wind and also concealed and protected the hexagon of cement piers which reached deep into the mountainside. The other visible structure, the top end of the optical tunnel — a water-cooled tube arranged on a polar axis to conduct the sun's image down 140 meters under the mountain — was a white-sheathed parallelogram tilted on a forty-five-degree angle to touch the tower's top corner.

These two structures, tower and tunnel hood, looked like something cut from clean paper and pasted together with toothpicks by an imaginative child. Over the decades since the telescope was abandoned, the Arizona climate had been kind to the structure. The sun could only bleach its sides whiter and, where the paint peeled, the prevailing wind scoured its metal surfaces bright before the infrequent rain could blot them with rust.

Under the hill, however, the facility had not survived as gracefully. Stray winds from the tunnel's open upper end had deposited little scalloping dunes of brown dust at the stations where the concave primary and secondary mirrors bent the solar image, now a full meter-and-a-half wide, around and back up and finally into the buried observation room and spectrograph pit. Here, at recesses ranging from ten meters under the surface down to thirty, had been the labyrinth of plates and cameras and diffraction grids that once massaged the solar disk into direct film views and thermally graded or wavelength-specific proofs.

These working precincts had fared the worst, as Po and his colleagues had discovered. After the McMath facility was given up, no one had thought to remove — or even plunder — the massive heliostat and the fixed mirrors in the tunnel. But all of the less weighty and more portable equipment had been broken up, bartered away, or sold off. The offices and observation room were cold, echoing cement boxes with their own thin dunes. Cut ends of exposed cabling and broken power conduits and water pipes extended from the bare walls. Even the light fixtures had been removed over the years.

Po looked overhead, into the last mirror positioned above the observation room and, through it, back up to the permanently misaligned heliostat. There a reversed image loomed, composed of ninety percent blue sky shaded with a tinge of haze in one quadrant, and ten percent a nail paring of the dusty green chaparral that surrounded the site, now curving above the sky in the mirror. The image swam overhead like a landscape seen through a porthole or a periscope.

"This place is a dump," Mosca said to the group in general. "Hopeless."

Sultana Carr must have followed his gaze, because she clicked her tongue to get his attention, then met his eyes through the gloom when he glanced down at her.

"Not so bad as all that," she said lightly. "The mirrors are sound. And unpitted — I checked *that* out already. When we replace the rusted clockwork up there with a really talented intelligence, the heliostat will track for us just fine."

"Wouldn't it be better to go into orbit?" Po asked. "Or to the Moon?"

The others in their team, all graduates from the JPL Institute who had studied and worked under the late Dr. Freede, stopped moving about and were waiting to hear the two acknowledged leaders argue this out.

"We'd never get the money to launch a new tube, or sink one this deep into the lunar landscape," Carr answered. "Or not soon enough. Starting from scratch like that would put us out of action for two, three years. We can get this facility up and running in six months, tops. . . . Besides, this setup will give us whole-light solar images a hundred and fifty centimeters across. That's wider than we could hope to get from any new facility built with current dollars. With plates this size, we can slice them up and analyze them any way we want."

"If we don't mind looking through about five hundred kilometers of dirty atmosphere. . . ."

"So, okay, there are tradeoffs." Sultana Carr shrugged. "If we do good work here, we can hope to launch a tube on the next wave of funding."

"Did you get Donaldson's promise on that?" Po asked. Hilary Donaldson was a NASA subdirector, one of Jamison's ultimate superiors and the highest level that Carr and her group had reached in the golden days of sorting out, after their warnings on the solar flare had proved too graphically accurate.

"She didn't say in so many words," Sultana admitted. "But the clear implication was there."

"Then we'd better make the best of this." Po grunted, scraping a toe in the dust across the vinyl tiles. "We're going to be here a lo-ong time."

The others looked around at the empty walls.

"And we won't be able to do ongoing magnetometer surveys," Po added after a while. "Not from down here. . . . And that's how we'll predict the onset of the next spot, you know. Freede's way. For that, we'll need a platform in close orbit around the sun, like *Hyperion*."

"Well, NASA didn't promise they'd launch anything near as grand as a ship, not right away. But they did agree to a string of automated probes, reporting to us through Vandenberg."

"We'll just have to make sure they include the cyber time to assimilate and collate the data," Po grumped.

Carr didn't answer him. Instead, she wandered off, pushing her cone of light ahead of her through a doorway cut into the hillside rock and down the hallway beyond.

"What'll it take to fix this place up, do you think?" Lowell Chen asked into the lull.

"That's what we're here to find out," Po said. "If the structural survey passes on the tower piers — which have been my personal big worry — then the rest should just be sweat and tears. . . . We'll have to put in all new equipment down here, obviously. And some of it we'll probably have to make ourselves — like the port framework, the diffraction grating, and the collimating mirrors for a hundred-and-fifty-centimeter spectrograph. They don't sell those at Pacific Instruments, I'll bet."

That brought a chuckle from the men and women who had gathered around him.

"Then there's the computer interface," he went on. "Nobody makes a charge-coupled plate that size. So we'll either have to spec one and do a special order from Singapore, or cobble up some kind of array from much smaller units. That would probably be the least expensive route."

"Po?" Sultana called from the doorway. "Down here?"

He went over and walked with her into the darkened corridor. Their flashlights made two roving dots crisscrossing on the concrete walls and tiled floors.

"This is the office complex," she explained. "Stripped now, of course. And I found some nests. Made by bears, or maybe people." When he stumbled beside her, she added, "Don't worry. They vacated some years ago."

"How can you tell?"

Carr shrugged and smiled.

"We're sure going to have a fun time clearing this place out."

She stopped at the second doorframe on the right, flicked her light into it. The room beyond was square, about four meters on a side. A line of bookcases stretched along the left wall, a bank of closets on the right. Po could just make out what looked like the porcelain surfaces of a private washroom behind one of the open doors.

"This is your office," she announced.

"Oh, come on, Sulie! I don't want an *office*." The place was huge by the Institute's standards. It had no window, of course, but the ceiling was high. You could teach a small seminar in there. "Next thing, you'll be offering me a title."

"I was thinking of Director of Operations. Unless you'd like to be Dean of Students. Over the next few years we're going to be getting a lot of requests from people wanting to study with us. You're a good teacher. . . . Besides, you always wanted Albert Withers' job one day, didn't you?" In the glow reflected off the far wall, she was grinning.

"Don't you think we're taking this whole thing a little fast, Sulie? I mean, we're only riding on the public hysteria caused by that solar flare. In another month, everyone will have forgotten the damage and disorder it caused. By then they'll be worrying about plagues or earthquakes or something else, and all that loose funding you're counting on will go to the bacteriologists or the seismologists or whoever is hot."

"You are forgetting the grantsman's first rule," Carr told him.

"Which is?"

"While the money is flowing, take it and smile."

"But it was only *one* sunspot, Sulie. A big one, to be sure, but an isolated incident just the same. You can't graph a curve with just one point of data."

"Then you didn't see the report this morning. . . ."

"No, I was too busy packing for our field trip here."

"Tsiolkovskii Observatory detected an anomaly and passed it along to NASA."

"Detected *what*, for God's sake?"

"A pair of spots, Po. Only little ones, really nothing compared to our Big Fellow. And they're so far up toward the pole — at about eighty-four degrees north — that the Wilson Effect makes them damned nearly invisible, foreshortened against the limb as they are. But still, sunspots is all they could be."

"So have we got a cycle under way?" Po could feel his heart begin to race.

"What else could it be?"

"Then . . . that changes everything."

"For a lot of people," she agreed. "All throughout the solar system. For one thing, people can expect a lot more interference with their communications and in their unshielded electronics. For another, the increased solar thermal output is going to change the climate in ways that the National Weather Office may not have anticipated. Such as, it wouldn't surprise me if the old folks were right all along about the Greenhouse Effect. It's certainly going to get a lot hotter here on Earth."

"I hear what you're saying," Po told her. "But still, aren't you getting just a bit ahead of yourself?"

"Hilary Donaldson called me first thing this morning with the news. She wants us to make good on that boast I made to Jamison — they must record everything there at Vandenberg — about our becoming a kind of solar weather bureau.

"I think we can expect funding support, also, from the United Nations, from the International System Survey, and from a coalition of corporations in transport and communications," Carr added. "Hilary offered to begin contacting them today and piecing together a cooperative forum. When this thing really gets rolling, Po, then we'll have probes, platforms, sight tubes, cybernetic assistance — anything we can think of, or have the balls to requisition."

Mosca stuck his head through the door and shone his light around the office space.

"Do you suppose this place is going to be big enough?" he asked.

Chapter 32

Invaders from the Beyond

> *Green* . . .
> > *Yellow* . . .
> > > *Red* . . .
> > > > *Violet* . . .

Point-Twelve Lightyears Beyond the Oort Cloud

The ship's hull pulsed around Red Halfspin Charm at frequencies passing up and down the baritone range of 10^{14} cycles. He never tired of feeling these waves of photon flux, which the ship's core held in gravitationally bound curves. Such energy! And such control of energy! From within, the hull radiated in all colors, in all visible dimensions, yet it could pass unseen because of those self-devouring curves.

Red Halfspin Charm knew that, should the hull constriction fail at this close distance to the new sun, the ship, he, and his crewmates would evaporate in a glare more intense than any supernova. And then any intelligence lodged on one of the many particle-energy nodes that surrounded this sun would see the light and be amazed.

So that must not happen.

He rebent his will to buffering the hull and encouraging the core. So intent was he on this exercise that he never felt the *ping!* of a higher-frequency electromagnetic burst impacting against the hull from outside.

"What was that?" asked Blue Twicespun Strange. His senses were much keener than those of the Charm Flavor. For that reason, a Strange was always the mission leader, and that was as it should be.

"I did not —" Red faltered and went quiet.

"We passed through a wavefront with energies exceeding 10^{20} cycles," Blue told him. "You are nearly blind in that range," the leader added, not unkindly.

"I was concerned with the ship."

"As you should be." Blue turned his full attention now on Yellow Spin Down, who was as concerned with where-we-are-going as Red was focused on where-we-are-now. "What do you see, Yellow?" the leader asked.

"I see the dawning, the shining, the passing and return-ing, which makes all things of itself." The Downs always did radiate a sense of their own self-importance in the order of things. "I see the lord of eternity — or of 10^{31} discrete cycles, which is close enough to make no difference," the quark added wryly.

"Does the star burn clear?" Blue asked impatiently.

"Yes, of course," Yellow answered too quickly. "I mean, with the exception of one blemish, which may be only the passing of a particle-body across my field of vision. I had thought to discount it — at least until we had moved closer."

"And what of that wavefront which just passed us?"

"Actually, it might be anything," Yellow temporized.

"And if it was not?"

"Then the blemish may be more than bad seeing."

"What do the meepers say?" Blue asked.

Ah, the meepers! Red Halfspin Charm had heard stories about these mindless creatures, massive constructs of charge and anticharge knit from the very fabric of a star's surface. They floated like lace across the bubbling sea of plasma, and the quark kin had programmed them to follow the magnetic anomalies there, which all middle-aged suns were prone to. Whole hadron-clusters of quarks must have destroyed themselves in placing just one of these meepers. And each of the midrange suns was rumored to boast thousands of these quasi-intelligences.

Excitement and hunger were wired into the meeper men-tality. They could draw strength and joy only from the interplay of conflicting field forces that built up deep within a star. As they played on its surface, they sang high-voltage arias in magnetic patterns that coded themselves into the solar wind. Then the quark kin could read those patterns from lightyears out and interpret them to discover the health of any nearby star. A happy meeper meant a sick sun. And that meant disappointment for any traveling quarks in the vicinity.

"Yes," Red beamed, "what *did* the meepers say about this sun?"

"I hear in them what I have not heard before," Yellow told them.

"Describe what you hear," Blue insisted.

"I hear a song of neither joy nor hunger. I hear a song of terror. It is a dirge of rending and passing away. I hear the finality."

"That is *not* as it should be," Blue commented.

"No . . . I thought not," the Down admitted.

"Yellow, that must be a sick star now. We should not be going there," Blue advised.

"Understood."

"You must bend us a new course," the leader commanded. "We need to move quickly at a high deflection. At all costs, we must avoid meeting up with the crowd of mesons and antiquarks that are sure to be mixed in with the scatter who are escaping that eruption. To join them would ignite just too joyous a reunion."

"Understood," Yellow repeated, and turned his attention in other directions.

Immediately Red began tweaking the ship's energies, shifting their position according to the new heading. They passed across the gravity waves that the nearby sun — at once so near and soon so distant — pumped out as extravagantly as it poured forth frequencies.

"So? Where to next, Yellow?" the leader asked cheerfully.

"I have a young giant on the list. He's impetuous, heady, and not at all reliable. But he should be fun — not cranky, like that Main Sequence dwarf we just missed." The Down Flavor was, by its nature, quick to reject what it could not have. "This fellow's good for at least 10^{30} cycles."

"That is as it should be," Blue told him. "Proceed."

THE END

worked and shrugged, and, shaking their heads, kept watching. Hear us! Sommerstein had been stuffed into his virtual reality helmet for seven hours, playing with all the possible transmission angles and breathing his own stale